Innocence

ALSO BY KATHLEEN TESSARO

Elegance

Innocence

KATHLEEN TESSARO

WILLIAM MORROW

An Imprint of HarperCollins*Publishers*

Grateful acknowledgment is made to reprint the following:

"If I can stop one heart from breaking" and "This world is Not conclusion": Reprinted by permission of the publishers and the Trustees of Amherst College from *The Poems of Emily Dickinson,* Thomas H. Johnson, ed., Cambridge, Mass.: The Belknap Press of Harvard University Press. Copyright © 1951, 1955, 1979, 1983 by the President and Fellows of Harvard College.

"i like my body when it is with your": Copyright 1923, 1925, 1951, 1953, © 1991 by the Trustees for the E. E. Cummings Trust. Copyright © 1976 by George James Firmage, from *Complete Poems: 1904–1962* by E. E. Cummings, edited by George James Firmage. Used by permission of Liveright Publishing Corporation.

HarperCollins books may be purchased for educational, business, or sales promotional use. For information please write: Special Markets Department, Harper-Collins Publishers, 10 East 53rd Street, New York, NY 10022.

FIRST EDITION

Designed by Cassandra J. Pappas

Printed on acid-free paper

Library of Congress Cataloging-in-Publication Data

Tessaro, Kathleen, 1965–
   Innocence / Kathleen Tessaro.— 1st ed.
     p. cm.
    ISBN 0-06-052226-7 (alk. paper)
   1. Single mothers—Fiction. 2. Rock musicians—Fiction. 3. Female friendship—Fiction. 4. Acting teachers—Fiction. 5. London (England)—Fiction. I. Title.
PS3620.E776I56 2005
813'.6—dc22
                                     2005040229

05 06 07 08 09 WBC/RRD 10 9 8 7 6 5 4 3 2 1

For my family

No coward soul is mine.

—EMILY BRONTË

Innocence

*T*HE FIRST THING you should know about Robbie is she's dead. She died in a car accident in New York—a hit and run—crossing the street one February afternoon to buy more Diet Coke. She really loved Diet Coke. Couldn't function without it. And she was never the type of girl to cross at a street corner.

The second thing you should know is that we'd lost touch years before that. Not exactly fallen out so much as given up on one another. We no longer saw the world in the same way. She refused to grow up and, at the time, I thought being grown up was a very serious, terribly important business.

I'm not so sure now.

She was larger than life, even at nineteen. Too large, as it turned out. But sometimes fate is mean in its portions of love, boldness; of heroism. The sweeping colours of the canvas are reduced to that irritating point precision of Seurat, the man with all the dots that join up from a distance, when what one wants is the audacity and eloquence of Michelangelo; that rare feeling that being alive is a grand and glorious thing.

There's an art to life. Some people have a talent for it. A boundless hope illuminates them. Where others are vague and tentative, they have only sharp, clear edges. Energy soars; lights burn brighter when they enter a room.

And that's the other thing you should know about Robbie.

She had that knack in spades.

*I*N HINDSIGHT, it was a mistake serving wine at the Thursday night adult education drama and poetry workshop. I'd imagined that it might help the group bond; loosen everybody up.

Mr. Hastings is certainly loose now. In fact, he's drunk.

He's decided to recite *The Waste Land*.

Again.

He reads it every week. According to him, it's the best poem ever written and can't be heard too many times. Some of us feel differently. But he's immune to any encouragement to broaden his poetic horizons.

So we sit, all eight of us, in a circle of old sofas and wooden chairs, gazing out over the rooftops of London from our attic room in the City Lit, listening to Mr. Hastings's now infamous weekly reading.

The fluorescent lights wink, the air vent wheezes and, outside, rain drums incessantly against the dirty windowpane. Below, the narrow, winding streets and alleyways of Covent Garden weave from one famous theatrical landmark to another; round the Theatre Royal and the Lyceum, through an elegant, affluent opening night crowd at the Royal Opera House. They duck past the Wyndhams the Garrick and the Duke of York's; squeeze down a low, dark passageway between the Vaudeville and the Adelphi, where stagehands and chorus girls shelter in the doorways, finishing their cigarettes just moments before curtain up, unaware that another great performance has already begun.

Mr. Hastings is a huge fan of a rolled *r*. He makes John Gielgud sound like a pre–Rex Harrison version of Eliza Doolittle. And he's not afraid of the odd shout; randomly notching up the volume on any word that takes his fancy. For a while, I thought there might be some sort of interpretive reasoning to it. I was wrong.

"April is the cruellest month, breeding
Lilacs out of the dead land, mixing
Memory and desire, stirring
Dull roots with spring rain."

Clive Clarfelt, whose thick, black quiff of hair has stood the ravages of time better than his face, tries to refill his glass. Mr. Hastings shoots him a look. Clive challenges him—even going so far as to snort in defiance. Mr. Hastings's eyes widen—something in the vein of Dracula hypnotizing a virgin.

Clive retreats.

And the reading continues.

The sound of Mr. Hastings's random, rolling voice, coupled with the suffocating warmth of the central heating has an almost instant narcotic effect. My heartbeat slows, my breath grows shallow. And my mind wanders . . .

Suddenly, silence.

I jerk up.

Mr. Hastings is moved to tears. He's wiping his nose on what he thinks is his hankie but is in fact Mrs. Patel's woolly winter glove. She's far too polite to mention this and smiles nervously as he mops his brow, then jams it into his breast pocket.

It's time to stage an intervention.

"That was just beautiful! Really moving! Don't you all agree?" I look around the room. The sound of my voice rouses the others; they blink like a group of nocturnal animals caught in a flashlight. "You read so . . . so *clearly*, Mr. Hastings, that I'm sure you've inspired everyone else."

A few nodding heads, even some helpful noises.

I take the plunge. "With that in mind, why don't we give someone else a chance? What about you, Brian?"

Mr. Hastings's smile disappears. "But I'm not done yet! There are twelve more pages!"

I count to three in my head. "Yes, but the thing is, it's such a long poem and we're really quite a large group today. I think it's best to press on so that everybody gets a go. Then maybe we can go back to the Eliot if we have time at the end." I look hopefully at Brian. "What have you got for us today?"

"A person simply doesn't interrupt Eliot!" He's taking this badly. "The whole *sense* of the piece will be lost! Fractured! Where was I?" And he accelerates, raising his voice.

> "What are the roots that clutch, what branches grow
> Out of this stony rubbish? Son of man,
> You cannot say, or guess, for you know only
> A heap of broken images . . ."

"Mr. Hastings, please!"

> "And I will show you something different from either
> Your shadow at the morning striding behind you
> Or your shadow at the evening rising to meet you:
> I will show you fear in a handful of dust."

"Please, Mr. Hastings!"

It must be the wine.

I'm normally quite adept at dealing with rebellious octogenarians. In the three years I've been teaching night classes at the City Lit, I've managed dozens of eccentrics and their artistic outbursts with little more than a handful of compliments and the occasional shiny object. But add alcohol and they turn wily; playing on your sympathy one minute and then pretending to be deaf the next.

"Mr. Hastings," I boom threateningly (or as close to threateningly as I can be bothered to get). "That's enough!"

He glowers at me.

"Now, Brian . . ."

"Where's that handkerchief, damn it!" Mr. Hastings gives Mrs. Patel a shove. "I sincerely hope you're not sitting on it!"

She murmurs apologetically.

I turn my attention back to Brian, a lanky young postal worker from Dulwich. Brian's a little shy and hasn't read yet in the group. I watch as he fumbles with a worn piece of photocopied paper and readjusts his tie.

"Yes?" I smile encouragingly. "What have you got there?"

"Well." He's a touch manic. "He he he he! It's nothing really," he squeals. "Just a little Emily Dickinson."

"*Jesus Christ!*" Mr. Hastings hisses.

Doris Del Angelo chips in. "I *adore* Dickinson!" And she glares at Mr. Hastings, who pours himself another glass of Bordeaux from the table in front of him, ignoring Clive and his empty glass, and staring at her breasts, which are, it must be said, quite amazing. She's in her late sixties and not afraid to showcase them in low-cut, form-fitting blouses. Each week they play a pivotal role in the dynamic of the group. She heaves them up defiantly. "I cannot *wait* to hear this poem!"

Should I attempt to remove the wine from Mr. Hastings? Visions of me wrestling the old man to the floor fill my head. Perhaps a tactical relocation of the bottle. Then I notice he's drained it.

Fair enough.

Back to Brian. "Don't be shy, Brian. Everyone has to start somewhere."

He smiles. "Actually, I think I'd like to stand."

He rises boldly. A moment later, his knees give way. He lands abruptly back in his seat.

"Ah, yes. It's a bit alarming to stand up and read for the first time, isn't it?" (The trick is to use these things constructively.)

"He he he he he!" He's hysterical. His hands are shaking.

"Why don't you have a go sitting down?" I suggest. "Just nice and easy. Easy does it."

The group waits while Brian gathers his strength.

"If I can stop one heart from breaking"

"Oh, *fuck!*" Mr. Hastings cradles his head in his hands.

"Please, go on, Brian. You're doing beautifully!"

"I shall not live in vain;
If I can ease one life the aching *[he he he!]*

Or cool one pain,
Or help one fainting robin *[strange twitch developing in right eye]*
Unto his nest again,
I shall not *[he he he!]* live in vain."

He's about to be sick or pass out.

"Well done, Brian! Really. Well done, you!"

Doris claps, her bosoms quivering enthusiastically. "Bravo, dear boy!"

A wave of fainthearted applause sweeps round the circle. Brian grins, blushing.

"And how did that feel to you?"

"Well, um! Unusual!"

"Well, it sounded bloody unusual too!" Mr. Hastings struggles to his feet.

"Mr. Hastings . . ."

"Damn Emily Dickinson!" He makes his way to the door, swaying like a sailor on the high seas. "And damn you all!" Grasping the frame, he wheels round. "I have not come all the way across London to listen to the musings of some morbid little American! Good night!"

It's unclear whether this last statement refers to Emily Dickinson or to me, but it's on the tip of my tongue to remind him that T. S. Eliot was a morbid little American too.

That's when I notice there's a wet spot on the couch. Mrs. Patel, ever vigilant for the possibility of an awkward moment, quickly covers it with her scarf.

Hastings's voice echoes down the hallway, bold and resonant. "Good night, ladies, good night, sweet ladies, good night, good night!"

Sitting there, staring at the scarf and the dreadfulness that lurks beneath it, knowing that the rest of the class are, in turn, waiting for my reaction to Mr. Hastings's mutiny, the thought enters my head again. I've been fending it off; deftly sidestepping it every time it appears. Only tonight I haven't got the energy to circumnavigate it any longer.

This isn't what I had in mind.

When I left my hometown of Eden, Ohio, fifteen years ago to pursue a career as an actress in London, this is definitely not what I had in mind.

And that's when I see her, lingering in the doorway.

It only lasts a moment, then she's gone. But it's definitely her. And she's smiling at me. Even from across the room, I can see the light, soft spread of her lips; an easy, graceful, teasing grin, as if to say, "So it's come to this, has it?"

Yes, Robbie. It has.

PART ONE

February 1986

I'M SEATED next to a redheaded woman on the plane. My supper of creamed chicken royal and boiled rice sits untouched in front of me. Instead, I stare at my new Keith Haring Swatch watch (a going-away gift from my boyfriend, Jonny). It's my first trip abroad. In only eight hours and twenty-two minutes, we'll be landing in London and a whole new chapter of my life will begin. Who can eat chicken at a time like this?

The redhead can. She's an old hand at foreign travel. Lighting another cigarette, she smiles at me.

"Oh, London's great! Great pubs. And you can have fish and chips. Chips is English for French fries," she translates. "They put salt and vinegar on them over there."

"Ewwww!" I say, ever the sophisticate.

"But it's good! You have them with mushy peas."

"Mushy what?"

"Peas!" she laughs. "They're sort of smashed up. You don't have to have them."

"Oh, but I want to!" I assure her quickly. "I want to try everything!"

She exhales. "Where are you from?"

"Eden, Ohio."

"Is that near Akron?"

"Actually, it's not near anything."

"And what are you doing? Studying?"

"Drama. I'm going to be an actress. A classical actress," I add, just in case she gets the idea I'm going to sell out. "I've been accepted into the Actors Drama Workshop Academy. Maybe you've heard of it?"

She shakes her head. "Is that like RADA?"

"Almost."

"Well, you're a pretty girl. I'm sure you'll be a big star." And she nods, drumming her long, pink nails against the shared armrest. "Yeah, London will be the making of you. It's a long way from Ohio, kid."

That's exactly what I'm hoping for.

I don't fit in in Ohio. I don't fit in anywhere yet. But back home, nobody seems to get me—apart from my boyfriend, Jonny. He's going to study graphic arts at CMU next term. He understands what it's like to be an artistic soul trapped in a working class town. That's why we get on so well. I pull out his going-away letter to me and read it one more time.

> I know this is going to be a completely amazing adventure for you, babe. And I can't wait to hear each installment. Write often. Never lose faith in yourself. And think of me slaving away over my drawing board, dreaming of you and your perfect, beautiful face until you get back . . . safe and warm in my arms. I'm so proud of you.

My darling Jonny.

We've been dating for nearly two years. When I get back, we're going to live together. In New York City, if things work out. Already I can see us: drinking coffee in the mornings, padding about in our loft apartment overlooking Central Park—sometimes there's a dog in the picture, sometimes it's just us.

Folding the letter carefully, I slip it back into the side pocket of my carry-on bag.

I think of my parents, standing next to one another at the departure gate of Cleveland Airport. They just couldn't understand why I needed to go so far away; why anyone would ever want to leave the States. I'm the only person in my family with a passport.

There's a whole, entire world bursting with beautiful language, enormous, crushing emotions and stories so powerful, they break your heart in two—just not in Eden, Ohio. How can I explain to them that I want to be part of it? To rub up against the culture that inspired Shakespeare and Sheridan, Coward and Congreve; the wit of Wilde, the satire of Shaw, the sheer wickedness of Orton . . . I want to see it, touch it; experience it all firsthand instead of reading about it in books, in between taking orders at Doughnut Express.

And at last, I'm on the verge.

Leaning back in my seat, I gaze out of the window. Somewhere, far below, my parents are driving back home now, thinking about what to have for dinner. And just beyond this expanse of blue, on a small, green island, people I've yet to meet are drifting off to sleep, dreaming of what tomorrow might hold.

The stewardess leans over, collecting my tray of untouched food. "Not hungry?"

I shake my head.

The next meal I eat will be fish and chips.

With plenty of mushy peas.

The Belle View Hotel and Guesthouse in Russell Square is considerably darker, colder and altogether more brown than the pictures in the brochure. The rooms, so spacious and inviting in the leaflet, are cell-like and lavishly appointed with tea and coffee making facilities (a kettle and teacup on a plastic tray) and a basin in the corner. Boiling hot water steams out of one tap, icy cold from the other. A certain amount of speed and physical endurance is required to wash your face but the reward is a genuine feeling of accomplishment.

However, the reality of shared bathroom facilities is another matter. No amount of counselling could prepare me for crouching naked in a shallow tub of tepid water while three large German businessmen wrapped in nothing but old bathrobes lurk outside the door. The whole experience is like a trip to the gynaecologist's, simultaneously intimate and deeply unpleasant. The English must have a relationship with their bodies that's alien to me; like a couple who are divorced but still living together in the same house; forced to be polite to someone they hate.

After bathing, and making myself an instant coffee (breakfast with the Germans is a bridge too far), the time has come. I'm ready to visit

the offices of the Actors Drama Workshop Academy in North London
and introduce myself to the people who are going to mould the rest of
my life.

It's further than I thought. I take a bus to Euston Station, a tube to
Camden Town and change lines before I find myself in Tufnell Park
Road. I wander up and down the long, residential street, which at this
time of the morning seems to collect old women glaring at the
pavement, dragging blue vinyl trolleys behind them. And then I'm there;
standing outside the United Kingdom North London Branch of the
Morris Dancing Association. This is the address. There's no mention of
the Actors Workshop anywhere.

A Glaswegian caretaker comes to my rescue. He explains, through
the universal language of mime, that I do have the right address; the
academy's somewhere in the basement.

The building seems empty. My footsteps echo down the corridor.
A creeping sense of doom grows in the pit of my stomach. This isn't
the hive of artistic activity I'd imagined, with students rehearsing in the
hallways, singing and dancing like extras from *Fame*. What if I've made a
huge, expensive mistake? What if I've travelled all this way for nothing?

I turn a corner and walk down the steps.

"Where the hell are the student registration forms! For Christ's sake,
doesn't anyone around here know how to do anything right? I want those
forms and I want them now! Gwen!"

I freeze at the bottom of the stairs.

A breathless woman in her early forties flaps past me, carrying a pile
of photocopied papers. Her hair's cut into a faded blonde bob and she's
wearing a navy wool skirt and a shapeless, rather bobbly green cardigan.
Round her neck, a collection of long gold chains, some with lockets,
some without, clink and rattle, swaying from side to side. "I can hear you
perfectly well, Simon. You're not playing to the back row of the Theatre
Royal Haymarket, you know." She heads into a small office.

There's the sound of paper hitting the floor.

"These are last year's forms! My God! What have I done to deserve
this? Just tell me, Lord! How have I betrayed you that I should be
tormented by such incompetence?"

I can hear her gathering them up again.

Her voice is quiet but lethal. "These are not last year's forms, Simon.

They're this year's. I know because I photocopied them myself. Now, if you're keen to continue in this vein, then you'll have to do it alone because one more word from you and I'm leaving. And you'll have to pick your own papers up next time."

She slams the door and marches into a larger room across the hall.

Maybe this isn't a good time.

As I turn to escape back up the stairs, the door of the office opens and a man in an electric wheelchair comes out. He's a tall man—I can see that even though he's seated—in his early fifties with a mass of wild grey hair. His legs are thin and strangely doll-like under the faded tweed suit he's wearing.

"Gwen!" he shouts, disappearing into the next room. "I'm a SWINE!"

"Yes, well, we know that."

"And you! Loitering on the stairs! Come in!"

I hesitate.

"Yes, YOU!" he booms.

"Stop scaring the students, Simon. We've had words about this before."

Moving closer, I poke my head around the corner. It's a spacious room with a large sash window that looks out at ground level to an unruly garden in the back.

"Hello." I feel like an eavesdropper who's been caught out—which is exactly what I am. "My name's Evie Garlick. I'm registered for the advanced acting workshop."

Simon spins around and shakes my hand. He has a grip that could strangle a child. "Welcome, Evie! Welcome to London and to the Actors Drama Workshop Academy! I'm Simon Garrett and this is my assistant, Gwen." He throws his arms wide. "Don't be deceived by these humble surroundings; these are just temporary accommodations while we wait for our new studios to be developed in South Kensington. Right next to Hyde Park and Kensington Palace. You'll love it. Please have a seat!" He gestures grandly to a folding chair in the corner. "Make yourself comfortable."

I sit down.

Gwen smiles at me. "Would you like a cup of tea? I'd offer you coffee but we're out of filters. Of course, I could make you an instant. Do you drink instant? Being American, I expect not. It's Nescafé." She unearths a jar from her desk drawer. "I've had it for quite some time." She shakes it, nothing moves; the granules have formed a solid archaeological mass against one side.

I smile back, grateful for her hospitality. "No, thank you. I'm fine."

"How was the flight?"

"Long."

"Oh yes." She wrinkles her face in dismay. "How terrible for you! How perfectly awful! I think there's nothing worse. Are you sure you wouldn't like a cup of tea?" she offers again, as if it might erase the memory entirely.

"No, really, I'm OK."

Simon sweeps up to me, braking barely an inch from my toes. "So, Miss Garlick! What makes you think you'd like to be an actress?" He's staring at me with unnerving intensity.

"Well." I know the answer to this question: I've been rehearsing it for nearly half my life. But still it comes as a surprise this early in the morning. "I have a real love of language and a deep appreciation for the dramatic tradition—"

"Nonsense!" he interrupts me. "It's about showing off! You like to show off, don't you?"

I blink.

I'm from a small, rural farming community. Showing off isn't something anyone I know would admit to doing.

"Well, for me it's more about unearthing the playwright's true intentions. Getting to the root of the story," I explain slowly.

He's having none of it. "Don't be coy with me, Miss Garlick! And showing off! Go on, say it!"

This has all the hallmarks of a no-win situation.

I wince. "And showing off."

"Good girl!" He slaps my knee. "Remember, all Shakespeare ever wanted to do was show off and make loads of money. All those wonderful plays, beautiful verses, astounding sentiments were to a single end. He wanted nothing more than to escape Stratford-upon-Avon, arrive in London and have the time of his life! I hope you intend to follow in his footsteps!"

He smiles at me expectantly. There's a sweet, somehow familiar smell on his breath. I try to laugh politely but a kind of snorting sound comes out instead. He doesn't seem to notice.

"Now," he wheels around. Gwen, balancing two cups of hot tea, expertly sidesteps him. He yanks open one of the filing cabinet drawers and pulls out an Instamatic camera. "Smile, Evie!"

I blink and the flash goes off. Out spits the picture. Simon throws the camera back in the drawer. "There you go!" He writes my name at the bottom in big block letters with a red marker. "Now we won't forget who you are!" he beams, sticking my picture onto a felt board with a pin. "Here she is! Evie Garlick! About to take the London acting world by storm! Now. Lots to do. Lots to do. Lovely to meet you, Evie. Did your parents pay by cheque?"

I nod.

"Brilliant! Boyd Alexander is your teacher. Won an Olivier last year for *Miss Julie* at the National. An expert in Ibsen. Brilliant director."

I nod again. I've no idea what an Olivier is. But I'm pretty sure *Miss Julie* is by Strindberg.

"Brilliant," I say. Obviously this is an important word to master.

"Absolutely!" He accelerates into the hall. "Gwen, when you're ready!"

"Yes! All right! Here you go," she hands me a slip of paper with an address written on it. "I've arranged for you to share accommodation with two extremely lovely girls who are staying on from last term. They're really very lovely, very dedicated. And just . . . lovely. I'm sure you'll be very comfortable . . ."

"Gwen! If you don't mind!"

"Yes, I'm coming! For goodness sake! So lovely to meet you." She turns and scurries into the next room, carrying the two mugs of tea, a large leather diary and a tin of shortbread.

And I'm alone, for the first time, in the offices of the Actors Drama Workshop Academy.

Which is costing my parents untold thousands of dollars. That I had to campaign for six whole months to be able to attend. Which is further away from home than I've ever been in my life.

Just those three things alone should make it amazing.

I close my eyes and try not to cry. Then I get up and look at my photo. Sure enough, one eye's open and the other one's closed. I look like a drunk singing.

Here she is, Evie Garlick. About to take the London acting world by storm.

I show up to the address on Gloucester Place, my new London home, wheeling my bulging suitcases (the ones encased in layers of brown packing tape to keep them from exploding). They got stuck no fewer than four times in the terrifying grip of the Underground escalator. During rush hour. The experience is akin to an extra circle in Dante's Inferno. Commuters vault up the steps on the left, the rest wedge in behind one another on the right. Tourists, however, suffer public humiliation as they grind the entire system to a halt by attempting to negotiate their bags unaided through the endless tunnels to platforms, which on the little multicoloured map appear to be all in the same place. In reality they're about as close as Amsterdam and Rome. The concierge at the Belle View Hotel insisted taking the Underground was cheap and easy. But I'm here now, hot, sweaty and considerably older than when I woke up this morning.

I take a deep breath and ring the bell.

A tall, slender girl dressed in a scarlet Chinese silk robe with a green facemask on opens the door. Her hair's wrapped in a towel round her head.

"I've got a date tonight," she announces, waving me in. "A real live English date!"

I'm not sure what to say.

"Cool." I drag my bags up the steps.

"You'll love this," she props the door open while I continue to wrestle with my luggage. "His name's Hughey Chicken! Isn't that terrific? I got his number from a friend of mine in New York. She says he's divine. You're here for the room, right?"

"Yes, that's right."

She holds out her hand. "I'm Robbie."

"Evie," I introduce myself. "Evie Garlick."

"Really?" She frowns and the green mask cracks a little. "Have you ever thought of changing your name?"

"Well, I—"

"We can talk about that later. I suppose you want to see it." She's heading off down the hall, the silk robe flapping round her thin ankles. Pushing the door open, she switches on the light. "Ta-da!"

I walk in and look around.

It's a cupboard. The kind of space that in America, they'd shove a washer and dryer into. There's a narrow single bed covered in a brown bedspread, a lopsided wooden wardrobe in the corner and a window that looks out onto a brick wall. The walls are covered in a sixties floral print of maroon and lime and the carpet was at one time pink. There are bald patches in it now; pale threadbare sections just visible by the dim light of the single bulb that dangles from the ceiling, encased in a dusty paper lampshade.

At seventy pounds a week, I was expecting something more. Something much more.

"Isn't it heaven? Everything you've ever dreamed of? Don't worry, my room's just as bad," she wraps an arm round my shoulder. "Come on. Let's get drunk."

I put my handbag down on the bed and follow her into the kitchen.

"Fancy a sidecar?"

"What's a sidecar?"

"Oh, Evie! Well, it's just heaven on a stick! Or in a glass. Or in our case"—she rummages around in the cupboard—"in two slightly chipped service station promotional coffee mugs." I watch as she blends together generous doses of brandy and triple sec and then crushes a wrinkly old lemon with her fingers. "Ice?"

"Sure." Her facemask, gone all crusty, is beginning to flake off.

"Cheers!" She hands me a mug. "Come with me while I wash this mess off."

I follow her into the bathroom and sit on the toilet seat, sipping my cocktail while she splashes cold water on her face. The bathroom is long and narrow with deep pile navy blue shag carpet. Every conceivable surface is covered in beauty products—cold cream, astringents, shampoos—used razors are heaped into the corners of the tub, along with an overflowing ashtray and several abandoned coffee cups. The air is heavy and damp, a sweetly scented fug of perfumed bath oil and rose petal soap.

I take another sip of my drink and watch as Robbie rubs off the mask. Her face is pale, lightly freckled, with no discernible eyebrows.

Bending over, she unwraps the towel from her head and a pile of white-blonde curls tumble onto her shoulders. She lights two cigarettes from the pack in her robe pocket and hands me one, leaning back on the sink and taking a long, deep drag. I've never really smoked before, never quite got the hang of it. But now, with the thick, sweet mixture of brandy and triple sec smoothing its way through my veins, it's easy to inhale without coughing. I roll the smoke around my palate and exhale slowly, just like Lauren Bacall in *The Big Sleep*.

Suddenly things don't seem so bad after all.

I'm free. Sophisticated; drinking in the middle of the day and hanging out in a bathroom with a girl I've only just met.

"Let's go sit somewhere where we can pass out in comfort," Robbie suggests, and I follow her into the living room. Dark and draughty, it faces onto a busy through road. The greying net curtains flutter every time a truck or bus whips by. She puts on a Van Morrison tape and throws herself onto the faded black leatherette sofa, dangling her long legs over the side. She isn't wearing any underwear. I sit across from her in one of the ugly matching chairs.

"So, what are we going to do about this name of yours?" She blows smoke rings into the air; they float, like fading halos above her head.

"Do we have to do anything about it? I mean, it's not that bad, is it?"

She raises an eyebrow. "You want to be an actress with a name like Evie Garlick? I can see it now: *Romeo and Juliet* staring Tom Cruise and Evie Garlick. Evie Garlick *is Anna Karenina*. The winner of the Best Newcomer award is Evie Garlick!"

She giggles.

"OK. Fine." I've lived with this all my life. "What would you suggest?"

"Hmmm . . ." She narrows her eyes. "Raven, I think. Yes. I like Raven for you. On account of your hair."

"My hair's brown."

"Oh, but we can change that, no problem. What do you think?"

"Evie Raven?"

"No, sweetie! Raven for your first name! Now let's see . . . Raven Black, Raven Dark, Raven Night, Raven Nightly! It's perfect! Raven Nightly. Now you're bound to be famous!"

I never thought of dyeing my hair. Then again, I haven't come all the way to London just to be the way I was back home. Still, it's a pretty big leap. "Raven Nightly. I don't know. It sounds like a porn star."

"And Tom Cruise doesn't? I think it's fantastic. And listen, I'm good at this; I've made up all my friends' names back home. My girlfriend Blue; she was the first person to start that whole colour naming thing."

"Really?" I've never heard of the colour naming thing.

"Absolutely! You don't think my real name's Robbie, do you?"

Suddenly I don't feel so sophisticated any more.

"My parents named me Alice." She grimaces. "Can you believe it? I had to do something and androgyny is so much more *now,* don't you think?"

"How old are you?" Maybe she's older and that's how she knows all this stuff.

"Nineteen. And you?"

"Eighteen. And you're from . . . ?"

"The Village."

I stare at her.

"New York City," she explains. "The Big Apple. Born and raised."

"Wow."

She's a New Yorker. And not imported; she's *always* lived there. I've never met anyone who actually lived in New York all their lives. It seems inconceivable that children would be allowed in New York; somehow profane and dangerous, like having toddlers at a nightclub. Surely the entire population consists of ambitious grown-ups from Iowa and Maine all clawing their way to the top of their professions in between gallery openings, Broadway shows and foreign film festivals.

"Wow," I say again.

She grins, basking in the glow of my small town admiration.

"I . . . I may be living in New York soon," I venture.

"Oh yeah?"

"I have an audition for Juilliard next month."

"I see." Her face is hard and unyielding, like a door slammed shut. "Those auditions are fuckers. Bunch of self-satisfied cunts, if you ask me."

"Oh."

A bus careers past, forcing a rush of cold air into the room. Robbie turns away. I follow her gaze but all I can see is an empty bookcase and the glossy black surface of the television screen.

"I mean, it's not like I'll get in or anything. It's just, it's Juilliard, isn't it? *Everyone* auditions for Juilliard!" I laugh, or rather, I make the kind of wheezing sound that could be a laugh if levity were involved.

We listen to the music and sip our drinks.

Suddenly she smiles and the door swings open again. "Hey, don't mind me! You're going to find it out sooner or later so I might as well tell you now: I'm a shit actress."

I'm stunned. "Oh, I'm sure that's not true, Robbie!"

She holds up a hand to stop me. "No, it is true. Believe me. I auditioned for Juilliard three times. And NYU and Boston and, well, just about everywhere else on the planet earth. Look, it doesn't even bother me." Her voice is breezy. "I've made my peace with the whole thing. Really."

At eighteen, I don't know anyone who's made their peace with anything, let alone a devastating admission of their own artistic limitations. It's threatening to me . . . how can she even say these words out loud? I've an overwhelming desire to change her mind.

"I'm sure you *are* good, Robbie! I mean, sometimes it takes years for people to grow into their type. And while that's happening it can be very awkward. After all, not everyone's an ingénue."

"You are, aren't you?" Stretching her legs out, she nestles back into the sofa. "So, tell me how you got started?"

She's changing the subject.

"I don't know." I lean back in the chair. "I did a play, in grade school. I was a little taller than the others . . . actually, I was put back a year. The truth is, I couldn't read properly or tell time or anything . . ."

I don't know why I'm telling her this. I've only known her about half an hour. But instinctively, I feel safe. There's an energy about her; a lightness I've never encountered in anyone before, like something's missing. And where a thick layer of convention and criticism would normally be, there's only air.

"That's dyslexia," she says, matter-of-factly.

"Really?" My parents were so embarrassed by my backwardness, it was never discussed. "Are you sure?"

"Trust me, I've spent more time in clinical physiological testing than you can imagine. Go on," she urges, making that sound normal too.

"Oh." I'm thrown by my unexpected diagnosis. "Well, when I was growing up, in the Virgin of the Sacred Heart Girls School, you were just thick. Anyway, there I was, a bit stupid and definitely spacey, taller than all the other girls and pretty weird looking because my mother really wanted a boy—she used to cut my hair short—and then I got the leading role in the school play because I was tall with short hair."

A tenderness washes over her features. "And you were good at something!"

I stare at her. "How did you know?"

"It's always the same. You want to be someone else and then you are and people applaud . . ." She grins. "Your secret's safe with me."

"It was the only time I can remember feeling like I belonged in my own skin. No one really wanted to hang out with me until then. And then my parents came along." I see my mother's bright smile, my father wearing a tie, sitting in the front row of the school auditorium. "They were proud of me. They'd never been proud before. That's when I made up my mind I was going to be an actress."

She's still and quiet; frowning at the floor.

I've said too much. The anxious, naked feeling I grew up with returns. Suddenly I'm back in school with my short hair and ugly uniform, trying too hard to make friends with the cool girls.

"I can tell the time now," I add quickly. "It just took a little longer."

She laughs; the frown vanishes and with it my awkwardness.

"What about you?" I ask.

"Me?" She presses her eyes shut. "I've been acting all my life!"

"So you must be good," I persist.

"You know what?" she sits up. "I'm not even that interested in it." And, leaning back, she wiggles her red painted toes, admiring her handiwork.

For a moment, I can hardly speak. "But . . . but, why are you here then?"

"Oh, darling!" She smiles at me indulgently. "Who in the world wants to get a job? And besides, I know I've got some sort of talent; it's just I haven't really found my milieu yet. It's all simply a matter of time. Never mind."

She lights a fresh cigarette, the glow of the flame illuminating her porcelain skin. "So, what I'm wondering, Raven . . ."

I flinch. "That sounds really odd to me."

"You'll get used to it. So what I'm wondering is, I have this great date with Hughey Chicken and he's got a friend he's supposed to meet tonight in Camden. So I'm thinking that maybe you'd like to come along too. A kind of double date."

"You mean a blind date."

"Yeah, well. I guess, if you want to look at it that way."

What other way is there to look at it?

"Actually, I have a boyfriend. He's a graphic artist at CMU."

She looks at me. "And . . . ?"

"Well, I'm not into being unfaithful or anything. I mean, we're probably going to live together when I get back."

"Relax! I wasn't suggesting you offer him bed and breakfast. We were just going to hang out. After all, it's London! Don't you want to meet people? Have fun?"

I hesitate.

Obviously the cool thing to do is say yes. But what if he turns out to be ugly? Or weird? Or even not ugly and weird but out of my league— handsome and cool? I think of Jonny; of his funny, crooked smile. If it's only to hang out, I guess it doesn't matter. He's not possessive. And it's not like I'm going on my own . . . But what would I wear? I've only just got here; I haven't even unpacked.

Robbie's smiling at me, swinging her legs. "So, what do you think? We're going to meet in this pub and then go on to see a band at the Camden Palace."

"I . . . I don't know."

"Rave . . ." She's already shortening it. I now have a nickname from a name that isn't mine. "Rave, the thing is, I don't know Hughey either. See? So it'll be fun. An adventure!"

I don't know why this makes sense but it does. (The sidecars may have something to do with it.) "OK, sure. To keep you company, that's all. But if it's all the same to you, I think I'll use my own name tonight."

She shrugs her shoulders. "Fine. But I wouldn't mention your last name if I were you."

The front door opens.

"Hello!"

"We're in here!" Robbie calls. "Getting drunk!"

A young girl in an ill-fitting brown coat peers in. She looks about fifteen, with heavy, straight, shoulder-length hair pinned back from her face by a bright pink barrette, and enormous round blue eyes. She's carrying a stack of books—a thick, leather-bound reprint of Shakespeare's first quarto, a Penguin guide to *Romeo and Juliet,* a copy of *The Seagull* and a well-thumbed edition of Chekhov's short stories.

"Hi." She crosses the room and holds out her hand. "I'm Imogene Stein."

I stand up. "Evie Garlick. Pleased to meet you."

"Evie's coming with me to meet Hughey Chicken!" Robbie beams, raising her mug.

"Better you than me." Imogene carefully places her books on the floor and shrugs off her coat. Underneath, her dress is a drop-waisted, pinafore affair, at least two sizes too big, and her shoes are the kind of solid, brown oxford lace-ups my grandmother favoured. "What are you drinking?"

"Sidecars. Want me to make you one?"

"Yes, please."

Robbie gets up and Imogene collapses onto the sofa. "I don't suppose you've got a fag?" she pleads. Robbie chucks her the packet before heading into the kitchen.

I watch as she lights up. There's something wrong with this picture. She looks like a Laura Ashley poster child but sucks deeply and greedily, throwing her legs over each other like a forty-year-old prostitute after a long night.

"So," I take a stab at conversation. "You've been out?"

Nothing like stating the obvious.

She passes a hand over her eyes. "Rehearsing. *The Seagull."*

"Yeah? Which scene?"

"The last one. You know, 'I'm a seagull. No, I'm not. Yes, I am.'" She takes another drag and for a moment it looks like she might inhale the whole thing in a single go.

"That's a great scene." I try to sound encouraging. "And a killer speech."

She nods, exhaling a stream of smoke from her nose. "Yep. I am a seagull. I *am* definitely a seagull."

We sit in silence.

Maybe she's a method actress. Method actresses take their work *very* seriously.

I catch her eye and smile.

She stares at me. And then, to my horror, her eyes begin to fill with tears.

Shit. If she thinks she's a seagull, we're in real trouble.

"I love him. I love him and he doesn't even know I'm alive!" She buries her face in her hands.

Is she in character? Should I be improvising with her? I stand up. "I think I'd better unpack or . . . something . . ."

"But I love him! I know he's the one! I just know it!"

Robbie comes back in and hands her a teacup minus a handle. "He's gay, Imo. Everyone knows it. Sorry. We're out of mugs." She refills my drink from a tarnished silver gravy boat.

"He's not gay!" Imo hisses. "Just English!"

"He wears cashmere socks, thinks football is violent, and lives with a man named Gavin. Who's an *organist*," Robbie adds. "Face it. He's gay. Of course, you don't have to believe me but I did grow up in the Village and if I can't spot a gay man then I must be blind."

"Who are we talking about?"

"Imo's scene partner, Lindsay Crufts. He's very handsome, extremely well-spoken and a total ass jockey."

"Robbie!" Imo glares. "Ass jockey is not a term I want to hear again to describe the love of my life!"

Robbie winks at her. "Golly, but you're cute when you're angry!"

"You know," Imo shakes her head, "for a girl who's about to shag some loser by the name of Mr. Chicken, you've got a lot of nerve!"

Robbie giggles. "You are so jealous!"

"Yeah, right!"

I'm on the edge of this conversation, dying to join in. I raise my mug grandly. "And while you're shagging Mr. Chicken, I'll be stuck shagging Mr. Chicken's mysterious friend!"

They both look at me and laugh.

I laugh too. But I don't know why.

Imo pauses for breath. "You don't have any idea what shagging means, do you?"

"Sure," I flounder. "It's dating, right?"

"Fucking," Robbie explains. "Shagging is English for fucking. Makes it sound like a carpet."

I dismiss it like it's old hat. "Yeah, I knew that. I just got . . . confused."
They exchange a secret smile.

I'm not sure I like them. I hate the way they both know how to smoke
and mix drinks and their bathroom's disgusting . . . maybe I should find
my own place.

There's a knocking, or rather a pounding, at the front door. "Hello!
Hello!"

"Shit! It's Mrs. Van Patterson, the landlady. Have you met her?"

I shake my head.

"She's a total nightmare. Dutch. And tight as they come." Robbie
prods Imo with her big toe. "You get it. She likes you."

"Does not!" Imo pushes her foot away. "You go."

"She hates me! At least you look like a virgin."

"I *am* a virgin," Imo sighs. She puts down her teacup and pulls herself
off the sofa. "Fine! Send the virgin. The virgin will do it!" And she
grumbles her way to the front door.

I lean across to Robbie. "Don't you think she's a little young to be
drinking?"

Robbie shakes her head. "She's nineteen. Not that you'd know it. Her
father's this big Hollywood agent. Bags of money. But her mother's a
total freak. Dresses her like a twelve-year-old, insists that she calls her
every day. She's a Born Again. Really into Jesus. It's so sad, really."

"But her name's Stein. That's Jewish, right?"

Robbie nods. "Ever heard of Jews for Jesus?"

I haven't. But I'm tired of being the odd one out.

I give an all-purpose response. "Fuck!"

"Exactly!" she agrees.

We can hear the front door open and she signals to me to be quiet.

"Hello, Mrs. Van Patterson. How are you this afternoon?"

"You girls are using too much hot water! The electricity bill is
enormous! It's outrageous how much water you use! The boiler is on a
timer! You must not press the immersion button. Ever!"

"But the hot water runs out every time we do the dishes. Or if one
person has a shower."

"Really! I've never seen anything like it! What are you doing? Bathing
every day?"

"It's been known to happen."

"Listen, don't you get smart with me! Twice a week is more than enough."

"Where I come from, it's completely normal to bathe every day."

"Where you come from, people are spoilt! Americans think the world is made of money! You girls don't know how lucky you are! Gloucester Place is one of the finest addresses in London. Have you ever played Monopoly?"

"Yes, Mrs. Van Patterson, I have."

"Well, it's like Park Lane. It's not on the Monopoly board but it could be."

"Hmmm . . ."

There's a weighty silence.

"Have you girls been smoking in there?"

"No, Mrs. Van Patterson! Of course not! Why? Can you smell smoke?"

"Yes, I can smell smoke!"

Imo lowers her voice. "I think it's the guys upstairs. I mean, it's none of my business. But I'm pretty sure I've caught them lighting up in the hallway a few times."

"Aha. I see. Right. You are a good girl, Imogene Stein. A nice, well-mannered girl. Much better than that roommate of yours. But you must not use so much hot water, ok? Right?"

The door shuts and we can hear Mrs. Van Patterson stomping upstairs.

Imo comes back in and sits down. "Well, another near miss for the House of Chekhov." She raises her teacup.

Robbie and I look at each other, then raise our mugs too. "I'm a seagull!" we chorus.

Imogene smiles. She's young and old, all rolled up at once.

"Yeah, that's me. I'm a seagull. So," she taps another cigarette on the side of the box and lights it, propping her legs on the coffee table. "Anyone fancy a nice, long bath?"

$\mathcal{S}$TANDING ON the front doorstep in the wind and rain, I fumble in my jacket pocket for my keys. And then I turn and check one last time.

No, she's definitely not there. Not hovering behind the laburnum or waiting on the other side of the gate.

Not that I really believe in ghosts.

But seeing Robbie is different.

She wasn't filmy or white or in any way vaporous or "ghostly." In fact, she looked normal, solid, wearing a pair of jeans and one of those ugly, orange sweaters she'd knitted when she thought her true calling was as a knitwear designer. (She never stopped searching for her calling; every year there was a new one. And that year we all got jumpers. I still have a couple— one in fuchsia and another in a kind of toxic-waste green. They manage to be both too tight and too loose all at once; I think the neck hole is really an arm hole and the arm holes, neck holes. She called it her "signature piece.")

By the time class ended, she was gone. I looked for her, walking to Covent Garden tube station; I half expected to see her trailing behind me, lingering in the shadows of Drury Lane or even standing on the train platform, reading a copy of *Vanity Fair*. She used to like Covent Garden, was forever picking up Australians in one of the bars in the market.

But she wasn't there.

And she isn't here now.

Of course, I must've imagined it. It's amazing what a little insomnia and a few missed meals will conjure up in a girl. I should be relieved. But instead, strangely, I'm disappointed. The older you get, the more friends you lose to marriage, children, work; to adulthood. Friendship itself becomes an apparition; a fleeting spectre, too quick to evaporate in the glaring light of day.

I turn my house key in the lock of the enormous scarlet-painted door.

Number 17 was once a formidable, cream-coloured, stucco-fronted Georgian property, very similar to all the other formidable, cream-coloured, stucco-fronted Georgian properties of Acacia Avenue, North London. Now, it's seen better days. It's the only house on the street whose garden gate squeals like an angry piglet each time it opens, or whose vanilla exterior is peeling away like shavings of white chocolate on a posh wedding cake. And, in a neighbourhood where neat little box hedges and topiary bay trees are de rigueur, the garden has definite romantic, wild, overgrown tendencies; much more Brontë than Austen. In summer, the fig tree drops its heavy fruit to form a thick, gooey compote on the pavement below, and each autumn the towering chestnut launches conkers at passers-by with eerie accuracy. A defiant, shabby grandeur has replaced its once impeccable façade. But in the five years I've lived here it's only grown more intriguing.

It's not your average house share. But then again, Bunny Gold, its owner, is not your typical landlord either.

When Bunny's husband, Harry, died unexpectedly ten years ago, it came to light that he'd been, in addition to a loving husband, father, a respected pillar of the Jewish community and owner of an extremely successful accountancy firm, also a chronic gambler.

He'd already cashed in his pension, life insurance and a great deal of their personal savings to meet his debts. Bunny, who'd spent her entire life in a cosy bubble of shopping, socializing and raising their only child, Edwina, was devastated. An affair would've been one thing. But leaving her in financial ruin was much worse. Above all, she was unprepared to part with her beloved home.

So she began to rent out rooms, although she'd be shocked to hear it described as a "house share." To her, our living arrangements are the result of an intimate form of artistic sponsorship; she's a patron rather than a landlord and will only let rooms to performers or artists whose work she admires. And at seventy-two, her enthusiasm for almost any form of music, painting, dance or drama, along with her remarkable appetite for the avant-garde, is nothing less than inspiring.

So, there's me, the actress/teacher, Allyson, an Australian opera singer/teacher, and our latest arrival, Piotr, a concert pianist/teacher from Poland.

And of course, the love of my life, Alex. We share a couple of rooms and a private bathroom at the very top of the house, overlooking the garden at the back.

We are the privileged few.

Postcards from all over the world regularly filter in from previous tenants, along with invitations for Bunny to visit them in Rome, Paris, New York, Berlin . . . I've known a few of them myself over the years. As Bunny says, "Evie, if this goes on much longer, one of us is going to have to propose!"

And she's right. I should get myself together and move on. But it's never quite as easy as it sounds. Whole years have evaporated, just waiting for the kettle to boil. Maybe one day, I'll be the one sending postcards, even if I only get as far as south London.

But right now, I'm just grateful to be home.

Dumping my bag and coat down on the reindeer antler coat stand in the front hallway (the work of a Norwegian furniture designer who lived here two years ago and now designs plastic chairs for Habitat), I make my way down to the kitchen for a cup of tea and a ferret round the fridge, only to find Allyson and Piotr arguing about lieder.

They barely notice me as I fill up the kettle and switch it on. Both are fairly formidable; it's like a scene from *Twilight of the Gods*. Piotr is incredibly tall and slender; he moves with a confident, swaggering ease, unusual for a man of his height. His dark hair's cut quite short at the back but still manages to tumble into his eyes, which are a warm shade of brown; the concentrated golden walnut of a tiger's eyes and equally intense. However, his hands are his most remarkable feature. They're Rachmaninov hands, vast and powerful; each one easily the size of a grown man's face. He's only been here a week, and I've never heard him say more than three words together. So it's quite a surprise to hear him speak in full sentences.

Allyson on the other hand is going through her Maria Callas stage. If Piotr's hands are his most distinguishing feature, Allyson's cheekbones are hers. They're like two evenly spaced shelves upon which her heavily made-up, green-grey eyes are balanced. Her long, auburn hair is scraped back into a perfect chignon and she's solidly, dramatically, emphatically curvy, or as she puts it, "ample yet agile" (the world of opera being much more image conscious than it used to be). But despite her impeccably groomed exterior, she possesses the mouth of a merchant sailor. After struggling in England for three years now, she's just beginning to cover roles at Covent Garden and sing a few major parts for Opera North and the Welsh National. That, along with a steady stream of young students, keeps her permanently occupied. But her real chance is coming next month. She's due to perform a recital of lieder at St. John's Smith Square and has had her heart set on being able to re- hearse with Piotr. But now it looks like she'll have to rehearse alone.

(This is one of the few advantages to shared housing: not all the dra- mas are your own.)

I move silently to the draining board and retrieve a mug.

"But *why*?" Allyson gestures wildly to the heavens; a move she used to great effect in a regional production of *Tosca* last March. "Give me one reason why not? For fuck's sake! I'll pay you whatever you like!"

Piotr leans against the kitchen counter, his hands in his jeans pockets; amused. "I've already explained to you. German is not a language that anyone should be singing! Ever! Italian, yes. French, ok. Russian, perfect! But German? Sounds like . . . like a noise you make when you, you know, spit!" And he demonstrates the noise.

I put the mug down. Maybe I'll give the tea a miss.

A slice of toast pops up in the toaster.

"But you play German music! You play Beethoven, Mozart, Liszt . . ." Allyson continues.

Piotr tosses the toast on a plate, opening drawer after drawer in search of a knife. I hand him one.

"Thank you. Liszt is not German."

He looks around.

"Don't be so pedantic!" Allyson accuses, pushing the butter dish across to him.

He sighs, spreading the butter thick. "When I play Beethoven or Mozart, I don't have to listen to German. I listen to music. When I have to listen to German, there's no longer any music." And he shrugs his shoulders; a rolling, slow-motion version that's somehow distinctly Eastern European. "I'm sorry."

Allyson turns away, unable to combat this curious logic with anything but a stream of obscenities.

Piotr, apparently oblivious, turns to me instead, munching his toast. "How was your class?"

"An old man walked out on me," I confess, sidestepping Allyson, who's spluttering under her breath in the corner. "He only ever wants to read one poem. One incredibly long poem."

"Good for him! So important to stick to your ideals, don't you think?"

He grins. Allyson growls threateningly.

"And you? When are we going to see you perform?"

I laugh, a nervous, high-pitched little trill. Suddenly I'm wrong-footed; an intruder in this conversation of artistic preferences and ideals. "Oh no, I . . . I don't really do a lot of performing any more. I'm really just a teacher now."

He raises an eyebrow.

I fumble about with a box of tea bags. Even without looking up, I know he's staring at me.

"I'm too old for all that nonsense," I say at last. "I gave it up long ago. Or rather, it gave up on me."

"And how is that?" He takes another bite.

It's far too late at night to unfold the facts of my failed acting career in front of a stranger.

But I make the stupid mistake of trying anyway.

"Well, acting isn't like music, Piotr. I mean, there are so very few jobs and so many people—"

He throws back his head and roars. "Ah, that's true! There are hardly *any* classical musicians in the world!"

I'm blushing. "I'm sorry, that's not what I meant. I just meant that . . . oh, I don't know what I mean . . ." I start again. "Well, I never got to play any of the parts I dreamt about. Never even got near them. I just ended up making B-rated horror films, a few commercials . . ."

"You were an actress." He shrugs his shoulders again. "That's what actresses do."

"No, that's what *unsuccessful* actresses do, Piotr."

"No," he smiles, "that's also what successful actresses do. It's all the same thing, really."

Like Allyson, I've come smack up against the World According to Piotr Pawlokowski. The rules are different here.

"Well, no . . ." I fumble, trying to articulate a yet unformed argument.

"You're American." He diagnoses my deficiency with a single wave of his massive hand. "You make too much of this idea of 'success.' No artist sees life as success or failure, profit or loss, good or bad. The point of art is lost if you measure it in commercial terms."

I blink at him.

"But it was awful," I bleat weakly.

He frowns, popping the last bite into his mouth. "And you believed it would be *fun*?"

There's a long silence.

I'd never thought about it that way before.

"Yes," I admit. "I expected it to be much more fun than working in an office or teaching pensioners or . . . or anything else, really."

He laughs. "Where did you get that idea?"

"Because that's the way it used to be." I can't help but smile to myself at the memory. "It always used to be more fun than anything else on the face of the earth."

"Don't you enjoy playing the piano?" Allyson comes to my defence.

There's that shrug again. "Sometimes. But *fun* isn't a word to describe a relationship with an art form that's embraced every aspect of the human experience for centuries." He looks at me sadly. "You Americans, I'm afraid, are like children—you don't like to grow up. What is it? 'The pursuit of happiness.' What is that? 'To be happy.' Where is the nobility in a life devoted to happiness? It's a shabby little goal."

"Lighten up, mate!" Allyson moves next to me; she loves confrontation. "No need to pick on her just because she's American!"

"I'm not picking on you," Piotr glances at me, then back to Allyson. "But there you go again! 'Lighten up!' Nothing must be serious. Everything must be small, fast . . . light!" He prowls the floor in frustration, reaching for the words as if they're hovering in the air around him. "You are the hero of your life—especially in art! Without adversity, obstacles, where's the hero's adventure? What's the point? Of course you do bad movies! Stupid commercials! So what? They're your dragons; you slay them, you move on.

You're bigger than those things!" He spins round. "What do you have to offer people, what experience, if life is only 'fun'?"

I open my mouth.

Then close it.

It's late; I'm overly sensitive. Instead, I focus on stacking the tea boxes in neat little rows. The silence builds, piling up between the three of us.

"That wasn't the only reason," I say. "My happiness wasn't the only consideration."

"God, Piotr!" Allyson shakes her head. "Could you be any more rude if you tried?"

"Rude?" He turns to her; baffled. "We're just talking. A conversation, right?" And he laughs, resting his hands against the counter. "What do you want? That we should stand here and flatter one another all night?"

There's a long pause.

"Oh. I see." His voice is sharp. "Of course, I didn't mean to offend you." For a moment, his eyes meet mine. I'm startled by the kindness in them.

He turns away. "I forget how important it is that we agree about everything all the time. I'll stick with the piano. Good night, ladies." He nods his head to each of us, a formal, slightly sardonic gesture, before heading up the steps; easily two at a time.

Allyson launches forward, nicking the mug I just put down and filling it with boiled water. "Well! Fuck me!"

The whole exchange has left me disorientated. I open the cupboard door, looking for something to eat. "I guess he has a right to his—"

"God!" She slams the mug down on the counter, half its contents splashing out over the sides. "I thought it would be brilliant to have a pianist in my own home to work with but I've never, not in my whole life, met anyone so fucking difficult!" Plucking a knife off the carving board, she begins hacking at a fresh lemon, throwing it into the water along with a large dollop of honey. "What a fucking diva! And what was all that about? Americans and happiness and . . . Jesus! I would've hit him!"

I need to go shopping. I close the cupboard door.

"His English is good—"

"Should be! He studied at the Curtis Institute in Philadelphia. Still bloody rude!"

"Thing is, Ally, I've been here so long—"

"Tits! I think I'm getting a cold!" She wheels round, glaring at me accusingly. "Does Alex have a cold? I'd better not be getting a cold, Evie."

I shake my head no, relinquishing any hope of actually finishing a sentence.

"It's the stress. The stress is outrageous! This concert is doing my nut in! Look at my glands, will you?"

I can't tell you how many times a week I have to look at Allyson's glands.

She sticks her tongue out. "Do you see anything? Is my throat red? Splotchy?"

No one is more paranoid about her health than Allyson. The kitchen counter is lined with vitamin bottles and herbal tinctures; her room emits a steamy, Arthurian mist from under the door, the result of a humidifier churning away constantly in a corner, and she sleeps more hours a day than a cat. Still, all her effort pays off: she has one of the clearest, most powerful singing voices I've ever heard.

I take a peek. "No, darling. It's fine."

"Thanks. Oh God, Evie! What am I going to do?"

"Well." I pick up another mug from the draining board. "You could always—"

"Balls! I'll have to call Junko again. But she's like a robot; she understands nothing of the power and passion I need for these pieces!" She looks at me. "You have heard about Piotr, haven't you?"

I shake my head and she leans forward, her voice uncharacteristically low.

"He's the one who walked out in the middle of the final rounds of the Tchaikovsky Competition in Moscow a few years ago!"

She stares at me eagerly.

I've no idea what she's talking about.

"It's the most famous piano competition in the world, Evie! He just stopped playing in the middle of his second concerto and left! When he was on the verge of winning!"

"But why?"

"It wasn't good enough . . . he didn't like the way he was playing." She rolls her eyes. Ally's competitive nature is so keenly honed that the idea is clearly anathema. I find it quite intriguing. "He's crazy, Evie! Insane! He was playing Prokofiev Three, with a full orchestra, and suddenly he just stands up and walks away!"

"So if he's crazy, Ally, why are you so keen on working with him?"

"Have you heard him? He was playing 'Gaspard de la Nuit' yesterday and I thought I would faint it was so heartbreaking...Oh fuckity fuck fuck fuck!" she collapses her head into her hands. (If Puccini had been composing for Allyson, "One Fine Day" would've become "Where the Hell Is He?")

I take a piece of cheese out of the fridge, turning this new information around in my mind.

"And now he teaches at the Royal Academy."

"But he could've been huge!" she mumbles.

We sit a moment.

Eventually, she looks up. "You know what we should do? We should go out, you and I; just the girls! We could go dancing or something!"

Every couple of months she does this; she launches into a campaign to force me into socializing, usually just after she's finished some big job.

"Well, maybe. I don't know, Ally. I think I'm a bit old for dancing."

"I'm older than you are," she reminds me.

"Yes, but you're, you know, trendy . . ."

"You could be trendy. Let's go shopping. It would be fun!"

She's staring at me with those huge, unflinching diva eyes.

"I'll think about it."

"You always say that. If I had your face and your figure—"

"Ally! Stop it!" Why am I so embarrassed?

"You're not even wearing makeup, are you?"

"Please!" I shake my head.

"I'm just saying, it's a waste! I'm going to stop asking one of these days and then you'll be sorry!" Opening one of the dozen bottles, she tosses a few pills into her mouth "So the old fart walked out on you, did he? You've mentioned him before—what's his name?"

"Mr. Hastings."

"Poor Mr. Hastings."

"Actually, he's a very difficult character," I point out, suddenly defensive.

"Yes, but you would be difficult too, wouldn't you? If you'd never lived out your dreams. Makes people crazy, Evie." She retrieves her drink and kisses me on the top of my head. "Night, darling."

Standing alone, I pour what's left in the kettle into my mug. There's not enough for a full cup, so I leave it. And I stare out into the vast, black space that's the garden in the rear.

I've never thought of Mr. Hastings as having dreams. Or at least not any that extended beyond making my class a misery. The revelation that he might endows him with an unwelcome vulnerability in my mind. This, along with Piotr's antihappiness diatribe, has finally tipped me over the edge. I'm exhausted and unexpectedly riddled with self-doubt.

I'm done slaying dragons for today.

Moving mechanically, I wipe down the kitchen counter before turning off the lights. And I have that feeling I get at the end of almost every day; the sensation of having left my body and watching it from a distance—a kind of physical déjà vu. Walking back up into the hallway, I'm floating, insubstantial; repeating the same evening rituals; pausing to make sure the front door's locked, checking and rechecking.

I turn to make my way up the stairs.

And there, sitting in the darkness of the living room, is Piotr.

He's at the piano. But there's no sense of impending action. No crinkle of anticipation, as if he might, at any moment, begin to play. Instead, a powerful calm surrounds him.

It's on the tip of my tongue to ask him if he's all right. To break the silence, smoothing it over with noise, questions and conversation.

But then an unexpected intimacy overwhelms me.

His stillness is revealing. It's as if he's unfolding very slowly before me; invisible layers dissolving into the shadows. The longer I linger, the more I see . . .

I step back.

This isn't an experience I should be having with a man I don't know. A man who doesn't even like me.

And yet a fierce longing clutches at my heart: to be in a room where I'm not alone and yet where nothing—no words, no movement, no explanation—is necessary.

Walking upstairs, I move as quietly as possible but the third stair from the top creaks unbearably. She's awake.

"Is that you, Evie?"

"Yes, Bunny." It's like being a teenager again.

"Did you lock the front door?"

"Yes, I did."

"Come in and say good night properly then."

I push open the heavy, wide door. Her room's spacious, with a set of small, adjoining apartments that take up the entire first floor. She's sitting, propped up in her lit-bateau bed on easily two dozen pillows, dressed in a linen nightgown covered by a pale gold bed jacket. Across her lap, an ancient edition of *Swann's Way* competes with the half-dozen copies of *Hello!* and *Tatler* that cover her bedspread.

Pulling off her reading glasses, she cocks her small, silver head to one side, examining me thoroughly. "Oh, Evie! If only you tried a little! A bit of makeup, a nice haircut . . ."

I stare at the carpet and smile. "Now, why would I want to do that, Bunny?"

She pats the end of the bed, inviting me to sit down. "You never know, darling. Lots of girls meet lovely men at work. That's where Edwina met her partner."

(Edwina, her only child, came out as a lesbian and moved to Arizona with a woman from her father's accountancy firm shortly after Harry's death. Bunny stayed with them for a month last summer. They run an extremely expensive, chic little gallery specializing in Native American art and are not, as she puts it, "unfashionably gay." "They're really terribly sweet," she assures me. "Discreet, with very flattering hairstyles. And it's such a relief not to have to humour them the way one must with a man. You know, Evie, as long as one of you can cook, it can't be that bad." I'm not sure she understands that it's more than just a convenient living arrangement; with Bunny it's almost impossible to tell.)

"Believe me, there are no lovely men where I work. Quite the opposite. And besides, you're forgetting that I have a perfectly marvellous man of my own. How was he tonight?"

She smiles. "As always, the best. Although his diet is appalling, my dear. I made some borscht tonight. Did you see it? There's a little left over in the fridge. I thought it might be nice, for Piotr, you know."

"But borscht is Russian, isn't it?"

"Yes, well, close enough. But Alex wouldn't touch it. Can you imagine?"

"Who in the world would turn down your homemade borscht?"

"Well, Harry didn't think much of it." She smooths away a crease in the sheet. "But then Harry had no taste. No taste buds, even. Too many cigars. Never allow Alex to smoke, promise me!"

"I'll do my best." I rise to leave and then stop. The mention of Harry reminds me . . . "Bunny, forgive me if this is in any way inappropriate and you don't have to answer me if you don't want to, but—"

She laughs. "My goodness, Evie! So *formal*!"

"I'm sorry. It's just . . ." How to put this? "Do you ever see Harry? I mean, now?"

She looks at me. "He's dead, dear."

I feel foolish. "Yes, I know, I was just wondering if you ever . . . I mean, if you believe that people can come back, you know, once they're . . ."

"Gone?"

I nod.

"Well"—she thinks a moment—"he sometimes makes an appearance in the mornings. Shuffles in wearing that dreadful old dressing gown and carrying a copy of *The Times*. Wants help with the crossword. Stuff like that. Chit-chat, really."

My heart dives forward in my chest. "And what do you do?"

"Well, the shit knows I'm not speaking to him." She picks up her copy of Proust again. "I just ignore him and he goes away. It's the cheek of it that's so annoying; the fact that he thinks he can just pick up where he left off."

She speaks without a trace of irony or insincerity . . . can it be true? At any rate, she's begun reading again—her hint that our conversation is over.

I drift over to the door; still full of questions, but unable to arrange my tangled thoughts. "Sleep well, Bunny."

"You too, darling." She looks up. "And honestly, if Harry starts hassling you for clues, just tell him to piss off. Never could spell."

"Right."

She goes back to her book and I close the door. Like so many conversations with Bunny, I have absolutely no idea if she's serious or just having me on.

As I pass by Allyson's room, I hear her humming softly. Something lovely. Something I don't know. Probably something German.

I climb the last flight, twisting the doorknob very carefully. Slowly, I creep through to the next room.

And there he is, sleeping. In his Thomas the Tank Engine pyjamas. Alex, my lovely, gorgeous, perfect four-year-old son. I lean down, softly kissing his forehead. And he shifts, brushing away the clinging attentions of his watchful mother, even in sleep.

I could spend all night staring at him, at the gentle curve of his forehead, the soft, smooth pink of his cheeks, the angelic (at least in repose) set of his mouth. Every day he grows more and more beautiful.

Like his father.

A cloud trails across the night sky. Cold white moonlight floods in through the window. Everything's illuminated, the countless toys scattered across the floor, the secondhand rocking chair in the corner, the brightly painted toy chest . . . Here is a world where nothing's lost for very long; where everything's retrievable. A fragile, temporary universe.

I settle quietly, as I do so many nights now, in the wooden rocking chair and watch.

He'll be bigger tomorrow and yet I'll have never seen a glimpse of him growing in the night. But I'm here, nonetheless. A sentinel, standing guard against a whole, impossible, unknowable future.

And here, in the stillness of my son's room, with the soft, sighing rhythm of his breathing for company, the thought enters again, uninvited.

Would I do it differently?

If I had to make the choice again, is this the fate I would choose?

I look out at the silent street below. At the daffodils bowed by the wind and rain.

It's a fragile, temporary universe.

And always has been.

T HIS IS IT," Robbie says.

We're standing outside a pub in Camden Town, called the Black Dog. The throbbing bass of the music inside pulses each time the door opens.

I waver.

"Come on," she says, swinging the door wide. She's a New Yorker; nothing can scare her. She gives me a little smile and I follow.

It's crowded; heaving. A Friday night mix of drunken Irishmen and City boys straight from the office. Jesus and the Mary Chain are wailing on the sound system. The bar is three deep. We find a corner at one of the low round tables.

"Do you mind if we join you?" Robbie asks. It's a group of girls, mid-gossip. They nod and wave their cigarettes at us. "Go ahead." We perch on the edge of our stools; I'm clutching my handbag in front of my chest like an old lady waiting for a bus. Robbie pushes it down to my lap.

"I'll get us a drink. What will you have?"

I fumble for my wallet. "Ah . . . I don't know . . . a beer, I guess."

She puts her hand over mine. "How 'bout a pint? On me."

And then she's gone, engulfed in the crowd. I smile at the girls across the table. They ignore me. Can they tell I've never been in a pub before? Does it show that I'm American? I readjust the embroidered vintage cardigan Robbie lent me and my Guess? jeans. Everyone else seems to be chicer, more convincingly put together. With bigger hair, shorter skirts and sharper shoulder pads. I'm the only one with a ponytail. Slipping the band out, my hair falls round my shoulders. I check my Swatch. Almost nine o'clock.

Robbie comes back, carrying two overflowing pints. "Here." She hands me one. I take a sip and almost immediately spit it back out.

"Jesus, Robbie! It's warm!"

The girls across from us stare at me like I'm a freak. Robbie giggles. "Yup," she says, settling onto the stool next to me. She whips out a compact and reapplies her lip gloss. I marvel at her poise. This is probably the sort of thing she does all the time back home in the Village.

I take another sip of my warm beer. "How will we recognize them?" I feel childish and stupid even asking.

"Well"—she pouts at herself in the mirror—"Hughey will be wearing a white shirt and carrying a copy of the *Evening Standard*."

I look around the bar. All the men are wearing white shirts and carrying copies of the *Evening Standard*.

"Robbie . . ."

"Just kidding," she slips her compact back into her bag and crosses her legs. "He's bringing me a bunch of flowers, so all we need to do is spot the sap with the bouquet and we're in business."

I'm impressed. "How romantic!"

She makes a face. "I told him to. Start as you mean to go on, Evie. I may be easy but I'm not *cheap*!"

I laugh and we sit, side by side, staring at the door. It opens and closes. More men in white shirts. More copies of the *Evening Standard*. Not a single petal in sight.

The girls across from us are laughing loudly, opening a fresh pack of cigarettes, flirting with the guys at the table opposite.

"How 'bout another?" I'm feeling brave.

"Sure." Robbie hands me her glass and I weave my way towards the bar.

"What it'll be?" the barman asks.

"Two more pints," I say, proud that I've mastered the lingo.

"Yeah, what kind, luv?" He points to a vast array of pumps.

I blink.

"Are they all the same temperature?"

He frowns. "Yeah."

I choose the pump with a picture of a harp on it. That seems pretty. "I'll have that one, please."

He raises an eyebrow. "Suit yourself." And begins to fill the glasses. It's black.

I panic.

"It's black," I say.

He hands me the glasses. "It's what you ordered." And removes the fiver from my hand. I wait for change but he turns to the next person. I guess that's it.

I walk back to the table with the drinks.

"I'm sorry, Robbie. It's black. I think it may have gone off."

"It's Guinness." She takes a sip and wipes the white foam from her upper lip. I hold mine warily. Warm and yellow is bad enough. "Don't worry." She nods encouragingly. "It's sexy. And Irish."

We wade through the Guinness. The music gets louder and so does the crowd. I go to the loo and come back. Then Robbie goes. She buys a pack of cigarettes and we bum a light. A couple of spotty City boys try to pick us up. The girls across from us leave with the guys at the next table. It's ten past ten.

I look at Robbie. "Well . . ."

She shrugs her shoulders. "I'm not worried." And she lights another cigarette, even though she has one burning in the ashtray.

At ten-twenty a man appears in the doorway. He's stocky, wearing a pair of round John Lennon glasses and sporting a shock of spiky, sandy-coloured hair. He's carrying a slightly crushed single rose in clear plastic wrap.

Robbie spots him and stands up. Walking over, she takes the rose from his hand. "This is not a bouquet, Hughey, is it?" She lets it drop to the floor, where it becomes a chew toy for someone's dog. "Now, are you going to buy me a drink or what?"

He smiles and wraps an arm round her waist. "I'd have come sooner if I knew that you were going to look like this."

"You should've seen what I looked like an hour ago." She shoves him in the direction of the bar. "By the way, we're drinking champagne."

He whistles under his breath and saunters up to the bar.

Robbie winks at me. "I told you it would be OK."

That's when I notice the guy behind him. Tall and slender, dressed in a faded suit and T-shirt, he stands, lingering by the door, running a hand through his long black hair.

He looks up at me, tilting his head sideways. "Hey." His voice is quiet but deep.

"Hey." My voice has gone quiet too.

He holds out his hand. "Jake," he introduces himself. He has soft dark eyes and the longest lashes I've ever seen.

"Raven," I say, holding out mine.

He wraps his fingers round mine. He holds them just a moment too long.

And I let him. As far as I'm concerned, he can hold them as long as he wants.

*N*o!"

"Well, what about some toast then? Most of the superheroes I know have toast for breakfast. Often with a little peanut butter and banana on it."

Alex crosses his arms in front of his chest. "Mummy, *nobody* knows a real superhero!"

"I know you, don't I? And you're going to have to sit down properly. No standing on the kitchen chairs. Now, with peanut butter or not?" I pop a couple of slices of bread into the toaster.

"Good morning, mate!" Allyson's dressed in a white towelling bathrobe. She swoops down on Alex, scooping him up in a great big bear hug. "Hey, mister! Where's my kiss!" she demands, tickling him under the arms.

"Ewww! Gross! Ugly Aussie girl germs!" He giggles hysterically. "Ewwwww!"

"No quarter, mate! Give it up! Say, 'I love Allyson!'"

"Never!" he screams, delighted. "Never, ever, ever! You stinky poofter!"

I whip round. "Hey! Where did you learn that word? That's not a word I want to hear again, do you understand me? Where did you hear that?"

He looks at Allyson, who in turn stares at her toes. "Sorry, mate. Must've been me," she admits. "I'm really going to try to clean up my language. Promise."

Sometimes I hate being Mom. "Well, it's not a word I want to hear again from either of you. Do you understand?"

They look at each other and giggle.

The toast pops up and Bunny breezes in, carrying a stack of old magazines, which she plops down on the kitchen table. She's always the first to wake, the one who puts the coffee on and rescues the milk and morning paper from the front doorstep. "I'm off," she announces. "Allyson, please pass me a plastic bag from that right-hand drawer, will you? I'm going to drop these by the surgery. I went the other day to have someone look at my toe and all they had were a bunch of copies of *Horse and Hound*. Can you imagine how depressing?"

I pass Alex his peanut butter toast, carefully cut into strips rather than squares, squares being for some reason entirely inedible. "What's wrong with your toe?"

Bunny pops an apple into Alex's school satchel.

He removes it again when she's not looking.

"Nothing, as it turns out. It just looked *odd*. And that's all I'm going to say, as you're dining."

Allyson and I exchange a smile; only in Bunny's world is peanut butter toast considered "dining."

"Oh!" Bunny swirls round, hands on hips. "And someone's been smoking in the house!"

"Smoking!" Allyson gasps, throwing her hand in front of her face for protection. "This is a nonsmoking household! We don't smoke in here!"

"Yes, but there were ashes in one of my favourite china planters; the one with the white orchids. I know it couldn't possibly be one of you girls." She eyes us sternly anyway. "I must have another word with Piotr. Damn, the dry cleaning! I'd forget my own head, girls." And she darts off, her high heels clicking against the flagstones of the kitchen floor.

Allyson glares at me.

It's my turn to feel like a child. "Stop it! It wasn't me! OK?"

"Well, someone had to do it! Probably that beast upstairs." She pours herself a coffee and settles down at the table. "It's a disgusting habit!" she continues, flipping through back issues of *Hello!* "I cannot live in a smoking household! It plays havoc with your voice . . . God, what are these people like! Look, Evie, 'My Plastic Surgery Torment' by Jordan Halliwell. Jesus! Just look at the size of those tits!"

"Ally!"

It's too late.

"Let me see! Let me see the tits!" Alex bounces up and down, brandishing a piece of toast and pulling at Allyson's sleeve.

She covers her mouth. "Oh, shit! Sorry, darling! I completely forgot!"

I flash her a look.

"Oh, bugger!" She giggles.

I'm fighting a losing battle. "Sit down, Alex, and finish your breakfast. We're going to be late and I've got a lot of work to do this morning." Whatever brief authority I possessed is quickly draining away. Alex ignores me and dances around the table instead, chomping on toast and repeating the word "tits" as many times as he can.

"Listen." Ally's desperate to make it up to me. "I'll walk him over today. Give me one minute while I pull on some clothes!"

"No, it's all right."

"Come on, Evie. Give me a break!" she challenges. "What can be so difficult about walking a child to school?"

"Well, he's got to have his gym things today and he needs to go in the side entrance rather than the front because of the road works on Ordnance Hill and he's not to give any of his lunch to that little Indian boy with the nut allergy; it was a close call the last time. And he's going to bug you about going into the newsagents for sweets but I don't want him having any, Ally . . ."

She's laughing at me.

"I'm serious!"

"That's exactly why you're so funny!" She rubs Alex's hair and he beams up at her. "I'll be two minutes."

She rushes upstairs with her coffee.

"And no more swearing!" I call after her.

"Mummy!" Alex yanks my sleeve. "I didn't *give* him the sandwich, Mummy. He *took* it," he reminds me.

I rub my fingers over my eyes. "Yes, darling."

She's going to buy him sweets, I just know it. She always does.

Oh . . . bugger.

And sitting down at the table, I nick a strip of Alex's toast, skimming through the abandoned magazines. These people live in another world . . . socialites, Hollywood actors, royalty, rock stars . . .

"Mum? Mummy?"

I look up. "What?"

Alex is watching me, his small face suddenly serious. "What is it?"

I stare at him.

Another face looks back at me.

"Nothing." I stand up, forcing my brain back into the present day. "Put your coat on, darling. It's time to go."

Allyson appears in a Cossack-style fur hat and long, grey wool coat—as always, every inch the diva. "Let's go, mate! Come on! Have you got your gym kit?"

"I need my crayons!" Alex bounds upstairs.

Taking a final swig of coffee, she puts her cup down on the table with a flourish. "And this time I promise: no sweets, no swear words and in school on time!"

"Yes. Fine." I move on autopilot, clearing the table of our breakfast things.

"Are you OK?"

I scrape the toast into the bin. "Yes. Fine."

Allyson leafs idly through the magazine pages.

"He's still a good-looking man. Even after all these years."

"I'm sorry?"

"That Jake Albery." She holds up his picture. "Still handsome, don't you think? God, I used to have such a crush on him!"

My heart's racing, hammering in my chest. I force the corners of my mouth upwards into a smile. "You're showing your age, Ally."

She laughs. "I know. I'm getting old. 'Oh, I lock it down, I lock it down, Baby Home Wrecker's in town!'" she sings, dancing over to the door where Alex waits, dressed and ready to go. Grabbing his hands, she whirls him into the hallway. "Oh, I lock it down, I lock it down, da, da, da, da, da, da, da!"

The front door opens and closes, sealing the world out.

Lingering at the sink, I make myself wash up the plates and mugs, slowly rinsing them under the warm water.

Then I turn the tap off.

Fold the tea towel.

And pick the magazine up again. As I knew I would.

So, he's back.

Allyson's right; he does look good—slightly tanned; the kind of gentle wash of colour that's the result of a couple of weeks in Monte Carlo or Beaulieu rather than a month in Mauritius—and effortlessly chic in a dark, tailored suit and crisp white shirt. But there's that familiar air about him, even in a photograph, a slightly edgy awkwardness as if even after all these years in the limelight he still doesn't quite fit in. He remains, as always, the outsider, one eye forever on the door.

His hand rests on the shoulder of a glamorous blonde. She has the same glowing tan, amply displayed in her sheer, strappy pink dress, and similar, expensively tousled bedroom hair. But her smile is harder; more focused. The cameras are on her and it's a moment she's been waiting for. She looks both terrified and intensely determined. Something in my stomach wrenches with recognition.

"Jake Albery seen leaving a private party at the Café de Paris," the caption reads. *"A back catalogue of songs from his hit band Raven is due to be released in May."*

Opening a kitchen drawer, I take out a plastic carrier bag and stack all the magazines neatly inside.

And then I stand there, staring at it.

If only it were as simple as that.

But it never was simple.

Right from the start I should've known.

OTHING HAPPENED."

"*Nothing?*" Imogene frowns.

We're waiting for our first day of classes to begin, sitting in the basement studio beneath the North London Morris Dancing Association. It's a vast square room with wooden floors and an old upright piano in the corner. Light filters in through small round windows near the ceiling; dust particles dance in the shafts of brilliant sunlight, slicing like lasers through the hazy calm.

"That's right. I mean, we just hung out. Went to see the band, talked." My cheeks are burning. I turn away, pretending to search for something in my brown corduroy handbag. All I can find is a mouldy old mint. I pop it into my mouth anyway.

Around us the room's filling with students.

"You're blushing!" She giggles. "You like him, don't you?"

I smile back at her.

Yes, I like him.

And I shouldn't. Jake's not my type of guy—not that I've ever met anyone like him before. There's something rough about him. I don't mean physically rough. But he has this dark undercurrent of raw energy I'm not used to; like anything could happen, any time. Besides, I'm not meant to like anyone except Jonny.

Jonny is my type; polite, clean shaven, on time . . . the kind of guy who celebrates the anniversary of your first kiss with flowers, even when he doesn't have any money.

But if I love Jonny, why do I keep thinking about Jake?

I wish he'd kissed me good night. Not just a peck on the cheek but one of those full-on face-devouring sessions that don't stop with kissing. But I can't tell that to anyone.

Robbie, on the other hand, happily disappeared with Mr. Chicken for ages.

"Enough about me." I'm determined to rein in these thoughts. "Show me which one of these fine gentlemen is Lindsay Crufts."

Now it's her turn to blush. "Where's Robbie?" she skirts my question. "You guys got back so late last night."

I shake my head. "I don't know. I heard her alarm go off." I check my watch. "And I pounded on her door before I left. She should be here."

A slender young man with soft, ashen hair walks in. He smiles at Imo and her whole face lights up. This must be Lindsay. But he takes a seat on the other side of the studio, folds his legs neatly over one another and fishes a worn copy of Shakespeare's sonnets out of the pocket of his tweed jacket. He reads intently, brow furrowed, nibbling away at his nails.

Imo gazes at him with unrestrained longing. I give her hand a gentle squeeze.

Soon the studio is full; there are about twenty of us and still no sign of Robbie.

At ten o'clock precisely, the door swings wide and Simon enters, wheeling expertly into the centre of the room. "Good morning!" he bellows. "Welcome to the beginning of the spring semester! I'm Simon Garrett. I've spoken to most of you, and shall, no doubt, speak to you again. However, if you have any questions or problems, either my assistant Gwen or I will be available to help you. Gwen!"

Gwen appears behind him, clutching a stack of papers, which she begins to pass around the room.

Simon whips one from her hand and raises it high. "Here are your schedules for the next three months. As you can see, we expect a great deal from you—in addition to your regular classes there are master classes, workshops, private tutorials and plenty of opportunities to see the greatest living actors of our generation in live performances. You're in London now, ladies and gentlemen. It's time to seize the day! If this is your chosen profession then you'll need discipline, determination, the ego of a dictator and the stamina of a decathlon athlete! We've provided you with the most extraordinary professional actors, actresses and directors as teachers. In return we expect you to be prompt, prepared and, above all, professional."

There's an awful hacking sound on the other side of the door; a kind of retching cough, followed by a long, woeful moan. "Jesus! Fuuuuuck!"

The door opens and a dishevelled, overweight man, somewhere between the ages of forty-five and sixty, stumbles in, an unlit cigarette dangling off his lower lip. His thinning brown hair is scraped back across his scalp, and he's wearing a wine-coloured pullover, grey suit trousers and a pair of well-worn black sneakers. He looks like a tramp. Standing just behind Simon, he pulls a gold lighter out of his back pocket. The cigarette fizzes into life. He inhales deeply.

"Greetings." His voice is deep and resonant; the rounded, poignant timbre of a fallen hero. "Pardon me. Have I interrupted your St. Crispin's Day speech, Simon? Once more unto the breach and all that? 'O! for a Muse of fire,' he roars, 'that would ascend the brightest whatever-the-fuck-it-is of invention!'"

"Not at all, my dear man!" Simon's all warm authority; they shake hands. "Just giving them an idea of what to expect." He turns his attention to us. "I'd like to introduce Boyd Alexander, who will be your principal acting instructor this term. Boyd has just returned from Russia where he's been working with members of the Moscow Art Theatre on a new production of *The Cherry Orchard*."

There's an audible gasp; the Moscow Art Theatre is legendary; the company Chekhov himself favoured.

"He's also due to direct the *Wars of the Roses* next season at the RSC, so we're very, very lucky to have him."

Boyd executes a little half-bow, nearly scorching himself with his cigarette in the process.

"Right!" He pulls a chair up and collapses into it. "Enough about me. Run along, Simon! Now," he glowers at us, "what I really want to know is, can you people act? Or are you just poncing about in London on your parents' credit cards for a few months?"

Gwen and Simon exchange a look.

Boyd waves them on. "Off you go, you two! And Gwen, a cup of tea wouldn't go amiss. Trust me," he purrs placatingly. "I am, after all, a professional!"

They leave. The rest of us are left clasping our schedules the way that lost tourists cling to maps.

"You were meant to prepare an audition speech. So, which one of you has the balls to go first?"

All eyes hit the floor.

He groans, inhaling again. "Fine. Shall we do it like this, then? How many Juliets do we have with us today?"

Three hands go up.

"Of course. Let's start with the Juliets. And how many of you have prepared balcony scenes? Please rise."

Two of the girls stand up; a small brunette with glasses and a rosy-cheeked redhead. Boyd leans forward in his chair, rubbing his hands together. "Now, my dears." His voice is sinister. "I want you to do the speech together at the same time." He points to the brunette. She's biting her lip. "You take one line and you," he turns to the redhead, "you take the next, do you understand?" She nods, tugging at her skirt nervously. "And yes, my darlings, this is a punishment because no one should have to sit through the balcony scene more than once on any occasion and also, as actresses, you should know better. Juliet has some stonking speeches filled with lust, death, suicide, ghosts, the whole bloody lot and you guys have chosen the naffest one of them all!"

They blink at him. The small brunette with glasses looks as if she might cry.

Boyd swivels round to the rest of us. "The first rule of being an actor is to grab the limelight. Make the most daring choices you can. Wherever you are, find a light bulb and stand under it! If you don't want to be looked at, if you don't want to be noticed, then you're in the wrong profession. And for fuck's sake, do something worth watching! Now that you've got our bloody attention, keep it! Right! Off you go!"

They stand, huddled together in the centre of the studio. The brunette starts, hands shaking.

" 'Romeo, Romeo.' " Barely audible, her voice is brittle and choked with tears. " 'Wherefore art thou Romeo?' "

"Stop!" Boyd barks, jabbing his cigarette out on the floor. He strides over, grasping her by the shoulders. "Are you going to cry?"

She nods her head, unable to form the words.

"Brilliant! Use it! Channel it! Feed it into the language! Finally! I've always wanted someone to do something different with this speech! What's your name?"

"Louise," she whispers.

"Speak up, girl!"

"Louise!" she shouts back, suddenly irritated.

And he smiles. A great, wonderful, warm, open smile.

His eyes gleam. Bouncing into the centre of the room, he flings his arms wide, throws back his head and shouts "Louise!" until the windows shake. Grabbing her hands, he whirls her round. "LOUISE!! LOUISE!!"

And she's giggling, laughing. "Wherefore art thou Louise?"

He catches the redhead's hand. "Go on!"

" 'Deny thy father and refuse thy name!' "

" 'Or, if thou wilt not, be but sworn my love.' "

The redhead spins round. " 'And I'll no longer be a Capulet!' "

They've caught the rhythm; we can feel it.

" ' "Tis but thy name that is my enemy;' "

" 'Thou art thyself, though not a Montague.' "

" 'What's Montague? it is nor hand, nor foot.' " They take each other's hands.

" 'Nor arm, nor face, nor any other part belonging to a man!' "

And so they dance, turn, vault around the room, throwing the words back and forth, volleyball in iambic pentameter. It becomes in turns breathless, urgent, fanciful—laced with longing, then drenched in desire; everything a young girl with her first crush would be, standing in the moonlight of her own private garden.

"I want you to remember this." Boyd pulls both his Juliets in closer. "I want you to remember what it's like to be alive, to be young; to have the most wonderful language ever written rolling about in your mouth— the flavour of the words on your tongue and this rhythm driving you. It's a sensual experience. Acting's all about the senses. Well done, both of you." He releases them.

They stagger, elated, back to their seats.

"So." He stretches his arms high above his head and yawns. "How many Hamlets do we have today?"

Tentatively, I raise my hand.

Imo looks at me.

"I see." Boyd gestures for me to stand up. "So, a bit of a Sarah Bernhardt, are we?"

I knew this would be tricky.

"And what, exactly, is your difficulty with the traditional women's roles?"

"They're boring." I'm pretending to be more confident than I am. "I'm not good at being young and pretty and . . . well, that's all they are; young and pretty."

He grins. Even sitting, he gives the impression of looking down from a great height. "Well, then. Let's see what you've got."

It's strange standing in the middle; quite different from how I imagined it. All eyes are on me and my heart feels like it's going to burst out of my chest, the adrenaline races through my veins. What is it he said? Make the most daring choices you can? Do something worth watching? Scanning the room, I suddenly spot the old piano. And a brilliant, bold scheme forms in my mind.

I push it towards the centre on its creaking wheels, then sit down and start to play, plucking out the tune to Mendelssohn's "Wedding March." I'll slowly build in speed and intensity, a macabre reference to Gertrude and Claudius's incestuous wedding, and then whirl round and hit them with the first line.

Da da da da . . . da da da da . . .

My hands start to shake.

I haven't played a piano in years.

The tune is only barely recognizable. In fact, it sounds more like the Captain and Tennille than Mendelssohn. But the longer I play, the harder it becomes to break off and swirl round.

I'm stuck.

Shit! I have to stop playing the piano! I have to stop! I'm panicking! I have to stop panicking and I have to stop playing the piano!

I twist round and nearly fall off my seat. A sea of bewildered faces greet me. I feel like a lounge singer. " 'To be or not to be,' " I shout, sounding remarkably like the guy who sells the *Evening Standard* outside Baker Street tube station. " 'That is the question!' "

OK. Calm down. I've begun. That's the main thing.

Only now I'm trapped behind the piano. I try pushing the bench back dramatically. But it makes a hideous, spine-crunching, scraping noise. The whole room gasps in agony. Once up, I attempt to recover by leaning nonchalantly against the side of it. The lid slams down and I end up screaming like a girl.

Sadistically, Boyd allows me to work my way all the way through. And when I finish, he just looks at me, arms folded across his chest. "Thank you, Miss . . . ?" He pauses, waiting for my name.

"Miss Garlick," I mumble.

The speech had seemed a lot more impressive in my room last night.

"Yes, well, Miss Garlick, I believe you've given everyone a valuable lesson about props."

There's a twitter of laughter.

I want to die.

"So, what's a nice girl like you doing wrestling with a piano?" He leans back in his chair.

I stare at the floor. "I don't know . . . I thought it would be . . . a good idea." I sound like an idiot. Why doesn't he just let me go? Why does he have to keep torturing me?

"How old are you?" he asks.

I pause. Is this a trick question? "Eighteen," I admit slowly.

"And what do you like to do?"

"Uh, well, going out, being with my friends . . ."

"You like boys?"

I flush. "Yeah."

"So pretty much the same stuff Hamlet likes: girls, hanging out with friends, being at school and away from home . . . normal student stuff. Only, of course, Hamlet isn't eighteen, he's thirty."

"Oh." This is obviously important. I only wish I knew why.

He looks at me, tilting his head to one side. "Doesn't that seem strange to you? You see," he continues, not waiting for my answer (perhaps already knowing that there isn't one), "long before the play begins, way before his father's murdered, there's already something wrong with Hamlet. He enters, fucked."

I'm not really getting this.

"That's what's so interesting. The hero of our tale is a loser. The most famous play in the world is about a guy who can't pull himself together, doesn't have a job, can't get the girl and who takes four hours to accomplish something he was told he needed to do in the first twenty-five minutes! And then he dies!"

I nod as if it's all starting to make perfect sense.

It isn't.

He leans forward eagerly. " 'To be or not to be' isn't about indecision—it's about failure. He goes through the whole speech, thinks about every angle of the question and then ends up back where he started. So, why does the world love Hamlet, Miss Garlick?"

I shrug my shoulders, inwardly kicking myself for not learning Juliet instead.

"Because," he speaks with sudden intensity, his face illuminated with feeling, "very few of us relate to what it's like to be a hero. But everyone understands what it's like to fail."

Boyd stares at me, searching my face for some flicker of recognition.

He's lost me. I avert my eyes, concentrating on the worn surface of the wooden floorboards, hoping he'll release me soon. I can sit down and be anonymous.

"Of course, there's a lifetime between eighteen and thirty," he concedes quietly.

"OK, right!" he shifts gears. "Let's get this speech moving." Standing up, he fishes around in his pocket and throws me a coin. "Forget the piano, OK? Let's keep it simple. Heads you live. Tails you die. Go on—toss it."

I throw the coin into the air, slapping it down on the back of my hand. "Tails."

"Is that what you wanted?"

"I don't know."

Boyd goes over, pulls Lindsay Crufts to his feet. "Here's the deal," he tells me. "You can either kill this guy or kill yourself."

I blink at him. "I'm sorry?"

"Go on, flip the coin! Heads, you kill him. Tails, you kill yourself."

Reluctantly, I flip the coin again. "Heads."

"Brilliant!" He gives me a shove. "Off you go!"

I look at him, horrified. "What do you mean?"

"Go on! Kill him!"

I turn to Lindsay. He smiles politely.

"Come on! What's wrong with you!" Boyd claps his hands. "Time's ticking! Let's go! Stab him! Strangle him! Hit him over the head with a chair! Do something!"

I'm completely paralyzed. "No!"

"Why not?"

"I can't!"

"Then kill yourself!" Boyd's circling me, fencing me in. "Go on! Do it! Those are the choices—him or you!"

"I can't!" I feel trapped, panicky. "I can't do either!"

"So say it! Start!"

> "To be or not to be: that is the question:
> Whether 'tis nobler in the mind to suffer
> The slings and arrows of outrageous fortune,
> Or to take arms against a sea of troubles,
> And by opposing end them? To die: to sleep;
> No more; and, by a sleep to say we end
> The heart-ache and the thousand natural shocks
> That flesh is heir to, 'tis a consummation
> Devoutly to be wish'd."

"That's it! Keep going!"

I press on, the language coming fast and easy now. The speech that, five minutes ago, had seemed like a nightmare of dragging time, tumbles out with a new urgency.

> "To die, to sleep;
> To sleep: perchance to dream: ay, there's the rub;
> For in that sleep of death what dreams may come
> When we have shuffled off this mortal coil,
> Must give us pause. There's the respect
> That makes calamity of so long life;
> For who would bear the whips and scorns of time,
> The oppressor's wrong, the proud man's contumely,
> The pangs of despised love, the law's delay,
> The insolence of office, and the spurns

That patient merit of the unworthy takes,
When he himself might his quietus make
With a bare bodkin? who would fardels bear,
To grunt and sweat under a weary life,
But that the dread of something after death,
The undiscover'd country from whose bourn
No traveller returns, puzzles the will,
And makes us rather bear those ills we have
Than fly to others that we know not of?
Thus conscience does make cowards of us all;
And thus the native hue of resolution
Is sicklied o'er with the pale cast of thought,
And enterprises of great pith and moment
With this regard their currents turn awry,
And lose the name of action."

Before I know it, it's over; done. And for the first time I feel as if I'm in control, driving the words forward instead of racing to catch up. It's an exhilarating, intoxicating sensation—like being behind the wheel of a powerful sports car. I wasn't sure I could do it. And now I want to do it again.

Boyd's rocking back on his heels. "Well, that's more like it!"

The door to the studio creaks open and Robbie, still wearing last night's clothes and clutching a takeaway coffee, tries to steal in.

Boyd swirls round.

"Ahhh! An Ophelia! My, my! You've *definitely* been picking the wrong sorts of herbs! And what's this?" he plucks the coffee cup from her hand, tosses the plastic lid to one side, and slurps loudly. "Mmmm! Milk *and* sugar! Perfect for a hangover, wouldn't you say?"

She smiles uncertainly and I retreat to my seat.

Wrapping a paternal arm round her shoulders, he leads her gently into the centre of the room. "Let me explain to you how this one goes. You can be late but you'd better be good. If you're crap, you'd better make certain that in future, you're on time. So, my dear (and, by the way, it's nice to know I'm not the only person in London who takes personal hygiene with a pinch of salt), I'd very much like to hear your audition speech."

He gives her his wickedest grin.

She, in turn, looks uneasily at the floor.

Silence extends in all directions; an excruciating, awkward vacuum of embarrassment. I feel for Robbie—wish that I could rescue her. But instead, the best I can do is look away, as if it's kinder to ignore her as she stands there, staring at the space between her feet as the moments drag by.

Then, very slowly, she lifts her head. Her eyes meet his. And when she speaks her voice is languid, almost drunk.

> "i like my body when it is with your
> body. It is so quite new a thing.
> Muscles better and nerves more.
> i like your body. i like what it does,
> i like its hows. i like to feel the spine
> of your body and its bones, and the trembling
> -firm-smooth ness and which I will
> again and again and again
> kiss, i like kissing this and that of you,
> i like,slowly stroking the,shocking fuzz
> of your electric fur, and what-is-it comes
> over parting flesh. . . . And eyes big love crumbs,
>
> and possibly *[a smile plays on her lips]* i like the thrill
>
> of under me you so quite new."

The room is silent.

She reaches across and removes the coffee cup from Boyd's hand, and winking, takes a sip.

No one dares move.

"And with that, ladies and gentlemen," he says at last, "I think it's time for a cigarette."

As the studio drains of students, Robbie sits down next to me. I turn to her, stunned. "I thought you said you were shit!"

She grins. "Oh, I can make a scene, if that's what you want. Now, on to more important matters. Who here thinks I should fuck the teacher?" She giggles and raises her hand.

Imo's practically apoplectic with indignation. "My God, Robbie! He's only about eighty! That's *so* gross!" she hisses. "Why can't you ever take anything seriously?"

Robbie sighs wistfully. "But he's sexy! Besides, our Mr. Chicken doesn't know his penis from his pancreas. Or my tits from my tonsils. Or for that matter—"

"Oh *please!*" Imogene stalks off, hands pressed over her ears.

I shake my head. "Bad Robbie. Down, girl."

"Oh, Evie!" She leans her head against my shoulder, stifling a yawn. "But being good is so boring! And besides, I'm ever such a long way from home."

Boyd walks over and sits down. "Good work today," he says, tapping me on the knee.

I look at him in amazement. "But I completely fucked up!"

"What you did took courage and balls. Anyone who wants to be an actor has to get used to making a prize prat of themselves. And in my experience, the bigger the talent, the bigger the flops. But it paid off, in the end . . . didn't it?"

My whole insides warm with pride.

"And you." He turns his attention to Robbie. "I'm a big fan of E. E. Cummings but I'm willing to wager that's just a little something you pull out of your back pocket anytime you don't fancy paying for your own drinks."

To my surprise, Robbie's pale cheeks are bright red. I thought nothing could faze her.

"Don't waste my time," he continues. "This isn't a nightclub in Soho and I'm not, despite appearances, a casting agent for the European porn industry. And next time," he adds, standing up and reclaiming the coffee, "go easy on the sugar."

That night, watching *Top of the Pops* and eating a supper of boiled rice, soy sauce and Singapore slings, Robbie composes her list of things to do. She's possessed, pacing the living room and waving her fork in the air.

"First off, girls, we need to get Evie here into Juilliard!"

"Guess that rules out my famous Hamlet speech."

She ignores me. "Second, we need to get Imo laid. Preferably with the homo, so a real challenge, that one."

"Hey!" Imo comes to life from the depths of the sofa, where she's been lying comatose for almost an hour, staring at George Michael dancing around in a pair of tennis shorts, singing "Wake Me Up Before You Go-Go." "Why am I second?"

"Because." Robbie pauses to take another sip of her drink. "Juilliard will change Evie's whole life, whereas getting laid with Mr. Nancy Pants will pretty much leave you back where you started."

"Oh." She leans back again, apparently satisfied but more than likely just pissed.

"And lastly, we need to devise a way that I can impress the new love of my life, Mr. Boyd Alexander."

"Try turning up on time." I flick a forkful of rice at her.

"No heckling! I'm on a roll! Now, how can we do this? What we need is an event . . . something sophisticated, sexy . . . something where we can all dress up and look fabulous!"

"You're blocking the television," Imo waves her out of the way. "I like George Michael."

Robbie shakes her head. "What is it with you and gay men?"

"Oh, no! I'm not buying that for one second! That's *definitely* one guy who's straight!"

"He's a babe," I agree, drenching my rice in soy sauce.

Robbie freezes. "I've got it! We'll throw a dinner party!"

"Do you think it makes any difference that none of us can cook?" Imo turns to me. "Sauce, please."

Robbie does a little pirouette, the contents of her drink splashing over the sides of her glass. "Leave it all to me! Why do you girls always think so small? Don't you understand? We have the power to be anyone or anything we want! The chance to change our whole lives in the blink of an eye! Anything is possible! Nothing can defeat the House of Chekhov! We will go to Moscow, I tell you! We will!"

I pass the soy sauce to Imo. "From Russia with love."

Robbie drapes herself into one of the large, leather chairs, sighing with satisfaction at the perfection of her own plan. "You know," she muses, unfazed by the fact that we're not really paying any attention to her. "I can't wait to be famous. I really can't. I just know I'm going to be good at it." And she leans back, her face a picture of contentment and easy, unruffled anticipation.

"Don't you love the word 'naughty'?" she continues, swilling her drink around like a character in a Noël Coward play. "I mean, the way the English use it? Even the way they say the word 'naughty' is naughty."

Imo and I are transfixed by Duran Duran's latest video in a way that prevents anything more than just shallow breathing.

"Well, I love it," Robbie whispers, half to us, but mostly to herself. "I can't think of anything more exciting than to be poised on the brink of committing acts of great daring and huge potential naughtiness."

I'M LATE. It's quarter past nine already and I'm still not out of the door. For the fifteenth time. I examine myself in the full length mirror of my wardrobe and attempt to readjust the little scrap of pale pink and blue silk Bunny gave me for my birthday. I try to tweak it with the same quick, sharp flick of the wrist I've seen Bunny and Ally use so many times to great effect, but the result is unpromising. I look like an airline hostess. For Air Kazakhstan.

I don't wear scarves; I never have. So why am I wasting precious time today playing with one that, until ten minutes ago, was firmly (if discreetly) headed for Oxfam?

I've lost my books. My room, normally a haven of cleanliness and order, has suddenly erupted into a full-blown mess. I can't find my papers. I tried to change my handbag to something slightly smaller and chicer and now have a purse I can't close, exploding with a selection of strange objects—mentholated breath mints, coloured pens, boxes of half-eaten raisins for Alex . . . The bed has all but disappeared; covered with piles of rejected clothes, the floor with unread sections of *The Sunday Times;* I stub my toe on one of Alex's transformer toys (a bright red superhero that morphs into insect/vehicle) and hop around, clutching it and swearing, and then realise my tights have run . . .

And I'm forced to conclude that there is no point to having extra time. I'm one of the women who don't know what to do with it any more. In fact, the whole day runs much more smoothly if I have no time; to think, feel or deviate in any way from my set routine. Women's magazines are always pontificating about the emotional rewards of luxurious baths, long walks, stolen hours spent reading or meditating or just being, whatever that may be. But what they don't allow for are women like me, who simply panic if given an extra twenty minutes in the morning; whose fragile balance of identity can no longer negotiate a world filled with unanticipated freedom in any form without transforming it immediately into an obstacle course of right and wrong choices.

All because Ally took Alex to school today.

Enough. The twenty minutes are long gone now and I'm late again anyway. Part of me is relieved to default to my normal panic stations mode. And as I tear the silk scarf off my neck, fling the contents of the cute handbag back into the enormous canvas holdall that's normally welded to my arm and shove my feet into a pair of black, stretchy pull-on boots that cover all sorts of leg wear disasters and have for years and probably will for years to come, I feel the comforting rush of adrenaline through my veins. Better the chaos you know.

I force myself to leave my bedroom, averting my eyes to the mayhem I'm leaving behind (there's no time, there's no time, the voice chants over and over in my head), and head downstairs, throwing myself down each flight of steps as quickly as possible. When I reach the bottom, I stop abruptly.

Is that cigarette smoke? Thick, heavy, unmistakable, emanating from the drawing room?

I push open the tall, double doors. It's empty; radiant with sunlight. I'd forgotten that it caught the morning sun or that it was so pleasant; so elegant and inviting. It's been weeks since I've seen it in anything but darkness.

But still the smell persists.

I move around the radius of the room.

Next to the marble fireplace, a Louis Quatorze chair and a small round table sit, basking in a square of warm light. The chair bears the imprint of a curled figure on its seat and one of Bunny's treasured collection of Halcyon Days enamel boxes is open; a small pile of ashes cooling in the lid.

"It's bad for you, you know."

I spin round. Piotr is standing in the doorway. He's just woken up, his dark hair looks particularly Byronic, his beard unshaven. He's wearing jeans and a T-shirt but his feet are bare.

"It isn't me," I assure him quickly. (There's no way of saying that without sounding instantly guilty.) Tilting the ashes out into the palm of my hand, I replace the lid. "I don't know who it is. None of us smoke."

He digs his hands into his jeans pockets. "It's OK." He grins; his eyes are almost amber in the daylight. "I won't tell your dreadful secret."

"No, but it really wasn't me!" I insist. "I don't smoke. Ever!"

He raises an eyebrow. "And yet you're holding a handful of ashes."

I pause. There's that strange feeling again, the same sudden rush of transparency I had last night. "I found them," I say, avoiding his gaze.

"I see." He stretches his long arms above his head, turning to run his fingers gently through the crystals of the hallway chandelier. A thousand rainbows appear.

"You don't believe me, do you?" I follow him out. This is too unfair and irritating. "Do you honestly think I secretly sneak ciggies in Bunny's front room, flick the ashes into one of her precious porcelain trinkets and then lie about it when I'm in danger of getting caught?"

He tilts his head. "Why not?"

"Why not?" I sound like a parrot. "Why not? Because it's . . . because it's naughty!"

I flinch. I can't believe I've just used that word in adult conversation.

Apparently, neither can he.

"You're a funny woman!" He laughs, rocking back on his heels. "I haven't met anyone like you in a long time!"

I don't even want to know what this means.

"I really don't smoke," I add dejectedly but it only makes him laugh harder.

"I'm making tea," he says at last, rubbing his eyes and pulling himself together. "Black tea. With sugar."

Is this an invitation?

"You do drink tea, don't you? Or"—he can barely contain himself—"I could just put it out on the table and then turn my back and if it should happen to go missing . . ."

He's off again.

"I'm late," I say, not moving; not quite sure what to do with the ashes in my hand. "I should've left ten minutes ago . . . and will you please stop laughing at me!" This seems to be a trend today.

The phone rings.

He holds his hands up. "OK! OK!"

It rings again.

"Excuse me." I stride purposefully across the hall to where the phone sits on a narrow table. "Hello?"

"Oh, hello! Who is this?"

It's Melvin Bert, the Head of Drama at the City Lit. The rounded, plummy tones of his Eton education are unmistakable. My throat constricts instantly, as a hand tightens into a fist.

"Melvin, it's me: Evie Garlick."

"How extraordinary! I . . . I was certain I'd dialled someone else . . ." He pauses. "But . . . but now that I'm through to you, I think you might do just as well . . ."

I shake my head.

Piotr nods. Crossing, he takes my hand gently by the wrist and tips the ashes into his palm. He smiles, his fingers warm against my skin.

He disappears down the steps into the kitchen.

I yank my concentration back. "What can I do for you, Melvin?"

"Well, the truth is, Edie . . ." He's never known my name. In the three years that I've worked for him, I've failed to register in any lasting way on his memory. "I need someone to take over Ingrid Davenport's class on the three-year acting course. She's been offered something at the National and at her age she really has to have a run at it!"

Ingrid's only fifty. But Melvin, despite his professional career administrating in the dramatic arts, has never been an actor. It continues to baffle him that anyone over the age of thirty would be interested in acting professionally when they could have a nice, comfortable job teaching instead. "As I said, I was originally going to ask Sheila, but now that I've got you on the phone . . ." His voice trails off, ripe with possibility.

This is a rare and exceptional opportunity; a chance to move out of the lower depths of teaching pensioners and night students; to pull myself into the proper, professionally accredited three-year drama course. Maybe even to direct. My heart surges with excitement. And terror.

All I need to do is to say something. Anything at all.

"Well, Melvin." I take a deep breath, determined not to betray my nerves. "That's a . . . an interesting offer . . . May I ask what times she teaches?"

There's the sound of him riffling through papers. "Let's see . . . yes, the first years are from eleven until one, then the third years are from two until four-thirty. She has private tutorials on Wednesday afternoons until six-thirty."

He pauses; a sharp, abrupt full stop. It shrieks for some sort of decisive, enthusiastic response. A clock ticks away in my head.

"Oh." My mind's reeling. "It's just, you see, my son is still in school," I fumble, thinking out loud, "and . . . I . . . I . . ."

God! Pull yourself together!

"Let me think . . ." I stall. "He's usually out by three . . ."

Melvin sighs indulgently. The clock ticks louder.

"I need to get from Drury Lane to St John's Wood before he . . . you know . . ."

I can't even finish a sentence! There's no way I'm capable of taking over Ingrid's workload.

"Melvin, I don't think it's going to work for me right now. I have to be available and . . . his schedule's very tricky at the moment . . ."

What am I doing? What am I saying?

"Yes, yes, of course. I understand." I can hear him tapping his pen. "Well, it was just on the off chance." He can't wait to get me off the line.

Suddenly I'm desperate again. "Oh, of course! I mean, if you want someone to fill in just for a few days or something . . . I mean, if there's anything I can do . . ."

"Yes, I'll keep you in mind," he says briskly. "Take care, Edie."

And the line goes dead.

I hang up.

Turning, I catch sight of myself in the antique looking-glass, hanging at the bottom of the stairs. A dim, filmy shadow clouds its surface like a phantom, compromising its clarity. Even the elaborate gilt frame can't redeem its grey face.

There I am, diffuse and uncertain, blinking back at myself. A wave of self-loathing engulfs me.

I've done it again.

Every time I'm close to getting somewhere, I back away from the edge of the cliff.

I've lost my taste for heights. But I don't know where or when it happened.

*D*ON'T YOU MISS your boyfriend?" Robbie's lying on her back on my bed, staring at the ceiling and dangling her legs in the air. She never spends any time in her own room at all, which is just as well, considering what a sty it is.

I'm unpacking my books; stacks of play texts and anthologies I've lugged all the way from the States. "Yeah, sure. But we talk a lot, so that helps."

She looks at me. "No, I mean, don't you *miss* him?"

My face flushes. "Yes. I suppose."

"Nice to know you're human, Evie Rose Garlick!" She gives my ponytail a tug. "Hey! I've been thinking. There's this great Fassbinder speech I think you should have a look at." She swings her legs round and sits up. "I'll be right back."

She pads off to her room.

"Look at for what?"

There are no shelves. I pile my books from largest to smallest against the wall.

They fall over.

"For Juilliard!" I can hear her sifting through the chaos.

I start again. Two piles this time.

"I already have my pieces."

She appears in the doorway, holding a battered volume. "But just look at this!" She flings herself back onto the bed. "It's amazing! Here. Read it out loud. You'll love it!"

I take the book. It smells musty, like she stole it from a library. "Which one?"

"The Model."

"'Sometimes I like to fondle myself. . . .'" I look up, shocked. "This is all about . . . about masturbating, Robbie!"

She claps her hands in glee. "Isn't it amazing? It's so sexy and raw! If you did that for Juilliard, they'd be floored, Evie! Nobody does that speech!"

"But it's . . . disgusting!" I say, unable to stop reading.

"It's Fassbinder. It's meant to be shocking. And you're so cute. You come across like such a good little girl . . . it would be amazing to turn the tables like this!"

"I'm sorry." I shut the book and hand it back to her. "I can't do that speech."

"What are you talking about? You're an actress, aren't you? What's wrong with it?"

I open my wardrobe doors. "It's so . . . so overt! And . . . tasteless, Robbie!" Picking up my laundry bag, I shake my clean clothes onto the floor. "I'd be too embarrassed to say those things!"

"But that's why you're an actress, right? So you can say all sorts of shit you normally wouldn't! Anyway, don't you ever get yourself off?"

"Stop it." I fold the pieces roughly. "And I'm not telling you anyway!"

She shrugs her shoulders. "Why not? I do. Everybody does. I have the most fantastic big, black, rubber vibrator. Want to see it?"

"No! I don't want to see it!"

"Want to borrow it?"

"No! I really don't!" This is the pile for ironing. "Stop it. You're being disgusting!"

"So, what do you use? The shower head?" She looks around the room. "A candle?"

"Robbie!" I pick up my ironing and march into the kitchen.

She follows. Obviously, she enjoys winding me up.

"Come on, Evie! Give!" She hauls herself up on top of the kitchen counter, oblivious to the piles of washing up. She watches as I struggle to open the ironing board. "What do you dream of? Two guys at once? Two girls at once? Dogs?" She bangs her feet against the cabinets like a naughty child. "You country girls are the worst!"

"I don't do any of that." I yank up the ironing board. It balances precariously. Then collapses again.

"Hmmm." She rubs her chin. "I know! Horses! Like Catherine the Great!"

"Stop it, Robbie!" I'm becoming upset. "I mean it."

"I'll bet you have a thing for big burly black boys . . . or maybe some sort of pervy incest thing . . . oh, Daddy, and all of that . . . nothing wrong with that, mind you."

"I'm serious! Please! I don't want to talk about this!" Pulling the board up again, I wrestle it into position.

"That's it, isn't it! You're a Daddy's girl, aren't you!"

"Robbie . . ." I want her to stop.

"Oh, look, Daddy!" She puts on a little girl voice. "I've grown out of my training bra!"

"Robbie!" I turn away.

"Are you crying?"

A hot, angry tear works its way down my cheek. I brush it away with the back of my hand.

"Hey!" She launches herself off the kitchen counter. "I didn't mean to upset you. Why didn't you just tell me to fuck off?"

I wish she'd leave me alone. "I can't." My throat's painfully tight.

"What do you mean you can't? I'm telling you to!"

"No, what I mean is, I can't!" Why does she have to make such a big deal of everything? "When I get angry or upset, I just . . . just cry, like some sort of fool! I can't even do it on stage! Whenever I have to get angry in a scene I melt down instead. I go numb and then . . ." I'm crying even harder now. "I just can't do it!"

"Why not?" She offers me a kitchen chair and sits down next to me. "What's the worst thing that can happen?"

"I don't know. No one will like me. I'll be ugly and vicious and evil and all this shit will come out and I won't be able to control it."

"Yeah?" She stares at me. "So?"

"What do you mean, so?" She's being deliberately obtuse. "No one will like me! I'll lose everything that's important!"

"It's bullshit." She wraps an arm round me. "Take me, for example. You could have a real go at me and I'd probably just think it was funny."

"You're not like normal people," I assure her. "I mean, don't get me wrong—I think it's great. I wish I could be as free as you and not give a shit. But I do!"

She gives me a squeeze. "You're too soft, darling. We have to toughen you up. Are people really that fragile in Ohio?"

I think of my parents. Silence at the dinner table; my mother sitting across from my father, pushing her food round and round on her plate . . . my father cutting his meat into hunks, forcing it between his lips, glaring at his water glass . . .

"No. People don't really get angry where I come from."

"Then New York will be good for you. The whole joint is seething!"

I sink my head against her shoulder. "I may not be going to New York."

"Oh, yes, you will! If I have anything to do with it! Besides, I need a chum I can torment day and night. Hey!" She turns to face me, suddenly excited. "What would Raven do?"

"Nothing." I roll my eyes. "She doesn't exist, Robbie."

She pokes me in the arm. "Yes she does! That's the whole point of alter egos. Come on, what would she do?"

I wish she'd just let this whole Raven thing go . . . Just because I used the name one night . . . I rub my running nose on the back of my hand. "I don't know . . . tell you to fuck off, I suppose."

"Great!" Standing up, she pulls me to my feet. "So tell me to fuck off!"

"But I don't feel it."

"So act it! Be Raven!"

This isn't going to work. "Fuck off," I mumble.

She's staring at me, hands on hips. "No, you're not going to New York. Come on, Evie, try harder!"

"Fuck off, Robbie!" I start to giggle. "I can't do it!"

She shakes her head, dragging me into the hallway. "Well, it's a start, I suppose. Come on!"

"Why? Where are we going?" I follow her into her room.

She flings her handbag over her shoulder, chucking a rapidly shedding fur jacket at me. "Catch! To Soho, my love! Let's get you the biggest, most obscene dildo we can find! And then we're going to stop at the all-night drug store and get some hair dye. It's time you started taking Raven Nightly seriously!"

I've never had a friend like this—someone so sophisticated, exciting and urbane that they don't even mind if I shout at them. I slip on the jacket, surveying myself in the mirror. Already I look different—cooler; much more grown up. None of my old friends would ever even dare to say the word dildo out loud, let alone buy one.

Robbie hammers on Imo's door. "We're going dildo shopping in Soho, darling! Can we get you anything?"

Silence.

This is the time that Im can normally be found talking to her mother long distance or leafing her way through the New Testament.

The door opens a crack. A twenty-pound note appears. "Something pink. And not too obvious," she instructs.

And then it shuts again.

"This place is a dive." Imo brushes her hand over the dirty tablecloth with disdain. "I don't know why we have to do this," she says for the ninth time in five minutes.

"Because," Robbie's eyes flit around the room. "This is where I'm going to teach you how to seduce a man. And we don't have much time. Sit up, Evie. And push your breasts out."

"I am," I say, irritated.

"Oh." She looks me over. "Yeah."

We're sitting in the basement room of a wine bar called Bubbles, located just around the corner from our flat on Baker Street. Everything's pink; the walls, the tablecloths, the chairs—a kind of bubble gum, Pink Panther pink, which only heightens the sense that we're extras in a low budget early 1960s film. However, instead of Rock Hudson and Doris Day bursting into song, we have small clusters of Arabs and balding businessmen enjoying the late-night talents of Rocco Rizzi and his vibraphone stylings. Rocco sits in his black tuxedo and white ruffled shirt on a small circular stage covered in pink shag pile carpet, a disco ball and strobe light dangling above his head. He's just launched into a particularly slow and heartfelt version of "Summertime." With extra vibrato.

"I love this song," Imo sighs. And she hums along, in her slender, slightly operatic soprano voice.

My wrap keeps falling off. I pull it up again. Tonight, we're all wearing treasures gleaned from Robbie's amazing wardrobe, which consists mostly of 1950s evening gowns, vintage cardigans and quite a lot of dead animals. The wrap is one of her prized pieces. It's made from two rather mouldy foxes that attach to one another by biting each other's tails; a trick accomplished with the aid of little clips glued underneath their tiny chins. One of them has had a beady glass eye replaced with a small black button. He looks particularly deranged. We call him Dave and the other Derek. Dave and Derek accompany us on most nights out, coming into their own after we've had too much to drink. Then they chat up strangers and perform lewd dance routines. But the chances of that happening tonight look rather slim.

We've already been here twenty minutes and nothing's happened.

The barman's back again. "Are you ladies ready to order yet?"

Robbie picks up the little cardboard menu of drinks with exaggerated enthusiasm. "We just can't decide between all these amazing cocktails!" she gushes. "Look, Evie! 'Sex on the Beach,' 'A Slow Comfortable Screw' . . . so many choices and so little time!" She laughs, a gay Scarlett O'Hara trill.

He's unimpressed. "Well, sooner rather than later, girls," he warns us, sloping back to polish glasses in the curve of the pink bar.

"We don't have any money," I remind Robbie. (Every time I turn round, the barman glares at me.)

"Money is cheating." She tugs at her white mink bolero, scanning the room again.

Two men with hair walk in and saunter up to the bar. They're reasonably young (below fifty), reasonably dressed (suits and ties) and laughing loudly as if they might be reasonably fun too. Robbie's eyes light up.

"Bingo!" She leans forward the way you strain over the edge of the platform for a long-awaited train. "Smile, Evie! Imo! Stop howling and smile!"

The three of us sit there beaming. Eventually their drinks are served. They turn round and find us grinning at them.

"Now look away!" Robbie hisses. "Imo, avert your eyes! That's right! Toy with them!"

So we all stare at Rocco instead. He gets excited and swings into a Simon and Garfunkel tribute, starting with a disco version of "Feeling Groovy."

"OK . . . and get ready . . . turn and SMILE!"

We swirl round, chairs scraping against the floor, and focus our collective bonhomie on the boys at the bar again. They seem perplexed but amused.

"Now, cool and casual, very cool, ladies," Robbie whispers, "and . . . back to piano man!"

"How long do we have to do this?" Imo asks, readjusting her black veiled pillbox hat, which doesn't seem inclined to move with her head at all but rather against it.

Robbie plays with the layers of crinoline on her New Look dress. "I really think that should do it, darling. Now remember, the trick is to keep the ball in the air!"

"What ball?" Imo frowns.

But Robbie just winks. "Watch and learn!"

Sure enough, two minutes later they arrive, flourishing a bottle of cheap house white and five wine glasses.

Andy's from Minnesota and his colleague, Greg, from Alabama. They're here on a sales conference. This is their first time in England.

We nod as if we've been here for years.

There's a certain disappointment on both sides to pulling fellow Americans; there's nothing glamorous or intriguing about travelling all the way across the world only to meet someone you could easily find in New Jersey. But the selection of glamorous characters in Bubbles is virtually nonexistent. And it's getting late. So we fall into all the usual things tourists discuss; how narrow seats are on airlines these days, what a disaster the food is, and why no one can make a decent cup of coffee.

"So, why are you guys wearing these getups?" Greg asks in his thick, slow drawl. He's younger than his friend, with pink, flushed cheeks and a wide, full mouth that doesn't like to close.

"We're actresses," Robbie says, sipping her drink daintily. To her, that's reason enough. But he continues to blink at us.

"Really?"

"Yes, we're larger than life," Imo adds, filling her glass again. She pushes her hat farther back on her head but still manages to drink through her veil.

"I see." He purses his lips and nods thoughtfully. "So, are y'all in character now?"

I don't like him. He seems stupid. And his sullen friend Andy keeps staring at me.

"We're always in character," I snap. If he mentions the exchange rate one more time, I'll run screaming from the building.

"So." Robbie, sensing friction, scoops the ball off the floor one more time. "Where are you boys staying?"

"We told you." Andy's tone is flat and bored. He thinks he's pretty cool with his Tom Selleck moustache and blow-dried hair. "Across the street at the Sherlock Holmes. How old are these anyway?" he asks, fingering Dave and Derek.

His hand brushes my bare arm.

I recoil.

Robbie catches my eye and I force my lips into a smile.

"Probably dead before you were born. And how old are you, Andy?" Flirting with men you hate is such hard work.

"Thirty-two." He looks at me with a firm, tough gaze, as if to say, "So what are you going to make of that?"

I make nothing of it. But smile again.

Robbie keeps nodding to the wine bottle. It's empty. Evidently it's my job to do something about it.

Rocco launches into "Bridge over Troubled Water." Imo claps her hands with glee. "Oh! This is one of my very favourites!"

She's drunk already. Imo's an infamously cheap date. She gets loud and excited and her head lolls about like a doll with no stuffing.

Andy rolls his eyes.

Greg laughs, making a kind of self-conscious gasping sound; pulling at his jacket. It was obviously his idea to come over with the wine.

"Gosh." Here comes some more sparkling social repartee. "Y'all have no idea how poor the exchange rate is! It's incredible! These drinks were a fortune!"

"Oh, they can't have been as bad as all that!" Robbie's playing Scarlett O'Hara again, which perhaps isn't such a wise move with a boy from the South, patting his knee playfully.

"You'd be surprised," he says, lapsing into silence.

Our gay, exciting evening in Bubbles wine bar is rapidly deflating. "Bridge over Troubled Water" is beginning to take its toll.

"Go ask him to play something more lively," I suggest to Imo. "Something a little less morbid."

And as she staggers up to the rotating pink stage, Robbie makes another attempt at a fresh bottle of wine. She tilts the empty one upside down. "Can you believe how quickly that went!" she laughs. "Now what are we going to do?"

Andy ignores her. "What are you doing tonight?" He's looking at me intently.

I shift away from him.

"Just things."

"What things?" he persists.

My mind goes blank. "I have to study."

"Study?" He sounds horrified.

"I'm a student," I add defensively.

And he laughs, rocking back in his chair. "Oh well, that explains a lot!" He drains his glass. "Come on, Greg. Let's get out of here."

Greg gapes at him like a fish. "What?"

"And now a little surprise for some Very Special Ladies!" Rocco beams at us. Imo's draped over him on the piano stool. Falling forward, she starts crooning a dangerously off-key version of "S'Wonderful" into the microphone. She's got a bad case of dolly head.

"How s'marvellous!" Robbie waves to the barman. "Let's have another round!"

Andy plows his hands into his pockets. "Are you buying?"

For a moment, the ball vanishes altogether.

Robbie sighs; looks at him hard. "Andy, do you like games?"

He sizes her up and then sits down again. "Sure. Why?"

"I have a good one." She undoes a large diamanté brooch from her dress. "Would you like to see how far I'm willing to go to get another bottle of wine?"

"Pretty far!" he snorts, leaning back in his chair.

She shrugs her shoulders, extending her thin arm across the table. "Shall we see just how far?" She flicks the brooch open so the long pin is stretched out like a blade. "I must say, your coldness has chilled my heart,

Andy. I feel desperate measures coming on. And I'm afraid I'm going to have to slit my wrist with this pin if someone doesn't buy me a drink soon."

She smiles sweetly.

We stare at her.

The barman approaches. "Yes?"

Robbie clenches her fist.

"You wouldn't dare," Andy sneers.

But she just winks at him. "I don't know about you," her voice is soft and smooth, "but I'm absolutely parched."

Without even looking, she draws the pin downward.

I gasp.

Andy lunges forward and grabs her hand.

"You're crazy!" he hisses, prising the brooch out of her grip.

"I'm thirsty," she reminds him. "And besides, who knew you could move so quickly. Not bad for an old man." And she pats his thigh.

Now he's staring at her with the same lecherous intent he was lavishing on me a minute ago. "I'm not that old," he assures her. "Fine. You win. Another bottle of house white," he barks at the barman, who shakes his head and disappears.

Robbie's shoulders relax.

Andy's still holding her wrist. "You're one crazy kid," he keeps repeating, over and over.

She frees her hand from his, leans towards him. "Would you like to see just how crazy I am?"

That's it. I grab her by the arm and pull her up. "Excuse me, we have to go to the ladies." And yanking her across the room, I practically fling her into the toilet. "What are you doing?" I yell. "Those guys are losers! What are you doing?"

She leans back against the wall and shuts her eyes. "I'm doing what I always do." She sounds tired. "Don't you want another drink?"

"No, not that badly! What would you have done if he hadn't stopped you?"

She ignores me.

"Robbie! What would you have done?"

"It's a game, Evie." She shrugs her shoulders, checks her makeup in the mirror. "It's just a game." She makes it sound simple; obvious.

"But . . . but you can't be seriously thinking about, you know, going off with him!" My indignation, which two minutes ago made perfect, unequivocal sense, now sounds unexpectedly clichéd.

"You're such a good friend to me." She kisses me on the cheek. "I like that."

I catch her arm again. "But . . ." I struggle to find the words. "But . . . I mean, you don't even like him . . . do you?"

She's distant; far away. "I do things I don't want to do all the time. I can't help it." She smiles sadly. "I'm bad."

I don't understand.

I let go of her arm.

Robbie strolls back to the table, a slow, rolling model's stride. As she draws closer, Andy rises, pulling her chair out for her and refilling her glass. He's taken off his tie, opened the top buttons on his shirt.

Imo and I don't stay much longer. During "Embraceable You," Imo declares loudly into the microphone that she thinks she's going to be sick. Greg quickly offers to see us home.

I wait up for her, sitting in the black leather chair in the living room, knees drawn under my chin, listening in the dark to the traffic and the sounds of the sleeping city. It grows later and, with each passing hour, quieter.

But still no Robbie.

The Sherlock Holmes Hotel is just around the corner in Baker Street.

"May I help you?" The night manager looks up from his paper.

"No, thank you." I settle into the corner of one of the chintz sofas. "I'm waiting for someone."

I must look ridiculous; with my nightgown shoved into my jeans under Robbie's rabbit fur jacket. But I don't care.

Nearly an hour later, the lift doors open.

She moves with the same dazed slowness of someone stumbling away from a car accident. An unlit cigarette dangles from her fingers. The mink bolero's askew and dirty; her pale lips swollen from where her lipstick has rubbed off.

I stand up.

She frowns, as if she can't quite place me.

"What are you doing here?"

I push open the glass door. An icy wind cuts through us.

"Come on." I hold out my hand.

But she just stares at me.

I don't know what I'm doing here. I've been sitting, waiting, wondering the same thing. And now it's four in the morning, the door's open, the night manager's watching us and I still don't have an answer.

"You're not bad, Robbie."

Suddenly she seems quite small.

I hold out my hand again.

"In fact, you're one of the best people I've ever known."

This time she takes it.

When we arrive home, I turn the key in the lock, pushing the door open as quietly as I can.

Imo's still asleep.

Outside, a bird sings.

We stand in the purple half-light.

"Good night," Robbie whispers. She leans towards me, her breath warm on my cheek.

I turn.

Her lips brush against mine.

And very slowly, very softly, she kisses me.

"THIS IS A STATION ANNOUNCEMENT. Southbound trains on the Jubilee Line are experiencing delays due to a signal failure at Finchley Road tube station. London Underground apologises for any inconvenience this may cause to your journey."

I'm still berating myself for this morning's conversation with Melvin, and now I'm stuck; one of nearly seventy hot, irritated commuters, jostling for position at St John's Wood tube station. Most of us have been here at least a quarter of an hour—that is, fifteen London Underground minutes, which are at least twice as long as normal minutes anywhere else. And we're doing what the English do to register our frustration; shaking our heads to no one in particular, folding our newspapers with extra violence, examining our watches with all the subtlety of a pantomime dame, so that we all understand how outraged and incensed we are by the utter inadequacy of the service provided . . . but without ever having to go so far as to say it out loud.

Finally, moving with no particular speed or urgency, a train emerges from the tunnel, already swollen with passengers. We crowd around the doors, surging forward as they creak open. Once all in, pressed up against one another cheek by jowl, we wait.

And the train sits there.

A minute goes by. And then another. Latecomers race from the escalators and squeeze themselves into the already overflowing cars. I'm wedged between two large, sweaty men; one with too much aftershave, the other without nearly enough. The latter raises his arm, reaching for the hanging strap. And I think I'm going to faint.

A distraction's needed. Reading my morning paper's out as I can't move my arms.

Only the advertisements remain. I look up.

An enormous black bird glares down at me.

"Sound and Fury: The very best of Raven," the poster reads. "Coming, May 2001."

I blink.

Suddenly, he's everywhere.

Then the inevitable happens. Just as the buzzer sounds and the doors finally begin to close, a homeless man with a guitar bounces on.

I avert my eyes. Please, Lord, make him move past. Make him go into another car.

But no. He smiles broadly, a great, toothless grin, unpacks the guitar (which isn't easy in a crowded train) and starts singing "Norwegian Wood."

" 'I once had a girl, or should I say, she once had me . . . ' "

His voice, rough with cigarettes and alcohol, scrapes across the notes; the very antithesis of the young John Lennon's.

The train lurches forward.

There's no escape.

Thing is, it's a difficult song to forget, once you get it into your head.

Round and round it goes, waltzing endlessly.

Round and round and round.

EGENT'S PARK ON an unseasonably warm Sunday
afternoon in April is littered with lovers; strolling hand in
hand, entwined around each other in the shade of newly
blossoming chestnut trees, or, if older, sitting next to one another on
benches, bent over sections of *The Sunday Times*. The world is in bloom,
great blazing fields of daffodils stretch along the pathways and the air's
full of cherry blossom, floating on the breeze like pale pink snow.

Lindsay Crufts and I are rehearsing outside. The day is too balmy, too
beautiful to be stuck indoors. And besides, the scene we have to present
tomorrow, between the famous writer Trigorin and the young aspiring
actress Nina in *The Seagull,* is set out of doors, on a day not unlike this
one. We're sitting on a grassy slope, amid a grove of slender silver birches
swaying in the sunlight.

Lindsay rises, regarding me with an expression of pained
seriousness (his indication that he's acting). " 'Day and night I'm
haunted by one thought: I must write, I must write, I must . . . the
minute I've finished one novel, I must immediately start another, then
another and another . . .' "

He stalks away, head bowed. " 'I write without stopping to catch my
breath, like a man running a relay race on his own. I can't help it. Well, I
ask you, what is so wonderful or beautiful about that? It's a hellish

existence. Here I am talking to you and getting all excited, and all the time I can't forget that there's a novel I haven't finished waiting for me.'"

He points to the sky. "'I see a cloud shaped like a piano. Straightaway I think, I must remember to put that in a novel or a short story, that fact that a cloud looking like a grand piano floated by. I smell heliotrope. Immediately I make a mental note: sickly smell . . . flower the colour of a widow's dress . . . mention when describing a summer's evening.'"

He wheels round violently. "'I can't escape. In order to bring honey to the masses, I am taking the pollen from my most beautiful flowers, in fact I am tearing those flowers from the ground and trampling on their roots. I am burning up my life. I must be insane.'"

I gaze up at him with a look I hope is full of uninhibited yearning and adoration, though in fact I was simply waiting for my next line and trying to keep my right leg from going numb. (These speeches are so long.) I borrowed one of Imo's floaty floral dresses for inspiration; when it comes to dressing like a virgin, she's the expert. But now it's wrapped itself round my ankle. I struggle to stand up and almost fall over. I'm neither delicate nor romantic.

Lindsay observes me disdainfully.

I finally regain my balance. "'Yes but surely when you're inspired, when you're actually writing, you get moments of real happiness?'"

He stoops down, plucks a daisy from the lawn. "'Yes, I enjoy the writing. I even like reading the proofs, but it's . . . it's as soon as I see the stuff is in print that I can't bear it. That's when I see that I've got it all wrong, that the whole thing's a mistake and that it should never have been written at all . . . I feel suicidal . . .'" He pulls the petals off one by one. "'depressed . . . Then the public reads it and they say: "Charming, shows talent . . . very nice but not Tolstoy" or "A fine piece of work but Turgenev's *Fathers and Sons* is a better book." And that's all I hear until the lid of my coffin is nailed down: "So charming . . . so clever." Until when I am finally dead my friends as they file past my grave will say: "Here lies Trigorin, quite a good writer, but not as good as Turgenev."'"

I take the flower (or what's left of it) and playfully jam it into the lapel of Lindsay's omnipresent tweed jacket. "'I'm sorry, but I don't understand you. You've obviously been spoilt by success. In return for the joy of being a writer or an actress I would be prepared to sacrifice the love of those I care for, I would face poverty and disillusionment . . . live in a garret and eat nothing but dry bread. I would endure being dissatisfied with myself and knowing my own imperfections.' " I throw my arms out, spin round, the blue sky races above my head. " 'But in return I would demand fame . . . real earsplitting fame! My head's spinning . . . . oh!' "

I collapse into his arms.

We stare into each other's eyes.

He leans forward, brushing my hair from my face.

I tilt my mouth towards his. His lips softly part.

"And scene!" he barks, releasing me.

I land abruptly back on the ground.

We walk back towards Camden Town tube station together. Conversation has never been easy between us. In the two weeks we've been working on this scene, we've barely spoken at all. I decide to take this opportunity to build up some chemistry between our onstage characters.

"So, how do you think it's going?" I ask, smiling brightly.

He nods his head vigorously about thirty-two times. "Good."

Maybe the best thing to do is stick to the material.

"Do you have any idea what they're talking about?"

"Sometimes." He looks at me. "A little."

We walk on in silence.

"They sure do talk a lot," I add, after a while.

He laughs, his narrow, formal features softening and for a moment he's almost handsome. "Yes, that's true," he agrees.

I smile back. We're almost there now. "Do you want to be famous, Lindsay? Or just well respected?"

He pauses.

We're standing outside Camden Town tube station, all around us the seething, alternative existence of Camden Lock swarms, with bizarrely dressed people peering and pawing over homemade jewellery stalls and hand printed T-shirts, weird wooden furniture, new age book shops; someone's playing a didgeridoo and the powerful scent of patchouli incense perfumes the afternoon air.

Lindsay smiles again, carefully removing the damaged daisy from his lapel. He hands it back to me. "Good night, Evie."

It's only three-thirty.

He's so odd, I think, making my way into the station, twisting the tiny flower between my fingers. How can Imo love him when he's so odd?

The escalators are steep and treacherous, rickety old wooden steps, descending slowly into the bowels of London. I slide in behind a pack of young girls on the right-hand side. And there's more music, echoing from the floor below, a busker playing "Norwegian Wood," only at twice the speed; a racing, driven ode to lost love.

I can see him now, twisting and turning on the platform below. His clear, bold voice slices through the murky half-light of the crowded tunnels. Coins clink in the open guitar case at his feet. The schoolgirls in front of me giggle, searching eagerly in their purses for spare change. I fish in the pocket of my jean jacket. He finishes the song and they applaud wildly. I look up.

It's Jake.

The escalator ends and I stumble forward.

He catches me.

"Have you started drinking without me, then?" His hands linger, wrapped round my waist; holding me as if I belonged to him.

Blushing, I take a step backwards and he releases me.

"It's such a surprise to see you . . ."

"Is that for me?" He grins, nodding to the coin in my hand.

I'd forgotten about it. It's not a pound coin; I'm certain of that. I just pulled out whatever was left in my pocket. What if it's a ten-pence piece? Or worse, a two-pence piece? I fold my fingers into a tight fist. "I had no idea it was you." I'm apologising in advance.

"So, you're not impressed with my singing?" He's teasing me now, pushing his black hair out of his eyes.

"No, of course I am!"

An endless tide of people swells around us.

"So." He touches me gently, pulling my wrist forward. "Shall we see how much you enjoyed it?"

I clench my fingers together even harder. "Before you do this, I just want you to know that I'm a huge fan of 'Norwegian Wood' and I was particularly taken with your interpretation . . ."

He laughs, prises open my fist. "Ah! Fifty pence!"

He's genuinely pleased.

"Well, this will buy you a lot more than a song!" He pulls his leather jacket on over his T-shirt and jeans, then bends down, collecting the rest of the spare change. He jams it into his pockets. "It's not every day I'm given such high praise. So, where shall we go to celebrate?"

I'm staring at him. "Pardon me?"

He places his guitar carefully back in its case and snaps it closed. "Did you think I'd let you off that easily?" He speaks with confidence, looking into my eyes, holding my gaze. He smiles. "I think I owe you at least one drink . . ."

Here he is, the man I think of constantly; the man whom I shouldn't be thinking of at all . . . the ghost of my waking hours . . .

"Or am I being cheeky?" He tilts his head to one side, puts on a posh accent. "Perhaps you have another engagement?"

"No! Oh, no!" I assure him. Suddenly I'm unable to keep pace with my life. It's as if someone's pressed the fast-forward button. I'm left stumbling in the wake of great events; moments I wish were preserved in amber, so I can wonder over them in secret, again and again.

"Well, then." He holds out his hand. "Shall we?"

I place my hand in his. It's warm and smooth, callused in places. And he leads me down, through the tunnels.

"Where are we going?" I'm intoxicated with excitement, like a small child, but doing my best to hide it. "All the pubs are closed on Sunday afternoons."

"I have a cunning plan," he promises, pulling me down another flight of steps.

"So, is this what you do? You play in the Underground?" We're weaving through the swarms of people.

"Exactly." He manoeuvres me to the end of the platform. "There's good money in it, if you hit the right station at the right time. Until the band takes off, of course. Nice dress."

I'm blushing again. "It's not mine. I borrowed it."

"I meant it as a compliment, Raven."

"Oh . . ." How horrible. How embarrassing and horrible. ". . . that's another thing."

There's a warm blast of air as the train rushes into the station. I brace myself. "I have to tell you, that's not my real name."

"Really?" He laughs again. There's the most charming dimple on his right cheek. "Are you operating under an alias?"

This is so humiliating. I try to sound breezy. "A girl can't be too careful. Especially on a blind date. Anyway, it's not Raven, it's Evie. Raven is just . . . just a name Robbie came up with . . ."

We force ourselves, side by side, into the crowded aisle. The doors close.

I reach up and grab the handrail, swaying as the train shoots into the darkness.

"So, the girl with the borrowed dress and the borrowed name, who wants to be an actress when she grows up. How will I know when you're telling the truth?"

I look at him sideways. "Is the truth awfully important to you, Jake?"

He smiles. "Now that you mention it, no, Evie. If, in fact, that's your real name."

We get off at Charing Cross, surfacing on the Strand.

"There's only one place to take a soon to be famous American actress."

Ten minutes later we're in the lobby of the Savoy Hotel.

The head concierge materialises, dressed in a morning suit. He stations himself across our path. "May I help you?"

Jake flings an arm around my shoulder. "No, mate. I think we're OK."

"Really." He curls his lip at us.

"Really." Jake smiles.

"If you're temporary staff," the man persists, "you should be using the back entrance."

Jake's eyes narrow. "We're meeting some people in the American Bar. It's through there, isn't it?" He takes a step forward but is blocked again.

"There is a dress code in the American Bar, sir," he informs us stiffly.

"Well, then." Jake raises an eyebrow. "Lucky I bothered to dress."

"And these are guests of the hotel, sir?"

Jake stops.

And stares at the man for a full minute.

"You know," he says, turning to me, "I'm really sorry. In fact, I can't tell you how sorry I am I brought you here. Sometimes this place is OK and sometimes it's so fucking amateurish I want to scream. As for you." He swings round. "Are they guests? No! They're not guests! They're complete fabrications of my overactive imagination!"

"Please, sir . . ." The concierge scans the lobby.

Jake ignores him. "They flew in this morning from L.A. Joel Finklehymen and Barry Inglesnook. From EMI. Do you want to look them up on your system? Can you spell Finklehymen or do you need me to do it for you? What's wrong? Never seen anyone in the music industry before?"

The man blinks, backing away. "No. No. Of course, sir. It's fine. I apologize. The American Bar is through there." He gestures feebly. "Would you like me to check your guitar, sir?"

Jake clutches the guitar to his chest. "Are you kidding? I don't want you going anywhere near my guitar! Do you know what this baby is worth? No? Of course you don't! You don't have a fucking clue who I am, do you?"

"No, sir," he admits, casting his eyes downwards. "I'm afraid I don't."

Jake shrugs his shoulders; lost for words. He turns to me in disbelief. "Raven, can you believe these people?"

"Honey . . ." I pat his arm placatingly, "not everyone watches *Top of the Pops*."

He stands, amazed, in the middle of the foyer. "Look," he says at last, "I don't have time for this. I have a meeting and now I'm late. Here." He presses a twenty-pence piece into the mortified man's hand. "Buy yourself a fucking newspaper and next time, mate, do your homework."

We make a grand exit, swaggering down the mahogany-lined corridor to the American Bar. I've never seen anyone with so much front. Except for Robbie. It's exhilarating. And for a moment, even I'm completely convinced of our sudden rise to stardom.

"Well, my dear," Jake says, as we near the doorway. "Welcome to the Big Time!"

We step inside.

It's empty.

Dark, plush and subdued, the only glimmer of the bright sunlight outside filters in through small, stained-glass windows tucked discreetly into the corners. The walls are lined with mirrors and prints of famous faces; but there's something House of Horrorsish about the constantly reflecting surfaces, the swirling design of the carpet and the squat little glass tables.

"Looks like Barry and Joel have stood us up," I say.

"Bastards." Jake throws himself down on one of the bottle green velvet banquettes and I perch across from him on a black upholstered cylinder.

A kind of ancient walking corpse drags himself from behind the bar.

He would be bald if it weren't for three very carefully placed strands of white hair. "And what can I get for you?" He moves so slowly, it looks like he's sleepwalking.

Jake examines the drinks menu, his eyes widening with dismay. "Two lagers, please," he says at last. "Is that all right with you?"

I nod.

"And some peanuts," he adds.

The corpse blinks. "We don't actually have peanuts, sir."

"Really? What do you have? Olives? Onions? A packet of crisps?"

"We have very small crackers, sir. In the shape of fish."

"I see." Jake pulls a face. "I'm not sure I like the sound of that."

"I could see if the kitchen have any nuts, sir. Some almonds, perhaps."

"Yes, speak to the kitchen, my good man."

When the drinks arrive, Jake pays for them entirely with small change, a process that takes about five minutes and includes several stops and starts but doesn't seem to faze the corpse at all. A few minutes later he returns, placing a small silver dish of blanched almonds on the table, elaborately arranged with sprigs of parsley between each one.

"This is very nice of you," I say, stealing an almond. My voice echoes in the thick silence of the empty room.

Jake leans back against the banquette, stretching out his long legs. "Do you think I'm being nice?"

I look up. "Aren't you?"

He shakes his head, staring at me steadily. His dark eyes have flecks of green in them. "Nice is for nice girls. I had other things in mind."

I can feel the colour rising in my cheeks again. I look away and say nothing, tracing my index finger very slowly along the cool edge of the glass table.

"It's OK," he adds, picking up his lager. "I can wait."

His cockiness is exciting and infuriating. "What makes you think I'm not a nice girl?"

I can't believe I just said that.

He laughs, throwing his head back. I blush even harder. But when he speaks, his voice is low. "The company you keep gives you away."

Suddenly, I feel uneasy.

"I have a boyfriend," I hear myself say.

"So you told me." He smiles again. "I'll bet he's nice."

I should be serious, indignant. But instead I'm smiling back.

I like the way he looks at me.

"Have you been here before?" I ask.

"Never," he confesses, letting me change the subject. "I thought it would be a bit more . . . lively. You know—full of famous people sipping cocktails . . ."

We both steal a glance at the corpse and giggle.

"Are you trying to impress me?"

A smile plays across his lips. "I'm pretty sure I already have."

"So, tell me something about your life," I demand quickly, pushing an almond around on the dish.

He sighs. "What do you want to know?"

"Let's see . . . what are your family like? Where did you grow up? What's your favourite song?"

"Born and raised in Kilburn. Two parents, on a good day. None, on a bad. My grandmother raised my brothers and me—along with Jesus, Mary and the Holy Ghost. Went to a Catholic day school, run by a bunch of disgusting old priests. Sang in the choir. Typical working class stuff . . ." He stops. "Do you know what that means?"

I throw the parsley at him. "You won't be inheriting the castle."

"It means I'll be buying my own bloody castle!" He flicks the parsley off his shoulder. "Now, the toughie; favourite song . . . either T-Rex, 'Twentieth Century Boy,' or Mott the Hoople, 'All the Young Dudes' or The Clash, 'Hateful' or . . ." he looks at me, "the one I'm working on now."

"Which is?"

" 'Limey Punk Rock Faggot.' "

I laugh. "Are you serious?"

"You don't like it?" He's staring at me closely. "I think it's kind of catchy."

He is serious.

I take a sip of my lager. "No, no it's great. Just . . . different. Let me guess; it's not a love song, is it?"

He takes a long swallow. "I don't write love songs. I don't believe in any of that."

"Oh." I try to sound as neutral as possible.

I push the almonds round and round in the dish.

He's just sitting there, watching me.

"It's a great title," I add. "Really original."

"You don't believe in all that, do you?" He sounds incredulous, as if I've just admitted writing a letter to Santa Claus.

"What?"

"Love."

"Yes, of course I do!" I'm aware of how uncool this is to say out loud, but I don't care. "It's the one thing I believe in above everything else. It gives life weight and meaning. How else can we leave the world better off than when we came in?"

And he smiles, despite himself.

"What is there to push us on? Encourages us to be anything more than what we already are, besides love?" I hadn't realised how strongly I felt. Now the words come rushing out like a hidden manifesto, gathering speed and urgency. "I want that experience. I really do. I want to be passionately, blindingly, uncontrollably in love no matter what it means; no matter how it ends! Before I die, I want to know what it feels like to give myself to someone absolutely; to think of them more than I think of myself; to be moved by what moves them . . ."

His face has gone blank.

I've gone too far; said too much. And now I wish I'd kept quiet.

It's too late now. I try to laugh it off. "After all, what else is there to believe in?"

He leans forward. "Fame. Fortune. Success. Not living in a fucking slum!"

This isn't the answer I expected. "Oh. Well." I shrug my shoulders. "If that's what you want . . ."

"It's not about what a person wants . . ." His voice is suddenly harsh. He sits back again. "You must come from a very good family to go to that la-di-da drama school!"

I glare at him, my anger rising. "They own a business. A business they built themselves! So, no. I don't think I'll be in line for the castle either."

"What kind of business?" he counters.

"An auto shop."

His face softens. "Sorry . . . it's just," he stops.

I wait for him to continue but he looks around the room instead, drinking his lager.

I should let the subject drop; what does it matter what he thinks?

But for some reason I can't.

I brush the hair out of my eyes. What would Raven do?

"So, you don't believe in love."

His eyes meet mine.

But this time, I don't look away. "I almost believe you," I say.

Something shifts beneath the surface of his features. "Why almost?"

"Because . . ." I take a sip of my drink. "You're lying."

We sit in silence.

I eat another almond; it crunches ominously. The temperature has cooled.

"Do you like this place?" he asks, after a while.

"It's a bit dark . . ."

"You're right." Taking a last gulp, he puts his glass down and stands up. "Let's get out of here."

And moments later, I find myself struggling to keep up with his long strides, as we weave through the empty corridors, all the while cursing myself. If only I'd just shut up, we'd still be there. But now it's all over; the hallways are like a dark maze and he's walking so quickly I practically have to run to keep pace with him.

We round a corner.

And then stop.

An immense ballroom opens out in front of us, bordered by dozens of round tables set for afternoon tea, with crisp white cloths and delicate gold chairs. Through the floor-to-ceiling windows, a panorama of London spreads before us; the River Thames shimmers like a slick sheet of cool crystal in the late afternoon sun. The view is dazzling, flooded with light. An orchestra's playing. And all around them, dozens of well-heeled elderly couples, dressed in their very finest, are waltzing, weaving in intricate patterns round the parquet wood dance floor.

I pause to catch my breath. "Oh! How gorgeous!" I lean my head against the frame of the portico.

"Do you like that?" He comes up behind me.

I nod. "Wouldn't it be wonderful to be able to dance? I wish I could."

We stand, watching.

Round and round they go.

"Come on."

I turn.

He's abandoned his guitar case and leather jacket. "Come on!" he insists. And taking my hand, he leads me onto the very centre of the floor.

"But I don't know how!"

He pulls me close.

"Just relax. And let me hold you."

My body softens against his.

He smells of cigarettes, the sweet perfume of laundry detergent and the distinctive, intensely warm scent of his skin. His heart's beating against mine.

"This is very nice of you," I smile.

"You think I'm being nice?" he whispers.

I nod.

We're hardly moving; swaying ever so slightly back and forth. And all around us, the old people are dancing, swirling and turning. The music swells; something familiar; a big band tune my father used to play, and he spins me, faster now.

I close my eyes, laughing.

And when I open them, he's staring at me.

"Is that the way you feel, then?" he demands suddenly. "About him?"

I look at him in surprise.

"No," I murmur, my throat clinging to the word, reluctant to let it go. "Not at all." I feel an unexpected stab of disloyalty.

His dark eyes soften. "Good."

He holds me tighter, lips brushing my hair.

And leaning my head against his shoulder, I close my eyes again.

I'M SITTING in the staff room of the City Lit, working on my prospectus for next term. It's like all the rooms at the City Lit, only there's a slightly posher mix of furniture here; someone had a brain wave one year to upgrade the facilities and went mad at Ikea. The sofas still sag and are covered with tea stains but they're bright blue with polished steel frames and there's a wobbly beech wood dining table and chairs, pressed up against the wall near the "kitchen."

The kitchen is like all institutional kitchens: terminally untidy. There's an ancient kettle encrusted with years of lime scale and an uninspiring collection of generic tea and instant coffee supplies. All the interesting offerings have Post-it's on them vehemently declaring ownership: R. FITZROY, the organic camomile tea reads, HANDS OFF! And next to it, a jar of acacia honey with the same threatening note. (This does nothing to deter would-be thieves.) Above the sink a laminated notice reads in bold black letters, PLEASE WASH UP YOUR MUGS AND SPOONS, THIS IS NOT A HOTEL! under which a stack of dirty cups and saucers sprawl. I recognize most of them from last week.

Above the wobbly beech wood table, there's a bulletin board, covered in important information I rarely take notice of. The only announcement that catches my eye is the weekly update from R. Fitzroy. *"Would the person who absconded with my Oriental blue and white china cup and saucer please return it immediately! It was a gift!!!!"*

It's this last, indignant line that intrigues me the most. Having never met R. Fitzroy, all I know of him or her (and I suspect it's a her) is the delicacy of their taste and the imprudent insistence of entrusting such sacred objects—the tea, honey and what's certain to be an exquisite china cup and saucer—to the wild, immoral elements of the City Lit staff room. Who would do such a thing? What kind of person brings anything of value here and leaves it overnight? And, more important, who gave them this precious token? A lover? A friend? Her mom?

Each week, I marvel in fascination at the fragments of R. Fitzroy's life as they unfold before me. I could easily look up the name on the staff roll and introduce myself, but that would be cheating. There's so little mystery in life as it is.

I remove the lid from my takeaway coffee and settle into the corner of one of the blue sofas.

Right.

Down to business.

The title of the course is Poetry and Drama; the Beauty of the English Language. A little nonspecific, I know. I've tried proposing more focused curriculums—the War Poets and the Language of Loss, or From Shakespeare to Mamet; the Evolution of Heightened Speech Through the Ages—but it's never taken off. What people really want is something more universal. A quiet, safe place to bring their favourite pieces. This course attracts a strange breed of students; the ones who haven't made it through the rigorous auditions for more advanced acting classes—older students; shy ones. My class is definitely not for professional actors. Or for young ambitious undergraduates. My class is for people who queue to stand at the back of the stalls to see *King Lear* at the National, even though they saw it two weeks ago, because it's their favourite play and they have nothing else to do on a Friday night. Or a Saturday night, for that matter.

I unpack my collection of poetry anthologies and play texts. Stacking them neatly, I arrange them in order of weekly classes: Shakespeare (two classes at least), Restoration Drama (special focus on the bargaining scene from *Way of the World,* the monologues from *The Rivals* and *School for Scandal*), a brief look at John Donne and the Metaphysical poets, and then a huge leap straight into Chekhov and the Romantic poets, for no better reason than I like them best.

I'm feeling quite smug and well read, surrounded by all my great literature, when Ellery King walks in. He's the fight instructor on the proper, full-time drama course. He moves with self-conscious, feline grace over to the wooden cubbyholes that fill the far wall, functioning as staff mailboxes.

I shouldn't stare.

Forcing my eyes back to my notebook, I pretend to be deeply absorbed in my own intellectually stimulating and highly worthwhile work.

"Week one," I write purposefully, "the dramatic interpretation of Shakespeare's sonnets. To include sonnets 154, 74, 12 and . . ."

Concentrate. What I'm doing is important and spiritually satisfying. I'm a teacher. A mentor. A guide on an intensely enriching spiritual journey of self-discovery.

"To include sonnets 12, 74, 154 and . . ."

"Hey." His voice is low and inviting. "Why don't I buy you a coffee?"

My head bobs up, cheeks flushed with excitement.

He's staring intently into the eyes of a young, leggy drama student, as if she's the most fascinating creature on earth. She says something and he throws his head back and roars.

Oh. My mistake.

He brushes his dark hair out of his eyes; drapes an arm around her shoulders, moving her towards the door. She nods like one of those toy dogs people put in the back seat of their cars.

I watch them leave. He hasn't even checked his mailbox, crammed full of post. I cast an eye to the far corner where my mailbox is. Nothing.

I close my eyes and feel the rapid beat of my heart pounding against my chest. This is ridiculous. He doesn't even know I exist. And if he did notice me, what would he see? A thirty-three-year-old single mother teaching adult education night classes? A woman whose stomach wrinkles up like an accordion when she sits down in the bath?

Get real.

I have more of a chance of seducing R. Fitzroy than I do Ellery King.

Flicking through my worn copy of the *Complete Works of Shakespeare*, I scan the first lines of the sonnets. Here it is.

Sonnet 129.

The expense of spirit in a waste of shame
Is lust in action; and till action, lust
Is perjur'd, murderous, bloody, full of blame,
Savage, extreme, rude, cruel, not to trust;
Enjoyed no sooner but despised straight;
Past reason hunted; and no sooner had,
Past reason hated, as a swallow'd bait,
On purpose laid to make the taker mad:
Mad in pursuit and in possession so;
Had, having, and in quest to have extreme;
A bliss in proof and prov'd a very woe;
Before a joy propos'd behind a dream,
All this the world well knows, yet none knows well,
To shun the heaven that leads men to this hell.

I look up at the place where Ellery King was standing; something of his aura lingers, hovering, glowing and vibrant, just above the grey carpet tiles near the door. For a moment I can almost smell the perfume of his tousled black hair and the warm heat of his tanned skin.

I close my eyes and inhale deeply.

Yes, we'll definitely have to work on Sonnet 129.

"You always go for the same type."

My heart stops.

I know that voice.

But I never thought I'd hear it again.

My eyes shoot open.

There, in front of me, is Robbie, dunking one of R. Fitzroy's precious organic chamomile tea bags into her missing blue and white china cup and saucer. She cocks her blonde head to one side and smiles; she's wearing the same orange jumper and faded jeans I saw her in the other day. Only this time she's closer . . . and speaking . . . and standing in a room full of other people . . .

All the air seems to have been sucked from my lungs; in fact, from my entire body. I cannot breathe.

"What are you doing here?" I clutch the armrest of the sofa for support.

"Pardon me," a man slips between Robbie and one of the IKEA chairs, making his way towards the kitchen.

"Of course." She moves to one side so he can pass.

"Oh, my God! People can see you!" I hiss, covering my face with my hands. They're shaking violently. "Jesus, Robbie! What are you doing? Get out of here! *Hide!*"

"OK, you need to calm down." She lowers her voice. "You're actually starting to make a scene."

"No, no! Just . . . just disappear again or . . . oh, God!" I press my eyes shut. "I'm going to be sick! Please go away, *please!*"

Instead, she sits across from me, calmly pressing her tea bag against the side of the cup with her spoon. "Oh, that's very nice! Whatever happened to 'Hi, Robbie! Nice to see you! How have you been?' Manners, Evie." She shakes her head sadly. "What's the world coming to, eh? Kids today!"

This isn't happening to me. She's in front of me; solid, real, her skin glowing with the warmth of life.

"You're dead," I say, as if trying to convince myself.

She sips her tea. "Just a little bit."

There's a long pause. We stare at each other.

She giggles.

"No, Robbie. You're *dead!*" I repeat accusingly. Perhaps if I say it convincingly enough, she'll disappear.

"OK, you've got me," she sighs, putting down her tea and holding up her hands. "I'm dead! Forgive me, but I'm a little touchy about the subject. Especially as you're alive, you have a beautiful son, you're sitting here in this hellhole farting around, lusting after that creep when you could be having a rich and fulfilling life . . . As I said, I'm a little touchy about the whole thing!"

I frown at her, offended. "What do you mean 'farting around'? Who are you to tell me how to live my life?"

She looks at me, hard. "Oh, I don't know. Who am I? Well, I'm the dead person who's come back from the underworld with the express purpose of telling you that you're wasting your time." She takes another sip. "How's that? Does that answer your question?"

"Underworld?" It sounds so ancient. "What ever happened to heaven and hell?"

She shrugs her shoulders. "We call it the underworld but really it's more like Grand Central Station on a warm spring night. A lot of milling about . . . departures, arrivals . . . that sort of thing. It's hard to explain. Heaven and hell are for amateurs. You know, I think this whole organic thing's just a load of hype. I can't taste the difference, can you? It's just like pee in a cup."

I don't know what to say.

It's all so ordinary and mundane. Here we are in broad daylight. I have coffee-mouth. She smells like cigarettes and Chanel No. 5. There's a guy at the sink behind us washing up cups and humming the theme tune to *Hawaii Five-O*. This is not a haunting. This is not the grand collision of life and death. And most of all, this is not happening to me.

I sit there, shaking my head and blinking at her. I really don't know what to do with this information. Or how I'm going to get past this episode and live my life like a normal person ever again.

"You're really weirded out, aren't you?" Her voice is surprisingly sympathetic.

I nod, incapable of forming a coherent sentence and unwilling to speak out loud, as if the sound of my own voice in conversation with hers is a kind of collusion, enmeshing me further in this whole bizarre, untenable scenario.

But despite my silence, she remains; crossing and recrossing her legs, drumming her fingers against the armrest, biting her nails. She never could sit still for five minutes.

The guy behind us finishes the washing up and moves on to a medley of Bernstein tunes, starting with "I Feel Pretty."

And I'm fairly confident I'm going mad.

After a while, she stands up. "I have an idea." She holds out her hand and then, after registering my obvious horror at the idea of touching her, places it very deliberately behind her back. "There's no need to be like that." She sounds hurt. "I didn't come all this way to harm you, Evie. As a matter of fact, it takes a hell of a lot of energy to be here at all."

That's when it strikes me; it's still Robbie. Dead or alive. Above everything, beyond everything—it's still just Robbie. She hasn't really changed. She's still all mouth, and miles of front—the same girl who died because she couldn't get through the day without at least a litre of Diet Coke.

I'm ashamed. "I'm sorry," I mutter. And, for the first time, I look her in the eye.

Yes, it's her.

But there is something different. A light, or rather, a radiance shining through her, as if, despite her apparent solidity, she's translucent after all. But (and this is the odd thing) she's not *unusually* translucent. And I have the fleeting realization that we might all be equally as transparent, if only we could see ourselves properly.

"Let's go for a walk." The air around her is still, oddly peaceful. "I have some things I'd like to tell you."

*I*F YOU'RE GOING to do this, you need to do it right. Understand?"

It's ten past seven on a Thursday evening. Robbie and I are the only students left in the building. Outside the sky is an inky, flat black and a slim sliver of moon is beginning to rise. The fluorescent lights glow eerily, blinking and buzzing above our heads.

I press my face into my hands.

There's a knock on the studio door and a disgruntled cleaner pokes her head round the corner.

"Five more minutes," Robbie begs, flashing her most appealing smile. The woman shakes her head, mumbles under her breath, but leaves us in peace.

Or what would be peace, if Robbie weren't holding me hostage. It's late; we've been here since our first class started at nine this morning and I'm tired and sweaty and in desperate need of one of Mrs. Van Patterson's forbidden baths.

I lift my head. "We ought to get back," I say.

But Robbie doesn't budge.

"Trust me on this, Evie. You only get one shot. And in ten minutes the whole thing will be over and you'll be back out in the waiting room with about a hundred other people staring at you. And they'll only call back five of them. Only five!"

I've heard this statistic before. In fact, I've heard the whole speech before. Many, many, *many* times.

"Every little thing you do has to be perfect." She's oblivious to my rolling eyes. "And I can't put my finger on it, but something's not quite right . . ."

This isn't what I want to hear.

I never asked her to help me; she just woke up one morning and appointed herself in charge of my Juilliard audition speeches. And for three weeks now, all we've done is gone over them and over them, again and again and again. At breakfast, walking to the tube station, over lunch, walking back from the tube station, at dinner . . .

At first I was flattered. That wore off a while ago.

I've never met anyone so determined.

Or so irritating.

Right now she's in what Imo calls her "Great Dictator" mode; her hair's pulled back from her face and she's wearing a pair of thick-framed reading glasses. (Imo and I strongly suspect they're fake.) She's holding a play text of *King Lear* in one hand, and a copy of David Mamet's *Sexual Perversity in Chicago* in the other, scrutinizing them; looking for clues. Finally she shakes her head. "Let's go over everything one more time."

That's it. I've had enough.

"No, Robbie. I've done them about fifty times already tonight. I'm finished." Dragging my aching limbs across the room, I retrieve my coat and bag. "I want to go home now. Come on."

"You don't get it, do you?" She hasn't moved and doesn't give the impression she's likely to. Removing her faux glasses, she regards me severely—her impression of a grade school librarian. "You have one little window of opportunity to change your entire life here; one chance to guarantee that you'll never have to go back to Ohio again except in a blaze of glory! And what? You're pissed off because you may have to work for it? That it may involve a bit of effort on your part?"

Robbie's the last person to lecture me on the importance of dedicated effort. Just because she's decided to show up for class on time, she suddenly thinks she's Lee Strasberg.

"Don't talk to me about hard work, Robbie! I've been slaving like a dog learning those pieces!"

She stands up. "And I'm telling you to do them again!"

"Why?" I throw down my bag and coat. "What's wrong with them?"

"They're just not good enough, Evie! I'm . . . I'm not sure why, exactly, but they're just not strong enough. As a matter of fact," she pauses, looking at the texts with a baffled expression on her face, "I still think they're the wrong pieces for you. Boyd and I were talking about them the other day—"

"*Boyd?*"

She smiles coyly. "Yeah, we were having a coffee together and I told him about your pieces . . ."

"You met him for a coffee? Alone?" I can't believe what I'm hearing.

She sighs dramatically. "Listen, it's just a coffee! We get on, OK? Anyway, I brought up that Fassbinder piece about a masturbating model and then he thought maybe if you did Isabella from *Measure for Measure* it would be a fantastic whore/nun contrast thing . . ."

"You know I don't like that piece! I told you I don't want to do it!"

"But, Evie, you're missing an important opportunity here! Like I said, you only get one shot . . ."

Her mouth is moving. I can hear the words but nothing's registering any more. I'm sick of the sound of her voice. Of her corrections, questions, stopping and starting me, bossing me around just because she did an audition once in her life . . . I can't believe she's seducing Boyd! For some reason, it's the last straw; a betrayal of something important and sacred. And now she wants me to change all my pieces so she can impress him.

That's it. I pick my stuff up again.

"You want strong? Well, fuck you, Robbie! I've had enough of your bullshit! It would be nice if, just once, you were enthusiastic and supportive instead of pulling me to shreds day and night! It will never be good enough for you! And you know why? Because you don't want me to succeed! You don't want me to get into a place that turned you down!"

She looks stunned. "That isn't true!"

"Next time, save yourself the trouble: buy a glove puppet. Then you can stick your hand up its ass and make it do as you please!"

I slam the door behind me.

The cleaner's there, leaning against the wall, smoking a fag.

She turns away.

I walk up the stairs alone.

For the first time in my life I've answered back. I'm not used to the rush of adrenaline and nerves. As I clutch the handrail, my hands are shaking.

This is a really bad night to be having a dinner party.

As soon as I walk in the door of Gloucester Place, Imo comes staggering out of the front room on a pair of Robbie's black stilettos.

"Shit! Evie! Where have you guys been? It's quarter to eight! They're going to be here in half an hour!"

I stop.

Her face is a primary school colour wheel; streaks of blue eye shadow, circles of pink blush, red lipstick, applied with all the skill of a child who can't draw inside the lines yet. Her hair's in a tight bun with a little curlicue wisp on either side of her face; the epitome of chic circa 1974. That, along with Robbie's slightly too large high heels and her very best *Little House on the Prairie* dress complete the impression: she's a little girl playing dress-up in Mommy's things.

It's cruel to let her make a fool of herself. How do I break the news that she looks ridiculous? The evening's been arranged so she finally has an opportunity to seduce Lindsay Crufts with her beauty and sophisticated sex appeal. That, and an enormous quantity of cheap wine. But unless he's even more curiously orientated than we think, all her hard work will be wasted.

As it happens, she's already too hysterical to care about my opinion anyway.

"There's no food, Evie!" She grabs me by the shoulders. "We have no food in the house! NONE!"

"What?"

I've been so wrapped up in my own problems that I haven't been paying attention to the whole dinner party thing.

I tug off my coat. It lands on top of a pile of other abandoned clothes in the front hall. "But I thought Robbie was going to sort it all out."

I walk into the kitchen and open the fridge. There's half a pint of old milk, some butter and a carrot. I look in the cupboards. A box of rice, pasta and four bottles of liquor—blue gin, green gin, white gin and a bottle of Cointreau with the cap missing—all of them nearly empty.

A lurching feeling builds in the pit of my stomach.

"See? Nothing! I told you! What are we going to do?" Her voice rises to a pitch normally only heard by dogs.

"OK. We need to be calm." (I'm not calm.) "How many people are coming?" (Are there any recipes that serve loads of people using only some rice and a carrot? I wish my mother were here.)

"It's us and about a *thousand* men!" She's plummeting over the edge. "Lindsay's coming! And that Chicken man, and some guy she buys coffee from in the morning named Carlo and that French girl Pascale . . ."

"The one who cries in every scene?"

Imo nods. "Robbie thought she would add 'colour and an international dimension to the conversation.'"

"But she can't open her mouth without weeping," I point out, which, upon reflection, isn't really wise at this juncture.

"I know! I *know!*" She's starting to shake; the two little curlicues bobbing up and down like alien antennae. "And Lindsay's coming! He's going to be here any minute! We're fucked! We're completely fucked, Evie!"

The true horror of the evening Robbie's masterminded begins to unfold. And the falling sensation accelerates dramatically. Pascale's crazy. The coffee man barely speaks English. Hughey Chicken has been leaving messages for weeks, all of which Robbie's been ignoring. And Imo . . .

Shit!

I fling open another cupboard.

We have three chipped plates, no clean glasses, nothing left to eat or drink, a flat that looks like Beirut and only twenty-five minutes to go.

I hate Robbie; with every fibre of my being, I despise her.

It's one thing to fuck about with me; to bully me and grind down every last particle of self-confidence I possess. It's another thing entirely to harm Imo; to get her hopes up and then to abandon her this way. I could kill Robbie for that.

But right now I have to do something to protect Imo from an evening of unremitting humiliation. I grab her hands. "OK, here's what we do. We're going to have to cancel. Do you have Lindsay's number?"

"What?" She stares at me blankly, suddenly coming over all Blanche DuBois.

"We have to cancel," I repeat louder, as if shouting will rouse her from this trance. "Do you understand, Imo? We have to make them go away!"

She snaps to. "But what if it's too late?"

"We may just have time. If we call now, they may not have left yet. I can do Pascale and we'll just have to send Hughey away . . . and the coffee guy too . . . hurry!" I give her a shove. She teeters into her room in search of her address book.

For a moment, I'm rooted to the spot. My most overwhelming instinct is to grab my coat and run. Instead, I focus: try to remember . . . Where did I put that tiny scrap of paper with Pascale's number on it? Did I keep it at all? My head hurts. I rub my eyes. Come on, concentrate!

The door opens.

"Hey! I could do with a hand here!" Robbie strolls in, her arms full of bags, followed by two Chinese guys carrying large boxes.

I stare at her.

"What's all this?"

"This? Well, this is our dinner party! Thank you." They drop their boxes on the long dining room table and, settling her own bags onto the kitchen counter, she pulls some money from her back pocket and tips them. "Thanks for all your help, guys. See you later!"

They smile, waving good-bye as they make their way out of the front door.

I open one of the boxes. Inside, it's piled high with Chinese takeaway cartons, stacks of chopsticks, fortune cookies, napkins . . . I watch as she unpacks the bags on the counter; one is full of ice and the other, some bizarre beer from Japan.

"Here." She hands me the ice. "Put the plug in the sink and dump this in, will you?"

When I'm done, she quickly forces the bottles in between the cubes, until the sink is overflowing with cold beer.

I'm astounded. "Where did you get all this?"

She's unpacking another bag, full of candles, in every conceivable size and shape. "Chinatown," she answers matter-of-factly. She turns to look at me. "You didn't honestly think we were going to cook, did you?"

I turn away. Every time I think I've got her pegged, she does something completely surprising. She's the only person I know for whom the unexpected can be considered business as usual.

I watch silently as she transforms the kitchen, whisking dirty dishes into a bucket she hides underneath the sink and piling the dining table high with fragrant, exotic treats.

It would never occur to me to do anything so bold or extravagant or expensive; there must be at least a hundred pounds' worth of food and drink here. Yet Robbie executes these grand gestures without even a bat of an eye. Half of me is jealous; if she hadn't arrived, I'd still be struggling to create a feast out of some rice and a carrot. The other half is pathetically grateful.

"How did you pay for it?" I ask sheepishly; by rights we should all chip in.

"Credit card." She drapes a scarlet silk scarf over the paper light shade in the dining room. A soft red glow washes over the room.

"Won't your parents be pissed off?"

She looks at me. "And what difference does it make to you?"

This is where I should make a move towards reconciliation. After all, what difference does it make how she does things, as long as it works out in the end? But there's a knot of resentment in my stomach that won't go away. I open my mouth to form the words but a fresh rush of anger flares up inside me instead. My good intentions evaporate. We have more urgent things to do. I concentrate on helping her lay out the food.

"My parents live for this kind of shit. I'm providing hours of entertainment and possibly the only bond of intimacy these people will ever share. Pissed off is what they do best," she adds pointedly.

Imo rushes out of her room, waving a pink plastic address book. "I've got it! I found it!" She stops. "What's this?"

Robbie's eyes widen. She looks at me in dismay. I can't help but smile back and the hostility between us relaxes. This is a common crisis.

Piling the candles into my arms, she whispers to me. "Why didn't you tell me she was dressed like Raggedy Ann? You decorate the flat. I'll sort her out! OK." She frog-marches Imo back into her room. "This might hurt a little but it's for your own good!"

The door shuts.

I rush around, filling every bare surface with candles, covering the ugly sofa with a marginally less offensive throw from my bed, doing my best to clear away the full ashtrays, piles of dirty laundry and mouldering cups of stale coffee and tea.

"How's it going?" Robbie calls.

"I don't know . . ." I stand back, surveying the results. "It still looks . . . bare . . . like something's missing!"

She pokes her head out. "Here!" She chucks me her lighter and I catch it. "Light all the candles. Turn out the lights. Take my Chanel No. 5 and spray it on the curtains. Put the Billie Holiday tape on a little too loud and then open a beer. I guarantee you, the place will look a lot better." She disappears again.

As I've been doing for the past three weeks, I follow Robbie's instructions one more time. In a matter of minutes the dingy, dark student flat is transformed into a seductive, scented, glimmering den of iniquity, with cosy dark corners, just right for intimate conversations and even more intimate assignations.

I pop the top off a bottle of beer and gulp greedily. I've had nothing to eat all day. Then I collapse into one of the black leather chairs. I see myself in the flat, blank television screen opposite; my dyed black hair tumbles down my shoulders in a mass of knots that haven't been combed through in days. My face peers out, pale and small. Yesterday's thick black liner and mascara are smudged around my eyes. My arms are twigs sticking out of my white T-shirt and I've been wearing these jeans for weeks. I take another swig.

I ought to pull myself together.

If only I had the energy.

"Ta-da! Here she is!" Robbie gives Imo a gentle prod into the centre of the room. Her long brown hair swirls around her bare shoulders, showcased in Robbie's black jersey Norma Kamali dress, which hugs her slim hips, then flares out like a flamenco dancer's costume. Her face is almost free of makeup; just softly stained lips and long dark lashes. And she's beautiful, refined; a Pre-Raphaelite Audrey Hepburn, although she still folds her long arms protectively round her waist. Is she afraid someone might notice she's not encased in a thousand yards of hand-smocked gingham?

I laugh in delight. "Im, you look amazing!"

She grins, turns and plants a kiss on Robbie's cheek.

The doorbell rings.

We look at one another.

Robbie grabs each of us by the hand. "The only rules are, ladies, that we are wonderful, wicked and witty. Apart from that, nothing else matters!" Then she sashays into the hallway and pulls the door open. "Why, hello! Oh, really, you shouldn't have!" she purrs, every inch the New York hostess.

As it turns out, Hughey Chicken, Lindsay Crufts, mad Pascale and Coffee Carlo aren't the only people Robbie's invited: Coffee Carlo brings three other guys—all gorgeous Italian students, dead ringers of Michelangelo's *David,* only wearing tight jeans and carrying bottles of red wine. Pascale brings her brother, Jean Luc, a Ceroc fanatic who, in addition to jiving with anyone who dares to stand still for thirty seconds, also thoughtfully raided the back garden of the squat where he lives to provide us with some of the most powerful home-grown grass known to man. And Hughey Chicken's rounded up some musical entertainment, which he promises will arrive any minute.

Best of all, Lindsay shows up wearing a suit and tie, carrying a bouquet of red roses. Imo shyly arranges them in the three empty gin bottles, while discussing various Chekhov translations and showing off her white shoulders.

The music gets louder and the guys from upstairs come down. We run out of Chinese and order pizzas. Empty beer bottles collect on every surface and spliff after spliff is passed around. One of the Italian Davids tries to make a move on me. And then on Imo. And then on Robbie. And then back to me again. He wanders over, shrugging his shoulders and smiling. "I really missed you." He settles down next to me with a fresh glass of wine. "I like you best, you know."

The doorbell rings. I make a move, but fail to navigate past Jean Luc, who twirls me under his arm.

Someone else opens it and Jean Luc presses me close, whirling me into the kitchen. I peer over his shoulder to see a familiar figure weaving his way through the crowd.

It's Jake, carrying a guitar case. He's not alone. Behind him, a tall, buxom blonde looks disdainfully at the assembled crowd. She's wearing strappy ankle boots and a flared miniskirt; her T-shirt torn in strategic places, like some video model on MTV.

Jean Luc scoops me up again, tossing me up in the air and catching me.

The entire contents of my stomach (three beers and two and a half spring rolls) somersaults inside me. Pulling away, I dive into the bathroom.

I look at my reflection in the mirror. What stares back could easily be one of the witches in *Macbeth*.

Shit.

Why can't I be the one with the Norma Kamali dress and all Robbie's expertise?

I grab a comb and start pulling it through my hair.

It's wrong, I know. The only person I should make such an effort for is Jonny. But I can't help myself. I'd give almost anything to be the cool blonde trailing behind Jake.

Someone's knocking on the bathroom door.

"I'll be out in a minute!" I shout, splashing my face with cool water. There's no way he's going to see me with panda eyes.

More pounding.

"I'm coming!" I unlock the door and one of the guys from upstairs falls in, not even bothering to wait for me to leave before he unzips his trousers.

There's music . . . live music . . . grinding rock chords, played with a confidence and skill that's somehow shocking in the mundane setting of our little flat. Drifting towards the front room, I poke my head round the corner. Jake's standing near the window, guitar slung round his shoulders, his lean figure almost doubled over with intensity as he plays. The room's gone quiet; even Jean Luc's still, mesmerised by this sudden unleashing of raw talent. The blonde is curled neatly at Jake's feet, looking up at him with the possessive smugness of ownership.

It's unfair. He's with her and I'm stuck with boring old Jonny . . .

Right. I may not have any designer dresses, but I can still do better than this.

I head for my room, open the door.

Someone's on the bed.

Two people, actually.

And there are groaning noises in the dark.

Great.

I clear my throat.

I cough.

I shuffle my feet, clear my throat and cough.

Fuck it.

I turn on the light.

It's Pascale and Lindsay Crufts. She's giving him a blow job. She glares at me, while he, on the other hand, is completely oblivious, head thrown back, eyes shut. She waves me away angrily, as if I've been incredibly rude to interrupt them.

I switch the light off and step back into the hallway, closing the door behind me. This is an image that will stay with me for ever; an excess of information I don't want or need.

"Have you seen Lindsay?" It's Imo, holding two glasses of red wine.

I shake my head no.

She frowns. "He was here only a minute ago." She wanders back into the front room, where Coffee Carlo invites her to sit down, nicking the second glass of wine and wrapping an arm around her shoulders.

This is a major setback to our plans. Who can I talk to?

I find Robbie in her room, changing her shoes and checking her makeup. "What?" she says when she sees me. "What's wrong?"

"Jake's here." I throw myself onto her bed. "And Imo's gay boyfriend is receiving a blow job right now from our own lovely Pascale!"

"No!" She starts to laugh. "Well, that proves exactly nothing about his sexuality."

"Imo doesn't know," I assure her. "But then Carlo's putting the moves on her right now."

"Good," she nods. "Carlo's not a fag. And he knows what he's doing. Pascale could be doing Imo a massive favour. Who would've imagined Waterworks had it in her?" Robbie turns her attention back to her hair.

The conversation is apparently over, neatly wrapped up as a simple partner swap. I watch as she reapplies her lipstick, smearing the edges gently with her finger to produce a soft, rosebud mouth. She's a cherub; pale ivory and pink. It would be a lot easier to make up with her if she weren't so pretty right now. A self-conscious silence stretches out between us. I stare down at the ruffled bedclothes; at the mascara stains on her pillow.

I force myself to take the plunge. "Listen, Robbie—"

She cuts me off. "Turn the light off when you go," she instructs. She grabs a faded denim jacket off one of the hangers in the wardrobe.

I'm angry again. How can she be so dismissive of this mayhem and chaos? Of Imo's feelings for Lindsay?

"Where are you going? Hey! You can't bug out now!" I shout. "We're in the middle of a party!"

"Yes I can." She heads for the door.

I grab her arm.

"What are you doing? What makes you think you can just fuck everything and leave like this?" My voice catches, my skin's hot. I'm not good at this. No one in my family fights; we go silent and sullen. But right now I feel like shouting.

Robbie pulls her arm away. "Grow the fuck up, Evie!" She looks at me with contempt. "That's life! Nancy Pants gets a blow job and Imo gets laid by a real man instead. Deal with it! At least Carlo's good."

I recoil. "Jesus! You slept with him! Is there anyone at this party you haven't fucked?"

For a second it looks as if she might cry, but her fragility freezes into a mask of revulsion. "I'm sick of the sight of you!" she hisses. "I'm sick of your whining, small-town, self-righteous shit! I fuck a lot of people. So what? A lot of people want to fuck me! At least I'm not simpering around, lusting after one guy while going on and on and on about some geek back home! 'Ooooo, we're going to live together in New York!'"

My eyes are stinging. "At least I'm not some stupid, wayward slut like you!"

I flinch; she's going to hit me. But she says, "I've got news for you: you're never gonna make it out of Ohio, baby! You haven't got the fucking balls!"

Then she turns and runs out. The door slams. But I'm the only one to hear it above the music, laughter, chatter and noise.

I bury my face in my hands.

It wouldn't matter so much if she weren't right.

I have to speak to Jonny. It's all gone wrong. I long for the sound of his calm, certain voice. Wiping my tears on the bottom of my T-shirt, I stumble out of the flat and into the hallway. There's a pay phone in the corner. Picking up the receiver, I press it to my ear. The line's dead. OUT OF ORDER a sign reads, taped across the top, printed in Mrs. Van Patterson's scraggly, old-lady handwriting.

Shit.

I lean against the wall. There's a roar of applause and cheering; Jake's finished another song. I don't want to talk to anyone right now except Jonny. Opening the front door, I fall out into the night.

There's a phone box around the corner. Traffic whips past. The wind's like a firm, flat hand pushing me backwards. I press on, shivering in my T-shirt. I pass a pub full of smoke and noise, next to a row of silent, empty shops. There's the phone box, a glowing red rectangle in the distance. I'm running now, pulling open the door, flinging myself inside. I pull out a couple of pound coins, jam them in. I dial the number and wait. Somewhere on the other side of the world, a phone rings.

"Hello?"

He sounds different, younger . . . far away.

"Hello?" he repeats.

"It's me."

"Baby! It's so great to hear from you! What's going on?"

"Nothing." Can he tell I've been crying? "I . . . I just miss you, Jonny, that's all."

He laughs. "I miss you too, babe. It's been really hard without you, if you catch my drift!" And he giggles wickedly.

This isn't what I want to hear. Why can't he be serious and romantic? And for the first time I feel embarrassed by Jonny; ashamed of him. He seems to sense this and tries to shift the subject. "Hey, how's that weird teacher of yours?"

I lean my head against the glass door. "Actually, he's OK. Quite good, really."

"Oh. Well. He sounded pretty strange to me."

Silence.

I can hear him stretching out on his bed. It must be early afternoon there. "So, you're up late. What are you guys doing? Just hanging out?"

"Well," I hesitate. "We've got a couple of friends over . . ."

"Sounds nice." His voice is distant; neutral. He waits for me to continue.

"Yeah . . . it is nice," I concede. Why am I so reluctant to fill in the blanks?

"And what about the girls?" he prompts me. "That Robbie seems pretty wild."

"We had a fight," I whisper, my eyes filling with tears again.

"What about?"

I don't want to tell him. He wouldn't approve of Robbie—wouldn't approve of so many things in London. Or rather, he wouldn't understand them. And it strikes me for the first time that we're not just on different sides of one world but living on totally different planets now. Something in me has shifted away from Jonny. It's moved into an altogether darker, more unfamiliar place. It's frightening. And at the same time exhilarating.

"Nothing really," I lie. "Just stuff."

"Oh." He can tell I'm avoiding him. "Is everything OK with you?"

I can't speak; my throat's tight.

I nod my head.

"Evie? Are you OK?"

"Yup. I just called because—"

The line starts beeping. "If you'd like to continue this call," a clipped English voice informs us, "please insert more coins now."

I panic. "Jonny!"

Beep, beep.

"What? What did you say?"

Beep, beep. Beep, beep.

"Jonny, I'm so sorry!"

The line goes dead. I'm alone, holding the receiver; the flat, insistent sound of the lost connection buzzing in my ear. I hang up, numb from cold, and step out of the booth.

There, leaning against the side of an abandoned betting shop, smoking a cigarette, is Jake.

He exhales slowly. "Hey."

"Hey." I step aside. "I'm finished now."

His eyes meet mine.

"I'm not waiting for the phone."

We stand there a moment.

He hands me the cigarette.

I take it, drawing it slowly to my lips. He takes off his leather jacket and puts it round my shoulders.

We walk, side by side, not touching, not speaking, winding our way in silence through the empty streets. I don't know where I am any more. I'm lost. And it doesn't matter.

After a while, he flags down a passing cab. Opening the door, he looks at me. "I want to take you somewhere."

I pull away. "Who's that girl?"

He doesn't even blink. "No one. Some chick Hughey thinks can sing." I get in.

I get in, knowing I've crossed a line. There will be more of them as the night goes on, things I've never done, things I never thought I'd do.

And I don't care any more.

He lives in a bed-sitting room above a bicycle repair shop in Kentish Town. It's one large room with a sink and a fridge in one corner and a mattress on the floor against the far wall. There are three more guitars balanced on stands next to one another, a portable amp, some sound equipment stacked in silver metal boxes, piles and piles of records and a sophisticated stereo system arranged on what looks like an old office desk, complete with a swivel chair. Ashtrays are everywhere. The walls are covered with posters of The Clash, Jimi Hendrix, Bowie, the Sex Pistols and the New York Dolls.

I sit on the swivel chair and watch as he pulls a tiny plastic bag out of his back pocket and takes out a small, framed mirror. I'm in a strange part of London with no money, no coat and no keys. He arranges the lines of coke, rolls up a tenner and hands it to me. And leaning forward, I do what I've seen people in movies do, pressing one nostril shut, sucking the powder up. Then I move to the other side. It's bitter, metallic; hitting the back of my palate like mercury.

He smiles and stands up, returning from the fridge with a bottle of vodka. And I take a sip, watching as he does the remaining lines.

He puts on Bowie's "Station to Station." It's the best music I've ever heard. Someone's pounding on the wall next door but after a while they give up and it stops. I feel languorous, the night has suddenly acquired a clean, hard edge. I'm no longer awkward and anxious, struggling to present a face to the world. I'm smart and sexy; more aware of my body, of every nerve of my being. And I love this music. Could listen to it all night.

I lean back in the chair and close my eyes. Kicking against the desk, I swirl round, spinning in darkness, delighted at the rush of freedom.

And then it stops.

Jake pulls me up. He presses his mouth over mine. And he tastes just the way I imagined he would. He's sweet and salty, all at once. The leather jacket falls away. He peels off my T-shirt and bra. I watch, floating somewhere outside myself, as he bends down, kissing my breasts. Arching my back, I weave my fingers through his long dark hair. He unzips my jeans. I step out of them. He kicks them out of the way and, a moment later, tears off my pale pink panties. They're the colour of cotton candy. My mother bought them. He pushes me back into the chair and I pull off his shirt, sinking my mouth into the warm flesh of his shoulder. Then he tilts the chair back and spreads my legs wide.

Jonny disappears; is obliterated.

Jake takes possession.

We snort more lines and he fucks me against the wall. Bowie plays on a loop again and again and again. He pulls me into the shower with him, rinsing my face clean, untangling my hair with surprising gentleness. He wraps me in a towel, carries me to the bed. He's hard again. I go down on him and then he turns me over.

"I wanna fuck your ass," he says.

And I laugh. Everything's so funny tonight. The coke's almost gone. We share the last lines. And everything, anything, feels good. He moves slowly, then faster and I think my head's going to explode.

It's 5:33 in the morning. We're lying still, tangled around each other, a mass of knotted limbs.

"I gotta go," I say.

"OK."

We lie there.

I make a move. He pins me to the bed.

"Not so fast," he whispers, kissing me.

It's 6:42.

"I really gotta go," I say.

He sighs. "OK." And throws an arm over me.

It's 7:20.

I'm stumbling around, looking for my jeans.

"Here." He hands me a cup of tea.

I get dressed. He lends me a black oversized jumper. My hair's dried into a strange, almost sculptural shape. I try to press it down with my hands, wetting them with water.

Looking out of the window, I search in vain for some familiar landmark. "How do I get home?"

He unrolls the tenner laying on the mirror. "I take you."

We stroll arm in arm to the main road. The air is delicate, clear and cold. We catch a bus, sitting on the top deck at the front. I rest my head against his shoulder.

At Baker Street we get out and walk. And as we approach the flat, he hands me a tightly wrapped piece of paper.

"What's this?"

He tilts his head to one side and smiles. "Consider it an invitation."

"To what?"

But he just leans forward, brushing his lips very softly against the curve of my cheek.

"Why don't you come in?"

"Na, I fancy the walk. See you later." He strolls up to the corner, a long, lean figure against the pale morning sky.

I wait until he rounds the corner before unfolding the little paper parcel.

"Welcome to Raven's World" it reads. And underneath, his address is wrapped round a small silver key to his flat.

I ring the bell, and after a while, a dishevelled Coffee Carlo appears, looking, ironically enough, as if he could use a cup of coffee. He's spent the night, along with Jean Luc, sleeping on the floor in the front room.

"Where's Imo?" I survey the damage from the night before with a curious sense of detachment.

He's sheepish. "She's sleeping. Quite alone," he adds, looking at me. "I didn't want to leave her here on her own all night."

My cheeks flush; I turn away. "I'm going to lie down," I announce, heading towards my room. "Just knock if you need me."

As I walk in, the image of Pascale and Lindsay pops into my mind again, sending an involuntary shiver up my spine. I examine the bedclothes cautiously, then peel them back. I kick my shoes off and curl up in my jeans and Jake's warm, woolly jumper.

So much to think about. So much to make sense of.

I'm made of glass; transparent and fragile. My head's buzzing. Even though I'm shattered, I can't sleep. I turn over onto my back and stare at the ceiling in the grey half-light.

Everything's different now. Everything's changed.

It's as if, after a lifetime of believing in gravity, I've been taught how to fly. The view's so indescribable; the air finer, more refined. I've been transformed from an ordinary person into a creature of rare gifts.

I'm in love.

It's exquisite; excruciating. A blinding, soul-searing light, illuminating even this shabby little room.

And I'm certain I'll never sleep again.

A knocking at my door wakes me.

I turn over, rub my eyes. I try to sit up. My head's too heavy. I fall back into the warm, soft pillow.

"Evie!" Imo hisses in the dark.

"What?" My voice sounds like sandpaper over cement. "What time is it?"

"Two-thirty. Something's happened to Robbie. We have to go now."

I sit up. The room spins. Every muscle in my body aches. "Where is she?" I ask, forcing my feet back into my shoes.

Imo's in the front hall now; I follow her. Coffee Carlo's holding her coat open. She steps inside. "Mrs. Van Patterson had a call from some hotel in Hyde Park." She refers to a piece of paper crumpled in her hand. "The Bristol, Seventy-seven Rutland Crescent." Carlo opens the door and, removing Imo's keys very gently from her shaking grip, locks it behind us.

Imo's scanning the street, looking for a cab. Carlo races down to the corner and flags one going in the opposite direction. We wait while it turns around.

"What did they say?" I feel sick and cold.

Imo shakes her head. "All Mrs. Van Patterson said was that she was in trouble. And she wouldn't leave."

"What does that mean? Wouldn't leave what?"

But she just shakes her head and looks away. I wonder, with a sharp stab of guilt, if she feels I abandoned her last night.

Carlo flings open the cab door and we climb in. My head's starting to clear; I pull down the window. A rush of cold air hits me. I inhale deeply. All the decadent glamour of the previous night falls away, a dark velvet curtain pulled open, tattered and filthy in the light of day. My imagination races ahead, trying to picture Robbie. The cab lurches and lunges through traffic. It's one of the longest journeys of my life.

Finally, we pull up in front of the hotel, a tall Georgian town house sandwiched in a row of similar buildings.

Carlo pays the cab while Imo and I rush to the front desk.

An irritable middle-aged Indian man is waiting for us. "We are not that kind of hotel," he informs us angrily, leading us up to the third floor, jangling a set of master keys. "The man, he checked out this morning. We do not allow prostitutes. He should not have brought her in. No guests. That is the rule. You get her and go, right?"

He unlocks the door.

It's a dark, narrow room, smelling of cheap cleaning fluid and too many cigarettes. The curtains are drawn against the afternoon sun; a narrow shaft of light cuts across the brown carpet. "Please, leave us for just one moment," I beg him.

He shakes his head but steps back anyway. "Ten minutes, you understand? That's all."

Imo and I walk in.

Robbie's curled in a ball on the bed, wearing the same faded fifties floral dress she was wearing last night, only the skirt's badly torn, her knees grazed and dirty. Her cheeks are covered in black trails of mascara but her eyes are strangely dead. She doesn't move.

I kneel down next to her and the sickly sweet smell of alcohol hits me. "Jesus, Im! She's completely pissed! Robbie!" I give her a shake. "Robbie! Are you OK?"

She blinks, staring at me as if from across a great distance.

Imo intervenes. She takes hold of Robbie's face in her hands, forcing her to focus. "Did you take something?" I've never heard her be so fierce. "Look at me! Did you take anything?"

Robbie shakes her head.

"Do you promise?" she persists.

Robbie nods.

"Then what happened?" Imo demands, letting her go. "What did that bastard do?"

Robbie turns her head slowly, looking first at Imo and then back to me. "Nothing. Nothing happens." Closing her eyes, she curls up, arms round her head. She's a child, crouching in a corner. "Nothing, nothing, nothing," she whispers. "Leave me alone!"

I look up at Imo, stunned. "We need to take her to the hospital!"

She shakes her head. "She's pissed, Evie. We hardly need a doctor to tell us that."

"But there's something seriously wrong with her!" I insist. "We should call an ambulance!"

Imo's expression is tough. "No. We need to get her home." She starts to collect Robbie's belongings, gathering her jean jacket and handbag; picking up her shoes from the floor.

I watch in confusion and then turn to the Indian man in the hallway. "I think we need an ambulance."

Imo intercepts me. "No! It's fine!" she assures him, yanking me back into the room. "You don't understand! This happened last term. In fact, it used to happen all the time. You have to trust me. I know how to deal with this. Before you came . . ." Her voice fades. She stops, overwhelmed. "It used to be much worse," she says quietly. "Now let's get her out of here."

She tries to lift Robbie up.

"Leave me alone!" Robbie shouts, pulling away. "Don't look at me!"

I stare at her tearstained face. She's familiar and unfamiliar; an unnerving facsimile of her former self.

The angry Indian man's shouting again. "They've drunk everything! The minibar is empty! That's a lot of money, you know! You owe me a lot of money! You're not leaving till I have been paid or I call the police, do you understand?"

"Fuck you!" Robbie lunges at him, nearly falling off the edge of the bed. Imo and I restrain her while Coffee Carlo deals with the Indian man and his unpaid minibar bill.

Carlo rings a friend of his, a man called Jim who delivers baked goods, who gives us a lift to the flat in the back of his van.

"No cab will take us," Carlo explains apologetically, looking at Robbie.

And Imo nods, pressing her hand over his.

When we get home, we put Robbie to bed, fully dressed, with a bucket next to her on the floor.

It's early evening before she comes to. I'm sitting, waiting, cross-legged on the floor by her bed.

She turns, groans, then struggles to sit up. "What are you doing?"

I gesture to a mug on the floor. "I made you a cup of tea."

"With sugar?"

"Yeah." I smile. "But I drank it about an hour ago."

She yawns, rubbing her eyes. "You've been sitting here that long?"

I nod.

"Why?"

"I wanted to make sure you were all right."

"Really?" She looks at me quizzically, pulling herself up onto her elbows. "Fuck! You haven't got a fag, have you? And a glass of water?"

I go into the kitchen and come back with both. She drinks the water in a single long gulp. Then we sit in the dark, passing the cigarette back and forth.

"Listen, about those things I said—" I begin.

"Forget about it," she cuts me off. "It's over, right?"

"Right," I agree, more than a little relieved to have got off so lightly.

"And hey, I don't remember you bursting into tears or anything!"

I smile. "You're right."

I'm dying to tell her all about Jake; about everything that happened.

She winces, passing a hand over her eyes.

I'll wait till tomorrow, when she's feeling better.

"Just promise me one thing," she sighs.

"What?"

Taking a long drag, she passes the cigarette back to me. "I don't want you giving up and becoming a hairdresser in Eden, Ohio. OK?"

"Oh! Yeah, right!" I laugh.

"I mean it, Evie. Promise me you'll see it through. Otherwise, I'm going to have to come after you!" Her face relaxes into a smile. "We could live together in New York. In the Village. Just you and me."

"OK, I promise."

She leans back against the pillows and shuts her eyes. "Did you put that bucket there?"

"Yeah."

"Why am I still dressed?"

"Why?" It seems an odd question. "Because we couldn't get you undressed."

"Oh."

She rolls over, her back towards me. "Did we have fun? Was it a good evening?" Her voice is small and muffled.

Is she joking?

"I don't know," I say, after a while. "Don't you remember?"

"Of course I remember," she assures me, quickly. "I remember everything."

I stare at the outline of her thin back. "Are you sure?"

But there's no reply.

She's asleep. Or dreaming.

Or both.

*W*ANT A FAG?"

Robbie's walking next to me down Drury Lane. Brilliant spring sunlight sparkles across shopfront windows. The sky is a near cloudless, clear blue. I feel like I'm floating; the ground disappearing under my feet. She offers me a packet of Marlboros.

"I don't smoke any more." My mouth is dry. I lick my lips but my tongue feels like cardboard.

"Really?" She seems surprised, as if the idea that smoking might be hazardous to your health is a complete revelation.

"I haven't smoked since I was pregnant with Alex; maybe before. I can't remember."

She takes out a cheap pink plastic lighter. "One of the advantages of being dead," she grins, leaning forward and cupping her hand round the cigarette end.

"Do you mind if we take it easy on the dead jokes?" I ask.

She glances at me sideways. "Am I making you uncomfortable?"

This is such a terrific understatement. And she knows it. She's enjoying the drama of the situation. "A little," I concede. "Just a little, tiny bit."

She laughs, smoke streaming from her nose. "My, but you're delicate! By the way, you never came to my funeral."

I was hoping she'd forgotten. "Yeah, I'm sorry about that." I'm focusing on the cracks in the pavement. "I was pregnant at the time. And broke. New York seemed such a long way away."

"Not that broke," she reminds me.

She's caught me out. One of the other advantages to being dead—you have access to the truth, the whole truth. This is the most bizarre social faux pas I've ever made. There's no alternative but to come clean. "You're right. I'm sorry. I was going through a bad time."

She takes another drag. "It was a bad time for me too."

We walk in silence.

I can hear my footsteps, brittle, fast. But I don't hear hers.

"You'd be surprised how much it matters," she says after a while. "You think that once you're dead, it would be the last thing on your mind. But it's one of those occasions where numbers really do count."

"Robbie, please!" She's not making this any easier. "I really am sorry!"

"Yeah. I know. You'd gone off me before then anyway."

I stop. "Listen, what is this? Have you come here just to guilt me to death?"

"Hey." She holds up a hand. "Lighten up on the dead jokes, please!"

This is unbearable. But, perhaps not surprisingly, it's exactly the way it used to be all the time. "You're just as difficult to talk to as ever!" I say. "Has nothing changed for you at all?"

She thinks a moment. "Did I mention I was dead?"

Something in me snaps.

I walk away.

"Are you denying it?" She runs to catch me up. "Are you denying the fact that you stopped returning my calls? Stopped writing? Stopped even sending me charity Christmas cards with pictures of sparrows in the snow on them?"

I wheel round. "People lose touch, Robbie! It happens. OK? So I'm a shit friend. Is that why you're here? To let me know I disappointed you?"

"Maybe."

We've stopped in front of a massive Freemason temple adorned with strange hieroglyphic symbols—eyes peering out of triangles and the like. It's like a badly made set piece from *The Magic Flute*. She's panting, struggling to catch her breath.

"You should know better than to make a dead smoker run!" She sits down on the front steps, dangling her thin wrists over her knees.

"What do you mean, 'maybe'?" I ask.

She sighs. "Well, actually, I'm not sure why I'm here. It's not clear yet. I mean, it's obvious you need help—anyone can see that. But I'm winging it at the moment." She scratches her nose with the back of her hand. "More will be revealed."

I stare at her. I'm being haphazardly haunted. By a dead school friend who doesn't even know why she's here.

She smiles, squinting in the sunlight. "Want to get a sandwich?"

"No. No, I don't." I pace up and down. I'm not sure what I expected but this certainly isn't it. "Anyway, can you do that sort of thing?"

She looks at me. "What?"

"You know, eat?"

"Sure. It doesn't taste like much: just so much texture and temperature. That's one of the downsides. I'd give anything to be able to eat a ham sandwich and really taste it. You don't know how lucky you are."

There's not a lot I can say to that.

The lunchtime pedestrians duck in and around each other, racing to make the most of their hour. The crisp spring air sharpens everything; everyone's more genial, vivid. We watch as the queue grows at the Italian deli across the street; girls chatting to each other; men in their shirtsleeves make jokes and flirt.

I sit down next to her. "You've been dead five years . . . why are you coming back now?"

She shrugs her shoulders. "Well, actually, I've been around a long time. It's just that you can see me now. You're the thing that's changed, Evie. Not me."

"I don't understand. I'm not the only one. Everyone else can see you too."

She looks at me kindly. "I don't think it's an understand kind of thing. And they can only see me because you can."

It doesn't make sense. But I'm not going to pursue the point; it disturbs me that I may have something to do with her sudden materialization.

She continues to puff away, in no particular rush, as if we're just a couple of office workers sneaking in a crafty fag. I keep stealing looks at her; trying to detect what signals that she's dead. But if anything, it's the lack of change that's so shocking. I'm older, dressed differently; even my perfume's changed. But the unnerving thing about Robbie is she's exactly the same. Not just ageless, but caught, from moment to moment even, as if the tape's being rewound right before my very eyes. It's a strange, profound feeling of being stuck; a weight hangs over us, like an unseen lid on a giant glass jar.

"What was it like?" I ask, after a while.

"What?"

There's no other way to put it. "Dying."

She's quiet for a long time. "Absolute." She sounds almost wistful. "There's an eventfulness to great moments; being born, falling in love, Christmas when you're small . . . Dying is an event, Evie. Maybe that's why Mom buried me in that weird blue prom dress." Her voice is gentle. "Taffeta with big puffy sleeves . . ."

I have an unwelcome image of Robbie's mother walking around Saks Fifth Avenue in search of a dress to bury her daughter in.

"But you're in . . . in one of your own creations." I gesture to her outfit. I'm trying to be tactful; even flattering.

She smiles appreciatively. "We always revert to type. Besides, no one can spend eternity in a prom dress."

I nod, as if I have complete empathy for her situation. In fact, all I can think of is, did she have to change her clothes or did they simply appear on her, like a chameleon changing colour? And if we do revert to type, what would my chosen outfit for eternity be? A baggy pair of Gap jeans?

"And were you, you know, ready for it?"

She frowns.

I try again. "You know, were you reconciled to the fact that your time had come?" (All these clichés are particularly awkward in conversation with someone who is, in fact, dead.)

"Well . . ." She takes a deep drag. "Thing was, it was an accident."

"The car came out of nowhere."

"Yeah." She stubs out her cigarette, grinding it underneath the heel of her shoe. "But it was more than that," she explains, exhaling slowly. "What I mean is, it wasn't actually my time, Evie."

She makes an "oops, these things happen" face.

"I don't understand . . ." My mind's gone blank. "What do you mean, you weren't meant to die?"

She makes the face again. It doesn't improve with use. I'm starting to feel ill at ease, in a situation that's more than a little uneasy to begin with.

Robbie stretches out her legs. "I think I was supposed to have a scare; a near death experience that was going to change my life. But then my trouser leg got attached to the front bumper and there was this terrific pull and then wham!"

I flinch.

She looks at me with curious amusement, unconnected to the impact she has. "Yeah, it did hurt," she adds, watching my face carefully. She knew I wanted to ask that, but didn't dare.

We sit a while, watching the traffic go by.

"Are you saying . . . ?" I'm not sure I really want to ask this question. I try to make it sound as casual as possible. "Are you saying that God makes mistakes?"

She inhales sharply. "It's a little more subtle than that. He isn't the only one in the picture. There are other factors to consider. It's not all down to him, you know."

I'm falling from a great height; a shocking new idea opens up before me. "What do you mean it's not all down to him? Who is it down to?"

She shrugs her shoulders.

Much more disturbing than seeing a ghost is bumping into one who nonchalantly informs you that God's a bit flaky and distracted. The feeling of panic rapidly gathers speed.

"But God's meant to be omnipotent!" I sound indignant; like I'm returning a faulty item to a store. I have nothing more profound at my disposal. In the grand scheme of things, I'm little more than an irate customer. "That means no mistakes ever, Robbie! Nothing's random. Everything's been thought out and planned well in advance."

She leans back on her elbows and laughs. "Jeez, Evie, where's the fun in that?"

This is a serious conversation. She's not taking it seriously.

My growing hysteria translates itself into a bad Maggie Smith impersonation. "God is not an area where I require levity! I want certainty, security.

The knowledge that there's some divine order involved in all this chaos. I have a child, Robbie! I can't live in a meaningless universe. Once you're a mother, God better have a fucking plan!"

She seems genuinely unruffled, which is infuriating. "But God doesn't make you do stuff, Evie. We're not puppets attached to celestial strings. He didn't push me in front of the car. And besides, the glory of being alive doesn't come from knowing that everything happens for a reason (which, after all, you're never going to be able to understand anyway, so where's the comfort in that?), or that there's some great traffic controller in the sky. In fact, what could be more beautiful than the fact that love exists in a random universe?"

Robbie never had children, never seemed capable of serious relationships. She doesn't understand what it's like to live or die by another's happiness.

"What are you saying?" My whole world's crumbling inside. "That all my prayers are useless? Not even God can protect my child?"

She stares at me with her open, pale green eyes; small, delicate features frozen in time.

A few more cars go by.

A biker.

The girls from the queue sail past clutching brown takeaway bags; ignorant and happy.

"How do I know you're not actually a messenger of Satan?" I demand, bitterly.

"Satan?" She laughs and shakes her head. "God, you're funny!"

But she doesn't answer the question.

I stand up, too upset to sit any longer. "I don't want to seem rude," I snap, "but what is it you want? Why are you here?"

She looks up at me, quite still. "You really don't know, do you?"

I fold my arms protectively across my chest. "No, I don't, Robbie. You said something about me wasting my time which, frankly, I find offensive."

"I was trying to get your attention. And you are wasting your time," she adds, before lapsing into silence again.

A few more minutes go by.

"Are you sure you don't want a sandwich?"

"No! I really don't want a sandwich!" I shout. "And you aren't answering any of my questions and this isn't funny, do you understand? I don't find any of this even remotely funny!"

But she just stares at me; detached and unreadable.

A cloud passes in front of the sun. The air turns colder. I tug my cardigan tighter and check my watch. "My life is perfectly fine, Robbie. I have class and there are a bunch of things I've got to do first, so I really have to get going."

A gust of wind pushes the cloud on.

She nods, an angel sparkling in the sun.

"Listen." My voice softens. "I really am sorry about the funeral. I was a shit not to come. I . . . meant to . . ." I stop.

She's right about what happened, about the rift between us.

"Forget about it." She smiles. "Maybe next time."

Shoving my hands into my pockets, I turn down Drury Lane, passing the girls with their sandwiches, picnicking on the steps of their office building. They seem incredibly young and fresh; laughing a bit too loudly; hungry for attention, for something exciting to happen in the next half hour of their lunch break.

I feel old. In half an hour, what little serenity I had has been snatched away. Now the universe is by turns bizarre, incompetent and unstable in a way I could've never imagined. My head aches. I feel suffocated and trapped. And on top of this, I must be hallucinating. That's the only explanation. Alex will be taken from me and I'll die, rocking back and forth in the corner of a padded cell without ever seeing him grow up . . .

The girls laugh again. I force my head down. I hate them. I hate everybody.

"Hey!" Robbie calls after me. "Do you ever regret not going to Juilliard?"

I stop. The girls look up at me.

"Did you know you were one of only twelve girls they chose that year out of over ten thousand applications?"

I turn round.

Robbie's leaning back on her elbows, just a whisper of a smile playing across her lips. "He didn't make it easy, did he?"

She says these last words so softly, it seems impossible that I should be able to hear them at all. But instead, they echo through my head; one of the few true things I've heard in a long time.

Traffic whips around me; a treacherous tide of perpetual motion under a still blue sky.

What could be more beautiful than the fact that love exists in a random universe?

"I have to go," I say.

o." He riffles through the stack of papers in front of him. "What have you got for us today?"

There are three of them; two men and a woman, sitting behind a folding metal table. The dull roar of the city is muted, somewhere far, far away. The room is stagnant; airless. With no windows, no furniture, just high white walls, an expanse of wooden floor stretching out in front of me. They tilt their heads up, chins raised, slightly expectant, but without the eagerness of anticipation.

I take a deep breath. I was terrified a moment ago; sick to my stomach and hands shaking. But now a strange stillness descends.

I look him in the eye.

Audacious acts foster confidence, Robbie says.

"Fassbinder, the model's speech from *Blood on the Cat's Neck* and Isabella from *Measure for Measure*."

They exchange a look.

"Fassbinder?" the man with the papers repeats. He searches through them again for confirmation. "Your application says *Sexual Perversity in Chicago.*"

"I changed my mind." I smile.

They frown.

"Say nothing you don't have to," Robbie advised. "The more you talk, the more you'll feel like a twat."

The woman leans forward. "Which Isabella? 'To whom shall I complain?'" There's a hint of condescension in her well-rounded voice; her impeccable vowels the result of years of teaching received pronunciation.

"No," I correct her. "It's one I pieced together from Act Two, Scene Two. 'So you must be the first to give this sentence.'"

She raises an eyebrow. "I see."

The third man pushes his glasses farther back on his nose and folds his arms across his chest; mild amusement plays across his features. "Well, then. Off you go."

I close my eyes a moment. A cool, clear calm comes over me. I savour the darkness.

"Make them wait," Robbie said. "Most people panic and begin too soon. The moment before you speak is often the most dramatic of all."

When I open my eyes again, something's shifted. They're sitting forward; looking at me with real interest. I'm not another girl from Ohio any more.

I'm an actress.

And then off I go.

It's six o'clock. I've been through three rounds of auditions, including movement and voice sessions. I'm exhausted. When I come out, Mom and Dad are waiting for me in the foyer. They've travelled up to meet me, to help me find my way around the city and catch a glimpse of me before I fly off to London again. They're sitting, reading books they've brought with them from the library at home, their coats folded neatly across their knees. And I suspect they've been there for hours—ever since I went in at ten this morning.

My mother smiles and they both stand up as I cross the marble floor. They seem older than before; eager to please and infinitely fragile surrounded by the aggressive pace of New York City. I'm not used to seeing them disorientated. Everything moves so much faster here and they're slow, baffled; out of step with urban life.

"So?" my father asks, removing his reading glasses. They're the kind you buy in a drug store; inexpensive fold away magnifying frames. He never used to need them. The book he's holding is on the creation of Israel and Palestine. Politics has always been his favourite subject.

"I won't hear anything for some time," I explain, wishing I didn't have to speak to anyone. "They have four days of auditions here and then they hold more in L.A." I yawn, leaning my head against his chest. I am grateful to see him.

"Seems a long time to wait." He rubs my hair. Then, noticing things in the way he does, days after the fact, he suddenly says, "I remember this being a different colour the last time I saw you!"

Mom is busy tucking her historical romance into her handbag; riffling about. "We have a surprise!" Her voice is gay, just bordering on hysterical. "Tickets to a Broadway show!"

Oh no. Not some dreadful musical about dancing cats. Not tonight.

She's brimming with purposeful energy. "We know you've been seeing a lot of wonderful plays in London, and you're not fond of musicals, although it's what New York does best," she adds. (This is an ongoing debate between us; I claim the musical isn't serious drama. "What's wrong with having a good time?" she says. She'd love to see one. The last time she was here in the 1960s, she saw Richard Burton in *Camelot*. She hasn't stopped talking about it since.) "But," she continues, a glint in her eye, "we've managed to get tickets for Glenn Close and Sam Waterston in something called . . ." She refers to the tickets again. "*Benefactors*. It's an English play," she says proudly. "About an architect. The seats are in the balcony but the man said they have a clear view."

"Mom! That's so cool!" I throw my arms round her. She smells of Anaïs Anaïs and Vaseline Intensive hand lotion; the way she's always smelt since as long back as I can remember.

She holds me tightly. "We're so very proud of you," she whispers.

"You're crushing me, Mom." I pull away.

"And after that, we're going to go to the best Italian restaurant in the world!" my father promises. "Where the waiters don't just bring the food to your table but they sing famous opera arias as well!"

I pull on my coat. "That's great, Dad. I can hardly wait."

And slipping my arm through his, I reach out, taking my mother's hand. Together, we push through the thick glass door, out into the windy evening.

My father walks ahead, raising a hand to hail a cab. The cabs in New York terrify me. The one we took this morning almost made me sick.

"In a few years' time, we'll be coming here to see you on Broadway," my mother predicts.

I smile.

"You know, Evie." Her voice is suddenly quiet. "You don't have to do anything you don't want to."

I don't know why she's saying that, why she's so serious.

"I know, Mom."

She pulls me close again.

And this time, too tired to struggle, I bury my face into her shoulder.

I feel unexpectedly small and frightened, like a child who doesn't want to go on the first day of school. I want to go home. We've come all this way, gone to all this trouble.

My parents aren't the only ones who are lost and overwhelmed.

The wind whips around us; my father's waving, a small figure searching through a constant sea of early evening traffic, surging all around us.

New York, the grandest, most ambitious city in the world, rises up, scraping against the sky . . . pushing harder, higher, ever higher, against the fading light.

Crossing the hotel lobby, I spot her instantly.

I would've recognised her anywhere; with her long, Modigliani limbs and ash-white hair, it's easy to see that she and Robbie are cut from the same, rare, delicate cloth. She's dressed in pale beige trousers, a cashmere twin set, and soft, tan ballerina slippers, custom-made for her narrow feet.

It's just two-thirty now. But she's already neatly ensconced in one of the overstuffed armchairs, legs crossed, jogging her foot up and down impatiently and working her way through a long black Sobranie cigarette.

Her grey eyes dart around the room. When I step forward, she doesn't look so much as catalogue me, taking me in from top to toe before wrinkling her face into a quick smile.

She stands. "How nice of you to meet me. Pamela Hale," she introduces herself, squeezing the tips of my fingers; her version of a handshake. There's a faint trace of a New England accent; a hint of girl's schools and debutante seasons in the controlled, even cadence of her voice. A yellow diamond, easily the size of a marble, sends beams of light shooting around the foyer with each movement of her flawlessly manicured hand.

"So nice of you. Really." And then she's looking at me again; a thousand bits of information gleaned, processed and indexed before I even sit down.

"So, are you enjoying New York? Have you been here before? Did the audition go well?" And inhaling deeply, she tilts her chin upward, watching me closely while I do my best to answer her questions. She nods again and again; her eyes never leave my face.

"Yes, I think it went well. You never can tell. And no, I've never been here before. It's so big, isn't it?" I ramble on; my nerves getting the better of me.

"So nice of you to meet me," she smiles when I've finished.

And I'm suddenly aware she's heard nothing. She's just been biding her time, keeping company with her own thoughts until my mouth stopped moving.

Sliding an enormous Saks Fifth Avenue bag out from behind her chair, she pushes it across to me. "Would you be so kind as to take this back for Alice? It's just a few things. Some shirts and a few trousers. Ralph Lauren. Casual," she adds quickly. "Nice pieces. She doesn't like the things I buy her. I know. But . . . but she should have something nice to wear. In case she goes somewhere . . . nice." She weaves her fingers together, pressing them down and up, down and up.

I stare at the bag in dismay. When she asked if we could meet so she could give me something to take back for Robbie, I had no idea it would be so large. There's no way it will fit into my suitcase. I'll carry it back with me on the plane.

"And how is she?" Her eyes bore into me.

I shift away from her as discreetly as possible. "She's great! She's been a huge help to me—coaching me for my auditions."

Opening her Chanel handbag, she takes out a gold cigarette case and lighter. "She's had enough practice," she snaps, forcing another Sobranie between her lips.

I watch as she lights it, flicks the lighter shut, closes her handbag. I've never met anyone like her—so beautifully put together, so naturally extraordinary looking, so agitated. We sit for quite a while in an uncomfortable silence.

I wish she'd stop staring at me.

"Was the traffic bad?" I'm desperate to fill the void with conversation. "I mean, is the Village very far from here?"

Her eyes narrow. "What would I be doing in the Village?"

I blink at her.

"Is that what Alice told you? That we live in the Village?" She manages to make the word "Village" sound as if it were a venereal disease.

"I . . . I may have got it wrong," I stammer.

She inhales slowly, calculating in her head. "I wouldn't believe everything she says if I were you. I certainly don't." She crosses and recrosses her legs. "So, how is she really? Has she been arrested? No, I guess I'd hear about that." Her voice is hard; drained. "Any abortions? Drugs? Black boyfriends?"

She's glaring at me as if it's all my fault.

"She's fine. I'm sorry." I stand. "I really have to go."

She looks at me. Then turns away.

Pamela Hale has examined me thoroughly.

I cannot help her.

She sighs and, opening her purse again, thrusts a thick roll of bills at me. "Please make sure she gets this."

I start to speak but she flashes me a look. "Just take it."

So I fold the money into my palm, afraid to be seen in the hotel lobby with so much cash. She stands up, stubbing the cigarette out in the ashtray; grinding it down furiously with her thumb. For a moment, it looks as if she may say something. Her brow furrows and her lips part. But she thinks better of it, presses her mouth shut.

Taking my fingers again, she squeezes them, just a little too hard. "So nice of you to meet me. So nice."

I watch as she leaves, struggling through the large double doors into the street. Suddenly she's all awkward angles, too long and too thin; like an exotic seabird—a flamingo or a crane—extraordinary to look at but clearly never made for life on dry land.

———

"Meet me."

"Where?"

"In Brighton. We're playing a place called the Cave."

I press my back against the wall. "I can't. I have rehearsal."

Silence.

Its ten-thirty on a Thursday night. I'm standing in the hallway, leaning with my head against the pay phone, watching as my credits roll by. I've been rehearsing all day for our end of term showings; Imo and I are doing a scene from *The Maids* and then I have a love scene from *Uncle Vanya* with a very short boy from Boston named Michael, who's just a bit too fond of onions. He's like a very smelly Kennedy. It's been a long day. I haven't seen Jake in weeks; first I was in New York and now he's been touring with his band, playing the wilds of Doncaster, Sheffield and now the jewel in the crown, Brighton.

"You could if you wanted to," he says.

I'm the one who's silent now. I'm already behind on my work, thanks to all the preparation that went into the audition. That was two weeks ago and, although I made it through to the final rounds, I still haven't heard anything. Every day I wait for a letter and as each day passes, I have a growing certainty of failure and all the anxiety that accompanies it. I stare up at a damp patch in the ceiling; at the peeling wallpaper and the hall light, which never seems to have a working bulb in it.

Everything's falling apart.

Jake and I are far away from each other. The weeks are racing by; the course will be over and I'll be back in the States—a fact which steals the sweetness out of every encounter with him. Soon we'll be permanently separated.

"Have you spoken to him yet?"

This is our other favourite topic: the Have You Broken Up with Jonny Yet conversation.

"No, not yet."

"Fuck, Evie!" I can hear him breaking open a beer; he takes a long swig.

"Jake, I can't just break up with him over the phone!" We've done this a thousand times. "We went out for two years! The least I can do is speak to him in person. When I get home."

"Why didn't you do it when you were in New York?" he demands.

"They're not that close together; New York and Pittsburgh. I didn't have time."

More silence.

"Come to Brighton."

"Jake . . ."

"Come to Brighton, Evie!"

I'm so tired I could collapse.

"I can't, baby! I just can't," I whisper. "Please . . ."

"Fuck this!"

The line goes dead.

I hang up the phone and drift back into the flat. I want to cry; I need to cry. But I'm even too tired to work myself up to tears. I stray into the kitchen and pour a glass of water from the tap.

There are roses on the dining room table; white roses, sent to Imogene from Coffee Carlo. He sends them every Friday; tomorrow there'll be a fresh bunch, with a simple card that just says, "When?" Robbie and I tease her about it: when what? He's already taken her out several times, so the obvious conclusion is more carnal. But Imo just smiles, arranging the roses in the vase she bought specially from a crystal shop in Burlington Arcade. "I'm still in love with Lindsay," she claims staunchly. But there's a soft, sensuous light in her eyes now, a cooler self-assurance that's blossomed in the warmth of Carlo's enthusiastic attention. When they're together, the chemistry is unmistakable. "When?" is the only question. Robbie and I bet it won't be long.

There's also an arrangement of red roses, wilting in their cellophane wrapping, shoved into a spare water pitcher and crammed into a corner of the kitchen counter. They're from Jonny. I still talk to him, still go through the charade of being boyfriend and girlfriend, all because I can't bear to break up with him over the phone. He knows something's up. That's why he sent the roses. Our conversations are brief, noncommittal; all a little too bright, a little too eager . . . hollow, unfelt noises. It's hideous and I hate myself for it. But surely it would be wrong simply to announce that it was over; I'd met someone else. I don't know any more. My head aches from trying to figure it out.

I go and sit on my bed in the dark, staring at nothing.

How can Jake and I be together? How can I break up with Jonny without breaking his heart? How can I make it all right when it isn't?

Of course there's a solution. An easy solution.

I should break up with Jake.

I'll never see him once I'm back in the States. It's hardly as if we're going to fly back and forth on the weekends.

Jonny would never need to know.

I bury my head in the pillow. If I get into Juilliard, I'll be too busy for boyfriends.

If I were smart, that's what I'd do.

But I'm not smart.

I'd rather die than leave Jake.

And yet there's no hope it will ever last.

I feel desperate.

It's half past two in the morning when the door buzzer goes.

I come to with a start, grope my way to my bedroom door.

The buzzer rings again; louder, longer.

Robbie sleeps through anything but Imo and I meet in the hallway. She's wide-eyed with terror. "Who can that be?"

"It's OK," I try to reassure her—and myself. "I'll take care of it."

"Hello?" I shout into the entry phone.

"Let me in!" the voice demands.

"Go back to bed," I whisper to Imo, my heart hammering in my chest. "It's OK."

She's baffled.

"Really," I say.

Long buzzing. Again; insistent.

Imo returns to the comfort of her bed.

I step out into the hallway and open the front door.

Jake's standing on the doorstep, head bowed, leaning against the frame. He looks up at me, a fierce, somehow fragile expression in his eyes. In the cold blue light of the street lamp, his aquiline features and long hair look like they're carved from marble.

No matter how well I think I remember, the reality of him is always devastating.

"What are you doing here?"

Is he high?

The icy air enfolds us in a black embrace.

"Do you want me to leave?" His voice is challenging.

I look away.

He grabs my wrist.

"Do you want me to leave, Evie?"

His black eyes are unblinking; his grip tightens. He pulls me closer. I smell the wind in his hair, the damp heat of his skin.

"What do you want? Do you want me to fuck off and leave you alone?"

He steps forward into the dark hallway. He's so tall; the street lamp casts an ominous shadow across the floor.

And then the door swings shut.

In the thick, close blackness of the narrow corridor, he envelops me, his warm breath on my face. "You're all I think about . . . all I want . . ."

I could pretend to struggle, to pull away. But I don't want to. He presses me against the wall.

"Tell me to leave." His lips are pressed against my ear. "Tell me to fuck off and leave you alone!"

I open my mouth.

His hands slide underneath my nightgown. I twist away, words catching in my throat.

He forces me backwards. "I'm in love with you . . ." His mouth brushes against mine.

I shut my eyes.

His touch is certain, sure.

He's tracing the curve of my neck with his lips.

"Go on, tell me to leave!"

I throw my head back; all the air has escaped from my lungs; I can't breathe.

"Say it . . ." he whispers, pulling me up.

I can't say it.

I'll never say it.

The nightgown floats, ghostlike, to the floor around my feet.

"I'm taking you," he murmurs. "There'll never be anyone else."

APPLAUSE THUNDERS through the hall. Allyson, resplendent in a gold sheath dress, turns and takes another bow. "Bravo!" we shout, cupping our hands around our mouths. Even Piotr, beaming broadly, looking smart in his dark suit and tie, joins in, shouting "Brava!" louder than all the rest.

It's her third encore. She turns to Junko and gives her a little nod. A hush descends and the familiar opening bars of Mimi's aria "Si, mi chiamano Mimi" from Puccini's *La Bohème* fill the air.

Bunny squeezes my hand. "Oh, this is my favourite!" she whispers. "There's nothing better than a tale of doomed love!"

We sit, transfixed. Ally's voice soars, singular and bright, unfolding like the petals of a rose, filled with love, hope and the promise of spring.

The evening's a terrific success. And there's a private party afterwards in the cellar restaurant below the hall. As the audience drains out, Allyson's surrounded by a crowd of admirers, laughing and chatting. She's clutching half a dozen bouquets from friends and students; her agent Clive sweeps her from one VIP guest to another, glowing with pride. Several important casting directors were in the audience tonight and now they're lined up, full of praise. Piotr's talking with Junko, towering above her, and Bunny flirts with a man in a bow tie I'm fairly certain she's only just met, patting his arm and laughing gaily as if they've known each other for years.

I stand near the door, waiting. It's unusual for me to be out in the evening like this; wearing a proper dress, makeup and hair done. I toy with the fringe of the emerald pashmina stole I borrowed from Bunny. She was so keen for me to look pretty tonight. And yet here I am, in this elegant building, dressed in a pale green silk dress I haven't worn in years, wishing I could vanish into thin air. I've lost the knack for social situations; it's like a muscle which, if you don't exercise, shrivels and dies.

Bunny catches my eye across the hall; she walks over. "Come on, Evie. Make an effort," she commands, pushing me forward. And, linking my arm through hers, she introduces me to the bow tie man, who turns out to be a reviewer with *The Sunday Times*. And then to a couple of Allyson's students.

"Bunny! Ohh-hoo!"

"Bunny!"

It's the shrill, singsong voices of Babe Heinemann and Belle Frank.

I veer round.

They're waving from across the hall.

"Hello! Bunny! Oh, look! Evie! Is that you? What? Have you got a dress on?" They're working their way over, weaving through the crowd in much the same way two small Chanel bulldozers might weave through an unprotected wildlife reserve.

There's nowhere to hide. My heart sinks but I wave in spite of myself.

There's no shame in this; Babe Heinemann and Belle Frank are a force far greater than me, and although each of them is only about four feet ten in their custom-made Ferragamos, they're much larger than life. And a pretty good match for death too.

They're twins, Bunny's second cousins. And they know all about death; are defined by its presence as a pivotal moment in their lives. They're widows. Proper, professional widows. The phrase "my husband, God rest his soul" comes as naturally to them as breathing. They consider Bunny a fully paid-up member of their exclusive club. Only she refuses to join in.

So they lavish their attention on me instead. (After all, a single mother is almost the same as a widow.)

Bunny leans over and gives Babe a kiss on the cheek. "So what did you think?" she asks.

Babe shakes her head. "Like an angel!" she sighs. "And it's nice to see you out and about for a change! You're a hermit, Bunny Gold!"

Bunny smiles, but says nothing.

"Evie!" Babe cuts in front of the bow tie man and grabs my hand, squeezing it affectionately. (We've suddenly become great friends.) "How are you?"

"You've lost weight! Is this new?" Belle's feeling the fabric of my dress, rubbing it between her fingers. "Last season or this?"

"Belle, for Christ's sake, let the woman talk!" Babe yanks me closer. "You *have* lost weight. You're skin and bone! I know that dress. Last season," she adds automatically to Belle. "I nearly bought one like it but you have to have *legs*. Now." She stares into my eyes with the intensity of a hypnotist. "How are you? *Really*. How are you bearing up?"

"Fine," I bleat, failing to dislodge my hand from Babe's powerful grip. "Everything's just . . . fine."

They continue to stare at me, waiting.

"Alex is well," I smile brightly. "Getting bigger all the time!"

"He's a lovely boy." Belle makes it sound as if I don't fully appreciate this fact. "You're a lucky woman," she adds in the same warning tone.

"Wasn't it a wonderful performance?" I grab Allyson's hand in desperation. "Have you met Ally?"

"Hello!" Allyson beams.

They look at one another.

Belle latches on to her arm. "My son has a crush on you!" she announces, so loudly that almost all conversation stops. "His name is David and he owns his own business!"

"How lovely." Allyson glares at me over Belle's head. "We must meet someday."

"Oh, absolutely!" I smile.

"You know, Bunny"—Babe turns her attention back to Bunny—"the first ten years are the hardest, take my word for it." She extracts a gold compact from her handbag and checks her lipstick; a thick pink shade she must've bought in bulk in 1974. "You need to get back into the world. And you *need* to get rid of that house." She stares at Bunny, her small, dark eyes unblinking. "Sooner or later you've got to let go."

A shadow of dismay ripples across Bunny's face. I want to reach out and reassure her. But Babe appropriates my hand instead, squeezing it vigorously. "Now. To the real business! Who can we find for Evie, eh?"

And she looks around the room, as if eligible men can be found unclaimed in dusty corners.

"Oh! He's tall! What about him?" She points to Piotr.

"God, no!" I say.

Piotr looks up, catching my eye.

He smiles. "God, no what?" he asks, walking over.

"Nothing," I say quickly. "Babe, this is my roommate, Piotr Pawlokowski. Piotr, this is Babe Heinemann, Bunny's cousin."

"Oh! So you're the Pole!" She grabs his hand, yanking him down to her level; he's practically doubled over.

"That's right. The Pollack, the American and the Australian. Sounds like a joke with a light bulb in it."

Babe pats his hand.

"He's cute!" she hisses to me.

Piotr looks at me. "Yes. You see. I'm cute."

Babe gives my arm a tug. "Isn't she a pretty girl? Look at that figure! Do you like children, Piotr?"

I'm going to pass out with mortification.

Or rather, I wish I would.

But he just laughs. "Yes. She's pretty and I'm cute. As for her figure." He stands back, appraising me. "I think . . . hmm . . . I think I should have a closer look. A private viewing, perhaps."

Babe giggles. I manage to wrench my hand free.

"OK!" My face is burning. "Enough!"

But he goes on. "Of course, you may not know this but she has terrible habits. She smokes when no one is looking and walks around in nothing but her bra and knickers when she thinks no one is home."

"No!" Babe gasps, delighted.

"That's not true!" I object. "I don't smoke! Ever! And when have you ever seen me in my knickers?"

"Don't say it's not true!" He turns to Babe. "I like to think it's true." He grins at me. "Something simple. White cotton knickers, maybe?"

Allyson grabs my arm, pulls me aside. "Thanks to you I've got a date with the midget's evil spawn. I'm going to have to leave the country now."

"Save me!" I hiss in her ear.

"Save you! I should kill you." But she drags me across the hall anyway, parking me in front of a squat toadish looking man in his late fifties, with thick, black-framed glasses and a permanently red complexion. "Here, talk to Felix. But don't be surprised if he talks only to your tits."

Later, at the restaurant below, my mobile starts to buzz. I duck outside on the front steps to take it.

"Hello?"

It's the babysitter, Karen. Nothing's more anxious-making.

"Is Alex OK?"

"Sure. Like, I'm just calling to find out if it's OK if I eat this chocolate thingy in the fridge."

I sigh with relief. "Actually, Karen, that's not mine. So would you leave it? I think there's some bread and jam . . ." I know how dull this selection sounds. I'm one of those women who never have any good babysitter grub.

"Oh."

There's a pause.

"You've already eaten it, haven't you?" I deduce.

"Well, sort of."

It's probably Bunny's; some expensive little delight from Marks & Spencer. "OK. Never mind now." I'll replace it tomorrow.

"Oh, and, just so you know, it wasn't me."

I look out at the even, Georgian architecture of the red brick houses that line Smith Square. "What are you talking about? What wasn't you?"

"I was coming down the stairs, after Alex went down. And, you know, the mirror, the big old one at the bottom of the steps, is broken."

"Broken?"

"Yeah, like there's this crack across it."

I shift uncomfortably in my high-heeled sandals. "Has anything else been disturbed? Is the window open? Is anything missing?"

"Na, I looked and like everything's locked. You should get some of those chocolate thingys," she adds, putting in a request for next time. "They're really good."

"Karen, do me a favour. Check on Alex again, will you?"

"No problem."

"I think . . . Listen, I'll call you back."

I click the phone shut. The best thing would be to go home now, just to make sure everything's all right. We came in Piotr's car but I can easily get a cab. As I'm looking around the square, I spot Bunny, sitting alone on a wooden bench in the gardens around the church. There's a curious quality about her; a kind of tranquillity, as if she's waiting for someone or listening to a conversation no one else can hear.

I walk over.

She looks up, startled. Then she smiles quickly. "Wasn't Allyson wonderful?"

I nod. "Yes, a triumph. Listen, there's been some sort of accident at home. I don't know how it happened, but the mirror in the front hallway is broken. There's a crack in it."

Her brow wrinkles, but she doesn't seem as upset as I had expected. "Yes," she says finally. "Yes, that makes sense."

"What do you mean?" I sit down next to her.

She's on the verge of answering, but thinks better of it. "Nothing, darling." She's unusually frail tonight, almost other worldly.

"Listen—" I begin.

"He was here," she interrupts me. "Standing just to the left of the organ."

"Who was here?"

"Harry, of course," she says, as if it were obvious.

"Oh." I'm listening closely now.

"It reminds me of the days just after he died. I couldn't sleep. Always hated sleeping alone. So I used to go to the opera and sit in the stalls. When they dimmed the lights, I'd doze off. It was warm, safe, dark. No one gives it a second thought if you fall asleep during the opera. In fact, there was a production of *Beatrice and Benedick* which used to send the entire audience into a coma at the end of the first act. I went to nearly every performance. I so hated being alone. So hated it."

I take her hand. A soft breeze dances around us.

"It doesn't matter about the mirror." She's very far away. "Things happen out of nowhere. They just happen."

"All the same, maybe I should go back, just to make sure everything's all right."

"Yes, I suppose so." Something of her old sparkle returns to her eyes. "Shall I ask Piotr to take you?"

I'm riffling in my bag, looking for my change purse. "No, I'll be fine. I'll catch a cab. I'm just going to say good-bye to Ally."

It takes another ten minutes to work my way through the clutch of people around Allyson and say my good-byes. The twilight sky's a dark navy streaked with black. The air's cool. I throw the pashmina over my shoulders and am searching for a black cab when Piotr appears, dangling his car keys.

"Bunny says you need to go home."

I'm flustered; suddenly all I can think of are white knickers. I scan the horizon, praying for a yellow taxi light. "I'm fine. I'll take a cab."

"Good." He lodges a hand in the small of my back, firmly pushes me across the square to where his car is parked. "I charge ten pounds to St John's Wood. But for you, fifteen."

He opens the door.

I glare at him, folding my arms across my chest.

He looks at me. "Are you getting in? Or do you want me to strap you to the roof?"

I get in. There's a special way ladies are supposed to climb into cars. I'm not certain how it's done but I realise I'm trying to do it now. He shuts the door, crosses and settles in on the driver's side.

"He's all right, Alex?"

"Yes, it's just that something's been broken. I'd feel better if I knew that everything was . . . OK."

"Right." He starts the car and backs out of the parking space so quickly, I have to hang on to the dashboard. He grins. "This is the way we drive in Kraków. You'll be there in no time. But I'd fasten your seat belt."

I take his advice. As we speed down the Embankment and across to Victoria, Piotr slips a disk into the CD player. And the grand opening chords of Tchaikovsky's first piano concerto fill the car.

We veer around Hyde Park Corner. I grasp the door handle for support.

"Listen, Piotr," I start, "I feel—" He narrowly avoids back-ending a Volvo estate. "I . . . I was a bit uncomfortable with . . . Jesus! Slow down!"

He looks at me. "You trust me, right?"

"Watch the road! Piotr, please!" I fling my hands over my eyes. "God help us!"

He laughs. "Good. Now, you were saying . . ." And whipping through the traffic, he swerves across lanes, gaining speed up Park Lane.

"I was saying that the way you were speaking to me, with Babe—"

"Flirting," he interrupts.

"Flirting. Flirting?"

"Flirting," he confirms. "Yes?"

"Well." Was he really flirting with me? "I just think it's inappropriate, considering that we're roommates."

He cuts in front of a bus at Marble Arch and pulls up sharply at the lights.

"Inappropriate," he repeats.

I feel awkward; I pretend to examine the CD case. "Yes. Perhaps it's a cultural difference but here, in London, when people live together, like we do, it's best to keep relationships . . ." What's the word I'm looking for? "Contained."

He considers, nodding gravely. "Yes. It must be a cultural difference. We Poles spill out everywhere."

"I'm serious."

"Yes," he snorts. "I know! You're always serious."

I can't believe what I'm hearing. "God, that's rich, coming from you, Mr. 'Happiness is a shallow little goal!'"

The lights change. "Happiness is a shallow goal. Shouldn't we strive for a greater range of experience in life?" The car lurches forward. "Anyway, you were irritating me."

"*I* was irritating *you*!"

He sighs, exasperated. "You're not the sort of woman who should be . . . be . . ." He taps the steering wheel, struggling for the word. "*Slinking* around! Teaching night classes! Pretending to be invisible!"

I'm cut to the core. "I do not slink!"

"Oh yes you do!"

"I do not! Besides, what business is it of yours!"

He turns into St John's Wood Road, gears grinding. "No business. Slink away!" he growls.

I'd give anything to get out of this car right now. I'm seething, sitting as close to the door and as far away from him as I can get.

"So. No flirting," he confirms.

"Right," I snap.

"So, not a good idea to tease you, then."

"Correct."

"And this . . . this idea of you wandering around in nothing but your knickers is absolutely, completely false."

"Piotr!"

"Just checking." He swerves into the High Street.

A thick silence wedges itself between us.

I will ignore him for the rest of the journey.

Turning the CD case over, I examine it intently. It's quite old, Russian; a photo of a gangly teenager on the front, with a defiant shock of spiky hair and hands two sizes too large for the rest of his body, poised at the side of a piano.

"Who is this anyway?" I demand.

He turns into Acacia Road. "Me."

"You're kidding!" I look at him, then back at the photo.

His face softens. "You like the hair, right? That's my rebellion phase. It didn't last long."

"Rebellion?" I can't suppress a giggle. The idea's ridiculous. It's hardly the Sex Pistols.

"Now you're teasing me!" he accuses.

"It's just, how much can one rebel against Mozart, Beethoven, Bach . . ."

Pulling up in front of the house, he switches off the engine and turns to face me. "You'd be surprised. It's only natural if you love something violently. Like the way it's impossible to sleep with someone you can't fight with. Rebellion is a type of love." And he smiles, a wide, easy grin; the small gap between his two front teeth lends his face a disarming, boyish charm. "Now, shall we go in and see what the babysitter who eats everything has left?"

As we get out, I remind myself I'm furious with him.

Karen's slumped in front of the television in what used to be Harry's old study. And judging from the assorted plates and bowls on the coffee table in front of her, she's worked her way through a considerable supply of the house food. She stands up, jamming her hands into her combat trouser pockets. "Hey," she greets us, rocking back and forth on her heels. She consumes more calories a day than an entire professional football team, but still only weighs about a hundred pounds. She has the kind of miraculous, angular adolescent figure that defies all the laws of nature.

First, I check on Alex, touch his cheek lightly and kiss his forehead. He's fine. Then the three of us examine the mirror. The cracked face looks as if someone's struck it, with a small object or even a fist; shards of glass radiate from a black central wound. We work our way through the house; nothing else seems amiss and I let Karen go for the evening. She ambles off, backpack over her shoulder, headed towards the tube station.

I close the front door.

Pale blue light floods in from the street lamp outside, a soft glow of light on the floor.

A slinking woman. Who pretends to be invisible.

It's not an attractive picture; not the image I've been trying so hard to project—of the sensible, responsible, capable woman, heroically looking after her only child.

Maybe Piotr's vision of a naughty girl, roaming about in her knickers, stealing secret ciggies does have a certain appeal.

Piotr's coming down the stairs. He stops on the last step.

I turn in the darkness.

"I should go now and get Bunny and Allyson." He flicks his car keys back and forth between his fingers. "We taxi drivers never rest."

But he doesn't move.

"Thank you for bringing me back. And for making certain everything is all right." I sound stiff and formal. "It's very kind of you."

He's silent.

He's seen through me, to a side of myself I'd rather ignore. "I didn't do it to be kind," he says, at last.

He goes to the door, opens it. He's so tall; the street lamp outside casts its long shadow across the floor. "I didn't mean to offend you." He looks up. "But you're not the kind of person who should be afraid. Of anything."

He speaks with such conviction. Yet part of me can't help but wonder who he's talking about.

Of course, what I should say is, "I'm not afraid!" with a defiant toss of my head. Or laugh, as if he's got it all wrong.

But instead the real question that rushes to my lips is, "Why?"

Why shouldn't I be completely terrified?

And for a moment I feel I am standing here in nothing but my knickers.

He closes the door.

I lock it, pressing my cheek against the smooth, cool wood.

And suddenly, inexplicably, I wish he were still here.

THE CAVE MAY BE a dive but at nine-thirty on a Friday night, it's packed to the rafters. Located under the Pier, it's a vast cavern with a long bar against one wall and a narrow stage against the other. There are a few round tables and stools but for the most part it's a dark, unfurnished basement, that can be cleaned with a garden hose and broom if necessary. Tonight it will be necessary.

It's wall-to-wall punters, drinking, dancing, shouting at the top of their lungs; girls with miniskirts and suede ankle boots; guys with Mohawks, spiky quiffs and pierced ears. Prince's "Let's Go Crazy" is playing and as we push our way past the bouncers, Jake waves to a group clustered around the bar. This must be the band.

"Hey," Jake shouts, wrapping an arm round my shoulders. "I want you to meet my girl!" They turn and I smile, pressing myself into his side, like Eve pressing back into Adam's rib.

There are three of them: Brian, the bassist, older than the others, pudgy, with soft features and thin blonde hair; Pat, the drummer, from Northern Ireland, wiry, mercurial and pale; and C.J., on lead guitar, black with thick dreadlocks and a cheeky, dimpled grin. C.J. has his arm draped over a very familiar blonde.

"This is Jazz," he introduces her.

It's the girl who came to the party with Jake.

"Short for Jasmine," she adds significantly, as if we're suddenly involved in an unconventional name competition and she's clearly won.

"How pretty," I smile.

What's she doing here?

She's wearing a short white jean jacket, a black and white polka dot miniskirt and piles of crucifixes layered round her neck. Underneath her jacket, the frilly lace of a corset peeps out. Her belt has a large gold buckle that reads FOR SALE. Suddenly this is the last place on earth I want to be.

Pat hands Jake a joint. He takes a drag, passes it on to me. It's bitter, strong, burns the back of my throat; I cough and splutter and they laugh while Jake slaps me on the back. I pass it on to Jasmine. She purses her lips in slow motion, inhaling with ease.

C.J. grabs another bar stool. I perch in front of Jake while Brian buys another round of drinks. Anxious sparks bounce around the conversation; everyone's smoking, finishing each other's sentences, stealing glances at themselves in the mirror behind the bar. Pat can't keep still. Dressed in shorts and a vest, his hands are in constant motion, tapping out complicated rhythms with his drumsticks against the bar, a glass, Jake's back . . .

"So, Evie," he says, looking at everything but me—the crowd, the stage, Jasmine's breast, my breasts . . . "So what do you think of our new name? Do you think it will make it? Yeah? Do you think, it's like, you know, the fucking thing, man? The shit? Or like, you know, what?"

I'm not sure it's even worth trying to look him in the eye, which is about as easy as dodging a bullet. "Yeah, The Thrust is a great name."

"Oh no!" He's staring at Jasmine's legs now, the door, back to the stage. "We changed it. Yeah, Jake's the man! What Jake says, fucking goes! Right?"

Jake flashes him a look and he whirls away to pound on a stack of old kegs by the door.

C.J. leans forward. "Andy wants to see you. He's giving me a lot of crap about the takings being shit on the door. Fucking look at this place! Liar!"

"Who's Andy?" I ask.

"The owner," Jake says, stealing a drag from Pat's discarded cigarette, left burning in the ashtray. "He never pays us, tight bastard."

Jake catches Jasmine's eye. She looks away.

Brian stands up.

I turn to Jake but he's laughing now, grabbing the joint back from C.J. "Brian, what the fuck are you wearing, man?"

We all stare at Brian. He hooks his thumbs in the waistband of his black vinyl jeans. "They're great, man! I got them at the market. I'm a fucking rock god now and you guys are just jealous!"

"You look like Michael Fucking Jackson!" C.J. sneers, pulling Jasmine towards him, burying his face in her neck. She yields limply, sizing up her profile in the mirror.

"You'll be singing another tune when I fucking land all the pussy!" Brian drags his hand through his prematurely thinning hair.

C.J. and Jake throw each other a look and then howl with laughter. There's something incongruent about the idea of Brian landing anything. I laugh too. Jake presses me close, his whole body shaking, clutching me the way a drowning man clings to a life vest.

"Fuck you!" Brian snaps, turning and forcing his way through the crowd. "You guys make me sick!"

"Fuck him," C.J. says, wiping the tears from his eyes.

"Yeah, fuck him," Jake agrees.

Pat's back, dancing around like a boxer, playing a tattoo against the barstool seat. "I gotta go to the loo again, Jake. OK, man? Like, I really need to go. So, are you coming with me? Yeah? Are you gonna come, man?"

Jake shakes his head, but rises anyway. "OK, Pat. But don't get too wired, understand? Just a couple, until after the set." He kisses my forehead. "Stay here with Jazz, OK?"

I hate the way he calls her Jazz. And I can't think of a more unappealing prospect.

C.J. drains his glass and bounces after them.

The crowd presses in, all elbows and brimming glasses of lager; I'm almost drenched by a giant guy balancing three pints.

I look around at the crowd, glance over at the stage, but apart from all the equipment, there are still no signs of life. So, I force another smile at Jasmine who stares back, a flat, dead look. She rolls her own cigarette, holding it aloft until one of the bar staff lean over and gives her a light. "So." She inhales. "Who the fuck are you anyway?"

This is the kind of girl Robbie would eat for breakfast.

"Well, *Jazz*," I take a beat. "I'm an actress. And I've just been accepted into Juilliard," I lie. "I'll be living and working in New York in a few weeks' time."

Saying that I'm in Juilliard is so wonderful; I feel ten feet tall and bulletproof. I only wish it were true.

She blinks at me sullenly.

I lift my right eyebrow. "And what do you do?"

"I'm a singer. And a model," she adds quickly.

"How lovely," I say, and I focus again on the stage.

The lights dim. A man dressed in a black T-shirt and jeans, sporting an impressive beer gut, takes the stage. "One, two, three, testing! One, two, three! All right, you lot! Pipe down!" His face is red with the heat and he struggles to catch his breath, mopping his brow with the back of his hand. "You know the rules: no throwing stuff, no crowd surfing and no spitting! And I mean it!" he shouts, pointing to six enormous bouncers by the door. The crowd boo and he shakes his fist like a classic pantomime villain, with about as much sincerity. "Shut it! And now, it gives me great pleasure to present, all the way from London, formerly known as The Thrust, it's Raven!"

I gasp. He's named the band for me!

Jasmine glowers at me.

The band stride on, self-consciously cool and moody; Jake pulls his guitar over his head and a small clutch of girls at the front scream with delight. Leaning forward into the microphone, he brushes his long hair from his eyes. "This gig's for Raven." He searches for me in the sea of faces. "The bird who stole my heart."

Then C.J. steps into the spotlight, launching into the grinding opening chords of "Limey Punk Rock Faggot" and the room goes wild.

My heart soars. They're above and far beyond all my expectations; Jake smiles at me and I feel I might explode with pride and joy.

There's a hand on my shoulder; I turn to find Hughey Chicken beaming at me. He leans forward and bellows in my ear, "So, what do you think?"

"They're brilliant!" I shout back. "Absolutely fucking brilliant! What are you doing here?"

He laughs. "I'm not a musician but I have talents! This is Alan Weathers." He introduces me to a man in his early thirties, deeply tanned and clean shaven, dressed in a sandy-coloured linen suit, worn with the sleeves rolled up so you don't miss the enormous Rolex watch.

He leans against the bar, holding a Perrier with as much casual grace as possible in a room filled with gyrating sweaty bodies. He smiles broadly. "Pleased to meet you!"

"He's from this great new label," Hughey continues. "They're called Virgin. Isn't that great!"

Obviously struck by the naughtiness of the name, he sniggers into his pint like a great, overgrown schoolboy. He's certainly larger and probably hairier than when he was eight but, other than that, I suspect not much else has changed.

"See! I'm always thinking, me. I'll have these boys signed in no time! Hey! How's Robbie?" he asks, his round face suddenly clouding over.

"So busy! School's a nightmare!" I lie and, changing the subject, gesture to Alan. "So, what does he think?"

Hughey nods his head to Alan, who gives him a thumbs-up.

Jake struts across the stage, throws his head back, triggering another screech of hysteria in the female fans. Hughey and I laugh, delighted and relieved. They're white-hot tonight.

Jasmine slides off her barstool, slips off her denim jacket, showing bare shoulders and a pair of plumy breasts, perched in her lacy bustier. "So, who's your friend, Hughey?" She licks her lips, leaning on the bar next to Alan. She looks up at him with her sharp blue eyes. He blinks. She offers him her hand. "I'm a singer too," she says, pressing close, rubbing her hand against his thigh. Any minute she's going to overflow that corset.

I don't care.

Jake spins through the heat and noise, a golden, glittering being— Orpheus playing in the underworld.

We're immortal.

Invincible.

In love.

THEY HAVE a ride called the Blade, Mum! In the Forbidden Valley, Mum! And it goes really, really, *really* fast!"

Alex is dragging his red and white school knapsack on the ground, his coat shrugged off, dangling around his elbows. He's dancing about four steps in front of me down Ordnance Hill Road, where I've just collected him from school.

"We're not going to Alton Towers, honey," I say for the fifth time in about three minutes.

"But *why*?" He stops dead, stumbling over the rogue knapsack.

"Because we can't afford to right now." I hate this reason and yet it's the reason for so many things. I reach down to take his hand. "Maybe another time."

He pulls his hand away. "There's another one, an even better ride, called the Black Hole! With a water park and a runaway train! You get to stay in this red castle and there are chips for dinner almost every night . . ."

Crouching down in front of him, I gently pull his coat back over his shoulders. "Alex, it's not that I don't want to go; it sounds wonderful. And when we do go, it will be a real treat. But we can't go right now."

He thinks a moment. "We could go tomorrow."

I stand up, mentally calculating our monthly finances again. There's very little room for manoeuvre. "I know, why don't I take you to the zoo tomorrow afternoon? We could make scary noises in the reptile house and watch them feed the lions—"

"We always go there!" He scowls. "That's so *boring,* Mummy! Everything we do is so *stupid!*" (He's developed a new way of saying things; a certain flair for the English language that, as an actress, I have to admire. He drags the vowels out; a kind of verbal cartoon. *Stupid* becomes *stuuuuuuuuuupid.* It's an eloquent—for a four-year-old—and exciting way of expressing himself that's just occasionally maddening for me.)

We round the corner of Acacia Avenue, the tall plane trees filled with lacy, fresh green leaves. They sway gently against the creamy white clouds racing above.

"That's very rude, Alex. And what we do is not stupid. It's fun." I sound like the very antithesis of fun.

I don't have the reserves to deal with Alex's endless requests—which I should be able to fill, long to fill and can't. The constant feeling of failure envelops me; smothers me; makes me tense. I snap at him. "And please don't drag your school bag on the ground!"

He ignores me, his small face a mask of sullen disappointment. He deliberately drags his knapsack through a puddle.

I reach down and grab his arm. "Alex! Did you hear me? I said, do not drag your school bag!"

He drops the bag. "If my father were here, he'd take me! If my father were here, we'd have the best times ever!"

There's that feeling again: the slap of an unseen hand across my face followed by a thick blanket of numbness, every time Alex mentions the word "father." I let him go. He catapults through the gate, runs up the steps and pushes open the front door. It stands, gaping open, like an affronted mouth. I watch Alex run inside; his entire being fuelled by a sense of frustration and betrayal.

Will there ever be a moment when that word won't tear my world apart?

"Ah, the joys of childhood!" Bunny's walking from the back garden, wearing a faded denim apron over her outfit, hands black with dirt, clutching the dead daffodils ruined in the rain last night.

I put on a smile and pick up the abandoned rucksack from the ground. I don't want her to see I'm having another bad day, all failure and guilt.

"I must say, darling," she continues, throwing the daffodils away in the black dustbin, "I'm only too glad not to be young any more."

She brushes the dirt from her hands.

"Didn't you have a happy childhood?" I'm eager to shift the focus away from Alex and me.

"Heavens, no!" She wraps an arm round my waist, leads me up the steps. "I was never suited to childhood. Full stop. There's an inherent hopelessness to being a child; a subordination of the will I could never stomach—even at four or five. People who go on about it being the best time of your life are idiots. No offence, darling. We all try to be good parents. Then some children are more docile than others." She closes the door, takes off her apron, folds it neatly. "And then there are ones, like me, who start raging against the light when they're five."

"So you were difficult, were you?"

She laughs. "I've always been difficult and will happily die difficult. My poor mother! Of course, it didn't help that I was also one of those easily stimulated children; far too apt to touch myself in public. It drove my mother mad. 'Where are your hands?' she used to say, over and over. I can't tell you what a relief it was to grow up and get someone else to do it all for me." She winks at me wickedly. "Now, shall I make us a nice hot cup of tea?"

I laugh; despite all her eccentricities, or perhaps because of them, she's cheered me up. "That would be lovely, Bunny. I'll be down in a minute."

I make a move towards the stairs. She stops me, putting a hand on my shoulder. "It's not as serious a business as you think," she says quietly.

I'm not quite certain what she means but there's a reassuring kindness in her face. I smile back, as if I understand completely, giving her hand a little squeeze.

Then, as she turns away, from the bright light of the entry into the cool shadowy hall leading down to the kitchen, she's suddenly an old woman. Head bowed, she clings to the handrail for balance, concentrating on the stairs. She turns the corner and is gone.

I climb up to the top floor. Alex, still in his coat, is sitting on the floor. His back is pressed against his bed, arms round his knees.

I rap on his door frame. "Knock, knock."

Silence.

I walk over and sit down next to him. His hands are clasped tight. They're covered with bits of paint and paste from today's art class; the resulting masterpiece is no doubt tucked into the infamous knapsack.

"I understand that you're angry at me," I say.

He doesn't move. And I can't find any more words; any promises to make that will soothe his upset. I have no clever quips to coax a smile. So we just sit instead, watching the play of light on the floorboards.

"Tell me again," he demands, eyes forward, fingers clenched.

I hesitate.

"Tell me the story again," he insists.

In my defence, I didn't know what to tell him. There comes an age, around three or so, when they start to ask questions. So I told him this. I'm not certain it's right any more; that it fits. But, of course, it's too late now. It's what I told him.

Because maybe some day, somehow, things will be different.

I begin, speaking slowly, softly. "Before you were born, before your father even knew you were on your way to join us, he set out on a long journey. He had to travel through uncharted lands, places where there is no map, where no one else had ever been before."

He flashes me an angry look. "Why did you let him go, Mummy?"

He's never asked that before. I pause, concentrating on the blue sky through the window. "I let him go because I couldn't keep him. When someone wants very much to have an adventure in life, it's impossible to hold them back, no matter how hard you try."

"But you loved him?" he asks. This sounds more like an accusation than a question.

I nod. "Yes, Alex. I loved him. And he loved me."

He leans his head against my chest, deflating slightly.

I put my arms round him. He nuzzles in close.

"And so your father went on a long adventure. And there were no phones and no letters. And he may be wandering still. Some day, perhaps he'll come back and you'll meet him. But if he doesn't, then he's surely watching you from heaven, and sending all good things your way."

"Like what?" His voice is muffled, coming as it does from the depths of my jumper.

"Like . . . warm sunny days or Michael Owen scoring a goal or when you lose a toy and you think it's gone for ever and then suddenly you find it again . . ."

"Like my Thomas engine."

"Exactly. Or when you have a lovely dream at night, so lovely you hardly want to wake up . . . these are all messages from your father, watching over you."

He looks up. "Do you think he likes me?"

I gaze into his large brown eyes. "Yes, Alex. It's impossible not to like you."

"And do you think that one day he'll come back?"

We sit a while, huddled together.

"I don't know, my angel. Anything is possible."

He's still. He's quiet now. But soon these answers won't be enough. I'm running out of time.

But for now, he's satisfied.

And I resolve that some day I'll take him everywhere he wants to go, no matter what the cost.

*S*UDDENLY I'M FALLING. The soft green grass gives way to a black, yawning chasm; cold, damp, infinite. I'm tumbling, plunging through the darkness. I open my mouth to scream. There's no sound. I throw my arms out. There's nothing to hold on to. Down and down I go, blind, mute, gathering speed . . .

I come to, gasping for breath. I focus on the ornate ceiling. There's the sound of waves crashing on the shore. My heart's beating like a stopwatch. But the bed is solid, real.

I turn my head. Jake's sprawled on his stomach, his face pressed into a pillow, arms outstretched; a fallen angel barely contained within the narrow frame of the cast-iron bed. He's unconscious, more deeply asleep than anyone I've ever known, as if someone had simply switched him off for the night. He's living out another, parallel life in a private, inaccessible universe far away. Is he falling too, reaching out his fingers to grasp something that's slipping away, before he can even touch it?

It's still early, maybe nine o'clock on Saturday morning. A thin shaft of daylight cuts across the wooden floor of our room at the Poppy Bed and Breakfast, through the heavy red velvet curtains.

My temples throb; a dull headache looms just behind my eyes.

Everything looks the same.

But something's shifted in the night; something important.

Carefully, I lift myself out of bed. Creeping as quietly as possible, I cross the floor to the armchair in the corner where all my clothes landed in a heap last night. Pulling on my jeans and a T-shirt, I grope around for my handbag, and slip into the hall. Downstairs, near the front desk, there's a squat pay phone, sitting on a table near the door.

Putting in a handful of coins, I dial and wait. It rings for ages. Finally, Imo answers.

"Hello?" I must've woken her.

"Im, it's me!"

"Evie! Where the hell are you? Are you OK?" She's wide awake now. "We thought you'd been abducted! Boyd's really pissed off. You missed rehearsal. And he says if you're not in on Monday he's reducing your part to a walk-on mute maid!"

"I'm fine. Honestly. I'm sorry about leaving like that, but really I'm fine."

"I tried to cover for you, said you were sick . . ." her voice trails off. And I can tell she doesn't approve of my behaviour. "I was really worried," she says again. It never occurred to me she'd be so upset.

"I'm sorry. I wasn't thinking. But I'll be back tomorrow. Jake had a gig, you see, and he really wanted me to come . . ." Suddenly, saying it out loud, it doesn't sound nearly as urgent or desperate as it had at the time. I abandon explanations and move to my real reason for calling. "Im, I don't suppose the post has arrived yet this morning? I was just wondering if there was anything there for me."

"I'll check." I can hear her riffling around on the floor. "Evie?"

"Yeah?"

Her voice is quiet. "There is something. It's a letter. From New York."

I swallow hard. "Open it. Please."

Paper tearing. Then silence.

It seems like whole minutes are ticking by . . . she's the slowest reader in the world.

"What? What does it say? Imogene!" I'm shouting. "What does it say?"

"Evie . . ."

"What! Just say it!"

"Evie, you're in. You've been accepted! You're in!" she squeals, laughing. I can hear her jumping up and down with excitement.

And suddenly I'm falling again. I close my eyes and the room spins.

What have I done? What on earth have I done?

I wander back to the room.

The bed's empty. There's no one here.

He must be in the loo. I sit down on the edge of the bed. Finally, I can hear him padding along the hallway, pushing the door open . . .

He smiles at me, standing in the doorway, wearing nothing but jeans. "Where have you been?"

"I got in." I'm staring at my hands, folded on my lap. There's a cold hard weight bearing down on my chest. "I got into Juilliard."

I look up.

He's frowning at me.

"In New York," I add.

And his face goes blank, with no expression at all.

"I'm going to Juilliard." Perhaps if I say it over and over, it will seem real. "I'm going to study acting in New York."

I sit, blinking at him.

"And this is what you want?"

I feel dizzy; far away. Why is he asking such a stupid question?

"I did the audition, didn't I?" It doesn't come out quite the way I intended. A sick tension knots in my stomach; I stare at the uneven patterns of the floorboards. "I'm an actress. This is what everyone dreams of."

He just stands there, looking at me.

What is he waiting for?

"Well? Aren't you going to say anything?"

He shrugs his shoulders. "Congratulations."

Suddenly I'm furious. "What's that supposed to mean?"

He narrows his eyes. "It means fucking brilliant, Evie! Fucking well fucking done!"

He turns away from me, starts to dress. He's pulling on his shirt, searching for a sock, yanking on his leather jacket.

Fuck him.

"Where are you going?"

"Out." He runs his fingers through his hair, glancing at his reflection in the dressing table mirror. He's not bluffing.

"Babe . . ." I slide off the bed and take a step towards him, hands outstretched.

He backs away.

I stand, watching with a growing sense of indignation; he's collecting the spare change from the bedside table, along with his cigarettes, lighter; pushing them into his inside jacket pocket.

"And what am I supposed to do, Jake? Exactly what is it you want me to do?"

He sidesteps me. "Do what you want."

He moves to the door.

I catch his arm. "I don't have a choice! I'm an actress!"

He twists it away. "That's what you keep saying."

"Jake!"

He swings round to face me. "For fuck's sake, Evie! What am *I* supposed to do? Huh? What the fuck am I supposed to do?" The bedroom door swings wide, banging against the wall. He heads down the hallway.

I race after him, the wooden floor cold and hard under my bare feet. "Jake, wait!" I grab his arm again, pressing myself close. There's a group of American tourists, senior citizens, weaving their way carefully into the breakfast room. "Please. Let's go back upstairs," I whisper. "Talk to me, please!"

His eyes blaze. "I told you," he speaks very clearly, very slowly, "that I want to be alone!" Then he twists his arm free with such violence, I'm propelled backwards, landing clumsily against the front desk.

"Oh dear!" A woman who could be my grandmother tries to rescue me from the floor. "Are you all right?"

I nod, wishing she weren't so kind; unable to speak without crying.

I go back to the room and wait, sitting on the bed.

An hour goes by.

I wash my face and change my T-shirt. Then I rummage around in my bag for something to eat. If I go out, I'm sure to miss him. There are a few spare packets of sugar, leftovers from buying coffee yesterday morning.

And another hour goes.

The sky is flat and grey.

I pull the curtains shut.

Lying on the bed in the darkened room, I curl myself round a pillow and cry. This should be the happiest day of my life. I should be happy. This is what I want. Isn't it?

Isn't it? I can't think any more.

And after a while, I fall asleep.

I don't hear the door open.

When I open my eyes, the sun is already starting to set. He's kneeling on the floor in front of me, watching me.

"You came back," I say.

He nods.

Another tear courses down my cheek. "Jake, what can I do?" I murmur. "What can I do?"

He takes my hand.

It's a slender thing, delicate; made of pale, almost white gold and set with a single glossy black pearl.

"Marry me."

Turning the key in the lock, I look once more at the ring on my finger. It's only two-twenty on Sunday afternoon and in three short days my entire life has changed for ever. And now, pushing open the front door of the Gloucester Street flat, I can hardly wait to tell Robbie and Imo the news.

The flat smells the same; of toast and damp carpet . . . I step over a pile of discarded magazines. "Hello! Anyone home?" I throw my rucksack on the floor in the hallway. "Girls!"

"We're in here," Robbie calls from the front room. She sounds subdued; probably hungover.

Already I'm beaming from ear to ear, I can hardly control my excitement. "I have an enormous surprise!" I announce.

Imo appears in the doorway, her face serious. She hasn't forgiven me yet for going away. "We have a surprise for you too—" she begins.

I grab her about the waist; twirl her into the centre of the floor. "Oh, but mine's so big it can't wait! Look!" I hold my hand up high. "I'm engaged!"

This doesn't have the effect I imagined.

There's an odd silence. Robbie's sitting very still, very upright, on the edge of the sofa . . . Imo's hand is on my arm, squeezing so tightly it hurts, and she's staring at me like we're spies in a World War II film and I've forgotten the code word . . . I follow her eye line, turning around.

And there, sitting in one of the black leather chairs and clutching a bouquet of red roses, a suitcase at his side, is Jonny.

His face is white. He blinks at me behind his black-rimmed spectacles.

"Surprise," says Robbie.

No one moves.

After about a minute, Robbie stands up, taking Imo by the hand.

And they leave, closing the door behind them.

It's early Sunday evening. I close the door to my bedroom very gently. And make my way into the kitchen.

Imo and Robbie are sitting at the dining room table, long-empty coffee cups in front of them.

"How is he?" Imo asks.

"He's sleeping now." I avoid her gaze, turning the kettle on and then off again. I don't know what to do with my hands. I pick up a dishcloth and wipe down the kitchen counter, before finally sitting on a chair at the far edge of the table. "I had no idea he was coming." I trace my finger along the bevelled edge. "It was awful," I add. "He cried."

Imo looks away.

"So, what's this all about, anyway?" Robbie's lighting a fresh cigarette, looking at me like she's Bogart or something.

After three hours of consoling Jonny, going over every painful detail again and again, this is the last conversation I feel like having. "Jake asked me to marry him," I explain, rubbing my eyes. "We love each other and he wants to marry me."

"Before or after he found out that you got into Juilliard?"

I sigh, exasperated. "What difference does that make?"

She and Imo exchange a look.

Instead of answering, she ignores the question, twirling the tin ashtray round and round with her middle finger. "You got into Juilliard, Evie. Where are you going to live? New York?"

Why is she making this so difficult? "I'm not going to Juilliard. We're going to live here. In London."

She sits forward. "How can you not go? It's everything you've ever wanted!"

"That was before I met Jake! Besides, things are starting to happen for him here. We can't just leave when his band's about to be signed!"

"If he loves you," she points out, waving her cigarette, "then he'll go to New York!"

"It's not like that, Robbie, and you know it! I can work here. I'm an actress. This is London: the home of drama. What's he going to do? Fly the whole band out?"

She glares at me. "He should wait then."

She doesn't understand anything. "I can't ask him to do that."

"Why not?"

"Because I'll lose him!" I shout.

"And what about us!" she shouts back. "We were going to live together in New York!"

"This man is the love of my life!"

"For fuck's sake, Evie! How would you know? You've only been alive five minutes!"

"What the fuck is wrong with you, Robbie!"

"You can't let me down like this, Evie!" Her voice catches. "You can't!"

Imo stands up. "Stop it! Both of you! You'll wake up Jonny. Besides, things are bad enough without you screaming at one another!"

Robbie pushes her head in her hands. "I just can't believe you're going to throw everything away like this!"

"What business is it of yours?" I demand bitterly.

"I said, stop it!" Imo bangs her hand on the table. She yanks Robbie up by her shirtsleeve. "You're coming with me. This is what gin was invented for."

Imo drags Robbie to the shop on the corner and they return with fresh supplies of liquor, cigarettes and cheap chocolate. She mixes us up a batch of gin and tonics, pouring out half the cold tonic water into a bowl, then filling the bottle back up with gin. We sit in front of the television, drinking and smoking, not talking, watching something strange and surreal, called the *Antiques Road Show*.

A man with a red nose and a lopsided bow tie is banging on and on, pointing out the merits of a Chippendale chair salvaged from a dentist's office in Inverness.

I feel queasy.

The thought of Jonny sleeping in my bed in the next room is nauseating; repulsive. His fragility and genuine confusion, the way he cried, his head on my lap—somehow it only adds to my physical aversion of him. It's wrong, I know. Hard-hearted and cruel. But I don't want to touch him any more, even to comfort him. I belong to Jake. And now, in the flesh, Jonny's just a small-town boy, in his FRANKIE SAYS RELAX T-shirt . . . he's not cool; doesn't even know what cool is. I want him to take his broken heart, his puppy dog eyes and leave; to catch the next plane home. But most of all I want to pretend it never happened; that I'm not the kind of person who destroys things without even thinking . . . just . . . because.

But I am.

And as long as Jonny is here, I can't escape it: it's a constant neon sign flashing on and off, in my brain. "It's your fault. You did this. You."

I pour another drink from the bottle on the coffee table. Robbie looks at me but doesn't stop me.

I raise the mug to my lips; it's a stronger mix than normal; Imo's not a great bartender—it's bitter and only lukewarm.

They hate me. I can feel it. They both hate me now.

I put the mug down and stand up.

"Where are you going?" Robbie asks.

I look at the floor. "I have to call someone."

She shakes her head. "I just hope he's worth it."

I stagger towards the door. And holding on to the frame, I turn to face her. "If you were really my friend, you'd be pleased for me."

She looks at me, hard. "You're fucking up," she says, turning back to the television. "You're fucking up your entire life."

"Yeah, well . . ." My eyes are stinging; I'm tired of crying and yet here they are, more tears. "It's my life," I say stupidly, childishly.

She ignores me. Imo's examining her fingernails.

What does it matter? I have Jake now.

I leave, stumbling into the hallway.

I take a deep breath, pick up the receiver and dial.

"Operator, how may I help you?"

"I'd like to make a collect call, please. To the States."

I give the operator the name and number then wait, listening to the phone ring far, far away. My head feels light, the hallway's spinning.

"Hello?"

"I have a collect call from a Miss Evie Garlick in London. Do you accept the charges?"

"Yes."

"You may go ahead."

I close my eyes and lean my head against the wall.

"Hey, Mom. It's me."

"Evie? What's going on? Is everything all right?"

"Mom, I've got something to tell you."

I T'S A CLOUDY, COLD AFTERNOON and I'm on my way to meet Allyson for an early supper in Covent Garden before my class. She says she wants to discuss something with me, most likely a detailed debriefing on her latest crush. There's a café behind the theatre that's easy for her to get to while she's on a break from rehearsals. I stop in a newsagent on St. Martin's Lane to buy a paper to read in case she's late. (She's always late.)

Waiting in the queue, my eye is inexplicably drawn to the cigarettes behind the counter, the ones with the huge warning labels declaring things like SMOKING KILLS and SECONDARY SMOKE HARMS SMALL CHILDREN in big black block letters.

What's wrong with me today?

I pull my change purse from my bag.

"Anything else?" the man asks.

I look around. JORDAN HALLIWELL'S SEX ROMP FIASCO the front page of the *Sun* screams. I've an almost uncontrollable urge to exchange my copy of the *Guardian*.

"No," I push the change across the counter. Educated women don't read the *Sun*. Educated women read serious articles about world affairs rather than titillating gossip about big breasted women and their lovers.

Standing to one side, I fold my copy of the *Guardian* and jam it into my holdall.

"Just this and a packet of Gitanes, please."

I spin round.

There she is, holding a can of Diet Coke, and grinning at me.

"Do you mind, darling?" Robbie nods to the waiting assistant. "I seem to have left without my wallet."

The man looks at me expectantly.

And I'm struck again by how incredible it is that other people can see her. It's reassuring; I'd much rather I wasn't the only one. But unfortunately, it doesn't make her impromptu appearances any more welcome. I've only just managed to block the last one out—an extraordinary feat of denial even by my standards. And now she's back again. The whole bottom of my stomach falls away and weightless anxiety takes its place. Fumbling in my purse, I find another fiver and hand it to him.

She follows me into the street, pulling a couple of wrinkled dollars from her back pocket. "Thanks. I so needed a fix! But you see, I only ever have what I had on me when I died. Dollars, I'm afraid." And she taps the top of the Diet Coke before pulling it open.

I wish I could be more pleased to see her but I'm not. She stands, apparently oblivious to the cold, dressed in what I'm beginning to think of as her uniform; the same old jeans and orange jumper, grinning at me.

"Listen, I have an appointment in five minutes," I lie.

"Fifteen," she corrects me, taking a gulp. "I'm going to walk you over."

I stop. "Do you have to? What I mean is, these . . . visits are really very disturbing."

"Oops!" She burps and giggles. "Pardon me! Listen, Evie, you're the one who brought me back. So deal with it. It's a bit boring having you spin out every time I show up. So anyway." She eyes me closely. "Who's been flirting!"

"I have *not* been flirting!" I correct her. She's thrown me. How does she know all this? "Piotr was flirting with me! But it's ok. I put a stop to it."

She rolls her eyes. "Why, Evie? For a moment there, I thought you were actually going to let your hair down and have a good time!"

"Why?" We duck down a back alleyway. "Because there's no point! And because those sorts of things are always a huge mistake and . . ."

"Don't you fancy him?"

I scowl at her. She's being deliberately perverse. "I don't know what you're talking about." I pull my trench coat tight around me.

She just laughs. "So tell me, darling, on exactly what date, at what time, were you transformed into a piece of walking wood? I'm curious."

I face her.

"OK, I don't know why you're here but if it does have anything to do with me then I have to say it isn't working for me at all. You have no boundaries, Robbie! You understand nothing about what it's like to be an adult in an adult world—with responsibilities and people depending on you . . ." She's grinning at me. "You're not listening, are you?"

She shakes her head. "Isn't it amazing?" She holds up the Diet Coke can. "No calories, no nutritional value, no point really, and yet so cunningly satisfying! A little like flirting, wouldn't you say?"

It's starting to rain; a light, irritating, unavoidable mist.

"OK," I sigh. "You've made your point."

"You didn't answer my question."

"I'm not likely to either."

We're passing my favourite shop. I automatically pause. It's still there— the cropped black leather jacket in the window. It's shiny and sleek, nipped in at the waist and wrists, with a thick belt that fastens with a stunning silver clasp. It's a work of art; tough, tailored and incredibly expensive.

"Hmmm, Mean Mommy! Why don't you buy it?" She drains her can and burps again.

I shake my head. "It's almost two thousand pounds."

"Looks like something a rock star would wear."

Digging my hands in my pockets, I pull myself away. "I wouldn't know."

And we walk on, Robbie slouching along next to me, content. Does she even feel the rain?

There's something nibbling at the back of my mind; a single persistent thought that won't go away. I look at her sideways. "You really hated me for a while, didn't you?"

She shakes her head. "No, Evie."

"You didn't come to the wedding. I didn't hear from you for a long time. Almost five years. I was so excited when I got your letter."

She grins. "Pretty smart of me to trace you through British Equity, huh?" She stops, digging out the packet of cigarettes. "It was a rough patch, Evie. I wasn't so well then. Don't take it personally."

I watch as she lights up, hunching over to keep the flame alight.

"You never told me exactly what was wrong," I remind her.

She carries on walking, pretending to be distracted by the passing window displays. "My mother took me in hand. I was treated for everything: drug addiction, alcoholism, sex addiction, unipolar psychotic depression with hallucinatory suicidal tendencies . . . you didn't know I was so fascinating, did you?"

I suppose I did know. But I hadn't realised just how serious it was. "I'm sorry. I just . . . I just regret that you never told me."

"It's not the kind of thing you chat about over the phone."

"I'm so sorry," I say again.

"Forget about it. Besides," she smiles at me, "you were busy. Being in love."

I smile back, although something in her tone cuts through me. "Yeah."

"So." She stops, leaning back against the outer wall of an apartment block. "Was it nice? The wedding?"

I roll my eyes, relaxing a little. "It was . . . interesting. My parents flew in on the day with a dress that my mother bought—at least two sizes too big. Jake's mother turned up pissed. His grandmother couldn't even look me in the eye. I'd never met his family before. There we all were in the Camden registry office . . ."

Suddenly I'm there again, in the square, empty room; rows of navy blue office chairs arranged on either side and my mother twisting her hankie, Jake's brothers trying to make him laugh, and Jake, tall and sure, holding my hands, looking into my eyes . . . "With this ring, I thee wed . . ."

"You went to Brighton for your honeymoon, didn't you?" Her voice rouses me.

"Yes. It seemed like the beginning of a whole new life. I know it sounds strange," I smile at her, "but it was so exciting. Even being poor was an adventure to start with. So many people were interested in the band . . . they had quite a following. And we were so passionate about each other. Any minute it seemed as if our luck might change."

She takes a final drag, throwing her cigarette to the ground; silent. And the old feeling returns, the unnamed rift between us. I never could discuss anything about Jake with her. I feel stupid for trying; like I'm trying to convince her of something.

"You never liked him."

Her face is impassive; she doesn't bother to deny it. Why did I ever imagine it would be any different—even after all these years?

"Not that you'd be able to understand," I add bitterly. "Sex was just a game for you. You've never loved anyone that way, have you?"

But she flashes me such a fierce look that suddenly I'm frightened.

"I have loved," she corrects me sharply. "I've loved more deeply than you can ever possibly comprehend! It's just I don't go on and on about it like it's a fucking fairy tale!"

And to my surprise, she strides off, rounding the corner before I can even open my mouth.

I look down the long avenue of shops, searching for some sort of internal bearings among the landscape of Long Acre.

There are none.

A fairy tale.

Maybe I did expect it to be that way.

And suddenly I'm reminded of the last time I saw her alive: that summer, June 1991.

The fairy tale had definitely faded by then.

For all of us.

PART TWO

June 21, 1991

N o, NO!" He tosses; throwing himself from side to side.
The room is black; I can't see.
"Evie!"

"Shhh." I roll over; only half awake. "I'm here. I'm just here. Lie back down," I whisper, pulling him to me. "Come and lie in my arms. It's just another dream."

He rests his head against my chest, hair spilling out across my breasts. "It won't ever happen," he murmurs, "and you'll leave!"

"Shhh. You'll wake the others." I stroke his head, pulling my fingers gently through his hair. "It will happen. As sure as I'm holding you now, it will happen. You'll be huge, famous, rich beyond all imagination, and girls will swoon when you look in their general direction."

"You're making fun."

"No, I promise you. It will happen." His heart's pounding; his forehead damp with perspiration.

"Tell me where we are . . . right now."

"Now?" I press my eyes together, gathering my thoughts and forcing myself into wakefulness. "Right now we're in . . . Rome."

"Rome? What does it look like?"

I pause. "The streets are narrow and twisted," I whisper, "the night air scented with lemons, and the rare, expensive perfume of beautiful women who sit by the windows of their ancient villas, staring out into the darkness, waiting for their lovers or the rain or both . . ." He's starting to relax, his limbs growing heavy. "Ancient cypress trees and faceless statues wait on every corner, silent and still, and we're standing, you and I, in the moonlight, on top of a mountain. The wind blows, warm and gentle against our skin . . ."

"Some day we'll go." He nuzzles deeper into my chest.

I hold him tight. "Yes, some day."

The others are already awake. I can hear them arguing in the bathroom.

They always argue about the same things; not enough takings, not enough publicity for the new show, having to live with us . . . She's in the shower and he's shaving. She always showers first because the hot water runs out and she likes to wash her hair. I'm far too familiar with every bit of their morning routine, as I'm sure they are with mine.

Jake's still asleep, stretched out so his feet dangle off the edge of the futon.

That's the other thing they argue about: Jake. Should he be here, shouldn't he; how he doesn't pull his weight. He's not an actor, so how can he contribute to the company? On and on and on . . . Their voices echo, bouncing off the tiles, and they don't bother to keep them down any more.

We share a room between the four of us at the back of the theatre— what used to be an old prop annexe. It's large but not large enough. There's a curtain hung on a drying line down the middle to divide it in half. But after almost a year of living, working and sleeping in the same space, there's really only so much a piece of cloth can do. All our possessions are stacked on top of one another; Jake has only two guitars now, he sold a couple to pay for studio time. But there are still boxes of sound equipment, books, black bin liners full of old clothes . . .

There's no point in getting up right now; the bathroom's clearly occupied. So I turn on my side, curling into the curve of Jake's stomach. Without even waking, he automatically throws his arm over me and pulls me closer. I love the smell of him in the morning.

It had seemed like such a wonderful, daring scheme. I met a girl named Hayley at an audition for a play last spring. I liked her immediately; she spoke about the passion of theatre, the importance of storytelling. She had soft brown eyes and short, cropped hair; she seemed vibrant and sensitive. Hayley and her boyfriend, Chris, a self-styled actor, director and playwright, were about to buy an old abandoned theatre, above a pub called the Angel in Islington. Chris went to Oxford. He plans to run the National Theatre some day soon. But in the meantime he'd inherited some money from his grandfather. They were going to form an intimate, raw acting company; living and working together to create a new dramatic experience—just like Peter Brook in *The Empty Space.* And the best part was there'd be no rent to pay; we'd remodel the theatre ourselves and live in the back rooms, performing new works in the evening, while devising and rehearsing during the day. They were looking for like-minded souls to join their band of artistic rebels.

The first play we performed was one that Chris wrote, *The Cell,* all about detainee refugees in a waiting room. I played a Polish girl who gets strangled by an IRA suspect (Chris) for protecting a mentally ill girl (Hayley). After that we did another one of Chris's plays, *The Bridge,* about homeless people living underneath a bridge. We all hung out near Waterloo Station for a week and I ended up playing a mentally ill girl who's raped by an old drunk (Chris), while his heroin-addict daughter (Hayley) looks on.

The critics have been slow to appreciate our work. Chris claims they've been brainwashed by television. He wants to do a piece, improvised fresh each night. There's a new one about mentally ill people being abused by their carers called *The Home.* But we've run out of money. So we're working on audience participation plays instead called *Cream Pie Classics.* Now we do very abridged versions of Shakespearean plays, dressed in plastic aprons. It's *Macbeth* this week. And for one pound a go, audience members can chuck a cream pie at you any time they want. That was Jake's idea. We've had to get in more actors but it's a huge hit with the late-night drinking crowd. It's the only thing we've done that's made any money. But Chris feels we're selling out; compromising our artistic integrity as a company. (Company direction is another thing we argue about. That and who's going to buy the groceries.)

"We should be making a statement!" Chris snorts, pushing his glasses back on his nose. He's got ginger hair and the kind of pale, copiously freckled complexion that flushes whenever he's angry. (He's always angry.)

"Theatre should change the world! Keep you awake at night! Get right under your skin!"

"Or pay the bills," Jake cuts in.

They don't get on at all.

I detach myself from Jake and slither out of bed. There isn't a kitchen as such; we use the sink in the bathroom and there's a hot plate and a kettle on the floor in the corner. I give the kettle a shake to see if there's any water left, then switch it on. There's no heating. The cement floor is cold under my bare feet. I scurry back to bed while it boils.

Jake's awake now. He smiles at me drowsily. Then he takes my hand, pushing down between his legs.

"Baby!" I murmur softly. "I have to get ready. Robbie's coming and I have an audition today—"

He puts his finger to his lips. "Shhh!"

And rolling me on to my back, he pulls up my T-shirt. "Go on," he whispers, "show Daddy what a good girl you are . . ."

The kettle boils.

Chris and Hayley are arguing on the other side of the curtain.

And Jake's moving slowly, silently inside me.

"Where's she going to sleep?" Jake lights a joint, watching as I shove our dirty clothes into a black plastic bin liner, ready to take to the launderette.

"Ajax says he's got a sleeping bag. Robbie can sleep on the stage. It just means she doesn't have to spend a night in a hotel and I get to see her . . ." I step over him, as he lounges, naked, in the middle of the futon. He smokes too much.

He takes another drag. "I don't like her."

I retrieve a pair of Jake's socks and what looks like a dingy rag but is in fact a pair of knickers, from behind a stack of paint pots. "Why?"

"She doesn't like me." He rolls onto his back. "That's enough reason, isn't it?"

"It's not true. She was just keen for me to go to New York. Besides, it's only one night." I tie the bin bag in a knot at the top. "I'll have to take this down later; I haven't got time now."

He props himself up on his elbow. "I need my jeans."

I look at him. "Then you'll have to wear them dirty. They're in there somewhere." I peer at myself in the old mirror leaning against a pile of mouldering books. I should pluck my eyebrows.

Shoving the joint into the corner of his mouth, he gets up, tears the bag open and dumps the whole lot onto the centre of the floor.

I swing round. "Jake!"

"I need my fucking jeans, Evie! We never have any clean clothes!" He shakes the remainder out.

I get up and start shoving the laundry back into the bag. "So take it down and do it yourself! What are you doing today anyway?"

"I've got stuff on." He finds the jeans, holds them away from his body, disgusted. "They're wet now! What the fuck!"

I throw the bag down. "What stuff? Jake, what stuff have you got on?"

He turns away from me, pulling on the jeans anyway. "Jasmine's having a party tonight," he announces, ignoring me. "The Sluts have been signed by Virgin, and C.J. and I are going."

"Oh. Are you?" My temper's soaring. "And when were you going to tell me? Robbie's only here for one night. I thought you'd hang out with us, not with some . . . some old flame!"

Jasmine's band, the Sluts, have been trailing around in Raven's wake for years now, sponging up the limelight with their derivative, Madonna-meets-Patti-Smith-in-a-see-through-bra kind of crap. And now they've been signed. Of all the bands in London . . . A thick, hot vein of hatred bubbles up inside me. I hate the fact that I'm jealous of her. I'd give my right arm not to care. But she's never stopped trying; she arrives before every gig Raven play, wearing something minuscule and obscene, passing around joints and lines of coke . . .

He yanks a T-shirt over his head, laughing. "Are you jealous?"

I stare back at him.

"It's business, Evie," he reminds me. "You could come, you know."

"I need some money." I turn back to the mirror.

He digs around in his pocket and throws a couple of quid down on the futon.

I look up. "I need more than that—I have to get a travel card and some lunch . . ."

"I haven't got any more."

"But what about—"

"I told you," he cuts me off, "I'll have more later."

He stalks off.

I climb up to the roof, the only place in the building that's private. But I'm not alone. Hayley's drinking a cup of black tea (we never have any milk), staring out at the city below, as it slowly awakens on another hazy summer's morning.

We sit, side by side, on a couple of old chimney pots, not bothering to make conversation. Downstairs, kegs of lager are being delivered, loaded into the basement of the pub below. Old Eileen, her hair in rollers, is waving her cigarette and swearing as two bewildered drivers roll them down into the cellar. She's always at her worst in the mornings—I feel almost sorry for them.

"Another day in paradise." Hayley smiles. There are dark rings underneath her eyes. She spots the book I'm holding. "Is that the play? How's it coming on?" She drains the last bit of tea from her cup.

"No." I shake my head. "I gave that up. Chris said it lacked a strong central message; it needed a theme, something other than love. It was a stupid idea anyway."

"I liked it." She stands up, rubbing her eyes. "It was fresh, romantic. The rock musician and the actress . . . they're great characters."

"Only I didn't know what to do with them. I couldn't make it work out happily."

"So make it work out sad. What's the difference? It's all drama." She stretches her arms above her head. "Is Jake downstairs?"

"Why?" My voice is sharper than I intended.

"Chill out, Evie!"

"Why, Hayley?" I can't help myself.

"God, I'm only asking!" She stomps across the roof towards the fire escape. She'll be in a mood all day now. "And by the way, it's your turn to buy supper!"

She climbs down the metal ladder. I rest my head in my hands.

It's still early but already the heat is sticky and unbearable. There are dark rain clouds massing in the corner of the sky. "Fair is foul and foul is fair" . . . lines from *Macbeth* march like soldiers through my brain. "By the pricking of my thumbs, something wicked this way comes."

I open the book.

It's small, beautifully made from soft black leather, properly bound, with thick, good quality paper. I found it in a sale bin at Liberty's. It looks like a journal, but it's not.

It's a collection of letters—to Jake.

But he doesn't know they exist yet.

There's so much I'd like to say, that never gets said. I don't know why it's so hard but the words get stuck. So I write instead. Some day, I'll leave it out for him. Or maybe one day he might open it by chance. And there it will be: a written testament of my love. All those times we spent fighting and struggling will vanish. I was thinking of him, believing in him all along.

Turning the pages, I find the last entry. It's almost full now. I date a new one.

"My darling J,"

I pause. What is it? What would I like him to know? I stare up at the sun, hot and heavy in the sky.

"I wish I had the power to change our lives. I wish that I could take away our difficulties and transport us to a safe, clean place, some time in the not so distant future . . ."

I stare at the words on the page.

Then I tear the page out, crumpling it into a hard little ball between my fingers.

He'll take it the wrong way; he'll think I'm criticizing him; telling him what to do. A faint feeling of nausea washes over me. The day is too sticky, too hot.

I force myself to concentrate again.

What will make him smile? Amuse him?

Jake the Famous Conquers Rome, I scrawl across the top of the fresh page.

> Rome is no stranger to heroes
> To passion, to art, to the annihilation of the senses
> And neither is my Jake
> Who is every bit a Caesar

As noble and courageous as David
Dauntless, dangerous, defiant

And beautiful

His slingshot draped loosely over his shoulder
Staring down Goliath, certain, sure

Naked and intense
(In or out of the bath)

Rome is no stranger to heroes
A thousand years pass in the blink of an indifferent eye
History loiters on every corner
Gods and goddesses eavesdrop on the conversations of passers-by
Longing to point tourists the right way round
Cemented in marble
Waiting for the next siege, the next triumph, the next big thing
And here he is
Strong and slim, like
Augustus, Daniel, the king of kings
And Rome is waiting. Smiling in the evening sun

Veni, vidi, vici!
The time is come.
It's what she was built for, made for, and yet still dreaming of

For Rome is no stranger to heroes

"You are my hero," I write at the bottom.

Some day we'll go there, to Rome. And he'll remember. He'll grab me about the waist, kiss my cheek . . . "Rome is no stranger to heroes," he'll whisper in my ear. We'll laugh, gazing out across the city . . .

I close the book.

As I make my way back down the fire escape, I look up at the sky. Sooner or later, it's going to rain.

*R*EACHING ACROSS the table, Allyson grabs both my hands. "I'm moving to Rome, Evie!"

She's sitting across from me in Brown's café in Covent Garden. It's started to shower properly now, in grey sheets, the windows fogging up. A thick, warm humidity hangs over the crowded dining room, where plates of cheap, hot pasta are served to weary tourists, crammed together at narrow tables. Our waiter plops a couple of glasses and a bottle of still mineral water down before swinging round to take another order.

"I'm sorry . . . Rome?"

Her whole face is radiant.

"I've got a job at Teatro dell'Opera di Roma! In *La Sonnambula!* Ian . . . you remember Ian, don't you? The baritone from Queensland?"

I nod my head numbly.

"Well, he's doing really well in Europe and now he's broken up with his boyfriend and he's got a fabulous flat right in the centre of Rome. It could be a base for me, Evie . . . The English don't really get my voice and there are so few chances here to build a proper career. I'm tired of covering for divas who can't act and can't sing while I wait around in the dressing room night after night! And anyway, I'm not getting any younger . . ."

Her voice washes over me. She talks on and on, telling me about her plans, about Italy and Italian men, of how many more opera houses there are in Europe and how well they pay . . . Our lunch arrives, two steaming plates of spaghetti that sit in front of us, untouched.

"You're leaving," I say, after a while.

There's excitement in her eyes; a passion igniting her features. I'm struck by how beautiful she is. "I've got to move on. I really want this, Evie! I've always wanted it; from as far back as I can remember."

I nod again.

I understand. Of course, I do; I remember what it's like to risk everything—to pick up and leave in pursuit of a dream. It just seems so long ago now; like something that belongs to another age and another woman, far removed from me.

I try to swallow. My throat's dry. Taking a sip of water, I hold up my glass. "Well done, you! Congratulations, darling!"

And she laughs, clinking her glass against mine. "You'll come and visit me, right?"

"Just try to keep me away!"

"And Alex too?" she presses.

"Of course!" I reach across the table, folding her fingertips into my palm. "You're doing the right thing. I'm sure of it."

For the first time since we sat down, her smile fades; a trace of fear flickers in her eyes. She holds my hand tightly. "You have to try, don't you? I mean, you never really know, do you, until you try."

I hadn't realised until this afternoon just how much I like her; how much I'll miss her. A vision of her room, bare and quiet, materialises; the empty space on the kitchen counter where all her endless vitamins and herbal tinctures used to be . . .

I pick up my fork, pushing the noodles around on my plate. "Jump first and look later. That's the way it's done!"

"I'm a little scared," she confesses.

"Don't be. You're a star, Ally. It's always been clear, from the first moment I met you. You have something special."

"Isn't that funny!" she twirls her spaghetti expertly round her fork. "That's what I thought when I first met you!"

"Really?" A rush of blood warms my cheeks. "So, shall we have a party for you before you leave?"

"Absolutely! But you'd better show up this time, OK?" She gives me a warning look. "Promise?"

"Promise."

"Our very own Evie Garlick!" she laughs. "Hey, that wasn't your stage name, was it?"

"No." I sigh. Some things never change.

She waves to the waiter. "I'm getting a mint tea. Do you want anything?" I shake my head.

"So what was it?" She waves again, unable to get his attention.

"Albery. Eve Albery." It's been so long since I've said it aloud; just the sound of it makes my skin go cold. I look away, just beyond the top of her head, in case something in my face gives me away.

But it doesn't.

She's more intent on attracting the waiter than unearthing my past.

"Wow. That's really pretty. Where's it from?"

"Just an old family name."

"Eve Albery," she repeats, savouring the open vowels in the way that only a singer can. "But you changed back."

"It takes so long to establish yourself," I explain, "that I didn't dare change it when I was working. But now I don't need it any more. That's all over."

She leans forward. "Come on, don't you miss it sometimes? Just a little?" I think a moment.

It's been a long time since I really thought about it; about what it used to be like, day in and day out—the waiting, the auditioning.

"No," I say finally. "I don't think I miss it at all."

I CHECK MY WATCH.

I'm going to be late.

There are twelve of us auditioning today, crammed into a narrow Soho office waiting room. We all look the same—variations on a theme of long dark hair and brown eyes. It's extremely disconcerting, when you're used to imagining yourself as unique, to discover you're just a type.

There're two girls here I see at every audition I go to. One's a rounder, more buxom version of myself, whom I think of as "Bubbly." Each time I see her, I resolve to eat less. Bubbly obviously thinks she's fat and has to make up for it by being super-positive and super-nice to everyone. She spends a lot of time befriending the receptionists, as if they're undercover casting operatives, secretly able to sway the director's decision. The other girl's older, probably pushing thirty, and disturbingly thin. I call her "Inch." When we fill out our details and measurements, she always asks, in her sharp, cut-glass accent, "Do you want this in centimetres or inches?" The answer's always the same, but she asks nevertheless, like an oracle tossing out riddles to fools. She carries a large bottle of Evian and spends a lot of time in the loo. She's recently taken up knitting. Before that, she used to do books full of crossword puzzles in ink, timing herself on her watch.

Bubbly, Inch and I pretend not to notice each other, which takes real skill in a room as narrow as this one. Instead, we're all focused on the most recent arrival, a slim vision of a girl, dressed in a school uniform, carrying a satchel. Is this fair? Can we really be expected to compete with the creamy complexion of a fifteen-year-old?

The room's decorated with a single, square black leather sofa, a glass coffee table and a huge Andy Warhol painting of Chairman Mao. Capitol Radio blares in the background. There's a young woman behind the receptionist's desk. The advertising world is too cool for normal office dress codes; she's dressed in jeans and a tank top, her hair in two skillfully uneven, blonde braids. She wouldn't look out of place perched on a bale of hay at the Grand Ole Opry.

I dislodge myself from the sofa where I'm wedged with three other girls and make my way up to the desk. "Excuse me," I don't want to speak too loudly, just in case the others can hear me, "but do you think I could go next? I'm meant to be picking someone up from the airport in an hour."

She sighs. "And you are?"

"Eve Albery."

She refers to a clipboard stashed just underneath her copy of *Marie Claire*. "Sure."

"Thanks." I walk back and force myself between the other girls. They glare at me for trying to sit down again. I pick up a copy of a trendy magazine called *The Face*.

My skirt's riding up. I tug it but it refuses to budge. It's Hayley's; a black polyester mix from Warehouse, paired with a blouse I bought from Oxfam. I look like a secretary. But then my agent, Dougie, wasn't very clear in his brief.

This isn't surprising. Dougie Winters is known in the business to be mad; not cute or crazy but genuinely insane. Originally from some minor aristocratic family, he's tall and thin with shocking blue mad eyes—the kind that roll about of their own accord, completely unrelated to the act of seeing. He owns a rambling basement flat in Hyde Park Gate, crammed with antiques and a considerable collection of poor quality homosexual pornographic art, quite a bit painted on vast swathes of black velvet. I've never seen him wear anything but shorts, no matter what the weather. And he's fond of carrying a walking stick. He struts around the flat in his bermudas like a majorette, whacking the stick around on anything from an elephant foot table to a Queen Anne writing desk. Now in his early sixties, he's been working in "the trade" as he calls it for almost thirty years. He has an enormous client list, largely due to the fact that he almost never turns anyone down—he's refreshingly untroubled by a client's CV, lack of experience, or even talent, but works instead on the premise that the whole industry is a numbers game. It's the one thing about him that's proved remarkably sane. He simply sends all of his clients up for everything. And, sooner or later, some of us are bound to luck out. But he's impossible to speak to, not only because he rarely remembers anyone's name but also because he's a shouter. Conversations go something like this:

"Got an audition for you! Tuesday! Commercial! Three P.M.!"

"That's great, Dougie! What's the address?"

"How should I know? Call the sec. What's-her-face will tell you!" Click.

His office is manned by particularly desperate out-of-work clients. The turnover is staggering; surviving even a day on your own with Dougie is impressive, let alone a week. I've never had to stoop so low, yet. But if things get much worse, I could be making Dougie cups of tea and dodging the walking stick before the year's out. It's been months since my last audition; almost a year since my last paid acting job—the role of "Hysterical Reporter" in the low-budget action film *The Bloodletting,* about a psychotic landlord and his young, female tenants. As I look around the room, I can't help but think the other girls, even Bubbly and Inch, exude a certain glow; an inner sheen that only comes when you've been working.

A giant stuffed bear's wheeled through reception.

I try to focus again on the magazine.

I really need this job. Once you get one commercial, it's easy to get more. And often the directors move on to bigger, better projects—film or television. If you're cute and do a good job, they remember you. "Hey, Bob, why don't we use that girl from the toilet roll spot? You know the one . . . What was her name? Eve?"

The trick is to stay positive; act like the job's already mine.

The girl next to me flips through the pages of Italian *Vogue.* She's got a French manicure; her long fingers look neat and chic. Why didn't

I think of painting my nails? They're probably looking for someone with great hands. Why didn't Dougie mention hands? I look down. Mine are chapped and callused, still covered in bits of black emulsion from repainting the theatre last week.

The door to the casting suite opens. Another girl with fantastic, clean hands emerges. She's blushing and smiling. "Thanks a lot, guys! Take care!" She laughs, waving playfully.

Shit! She's got it.

She's definitely got it—she's calling them "guys."

We all watch as she smiles triumphantly, nodding to the girl with the braids. "Thanks. See you later!"

She knows her too! She obviously does loads of commercials. Shit, shit, shit! Why are they even going through the charade of seeing the rest of us?

The reception desk phone rings.

"Eve Albery," the braid girl calls out. "You're next."

Wrenching myself up, I pull down my black skirt and button my jacket. There's a little run starting in the bottom of my tights. It's too late now.

Please, God. OK, deep breaths. It's mine. This job is mine.

Remember: good-natured yet seductive, cool but boundlessly enthusiastic . . .

I smile, knock on the door, then push it open.

It's another tiny room, quite dark, with blackout blinds drawn against the summer sun. There are two men, an older man with a beer gut, wearing a black T-shirt with a triangle on it that says SERVICE, UNITY AND RECOVERY, sitting behind the camera, and a younger guy, with short brown hair and a long, angular face, who can only be in his early twenties. He's dressed in jeans and a leather jacket, a kind of advertising world James Dean. As I walk in, he stands up and shakes my hand.

"Jason Wiley," he introduces himself. "And you're . . ." He searches through the vast pile of CVs and photos on the table in front of him. "Carole?" he ventures, picking one up at random.

"Evie. I mean, Eve," I correct myself. I'm not used to the name change yet.

"OK. So, Eve," he sounds incredibly, almost paralytically bored. "What I need you to do is to stand here," he grabs me by the shoulders, wheels me in front of a sky blue background screen. "And I need you to take your jacket and top off."

"I'm sorry? Did you say my top?"

He spins round to the cameraman and shakes his head. "See? What did I tell you?"

Then, rolling his eyes, he turns back to me. "I need you to take your jacket and top off. OK?"

I smile apologetically, "It's just my agent didn't mention any nudity . . ."

He's becoming annoyed. "Well, they wouldn't," he snaps, "because there isn't any. This is a deodorant ad, darling. So we need to have a nice long look at your armpits." He riffles through the papers in front of him, searching for something important; something interesting. "Now, if you don't mind."

I look at the man behind the camera.

He grins at me. He's got gold front teeth.

"Don't mind Boris, darling. He's seen it all before. You can put your things here." Jason points to a black metal chair.

I hesitate. I can't remember what bra I'm wearing or what condition it's in . . .

Jason continues to stare at me.

If I turn my back to undress, I'll seem prudish and self-conscious. And no one wants to hire a prude. So I fix my face into an expression of bland pleasantness and unbutton my blouse. Even though it's June and warm outside, my flesh is goose-bumped and cold. I fold my clothes carefully on the chair. It seems to take for ever, like I'm moving in slow motion. Perhaps it would be sexier, more appealing if I nonchalantly tossed them there. It's a little late for that now. I wish I could stop thinking . . .

"Great. Now, take a step forward please, darling." Jason starts waving his arms at me like ground staff at an airport. "Into the light, that's it! Stop!"

I stop. The two of them stare at my image on the video screen.

Jason scowls. "What do you think?" he mutters.

Boris points to something, presumably on my body, and shakes his head.

Jason narrows his eyes. "I see what you mean." He looks up. "Can you lift your arm for us, please?"

I lift my arm.

"Higher."

Boris raises his eyebrows.

"Nice," Jason says, tracing his finger along the screen. "This here. Good. So, Eve. Do you wax or shave?"

"Shave." Is that the right answer? "But I can wax, I mean, if that's what you prefer." God, I sound too eager. Act cool!

"And is that a Wonderbra?"

"No," I frown. "I think it's . . . it's a Playtex, something like a Natural Shaper . . . from the States . . ."

"I'm not thinking of buying one, dear. I'm just wondering if those are real or if you've been helping nature along."

I blush. "No, no, they're real."

"Bravo." He crosses, hands me a stick of deodorant. "Now, I want you to apply the deodorant. But slowly, sensually. And we need to see your face. So I want you to keep it in profile, just here." He shoves my nose into the crook of my arm. "Got it? Face stays put. Do you think you can do that, darling?"

I hate the way he keeps calling me "darling." But I laugh as if the whole thing's entirely too delightful for words. "I'll give it a shot!"

I start rubbing.

"No, no, no, no, no!" He's waving his arms again. "You have had an orgasm, darling, haven't you? At some point in your life?"

Boris can't contain a snigger.

"I'm sorry?" Jason prompts, cupping his hand over his ear in response to my silence. "I can't hear you?"

I bite my lip. And nod.

"Well, you'd never know it! Could we have some *real* action now?"

And so, for the next five minutes, I roll the plastic stick around under my arm, closing my eyes and gasping with pleasure—only not so much pleasure that I'm compelled to move my head in any way—while Jason shouts things like, "Open your mouth! Wider! Soft lips! *Yes,* that's it! Softer! Is it satisfying you? Yes, darling! I think it is!"

Just when I think it can't get any worse, Guy arrives.

Guy is the nineteen-year-old runner who's been sent out to buy sandwiches and coffee. And he's got the ruddy good looks of an extremely posh Eton schoolboy, which is exactly what he is. Tall with yellow-blonde hair and dimples everywhere that dimples are possible when a person smiles, he puts down the provisions and then loiters next to Boris, gaping at me on the video screen.

"Guy, we need a sniffer!" Jason announces.

"OK. Right." Guy slouches over.

"The last shot we need is of a male model sniffing your armpit," Jason explains.

I blink at him.

"Is that a problem?" he asks threateningly.

"No, no, it's great! No problem at all!" I lie, as if I can think of nothing nicer than having a pubescent boy wedged into my armpit for the afternoon.

"Guy, take your shirt off."

"Yah." Guy strips it off, which I'm certain is entirely unnecessary, then leans his beautiful bedimpled face into position.

I'm starting to sweat; I can feel the dampness building between my shoulder blades. Shit. Did I put on any deodorant today? "I'm so sorry," I whisper. "Really. So sorry!"

Guy smiles at me with his clear, grey-blue eyes. "Na, it's like, cool."

"No talking!" Jason shouts. "Now sniff, Guy! Sniff!"

Ten minutes later, I'm tucking my shirt in, shaking Jason's hand good-bye.

"Take a tip from me." He grips my hand tightly. "You've got to learn to be more adaptable. Understand? You've got a nice pair of tits. But that frown is going to cost you work."

I should say something. Something along the lines of, "Piss off, I don't want your filthy, humiliating job anyway, *darling*!" But instead I blush and murmur, "Thank you," nodding solemnly, as if he's just given me the secret of the Holy Grail.

I open the door.

In a single movement, the entire waiting room full of girls swivel round to stare at me.

"Hey, thanks, guys!" I wave, buoyant, full of smiles. "That was great! See you soon!"

I wink at the braid girl. "See ya!"

And making my exit, I push through the door into the safety of the empty corridor beyond. Leaning with my back against the wall, I close my eyes. This is the last time. The very last time.

But I know I'm only kidding myself.

Someone's coming.

I pull myself up and pretend to be waiting for the elevator.

It's Guy. "Hey!" His cheeks are bright red. "I just thought, if you ever, you know, want to hang out." He tilts his head to one side and hands me a scrap of paper.

"Guy!" Jason's voice thunders through reception.

He lingers a second longer. "And just to let you know, you, like, smell totally amazing!"

Then he's gone.

I stand, holding the little scrap of paper. Then I lift up my arm and have a sniff. Not as bad as I thought. I press the lift button, slipping the number into my handbag. It's the nicest compliment I've had in a long time.

The arrivals area at Heathrow is crowded with excited children, anxious parents and eager lovers. Taxi drivers lean, with glazed expressions, holding signs, searching for people they have yet to meet. I make it just in time to see her come out of the customs hall. She is, as always, eye-catching, dressed in a pair of black fitted trousers and the ugliest, green knitted top I've ever seen.

I wave. "Robbie!"

And she spots me, wheeling her thick, battered vintage Louis Vuitton case behind her. "Evie!" She wraps me in a scented embrace; Chanel No. 5. And suddenly, it's just like old times.

"I'm so glad you're here!" I hold her close. "It's been ages!"

"Years! Can you believe it?"

I give her another squeeze. "I'm so glad you're here," I say again.

"Darling, what are you wearing?" she laughs, holding me at arm's length.

I shudder. "I had a casting today. A deodorant commercial. I can't tell you how cringe-making the whole thing was. And please, just for five minutes, don't call me darling!" I start to head towards the train but she pulls away.

"Let's take a cab; I'm shattered," she pleads.

"I . . . I didn't think, Robbie . . . it's just, I haven't been to the bank yet."

"I have cash." She surges ahead to join the queue.

Opening my handbag, I peer into my change purse. Two pounds and fifty-seven pence rattle around in coins. Clicking it shut, I wander after her.

She leans back in the cab. "So, how's married life, Evie?" She gives me the same naughty little smile everyone does when they use the phrase married life, as if it's merely a euphemism for masses of sex.

I nod. "Great! Lovely. Where did you get your jumper? And how can you stand to wear it in this heat?"

"I made it!" she laughs, looking at it as if she still can't quite believe the genius of her own handiwork. "I made you one too," she adds gleefully. "I've discovered a whole new side of myself that's intensely visual. It's amazing! And I love the feel of the wool between my fingers . . . it's so . . . so . . ."

"Woolly?" I suggest.

She wrinkles her nose at me. "I was going to say grounded. Earthy. Did I tell you I began a textiles course? I'm doing really well. In fact, I'm a genius. Last week, I made a coat entirely out of recycled plastic bags. They're using it in the end of term show. Of course, it smells a bit and makes a horrific noise if you move, but my professor says I'm inspired."

"Did you sleep with him?" I tease.

She smiles, digs a packet of cigarettes out of her pocket. "No, not this time." She tears the cellophane. She looks bloated; her grey-green eyes are washed out. Maybe it's jet lag.

"Although I should," she adds, giving me a wink. "He's short."

"And this is a good thing?"

She lights up. "They're so eager to please."

"I wouldn't know!" I laugh. The smell of the smoke is sharp and acrid. "Robbie, roll down the window, will you?" I press the button on my side.

"What's wrong?"

"It's the heat." I take a deep breath.

She holds her cigarette daintily out of the window. "My very own Princess and the Pea. So, thanks for putting me up tonight. Boyd's not back from Moscow until tomorrow."

And she winks again.

I shake my head. "What are you doing, Robbie?"

"What I always do." She shrugs her shoulders lightly. "He's sweet.
I like him. We get each other, Evie." She takes another drag and looks out
of the window. "He's taking the Moscow Art Theatre to the Edinburgh
Festival. He needs company. And frankly, so do I."

There's a lost quality in her voice; a sudden sadness. I turn to look at her
again. She's collapsed against the seat, gazing out of the window, chewing
unconsciously on her bottom lip. There's something different about her; a
vagueness, a strange sense of resignation. We lapse into silence.

London races by, grey council flats punctuated by vivid patches of
green, then more grey towers, stacked as uneasily as a child's building
blocks—haphazard, makeshift. Laundry's strung out on rows and rows
of balconies, flapping in the heat of the late afternoon sun. A mass of
dark clouds gather ominously in the east; black, like a murder of crows.

When we arrive, Robbie pays the driver as I drag her suitcase from
the back of the cab. "Well, at least we don't have to go far to get a drink,"
she observes, pointing to the pub.

"That's true. Look, I hope you're not expecting anything too
sophisticated." I unlock the side door and heave the case up the stairs.
Pushing the door open, I turn on the lights. "Hello?" I call out. There's
no response; for once it's empty. I feel a rush of relief.

"Here, let me show you around," I offer, putting the case down by the
ticket desk.

Robbie strolls past me, through the small foyer into the biggest room,
the theatre itself, with its raked metal seats and large empty floor space.
"So, this is it." She turns. There's an expression of unmistakable pride on
her face. "How does it feel? Doing what you love?"

I shrug my shoulders, suddenly shy. "I'm not sure getting pelted with
cream pies in the middle of *Macbeth* is what I love. 'Out, damned spot' is
particularly messy because you have to be so static."

She laughs. "Can't you duck?"

"Ahh! That's cheating." I push aside the curtain that separates the
wings from the backstage area, the bathroom and the prop annexe. "And
here's our little home!"

She follows me into the back room, looking around at the two
mattresses on the floor, the piles of clothes and personal belongings,
stacked among paint pots, gels, light rigging, scaffolds and old scrims.

"Intimate," she concludes.

I'm embarrassed, seeing it through her eyes. I quickly pick up a couple of dirty ashtrays and an empty teacup Jake's left on the windowsill, as if that will suddenly make it more amenable. The air's stale and hot. I open the window. "You've got the stage area all to yourself," I promise. "Ajax is bringing a sleeping bag," I add, as if this is an alluring prospect.

Robbie's naughty smile returns. "Is he cute?"

"Only if you like ferrets." I pull off my jacket. "I'm just going to change my clothes. What do you want to do? Do you want to crash out for a while? You can sleep here." I unbutton my blouse.

She shakes her head, looking through the spines of the books piled on the floor. "No, I'm going to push on through. My God, Evie! Your tits are amazing! I don't remember you having such amazing tits . . . so firm and round . . . Can I touch them?"

"Piss off!" I laugh. "And stop staring at them, you perv!"

She leans up against an old metal filing cabinet. "Lucky old Jake! Speaking of which, where is the beast?"

I pull on my jeans. "Oh, I think he's got some stuff to do today . . . session work maybe. I'm not sure when he'll be back. These things go on for ages . . . you know how it is."

She's opening the filing cabinet drawers, riffling through them, quite unabashed. "And the band? Any closer to being signed?"

I consider asking her to stop but she'll only look when I'm not around anyway; I might as well be present for whatever she finds. "They lost their bassist. And they're so hard to find. Everyone wants to play lead guitar; they're like gold dust."

She's got my passport. "Look!" She holds it open. "You're such a baby! You used to look like that, you know—all eyes."

I take back the passport and shove it in the drawer. "So what do you want to do? As long as we don't go anywhere or spend any money, the sky's the limit."

She swirls round. "Let's get drunk."

"I really haven't got any money," I confess.

"Well then. Let's slip downstairs and get pissed instead. It's on me." She slides her handbag over her shoulder. "Just like old times."

THROUGH HERE, please!" Bunny orders, shouting at the top of the kitchen steps. "Evie! Will you show them where it goes?"

I open the kitchen door and instantly a wave of music from Piotr's rehearsal with his new chamber music trio floods in. It's surprisingly immaculate for a first run. Two men carrying cases of wine and beer struggle down the steps.

"My goodness!" I laugh. "There's so much of it! Are you trying to get us all pissed, Bunny?"

"Let me see!" Alex bounces up to examine the bottles more closely.

It was damp and dreary earlier on, so Alex and I holed up in the kitchen. We've been colouring in a large banner for Allyson's party tonight and watching his favourite Thomas the Tank Engine video, munching popcorn as we go. The Mendelssohn piece the trio are playing makes a pleasant change from the Thomas theme tune I know so well.

"Here's just fine." I direct the men to one of the only surfaces in the entire kitchen not covered in party supplies.

Bunny rushes down after them. "Good! Excellent! Oh, I hope there's enough! Do you think there's enough?" She turns back to the deliverymen. "What else have you got? Is there any more in that van of yours?"

They look at one another. "Well, it's already been bought by other people . . ."

Ally's invited easily eighty people tonight and Bunny's beside herself with nerves. She must've entertained all the time when Harry was alive but now she's out of practice, obsessed with each last-minute detail. Ally, on the other hand, has removed herself from the fray and taken the day off to have her hair done.

"It's fine," I intervene, taking her arm gently. "There's more than enough. Besides, darling, people always bring bottles to parties."

"Do they?" She seems unsure. "What if they bring nothing but flowers and I don't have enough vases?"

She looks up at me with such a forlorn expression that I laugh, kissing her forehead. "Trust me. Alex and I will help you. Come on, peanut!"

"I'm not a peanut!" he corrects me. "My name is Alexander. Alexander the Great!"

"Fine, Mr. Great. Will you please pass me the white wine bottles, one at a time?" I open the refrigerator.

Bunny wavers in the centre of the kitchen, her brow furrowed, watching as we stack the bottles inside. "This isn't right," she concludes, after a while. "I think we should go to Harrods."

"Harrods? Why? Thank you, darling."

But she just frowns at me.

"Bunny?"

"Because," she says firmly, "when you have a party, you go to Harrods. For olives and crisps and chocolates and . . . and . . . it's just what's done, Evie!" It's not like her to be so abrupt.

Alex looks at me. I look at him.

"All right," I say slowly, slotting the last bottle on top of the rest. "We'll go to Harrods. Alexander, will you get your coat?"

He leaves. I close the refrigerator door. Bunny's still standing in the middle of the room, her lips tightly pursed, arms folded across her chest.

"What's wrong?" I ask.

She glares at me, then her face softens. "I'm fine." An undercurrent of annoyance still crackles in her voice. "It's just, look at all this!" She points at the packages of tortilla chips and pretzels; the Tesco's sausage rolls, dips and cheese sticks . . . "A party is an event! People nowadays don't understand the importance of the little things, the details! This isn't the way it's done!"

I should be used to this sort of diatribe by now; she's been acting strangely all week—one minute bossy and cheerful, the next snappy and sullen.

And apparently there's only one thing for it.

We're going to Harrods.

Piotr wanders in, looking shattered.

"How was it?"

He turns on the kettle, sighing. "Well, now at least we know what to work on." And leaning back on the kitchen counter, he smiles at Bunny. "Everything ready?"

"We're going to Harrods," she informs him briskly.

"Bunny believes we've forgotten something," I add.

She flashes me a look. "I don't believe, Evie, I *know*!"

I don't know why, but I'm the one getting it today.

Piotr catches my eye. "Good idea." He turns the kettle off. "I need socks. I'll come too."

It's nearly four o'clock on the day of the party and we're wandering around the Egyptian room of Harrods, navigating dazed clusters of tourists. Not one of us really knows what we're looking for or why we're here. Bunny insists she remembers the way to the Food Hall and refuses to ask for directions. We trail after her.

"Harrods is *not* what it used to be!" she snaps, sidestepping a fat American, already wearing shorts, even though there's nothing remotely warm about the weather. "It used to be exclusive, discreet; the staff addressed you as 'sir' or 'madam.' You were served. And you knew it. Now look!" She gestures to a faux bust of Nefertiti. "That looks like Elizabeth Taylor with a bath towel on her head! Where's the Food Hall? It used to be just here . . . I don't understand . . ."

Alex clings to my hand. He senses something's wrong without being told.

"Bunny, why don't you tell us what you want and then we can buy it?" I suggest. "Maybe you and Alex could sit and have an ice cream and Piotr and I will do all the legwork—after all, it's so crowded today." I'm speaking to her in that tone of voice I reserve for Alex when he's over-tired.

She dismisses me. "I've been coming here since before you were born! I know what I'm doing!"

We take another turn and end up in the leather department, thankfully uncrowded. It's also remained relatively untouched throughout the years. The wood panelling still gleams, while the mahogany and glass display cases lined with crimson and black velvet cloth still show alligator handbags and glittering evening bags.

These familiar surroundings seem to have a calming effect; Bunny's pace slows. She wanders over to one of the counters devoted entirely to leather gloves. She presses her hand against the glass. "My mother once confessed she'd had a dalliance with the man in the glove department." Her voice is dreamy. "Apparently he used to hold her hand in such a way that she was paralysed with lust; sliding only the softest, most expensive kid gloves very slowly over her fingers. They met every Tuesday at the Basil Street Hotel for an entire summer and she managed the whole affair without ever knowing his first name. Her glove collection was unparalleled." She looks sad. "Everything's changed."

I put my hand over hers. Once upon a time, it would've been covered in a soft kid glove. She holds it tight.

"I used to be able to entertain at the drop of a hat. Harry and I could be at each other's throats and I'd still pull it off. Now all I throw are going-away parties." Her shoulders fall forward. "I'm tired, Evie. I'm tired of saying good-bye. And I'm tired of doing it with a smile on my face."

"Right!" Piotr steps forward. He flashes Bunny a smile and links his arm through hers. "Step this way, please!" He escorts her into the next room, fine jewellery. "Alex and I have been talking. We're going to do the shopping, right?"

"That's right!" Alex beams, mimicking Piotr's authority as best he can; clearly pleased to be included in the male/hunter-gatherer section of the expedition.

"While you sit here!" Piotr instructs, leading her into a luxurious showroom for Boodle and Dunthorne, complete with cut-glass chandeliers and cream suede leather sofas.

Bunny blinks at him, stunned. A smart-looking gentleman in his early forties materializes from the back room. "May I help, sir?"

"Yes," Piotr straightens to his full height, tosses his hair back from his eyes. "These women need to see diamonds. Big diamonds. And lots of them!" He clasps Alex's shoulder. "My colleague and I will be back. But until then," he takes out his wallet and whips out a card, handing it to me with a flourish, "they can have anything they want!"

"Yes, of course!" The man smiles, gesturing to the elegant sofa. "May I start by offering you ladies a glass of champagne?"

I watch in amazement as Piotr steers an exuberant Alex out of the room, then look down at the card in my hand. It's a library card for the Sorbonne in Paris. I stuff it quickly into my coat pocket before anyone else can see.

Bunny settles back in the settee, running her hand wearily over her eyes. "Actually, champagne *would* be lovely. But not too dry!" she pleads. "I'm like the Queen; I have a weakness for sweet wine!"

"But of course!" He disappears into the back room, then returns with a bottle of Taittinger on ice.

He pops the cork and Bunny relaxes next to me, leafing through a catalogue casually, as if her only intention all day long was to go jewellery shopping. And suddenly the afternoon is transformed into a glamorous, festive event; rescued from the claws of chaos by Piotr's bold, affectionate gesture. I take the offered glass, wondering again at his mass of contradictions. How did he know this would soothe Bunny's fraying nerves? Has he bought diamonds before? And, more importantly, for whom?

"Cheers, ladies!"

We sip quietly while the assistant unlocks one of the display cases, taking out a tray shimmering with stunning solitaire rings.

"Oh, Evie!" Bunny sighs, her eyes gleaming with delight.

He grins wickedly. "Let's start small, shall we?"

It occurs to me that this is just the sort of extravagant outing Harry would've treated her to in times of crisis; in the days before honesty, in all its clumsy, intrusive forms was believed to be the only passport to intimacy.

One thing is certain, as I sit, sipping champagne, diamonds dangling from my fingertips, it's clear that there's no substitute for romantic imagination and daring, absurd acts of unexpected kindness.

And I'm reminded of Robbie. So much so, I almost expect her to appear, grab a glass of champagne, and insist upon viewing the tiara collection.

I wait, feeling, for a change, that it might be nice to see her again; she'd make Bunny laugh and flirt outrageously with the salesman. For a moment the air is charged with possibility.

The minutes roll by; the sensation slips away.

I twist an enormous diamond ring around on my finger.

And I miss her.

*T*HE REGULARS at the Angel are a pack of old Irishmen, Paddy O, Mick the Tick, Evil Joe; they're already well away when Robbie and I arrive; heads nodding, eyes at half-mast, tucked into dusty corners where the damage is limited when they fall over. Ian's behind the bar. He's the owner's nephew, from Dublin, in London for the summer. In his early twenties, with dark hair and round, bright blue eyes, he's funny, shy and sharp, dreaming of a career as a stand-up comedian. I can tell when he's flirting because he launches into his set—joke after joke, eyes gleaming. As Robbie and I settle down at the bar, he mixes us up a round of rum and Cokes on the house, treating the delighted Robbie to all his best lines.

Eileen, the owner, comes down, chain-smoking, her bleached blonde hair twisted into a formidable beehive. She's in her fifties, wraith thin, with a hard, lined face. Her skin is almost orange, from regular sun bed sessions in the salon round the corner. She mixes herself a large G and T and yells at Evil Joe, who was, according to Ian, once the love of her life, many, many years ago. Now he just blinks at her, offering to light her already lit cigarette, then cowering in the corner, running up a tab he never pays. She assures him, through vivid, detailed description, that he's nothing, the lowest of the low and always has been as long as she's known him. And when she's made her point to her satisfaction, she tops up her drink again and stomps back upstairs.

"The course of true love." Ian sneaks a couple of packets of peanuts over for us.

As evening rolls around, the pub fills up and Robbie comes back to life, filling me in on the details of Imogene's engagement to Coffee Carlo. She figures it was always inevitable. "He's *enormous*," she confides, catching Ian's eye. He blushes and pretends to be wiping down the bar. "I just managed to escape myself, Evie. He's really the most delightful freak of nature and when you consider that she was a virgin . . . well! Also, being Italian, he's the perfect mix of the profane and the sacred; whore, Madonna, whore, Madonna . . . she loves it! I'll bet she still has a few of those old Laura Ashley dresses tucked away in her closet for rainy afternoons . . . He's talking about opening a coffee shop business." She shrugs her shoulders. "It will never take off. But he's so stubborn."

Her voice is swimming round and round in my head; a kind of droning monologue over the building agitation in my brain. "Let's sit near the door," I suggest. "The heat and the smoke are starting to get to me."

She picks up our drinks. "Are you all right?"

"I'm just tired."

We move to a table near the door.

It's nearly six-thirty. I need to shop for supper. It will have to be pasta again. Pasta, tuna and tinned tomatoes. And an onion, if I have enough money. Just the thought of it makes me queasy. The heat is stifling. I add more ice to my drink; it sits there, melting. Soul II Soul come on the sound system and Robbie sways back and forth, chattering on; I nod my head and smile.

I wonder where Jake is. What he's doing.

I twist the pearl ring round on my finger.

Robbie takes my hand. "Do you wear that all the time?"

"Of course I do!" I stretch my fingers wide. "It's my engagement ring. And wedding ring, for that matter."

"You can't do that with pearls. Look, Evie." She points to the dull surface. "It's wearing away. They're not strong enough for everyday life; they're too fragile. Pretty soon you'll have nothing left."

I pull it away from her. "How do you know?"

"Everyone knows that." She's looking for her lighter. "It's common knowledge."

Eileen saunters over to collect our empty glasses. Then she stops, her mouth turns down at the corners; she waves her cigarette in my face. "You best keep that man of yours out of here, do you understand? I'll not have that type of thing going on in my pub! A drink is one thing, do you get what I'm saying?" She continues to glare at me with her watery grey eyes.

I recoil. "I don't know what you're talking about!"

"You know what I'm saying," she assures me. "You know exactly what I'm on about!" And she reels back to the bar, leaving the glasses for Ian to clear. I watch as she tops up her drink and then sits in the corner with Evil Joe.

Robbie frowns. "What was all that about?"

"She's pissed. That's all." I push the table back and stand up. "Let's get out of here. I have to go to the market anyway."

As we round the corner with our shopping, I hear music and voices coming from the open windows of the theatre. It is, as always, the loudest building on the street.

Robbie and I climb the stairs and open the door. Hayley, C.J. and two guys I don't recognize are all sitting on the stage, on a sofa and a couple of chairs, like some kitchen sink drama; C.J.'s plucking out an alternative guitar solo to "Brown Sugar" and Jake's concentrating, rolling a joint. The floor's covered in empty cans of Tennant's and there's nothing but a thin film of powder left on the mirror balanced on Hayley's knees.

Jake looks up; he's high. He smiles at me, then his eyes narrow as he spots Robbie.

"Welcome home, babe." He swaggers over and kisses my cheek. "I told you she was beautiful." He wheels me round to face his friends. They smile. "This is Gary and Smith," he introduces us. "And of course, all the way from New York City, my wife's dear friend, Robbie."

C.J. waves. "Hey, Evie!"

I ignore him. He's here so often, it's like having a pet.

"So when did you get home?" I try to make my voice sound pleasant and easy, as if I'm some 1950s hostess, entertaining my husband's business colleagues. I don't want to fight in front of Robbie.

"A while," Jake says. "These guys are touring with Eric Clapton through Europe next week." He lights the joint, inhales, then passes it to Smith. "Hey! We're going to have some new photos taken! Gary knows this shit hot fashion photographer who'll do the whole thing for the price of the film. We're meeting him tonight . . . Isn't that great?" There's always some new plan to take over the world, especially when he's high. "I'm starving, babe. What have we got to eat?"

Smith asks Robbie how long she's in town for, C.J. and Gary start arguing about fingering . . .

"Babe?" he repeats. "I'm hungry." And he stands up, draping himself around me. He leans too heavily, smelling of sweat and aftershave.

I shrug him off. "There isn't enough food," I say quietly. "And where did you get that stuff?"

He grabs me again. "Don't pull away from me," he warns.

"You told me you weren't going to do this any more!"

He lets me go. "I'm looking after things." This is his standard reply. "You don't need to worry; I'm looking after everything."

I put my bags on a chair and bend down, picking the empty cans off the floor.

Robbie's laughing. Gary's got the guitar now; he's strumming away. C.J.'s rocking back and forth. Hayley's just blinking, staring dully into the middle distance.

"What does that mean, Jake?" I look around. The stage, reasonably clean when I left, now looks as if someone's emptied a garbage bin in the middle of the floor—paper, ashes and cigarette butts, a half-eaten packet of crisps . . . Robbie's meant to be sleeping here tonight.

"Look at this place!" I've got my hands on my hips.

"Fine. You know, you could always believe in me, for a change! Have a little faith!" He grabs his jacket from the back of the chair he was sitting on. "Come on, guys. Let's go get something to eat. You're buying, C.J."

"Aw, shit!" C.J. protests but stands up, nonetheless. Gary and Smith stand too, leaning against each other for support. Smith stumbles and knocks into the chair. The groceries and my handbag tumble down, the contents rolling all over the floor—keys, tuna, makeup, tomatoes, tampons . . .

"Shit! Sorry, man." Smith bends down in slow motion, picking things up, swaying like a willow in the breeze.

"Leave it," Jake orders. He grabs fistfuls of stuff, jamming it back into my bag.

Then he stops.

He's holding something. A scrap of paper. Standing, he unfolds it and then looks at me. "What's this?"

It's Guy's number.

I flush. "It's nothing. This kid, at the audition . . . it was for deodorant and . . ." Everyone's staring at me. "Actually, it's quite funny. You have to mime putting on this deodorant and then some male model sniffs you—I mean, under the arm—but of course, they didn't have the male model, there was just this runner who's about twelve." Robbie laughs; C.J. and Gary are smiling. "So, here I am standing in my bra with this kid sniffing my armpit . . . and I'm starting to sweat . . ." They're laughing, I'm laughing. The only person not laughing right now is Jake. "Afterwards he gave me his number. He was just a kid," I say again.

"So." Jake's voice is flat. "Why didn't you throw it away?"

They all look back at me; it's like a match at Wimbledon.

"Because I just wanted to get out of there. And there wasn't a bin. And . . . and I needed to get to the airport."

His eyes haven't left my face. "What do you mean you were in your bra?"

"Come on, man!" C.J. laughs and pulls at Jake's arm. Jake yanks it away.

"Like I said, it was for deodorant," I explain. "They wanted to look at your armpits. Jake, don't be stupid!" I plead.

"I'm being stupid," he repeats. "I'm stupid."

"Jake . . ." This is exactly what I was hoping to avoid tonight. "You don't understand!"

"No, I don't. I don't understand what my wife is doing in her bra in the middle of fucking Soho!"

The room's silent.

"What are you saying?" I ask.

He glares at me. "I don't trust you! That's what I'm saying!" He crumples the number in his fist and tosses it at me. "Go call your boyfriend!"

"Jake!"

"You used to be something!" He paces the floor. "Something out of the ordinary! With your long flowered dress . . ."

"What are you talking about?" Tears sting the back of my eyes. "I'm still the same! But that wasn't my dress, Jake! I never wore long dresses!"

He grabs my wrist, pulling me close. "So was it just talk? When you said you wanted to love someone so much that nothing else mattered! Was it?" I've never seen him so upset. "No matter what happened, that's what you said!"

He lets me go.

"Jake!"

But he storms off, slamming the door. The rest, C.J., Smith and Gary, quietly filter after him.

Hayley blinks at me. "That was a really good scene."

I'm shaking. I sit down on the sofa, cradling my head in my hands.

Hayley slides off, crawls over to pick the tin of tuna off the floor. "Can I eat this?" she asks.

I nod. Peeling the lid back, she begins picking it out with her fingers. The overpowering smell of tuna fills the room. And suddenly my stomach's churning. I rush out, making it to the loo just in time.

When I come back, Robbie's in the foyer, standing by the window, looking out onto the street below. Dusk is drawing in, purple streaks across a lavender sky. The birds are singing the way they do on warm summer evenings.

"How late are you?"

I stare at her back.

How does she know?

"Come on, Evie." She faces me. "How long has it been?"

I look down at my hands. "Nearly two months. I thought it was stress . . ."

She turns again and gazes out at the church across the street. A dull growl of thunder echoes in the distance.

"Do you want it?" Her voice is weary.

I don't know the answer; it seems an impossible question, not a question a person should even ask when they're married.

"Have you told him?" she persists, ignoring my silence.

"No. Things have been difficult. It isn't the way I thought it would be," I add stupidly.

"What isn't?"

"Any of it." I haven't got the energy to go over all the optimistic, childish expectations or the inevitable disappointments. I shake my head, staring numbly at the floor. "Nothing's the way I imagined."

She doesn't try to argue with me; to offer advice or even a halfhearted pep talk. Instead, she leans back against the windowsill, standing very still, for a long time.

The door opens. Chris, huffing from the exertion of climbing the stairs, trundles in, his white skin dotted with beads of perspiration. He's wearing long shorts and a white shirt, soaked through under his plump arms. His bushy red hair sits like a small fox or an exceptionally large squirrel on top of his head. He's got a thick file of papers in one hand and a rapidly melting pink Popsicle in the other.

"I've just come back from the accountant. We're fucked!" He eyes Robbie up but waives the option of a civilized introduction. He thrusts the Popsicle back into his mouth instead. "What's for dinner?" He goes over to the desk, checks the answering machine. "Who turned this off? Jesus! Do I have to do everything around here?" It beeps loudly as he switches it on. "How the fuck are we going to take any bookings? And from now on, we're going to get up every morning with the dawn and do Tai Chi. As a company! Brook does it," he adds. "And we need to start gelling, understand?" He waves the Popsicle at me. "We need to start functioning as a single entity, OK? Like we can read each other's minds on stage. Otherwise, there's no point. We're as useless as the fucking RSC! Where's Hayley?"

"Chris, this is my friend Robbie . . ."

He strolls away from me, into the theatre. He's always in a bad mood, always banging on about gelling. I'm sick of gelling. The only time I've seen him happy is when he's taking a bow.

"For fuck's sake! Look at this place!" He'll make the perfect Lear some day; ranting and raving is what he does best. "What is this? Fish? Disgusting!"

Silence follows.

Robbie turns to me. "Charming. And so sexy!"

I smile.

Then he storms into the foyer. His fury's electric. "Where's Jake?" he hisses. "Tell me, Evie! Where the hell is he?"

He's such a drama queen. "I'll clean it up," I sigh. "Calm down. He's out."

Instead of calming down, he grabs me by the arm, drags me into the next room.

"Hey!" Robbie cries.

He's pulling me forward; nails digging into my upper arm. He flings me in front of the sofa.

Hayley's lying down; she thinks something's funny. He yanks her up by the arm.

"There!" he shouts, pointing to a telltale red mark near the crook of her elbow. "Do you see that? Do you? That's it, Evie! It's over! He's out of here! Do you know how long it took us to clean her up last time?"

I stare at Hayley, who rolls onto her back.

"Fuck you," she whispers to Chris, sweetly, then laughs again.

I can't seem to connect the dots in my mind. "But . . . but why do you think that's got anything to do with Jake?"

Chris hauls Hayley up, then wheels round. "What are you, blind? Everyone knows Jake deals, Evie!"

"No. No he doesn't." I sound small; like a child. "He stopped. And anyway, it was only weed."

"I want him out of here!" He's carrying Hayley into the back room. "Or I'm calling the police!"

It's all wrong; some sort of mistake.

Jake promised.

I turn to Robbie.

She puts her hand on my shoulder. "We need to find him."

Mink Bikini is located underneath the arches in an alleyway behind Portobello Road. It looks like all the other car repair workshops and scrap yards, only the constant driving bass of the music and the wild dress code give the game away. It's the kind of unmarked club that repels tourists and hen night parties; here, only the ultra-cool are admitted; smoking and scoring in the shadows, well away from the light above the door.

Even though it's still early, the party's picking up speed. Robbie and

I aren't really outfitted for the scene. We're stopped at the door by two enormous black bouncers, dressed in black leather bondage gear.

"Are you on the list?" one growls.

"We're the fluffers," Robbie grins, with her characteristic combination of profanity and charm. "We'll be getting to work in a minute, if you want to watch."

They smirk and let us by.

"What are fluffers?" I ask.

"You don't want to know," she assures me. "But let's move quickly, OK?"

It's almost pitch-black inside. But the bar is lit by electric-blue tubes under glass, the stage is bathed in an indigo glow. The dance floor's crowded with beautiful people. A searchlight swings in all directions; famous faces appear for a second, then disappear; the music's brutal and sharp, layers of relentless sound. In front of us now, an exquisite young girl with long auburn hair and ivory skin, wearing nothing but a scrap of silk, like a nappy, is passing around shots of a blue liquid, served in plastic baby bottles. Everyone's swaying, sucking, screaming to be heard.

I turn to Robbie. "We'll never find him; I can hardly see."

"Stay close," she instructs, pulling me through the crowd.

She stops just to the right of the stage, where another couple of bouncers are waiting; more soberly dressed this time in black jeans and T-shirts. One of them steps up as we approach.

"We have a delivery," Robbie shouts over the music. "We're expected."

He looks us over. Our faces are blank, impassive.

Then he pushes the door behind him open. We walk through a long, cold cement corridor, smelling of damp, packed with rigging and sound equipment. The door slams shut. There are voices, echoing, somewhere down the hall. Above them all, I recognize Jasmine's razor sharp laugh.

"I can't do this," I tell Robbie.

She grabs my hand. "We have to."

The dressing room's full of men; middle-aged men in suits, younger men in jeans, lounging on sofas, leaning against the water cooler, all staring. Jasmine and her band are holding court. She's wearing a see-through, skintight plastic jumpsuit, with a flesh-coloured thong and black gaffing tape over her nipples, à la Wendy O. Williams. She leans back, legs spread wide, smoking a spliff.

She looks up, sees us in the doorway. "Oh! Look what the cat dragged in! How nice of you to come!" she purrs. Her hair's bleached and shorn, her eyes bloodshot and swollen; heavily outlined in layers of black eyeliner. It hardly matters; no one's looking at her face. "Have you come to congratulate me?"

I swallow hard. "Actually, I'm looking for Jake."

"A lost husband!" She inhales again, turning to face her audience of admirers. "Seems I'm collecting them tonight!"

They laugh.

I'm the floor show.

Robbie squeezes my hand.

"Are you two together?" Jasmine waves her joint at us. "Now, even I might pay to see that!"

More sniggering.

"Is he here?" I say quietly.

She turns, admiring her reflection in the mirror. Narrowing her eyes, she picks up the black eyeliner. "Why don't you have a look for yourself?" She nods to the bathroom door.

I walk over to the battered metal door and turn the knob.

The first thing I notice is the smell, a burning sickly sweet odour, stronger than the stench of urine. It's darker than the dressing room; the only light comes from a flickering bulb above the mirror. As my eyes adjust, I make out two shapes. Jake's leaning against the sink, holding his arm out. Smith's concentrating, filling the needle . . .

Jake looks up.

His expression is more disappointed than surprised. "It's from L.A., baby." His voice is hoarse. "Once in a lifetime stuff. We'll make a fortune . . . an absolute fortune . . ."

Smith doesn't even pause. He moves swiftly, jamming the needle in. Jake closes his eyes and exhales.

I shut the door.

Jasmine licks her lips. Her skin's flushed and sweaty under the plastic. "Did you get what you came for?" She looks in my direction but her eyes fail to focus.

I walk away, Robbie trailing after me.

———

218 ∾ KATHLEEN TESSARO

The warm night air is close and humid. I watch Robbie smoking her cigarette, pacing up and down between the chimney pots. I'm sitting, dangling my legs over the side of the roof.

It's not such a long way down. Just a couple of floors.

"Let's get out of here." She throws her cigarette away. "Come on, Evie."

There's a little square of pavement between my feet, just a few dozen yards below. "Where?"

"Come on. Get up."

I look at her, in her misshapen green jumper. "I don't think I can." I stare down at the pavement again.

"That's why I'm here." She pulls me back from the edge. "Let's go."

Standing on the street corner, bags in tow, she waves down a black cab. "Take us to the hotel where Oscar Wilde was arrested, please."

"You mean the Cadogan Hotel," the man smiles. "There's a poem about that somewhere!"

"Typical," she sighs.

We climb in.

"We're going to sleep in a proper bed, have a delicious meal and drink champagne in the bath," she promises.

"There's no way we can pay for it," I object.

"Yeah, but we're fucked, you and I. So we might as well have a party, OK?"

I should argue with her. I should protest and make the taxi pull over. But instead I lean back in the seat and roll down the window.

Maybe she has a point.

It's another London that whisks by; a London of green garden squares and red brick mansions; of boutique shops and designer clothes; a clean, polite, well-spoken London, with a boarding school education and tickets for Glyndebourne.

I linger in the corner of the lobby while Robbie speaks to the clerk at the reception desk. She takes out a credit card and her passport, pushing them across the counter with great confidence. And we're led to a suite with views over Cadogan Square.

It's so beautiful. No dust or filth or piles of clutter; it's untainted, orderly; immaculate. There's the cavernous marble bathroom, with the claw-and-ball-feet bath, the tiny bottles of hand cream and scented

shampoo, piles of thick, white, oversized towels; here's the carved
mahogany bedstead, high ceilings, tall, narrow, infinitely refined french
doors. Robbie opens them. Summer rushes in on a single breath, filling
the room. It's not the summer I know; stale air and sweat; but the
perfume of honeysuckle, clean sheets and freshly mown grass from the
square below.

Robbie goes into the bathroom to turn on the bath. I sit on the
corner of the bed, my hands underneath my thighs.

I want to weep. But all my tears have gone.

"Look, darling." Robbie's back, holding the thick room service menu,
page after page of elaborate entrees. "Look at all the wonderful things we
can have!"

She orders champagne, a pot of Earl Grey tea, hamburgers with extra
chips and tiny English strawberries and vanilla ice cream. I haven't the
heart to tell her I've lost my appetite.

I sit, immersed in the warm, scented water.

Her handbag's collapsed on top of the toilet seat, the hotel receipt
poking out of the top. Shaking the water off my fingers, I reach down to
have a look. But when I pull it out, a slim vial of pills rolls out onto the
floor.

"Lithium," the inscription reads. "To be taken twice a day." And there
are more. Inderal. Prozac. These are real prescription pills, not
recreational ones.

"I'm running you a bath too," I say, when I come out, wrapped in one
of the fluffy white robes. "Do you want me to sit with you?"

"No." She turns away. "I won't be long."

True to her word, she appears shortly after, a vision of Victorian
modesty in a long-sleeved floaty white nightgown; the kind of thing Imo
used to wear. We lie, side by side, my dark head on one pillow, her fair
curls on the other.

"Come to New York, Evie. We can have the baby, you and I."

I'm so tired; my eyes ache. "Let's not talk about it now."

"I'd love to have you back again—we'd have such adventures."

"What are those pills?"

"Just pills." She rolls onto her back, eyes closed. "Sometimes the
water gets too high."

"What do you mean?"

She looks like a statue; like one of those monuments laid out in St. Paul's.

"Virginia Woolf drowned herself in a river . . . It's nothing. I had a rough patch. I hate them; they make everything . . . flat."

"I'm sorry." I touch her hand. Her skin's cool and dry. "I'm so selfish."

She opens her eyes again and smiles. "Actually, it's nice to be the one with the answers for a change."

At home, on the outskirts of Islington, you can always hear the grumble of some domestic disharmony brewing in the background of the night. But here in Knightsbridge, the linen sheets are cool and crisp against our skin, the bed firm yet yielding; every intimate comfort met as if it were our birthright. Even the traffic outside is unhurried, quiet.

Around five, I wake to birdsong. The air's unexpectedly fresh. It must've rained in the night. Robbie lies motionless beside me, curled into a half-moon around her pillow, as if it were a lover she won't let go of. The sleeve of her nightgown has rolled up around her elbow in the night.

Carefully, silently, I pull the sheet over her again.

Lying back, I gaze at the golden glow of sunlight as it takes possession of the morning sky. And holding out my arms, I imagine the weight of a small, warm body pressed against my chest.

*A*LEX IS SKIPPING across the room, holding on to Piotr's hand, taking five rubber ball steps for Piotr's one, dragging a signature green bag along the floor. Every fibre of his being is electric; it's like watching a firefly bobbing in the night sky, illuminating everything around him.

A familiar, almost painful sensation burns across my chest; pure love. Still wearing his Thomas the Tank Engine pyjama top, the one he won't be parted from, with his unruly hair that can't be tamed, no matter how hard I try, his dimpled cheeks and fearless, unrelenting immediacy, my son is a force of nature; raw, potent and miraculous to behold.

Letting go of Piotr's hand, he barrels into the Boodle and Dunthorne showroom, throwing himself onto me.

"We got *everything*!" He laughs, burying his face in my lap.

I quickly kiss the top of his head before he squirms away, desperate to touch as many jewels as he can before the assistant ferries them to safer ground.

"So." Piotr grins, carrying two bulging bags of his own. "Which one will you have?"

He leans casually against the counter; completely untroubled by our deception.

I can't resist the temptation to ruffle his unflappable exterior. I pluck the largest of the solitaire rings from the tray and smile sweetly. "I like this one."

Bunny coughs.

But he just smiles back. "Put it on," he suggests.

Slipping it over my finger, I hold up my hand. "What do you think?"

The assistant has gone rigid with anticipation.

"Mummy, are you buying that?" Alex pulls at my arm to have a closer look. "Are you?"

Piotr looks at me.

I look at him.

He's enjoying this; I can tell by the glow in his eyes, the soft curve of his lips.

"What do you think?" I ask again, as calmly as if we were discussing what sandwich to have for lunch.

Bunny drains her glass and stands up. "Would you look at the time! We really must make a move!"

But Piotr holds his ground. "I think you can have anything you want," he says and, turning to the assistant, he digs out his wallet. "I sincerely hope it comes in a velvet box?"

"Mummy?"

My face is flushing; it's all I can do to keep from laughing out loud.

"Oh yes! Certainly, sir!"

I slip the ring off, put it back on the tray.

"Actually, I've changed my mind." And taking Alex's hand, I stand up. "It's not really what I was looking for."

Piotr's eyes are unwavering. "What are you looking for?"

And walking over to him, I do a very uncharacteristic thing, in a day full of uncharacteristic events. Slipping my arm through his, I kiss his cheek, very lightly. "Not diamonds," I say softly.

The assistant nods, deflating.

"Thank you," I add. "They're all so beautiful."

"Yes, thank you!" Bunny smiles, taking Piotr's other arm. "The champagne was delicious!"

"A pleasure." The man bows, his professionalism always intact. He begins carefully replacing all the rings in the right order.

Then Alex takes something out of his bag and hands it to him.

"Oh!" The man blinks in surprise. "What's this?"

It's a golden box of chocolates, tied with an elaborate black silk ribbon.

"I chose them!" Alex announces proudly. "There are no nuts and no marzipan!"

And then he races back to join us, clinging to Piotr's leg, laughing with delight.

"You're full of surprises," I say, as Piotr steers us all towards the nearest exit.

I can feel his eyes on my face but concentrate instead on how easy it is for him to walk with a four-year-old balanced on his shoe.

He draws me closer, swerving past a clump of Germans paralysed with admiration in front of the fish counter.

"So are you."

*J*AKE AND I ARE SITTING on a park bench in Soho Square. It's a warm, beautiful summer's day; the leaves on the high plane trees rustle in the breeze. There's not a cloud in the sky. Bodies are stretched out on the lawn, office workers taking in the sun before they head back to their desks.

Jake's hunched over, arms resting on his knees. He's wearing his leather jacket, even though it's far too warm, and shades against the sun. We watch as a small child, a little blonde boy of two or three, chases a pigeon across the footpath, a hopeless pursuit and yet all the while giggling with delight.

When he speaks, he doesn't look at me, his right arm cradling his battered guitar case. "Why are you making such a big deal out of it? It's nothing—a way to make some cash. We could move out . . . get a place of our own."

I've heard all this before.

"It's under control," he adds. "It's not like I have a problem."

"So stop."

"I have."

I twist my ring round and round on my finger. "I don't believe you."

"Jesus, Evie!" He looks at me, but I can't see his eyes behind the mirrored shades. He's out of money, the dole cheque long gone. His hands are shaking. "We can't do this, you know that, don't you? You don't understand how hard it is."

"If you cleaned up, we could!"

"No." He shakes his head. "I want it back the way it was—just you and me."

"It's part of us—"

"I don't want a baby!" he snaps suddenly. "I don't want another fucking mouth to feed! Any day now, the band could be signed. And then what? Besides, I'm not doing anything that Keith Richards doesn't do every day of the fucking week!"

"Only you're not Keith Richards, are you?" I snap back. I'm hurt and scared; I want to hurt him too.

He runs his fingers through his hair, then covers his face with his hands. He sits that way for a long time. "You know nothing," he whispers at last. "Please, Evie! This is what I want, so badly . . . I really do!"

"Exactly what do you want?" I'm crying. I don't want to but as I wipe away one tear, another one follows in its wake. "Do you want me? Us?"

"Don't do this . . ."

"I am doing it! I can't live like this any more!"

I wait for him to say something. Anything at all.

But he just sits there.

I stand up.

"Baby?"

I can't look at him.

He gets up, pulls me close. "It's not that big a deal," he whispers. "Most girls have them . . ." I struggle but he holds me closer. And for a moment, I let him, burying my face into his chest. This used to be the safest place in the world. "Come on, babe. Take it easy." He strokes my hair. "Where are we now, huh?"

The laughing little boy stumbles and falls; his cries pierce the air. His mother pulls him up roughly, yells at him and puts him back in his stroller.

"We're nowhere." I push Jake away.

"Evie . . ."

"It's my baby! I'll do it." I can hardly see now; can hardly speak. "I don't want anything from you. Ever."

I start walking.

And then, suddenly, I'm running.

It's a warm, beautiful summer's day.

High in an office overlooking Soho Square, the pictorial editor of a magazine called *The Face* is flipping through a photographic portfolio. The photographer waits patiently, staring out of the window at the square below; cataloguing the figures there in his mind: two lazy strolling street sweepers, a woman with a pushchair, a girl, running . . .

The editor turns the page; a young man stares back at him; angular, defiant, a guitar draped across his bare chest. "Who's this?"

The photographer turns back from the window. "Oh, that! That's a favour I did for a friend. Some band called Raven. That guy was unbelievably photogenic."

"Has it been published?" the editor asks.

He shakes his head.

"Well." The editor leans back in his swivel chair, props his feet up on the desk. "I think we have a cover."

Two weeks later, right in the middle of a Friday night Cream Pie Classic of *Othello,* I start to bleed. At first the audience think it's some sort of effect but then I faint on top of a guy in the front row. A guy holding a cream pie.

In the ambulance, a young Australian paramedic holds my hand. He gives me an injection and tells me to count to ten out loud. I get to five.

When I wake up, I'm on a ward. I try to turn my head, but the pillow's stuck. I raise my hand to my hair; it's sticky, still covered in whipped cream. And then I notice there's a drip in my arm.

A doctor appears at the end of my bed, surrounded by students.

"Hello," I say. There are such a lot of them.

He picks up my chart. "Female, twenty-four years of age. Infection and complications resulting from a miscarriage. Treatment would be?" he asks a pretty red-haired girl.

"Standard D and C followed by a course of antibiotics?" she suggests.

"Good. But in this case the infection was complicated by a secondary long-term venereal disease. There's lasting damage."

The redhead looks at her notes. "And that means?"

He puts the chart back on the end of the bed. "She's infertile now."

*G*OD, THE SLUTS! Whatever happened to them?"

"Hey! Turn it up, will you? Come on, Evie! Dance with me!"

Ally grabs my hands, trying to entice me onto the makeshift dance floor in the front room. It's after one in the morning and the house is still heaving with people, spilling out into the hallway, swaying to the music.

I step back. "No, thanks. Maybe later!" I shout above the din.

"You always say that! One of these days, baby, you're going to have to let your hair down!" She twirls into the midst of the throng where Andrew, a big black baritone, shimmies up to her.

"Why don't we go aaaaaaall the waaaaaaay!" Jasmine's voice howls, above the grinding bass.

She grabs his hips, throws her head back, laughing.

I slip through the crowd, stepping over the bodies perched on the stairs, deep in conversation, climbing up to the top floor. The music still thuds dully, but Alex remains fast asleep, sprawled across his bed. He was up until ten-thirty, running around in his pyjamas, eating too many crisps and trying to steal drinks. Allyson made a huge fuss of him, calling him her boyfriend and introducing him to everyone. Eventually I tracked him down, curled up underneath the piano, his cheek pressed against a pile of sheet music.

Closing my bedroom door, I wander back down the steps.

The first half of the night was easy: I spent my time filling glasses and taking people's coats . . . but now that we've moved into the disco part of the evening I'm at a loss. It's too noisy to sleep, not that I'd be able to . . . The air's hot and smoky. Pausing on the landing, I open another window, letting in a blast of cool air. I lean out.

"Don't jump."

Piotr's walking up the stairs, holding a beer. In his black shirt and jeans, he's handsome, sure of himself.

I smile.

I've been avoiding him.

He's the reason I'm wearing this silky, lacy camisole; bare arms hooked into new, fashionable low-rise jeans . . . All night long I've known when he was in the room, who he was talking to, when he left. If I raised my eyes, his would be there to meet them, dark, certain. The tension, sudden and mysterious, grows tighter.

It's dangerous.

"You take the fun out of everything," I say, looking out into the night.

He stands next to me.

Just being close to him sends a rush through my veins, warming my skin. He's wearing cologne; it smells of cedar and incense; fiery, profane, sexy.

"You don't dance either?"

I shake my head.

"I'm bored." He sighs, rubbing his eyes. "Come. Talk to me."

"I can hardly stand up, let alone speak," I'm objecting. But not too hard.

The bathroom door swings open. A couple of girls stumble out, clutching each other about the waist, giggling hysterically.

He takes my hand. "Come on."

I let him drag me across the hall into the relative quiet of his room.

We stand in the dark. The moon shines from behind a mass of black clouds; a clear, other-worldly glow illuminates the large double bed.

He closes the door. "Lie down." His voice is deep, intimate. "Talk."

I brush my fingers along the cool iron bedstead. "Why?"

I want to be close to him; I want it too much.

"Because," he stretches out, watching me, "it's what I want, Evie."

There's a certain way he says my name, with those distinctive, heavy vowels; it makes my breath stop, seizing a moment in my chest. This is foolish, I think, lying down next to him. I'm not a child. This is what's clearly known as a compromising position. Yet there's a slow, deliberate sensuality to my movements.

The pillow's cool under my cheek. It smells of him.

"Tell me about Paris." I turn to face him.

"The library card." He smiles; that charming gap-toothed grin.

"Yes."

He exhales, as if forcing the memory away from him "I did what everyone does in Paris. Studied. Fell in love. Grew a beard. Shaved it off. Grew a moustache. Shaved it off. Oh, yes! I also learned how to make Quarter Pounders with cheese at McDonald's on the Champs-Elysées . . ." He laughs. "Le Big Mac."

"Did you wear a uniform?" I tease.

He nods. "With a hat. Very attractive."

"Why Paris?" My voice has dropped.

"I was unhappy. If you can't be happy, at least you can be in Paris." His eyes shine in the darkness. "Take your hair down, Evie."

He's so bold.

"Why?" I ask softly.

"Because it's what I want."

I'm like some nineteenth-century courtesan taking requests . . .

Reaching up, I give the band a little tug. My hair tumbles down, long, dark and silky across the pillow.

"So you were unhappy . . ."

He curls a lock round his finger, very slowly. "I lost my way."

"How?"

"It's a long story."

"Tell me."

He sighs. "I did a competition. The Tchaikovsky Competition in Moscow. In the final round, I walked out."

"I know."

Reaching out, he brushes a tendril back from my face. His fingers linger, caressing my cheek. "Do you?" His eyes search my face. "I played like a monkey . . . performing. In the middle of the second concerto, I couldn't stand it any more. I stood up and left. And then the nightmare began. It seems nobody does that. It was a scandal. As soon as I came off the stage, there were agents, record companies . . . It was worse than winning. Now I'm supposed to be daring, different. A rebel. But I knew nothing of what it would be like, playing night after night, travelling, reviews . . . At every concert the audience only wanted to see the pianist who walked out on the Tchaikovsky. That was who I was." His face clouds. "Before, I never thought of myself when I played; afterwards, that's all there was. My freedom was gone. I was lost."

"So you went to Paris and grew a beard?"

He traces his finger along my lips. "Yes, Evie."

"And fell in love."

He nods again. "Yes, Evie."

"And now?" I'm speaking just above a whisper.

"And now I teach and play chamber music and think too much . . ."

"Piotr . . ."

"Yes?"

"I think you're remarkable."

For a moment, he's very still, looking at me. Then he slides his hand beneath the small of my back; scooping me into his arms. I press my cheek to his. "You're extraordinary, exquisite!" I lace my fingers through his thick hair. He holds me close. And the transparency that's threatened since the first moment I met him shatters. "I'm lost too . . ." I whisper.

He takes my face in his hands. "No."

And then he kisses me . . . again and again and again.

"You're not leaving here tonight," he murmurs. "You know this."

He covers my neck with delicate kisses, then the warm curve of my shoulder.

I close my eyes. "Why?"

The camisole slips away.

"Because," his lips are everywhere, "it's what I want."

Jake's on the doorstep, knocking to get in. The sky's black, wind howling. I can't hear his voice over the gale but I know he's calling; pounding his fists against the door.

I try to move but my limbs are made of lead. There's something pressing down on me, a great black weight.

He's calling. The storm's breaking.

And I can't move.

"The water's high!"

I look up.

It's Robbie.

She's sitting on my chest, crushing my rib cage, knitting. Long red yarn twists round her thin fingers, staining them pink.

"It's too high!" She laughs.

Her mouth gapes open; a black hole. She has no teeth.

And suddenly it's not Jake's voice but Alex's. "Mummy! Mummy!"

I try to push her off.

"Mummy!"

My legs won't move.

"Mummy!"

I come to with a start.

"Mummy!"

I jump out of bed. It's cold. I'm naked.

This isn't my room.

"Mummy!" He's crying.

Piotr sits up.

I have no clothes on and not enough hands.

"Alex!" I plead. He can't see me like this.

Piotr swings his legs out, pulls on his jeans. "Stay here," he orders, opening the door.

My heart's galloping, bucking against my ribcage. Where are my knickers? I search for my top, pulling it on. What if he's not all right?

I stumble over my shoes, yank on my trousers . . . I can hear Piotr talking to him, taking him downstairs to the kitchen. "She's going to be back in a minute," he says soothingly. I peer through a crack in the door, watching as he carries him down the stairs. Alex rubs his eyes with his fists; tears on his cheeks.

My chest snaps in two with guilt.

My little boy's been crying, alone in his room for God knows how long.

As soon as they round the corner, I race up to the top floor. I check the alarm clock. It's six-thirty-five in the morning. Throwing on a fresh shirt, I head down to the kitchen.

"Mummy!" Alex runs into my arms. "I woke up and you weren't there!" He clings to me.

Here is my whole world. My entire universe. This little body, pressed against mine.

What was I thinking of? How could I have been so reckless?

"I'm making toast," Piotr says casually. He's standing at the kitchen counter, slicing a loaf of bread.

"No," I say sharply, "I'll make it."

"Evie . . ."

"I'll do it." Scooping Alex up, I sit down in one of the kitchen chairs with him on my lap. "I'll look after him."

"He's not a baby," he sighs.

He doesn't understand; he'll never understand.

"And neither am I. I'm fine on my own!"

"Evie!"

"Please, Piotr, just leave us alone!"

Alex is crying again. Piotr flings down the bread knife and walks out. I'm left holding my son; the smell of burning toast fills the kitchen.

The door slamming upstairs is like the door slamming in my heart.

And I know this feeling.

It's safe. Numb.

I've been here before.

I bury my face in Alex's neck.

And I don't care.

Doris looks up at me, standing in the centre of the room, script in hand. "That was just dreadful!" she confesses, giggling self-consciously.

She's right.

The rest of the group look away, clear their throats; anything not to laugh.

"No." I'm searching for a more constructive way to put it. But her Scotty dog jumper and long chandelier earrings are just a bit distracting. Her legendary bust makes the dog's face into a kind of Elephant Dog, with a head five times the size of its body. I force my eyes back to her face. "It's a difficult speech, Doris. It's all about the character's hidden motivations."

She shakes her head; the earrings rattle like wind chimes. "I just don't understand it! I mean, 'I am a seagull'? What's that all about?"

"Well." There's no simple answer. And today I desperately wish there were. I rub my eyes. "Why do you think you say it?"

"Because I'm crazy," she decides. Nods her head. The earrings chime.

I wrinkle my nose.

She tries again. "I don't know. I suppose I think I am a seagull."

"And what does that mean?" I prompt.

"That I'm crazy?"

I take a deep breath. Chekhov isn't easy to teach, at the best of times. And *Uncle Vanya* would've been better for this lot; closer to their own age range and experience. But I haven't prepared *Vanya*; for a week now, I haven't been able to concentrate on anything more taxing than the back of a cereal box. *The Seagull* seemed a safe bet—something I could do in my sleep. But I hadn't reckoned on Doris Del Angelo's inquisitive enthusiasm.

"What do you think it means?" She throws it back at me.

"Well . . ." I can't really tell her I don't know. I've been looking at this speech for around fourteen years and I've no more idea of what's going on than I did when I first read it. I'm meant to be the expert. So I do what all teachers end up doing on bad days; I dodge the question.

"Doris, I can't tell *you* what *I* think it's about. In order for the associations to have any real power for you as an actress, you have to make your own connections, find your own meaning."

"Oh."

I think she's on to me.

"The important thing is that you ask yourself the questions." I try to round the whole thing up. "And if you can keep the language in the moment, you'll find the scene becomes much more powerful."

Her brow furrows.

Clive sits forward in his chair. His quiff is particularly voluminous this evening. "What does that actually mean?"

Shit. Sometimes I swear they gang up on me.

I look at the floor, like maybe the answer's written between my feet. "What it means," I say slowly, feeling my way blindly into some sort of response, "is that something that's happening right here, right now, between Nina and Konstantin is motivating that line. You're trying to tell him something; explain something to him; something important. And the best way you can put it is, 'I'm a seagull.' You're not zoning out and having a crazy moment; you *may* be crazy but it's all very real to you and you're really trying to actively communicate this idea to him."

She's frustrated. "Yes, but *what* idea?"

I should have called off sick.

"That you're a seagull." I stop.

I start again. "OK. Let's look at the evidence. You've come to Konstantin. And he keeps telling you that he's in love with you; that you're amazing, that he kisses the ground you walk on."

"Yes . . . ?"

"He acts like you haven't changed, but you have. And you want him to know that."

"But to know *what*?"

I look at the sea of expectant faces. The air's thick with dust, warm and heavy. The sound of the room fan whirrs incessantly in the background.

When I speak, my voice is surprisingly hard. "That you're a seagull, Doris. That you're not a beautiful, talented young woman on the verge of a thrilling acting career, in love with a clever, famous man. You've lost your lover. Your child has died. And now you're a second-rate actress in the provinces. You're a seagull. A dead thing. An awkward, shrill bird that someone saw and shot for no better reason than because they could."

The room's gone quiet.

"But you're still stronger than that. Every time you feel like giving in, you pull yourself up again. 'I am a seagull.' And then you say, 'No, that's not it.' You refuse to give in. Even though you've lost everything."

She stares at me. In fact, the whole room's staring at me. I cradle my head in my hands.

What's the point?

"It's the ability to endure." Mr. Hastings drops the words into the silence like a pebble into a still pond.

I lift my head. "Pardon me?"

"She says," he repeats softly, "it's the ability to endure."

A light goes on in Doris's eyes. "Yes, that's true," her voice brims with excitement. " 'The main thing is not the fame, not the glory, not all the things I used to dream of,' " she quotes, " 'it's finding the strength to go on. How to bear your cross and have faith.' "

My chest tightens.

" 'And when I think of my vocation,' " Mr. Hastings adds, finishing the speech, " 'I do not fear life.' "

The room's too hot. I push my chair back. "Let's take a break. Ten minutes, everyone."

236 ~ KATHLEEN TESSARO

And without pausing, I dive into the hall.

"Don't you think that's right?" Doris follows me out, rushing in her high-heeled boots. "She's a real actress now. Isn't she?"

"Yes, that's right." There's a humming in my brain.

"Her suffering's made her stronger."

"Absolutely."

She puts a hand on my arm. "Are you all right?"

"I'm fine," I say, touching her hand. Then I pull away. "I just have to do . . . something."

I walk. The hallways snake like a maze between the classrooms; there are noises, snatches of other classes; stern, confident voices informing eager students. There's a wrenching in my chest. Here's the side door; leading to the alleyway. I push through, into the cool, black night air. Above me, stars blink. I lean with my back against the wall and close my eyes.

And when I think of my vocation, I'm not afraid of life.

"You're not a fucking seagull, Evie."

"Leave me alone, Robbie." I don't want to open my eyes; I'm not willing to engage in this madness again.

"I'm serious, Evie."

"What do you know about it, huh?" I say, looking at her.

She's standing there, in that stupid jumper, hands in her jeans pockets.

I rush on, not waiting for her answer. "You never even bothered to live out your dreams—you foisted them on me to live out instead! Isn't that why you're here? Because I failed you? Well, you needn't bother! I already know that! I don't need you swinging back from the underworld every five minutes to tell me I fucked up!"

"You're unhappy," she says, as if it's some stunning revelation.

I can't control the tears any more. "Of course I'm unhappy!"

"But why? You're in love, aren't you?"

"No, I'm *not*!" I snap vehemently. "I just did something stupid, that's all! Something foolish!" What's the point in explaining to her? "I should've been more careful."

"But that's just it, Evie . . . you're too careful! When did you start being so careful? So frightened? Where's the girl who risked all . . . dared all?"

"That was you, Robbie, not me! Remember?"

"No, it was you," she says firmly. "It was you."

I turn away.

How can I make her understand when I don't even understand it my-self? This ambivalence and then the tidal waves of feeling that shift, with-out any warning, to destroy whole internal landscapes in a heartbeat, leaving me lost? I'm like a kid, struggling to build a tower of blocks only to kick them all over for a thirty-second rush of power and freedom. Only they aren't blocks; it's my life.

"When I let myself go, bad things happen, Robbie."

"What are you so afraid of?"

"I'm afraid of myself!" I wipe the tears away with the back of my hand. "You don't know what I'm capable of!"

"Then tell me!"

"No!" I shake my head. "No. I have to go."

I yank open the door.

But she won't stop. "Come on, Evie! When was the last time you let your guard down? Can you even remember?"

I shouldn't rise to the bait; but instead I swing round, facing her across the narrow alleyway.

"I can tell you exactly when!" I shout bitterly. "Five years ago! June twenty-first, 1996!"

I step inside. The door slams shut.

My heels click fast along the floor.

But now the seed's planted and it grows.

The class continues. I nod my head; make the appropriate gestures and sounds.

But I'm not there.

I've been transported back in time, to that morning five years ago, every detail fresh as yesterday.

If only we could choose which memories we keep and which ones we discard for ever. But instead, the mind clings to events that baffle; watch-ing them, like a movie, over and over. But without the power to choose a different path.

PART THREE

June 21, 1996

I OPEN MY EYES.

The house is quiet.

Lying on my back, I stare at the play of light through the bedroom curtains; golden shapes dance on the carpet. From the garden outside, the perfume of new roses drifts in through the open window. Another perfect summer's day.

I hate mornings.

Reaching over, I pick up the little enamel pill box. The one I bought in the Stratford-upon-Avon gift shop, with a quote etched into the lid: "To sleep—perchance to dream." I shake it, listening to the pleasing rattle of the pills inside. There's quite a collection now; sleeping pills from three different doctors, two in London and one here in Warrickshire. I'll never have to spend my nights alone and awake. Just knowing the promise of eight hours of guaranteed unconsciousness is right here somehow makes everything more bearable.

I put the pill case back on my bedside table and roll over. There's an undertow of hangover pulling at my brain. Nothing a few paracetamol won't cure. Opening night parties are infamous for drunkenness and promiscuity. I got off lightly. Or was it heavier than I remember?

I remember flirting with Anthony Kyd and that young Fiennes kid . . .

then again, who wouldn't flirt with the Fiennes kid? Nothing happened.
I'm almost sure.

Not that it matters.

I'm meant to be in love.

Meant to be.

I close my eyes.

My heart's a cage. Shut tight.

Evan's a lovely man. Handsome. Or so my girlfriends tell me. He's
older, thirty-three; works in the City for Deutsche Bank in human
resources. I met him almost a year ago, filming a corporate training video.
He was soft-spoken with kind eyes, sitting in for the client; making jokes
about the catering and teasing me about the navy wool suit I had to wear.
Solicitous, gentle. Nice.

Maybe too nice.

There's a dark, cold current pulling me down. I spend all day fighting
against it. Pretending I'm good. It takes tremendous energy and
vigilance. But some day soon I'll give up. It's only a matter of time.

There's a packet of cigarettes crumpled on the floor. I don't
remember buying them. I lean over, pick them up, jam one in my mouth
and light it.

Evan finds me fascinating. I don't know why. The less interested I am,
the more devoted he becomes. He wants me to move into his flat in
Madia Vale. I've said I'll think about it. Maybe when the Stratford
season's over. But the truth is, I don't care. Even the sex: I set him these
tasks; once I tried to get him to hit me but he wouldn't . . . I play a part,
watching myself from a distance . . . "Stop!" I say, when he tries to speak.
"Just fuck me." He does. I twist away, shut my eyes and wait to feel
something. Afterwards, he can say what he likes; tell me about how
wonderful it is to be so free . . . I feel trapped. And confused.

Yesterday's paper lies in a heap on the other side of the bed; the
passenger side.

It was five years ago today. June 21.

Evan says he doesn't mind.

He's never really wanted children. "We can always adopt anyway." He
talks like that; like we'll be together for ever.

I inhale hard.

He says he doesn't mind.

Taking a long, deep drag, I stub the rest out in an old coffee mug. That's my last one.

I'm going to be good now.

The season's only just begun. "Now is the winter of our discontent made glorious summer . . ." A two-year contract with the Royal Shakespeare Company, first in Stratford-upon-Avon and then in London. Two whole years of the kind of stability and financial security that most actors can only dream of.

I'm lucky. Lucky that Boyd Alexander was one of the directors; lucky that he remembered me. I'm in three plays this season; *As You Like It, The Rover,* and *Richard III,* which opened last night. They're small roles and I understudy quite a few larger ones but it's a start. I'm lucky.

Lucky, lucky, lucky.

There's that dark undertow again.

Get up. Get out of bed.

Stop thinking and move.

I force my legs out and swing my body upright. That's right: have a pee, brush your teeth, make coffee . . .

Downstairs in the kitchen, I switch on the radio and open the fridge. There's nothing there but coffee, milk and jam. Half a dozen pots of jam. I haven't got much of an appetite. Besides, I can always get something in the staff canteen. Measuring out the coffee into the filter maker, I fill it with water, then wander into the front hallway to pick up the post.

It's a funny place, my little rented cottage; everything a proper large house would have, scaled down. It sits back from the road, at the bottom of a three-acre garden of a much larger, much grander country house called the Old Rectory. The owners built this as a granny flat in the late seventies and now rent it out to performers at the RSC. They obviously don't need the money, it's more a talking point in local conversation; people here have actors the way the rest of the world has pets. "Oh yes, mine's in *The Tempest* and *Lear.* Eats mostly baked beans. Fairly clean— wonderful diction!"

My landlady's a woman called Amanda in her early fifties with short blonde hair. Her children are all grown-up and her husband is always on business trips (I suspect he has another family somewhere). She invites me almost every day to come "up the garden path," as she calls it, and have a glass of wine (or four), even though I'm always in rehearsal or performing. She asks anyway, her voice bright, almost metallic with cheerful desperation.

There's a large brown envelope waiting for me on the doorstep—my post forwarded from London by my flat mate, Kelly. I've rented my room out to a Japanese girl, who's come over for a year to learn English, but I've kept my old address. I tear the envelope open—a catalogue from some clothing company, a voter registration card, a schedule of teaching classes from the Guildhall . . . and another letter from Messrs Strutt and Parker of Mayfair.

Again.

Why doesn't he just leave me alone?

I walk into the kitchen, lean back against the kitchen counter, turning the letter over in my hand. It's expensive, heavy, watermarked paper, signalling the expensive, heavyweight services provided. I should throw it away; that's what I normally do. But this one's more solid, thicker than most. There's something perverse in my mood today (most likely the hangover).

I tear it open.

Dear Ms. Albery,

Please find enclosed a letter, forwarded to you on behalf of our client Mr. Jake Albery.

I hope all is well with you,

Yours truly,
Alfred Albert Manning, Esq.

As promised, another letter waits inside. It's written on hotel stationery, doubtless composed on one of Jake's many sell-out tours. It's embossed "Hotel Del Coronado, San Diego." Maybe he's recording another album; his third. My name, "Evie," is scrawled across the front, underlined emphatically. My stomach lurches at the recognition of his handwriting, followed very quickly by a sense of outrage. He has no right to call me Evie. My friends call me Evie.

I slip my finger underneath the seal and force it open.

There are two closely written pages; the paper's filmy; like tissue paper. "Evie-Ex," it begins quite abruptly.

I don't know why I bother writing to you. All you do is ignore me. You should take the money. You can get a place of your own. I never looked after you. And now I've got the money, so let me do this for you. You can have whatever you like—a flat in Chelsea, in Mayfair, in bloody Eaton Square . . . ? I don't care . . .

The handwriting's sloping and erratic, crowding together, then veering off the page.

We're not finished . . . it's not over . . . you can have whatever you want . . .

I crumple it between my fingers; it's the same as all the other letters . . . the same thing, again and again. Now that he's made it, he thinks he can erase the past.

I throw it in the trash, on top of the cold used coffee grounds, adding Alfred Albert Manning's letter with it.

These things unsettle me. I don't know why I do them.

Reaching over, I pour myself a cup of strong black coffee and try to focus. There's an understudy rehearsal today for *Richard III;* I'm covering Lady Anne. Boyd will be there, so I need to be on form. Should also think about groceries for the weekend; Evan will be coming . . . I rub my eyes. It's such an effort to think about him; for some reason he just won't stick in my mind.

"It's twenty past ten and a beautiful Thursday morning . . . You're listening to 105, Radio Warwick and this is Raven . . . 'Baby Home Wrecker'!"

I reach across, yank the little portable radio out of the wall and throw it in the trash too.

I never saw Jake again.

After I came out of the hospital, I never spoke to him or made contact. He'd moved out before that; Chris made him. For a while he crashed on C.J.'s floor and then he was seen, Hayley said, hanging out near Jasmine's flat in Westbourne Grove . . .

It was a shock, when the magazine came out. Suddenly he was everywhere; the band was signed; almost immediately they were on tour, supporting Guns and Roses in America. That's how it happens; what success looks like.

Like absolutely nothing. Until it hits.

Then there were letters, phone calls . . . I ignored them. After a while they died down.

Then they began to look official.

Divorce is easy, which seems ironic, considering how difficult it is to be married. But all I had to do was sign a few papers and wait.

And then, out of the blue, they started again. They came through his solicitor, some with cheques in them, some just letters. One even had a first class plane ticket to Hong Kong. They always seem to know where I am, what I'm doing. They follow me around the country.

But I don't want anything from him. Ever.

Of course, I'm aware of the women; the "episodes," the cars, the drunken brawls, the court case in Arizona with the sixteen-year-old, the models and the models' sisters . . . but only peripherally.

I stay away from all things Jake. He isn't, although I'm sure it would cut him to hear it, as omnipresent as he'd like to be. Anyway, from what I gather, he's changed. And the music's full of keyboards now; overproduced. Sometimes in a bar or in a store, I can't help but hear it.

The best thing, in fact, is to imagine it never happened; I pull my memory up short, like a dog on a lead, whenever it strays into the past.

My heart is a cage.

There is no key.

Later that afternoon I'm backstage in the dressing room, sharing a cigarette with an older actress, Eloise Kurtz, who's covering for Margaret. The rehearsal's almost over and we're both dead; I've been dead for at least an hour and am now busying myself Sellotaping my good luck cards up on my mirror. Eloise is reading the paper. Most of an actor's life is spent waiting; we've become experts at dragging even the most banal activities out for hours at a time. There's a delivery of flowers from my parents, who are coming to visit next month, and even a telegram from Robbie. "About bloody time!!!" it screams. She's been studying yoga in India; says it's the next big thing. She claims she's mellowed but I doubt it. I'm not very good at keeping in touch with old friends any more; I seem to do better with strangers nowadays. Evan's long-stemmed red roses are elegant, in excellent taste and predictable. He wanted to come last night, but I put him off.

I'll ring him later.

Over the tannoy, Richard's calling for a horse and there's the sound of actors scuffling and shouting, trying to depict a major climactic battle scene, even though there are only three of them on stage.

Eloise folds the paper over. "So, are you going to book a holiday this year?"

David, the stage manager, knocks on the door. He's tall, thin and balding, with thick black-framed glasses and a sharp, witty sense of humour. "Good news and bad news, ladies!" he announces. "Seems Janice ate a bad prawn for lunch. So, mazel tov, Eve! You're our Lady Anne tonight!"

I stare at him.

I've only had two rehearsals and Lady Anne's first entrance is notorious; you have to come on all guns blazing, or the entire scene and the first major set piece of the play falls flat on its face.

Eloise registers my horror with delight. At last, a real drama. "Oh dear! You're about to pop your cherry! I'd best go get you a cup of tea." And she hares out, stopping at every dressing room down the long hallway to deliver the news. Nothing's more delicious to Eloise than a fresh morsel of gossip.

David comes up behind me and rubs my shoulders. "You can do this, darling. It's the second night, after all. There are still press due in and it will give the show a lift. Second nights can be so flat."

I nod, looking blankly at my reflection in the mirror.

I have every intention of conquering the world; I just hadn't intended to do it today.

Boyd comes to visit me at the half hour call.

He sits, watching me put on my makeup.

"Ready?" he asks.

"Ready," I lie, smiling back at him in the mirror.

"I want you to take it up a notch."

"Done," I promise; with my nerves right now, everything will be up quite a few notches.

"And don't let Anthony upstage you," he advises. "He's a shit like that."

I nod. The most important thing is that I should remember all my lines. Next: that they should be in some sort of order.

But I don't want to tell him that.

Improvising in iambic pentameter is an art I haven't yet mastered; it's the Victoria Cross of stage acting. Of course, the only way you learn how to do it is by falling into the abyss. It's already yawning before me; I have visions of opening my mouth and no sound at all coming out. They'll bring down the curtain, refund all the money, take me out to the parking lot and shoot me.

However, I'm surrounded by help. My fellow actors rally round; bring me sandwiches I don't eat, tell me funny stories I can't hear; they're helping me with my makeup and hair; wrapping compliments round me like a protective cocoon.

The wardrobe mistress arrives. Janice's gown is too big for me and they haven't had time to make the understudy costumes. She's pulled something from stock; a heavy black velvet dress with a long train. It weighs a ton. I hold on to the door frame as she laces me into the corset, wedging her knee into my back, pulling tight. Then the wig mistress fixes the veil; yards of sheer silk, tumbling down my back.

"Sold out tonight!" David calls, rushing down the hall.

It doesn't even occur to me to ring Evan. And by the time it does, I'm too terrified to speak.

The house lights go down. Cue the music. And I'm standing in the wings, trying not to vomit.

A spotlight rises stage left and Anthony begins.

"Now is the winter of our discontent
Made glorious summer by this sun of York;
And all the clouds that lour'd upon our house
In the deep bosom of the ocean buried."

Behind me, the pallbearers of Edward's body queue up, having just come out of the greenroom where they watch television and smoke. They're on strict orders not to corpse me tonight.

"Good luck, Evie!"

"Break a fucking leg!"

> "But I, that am not shap'd for sportive tricks,
> Nor made to court an amorous looking-glass;
> I, that am rudely stamped . . ."

Michael, who plays Berkeley, leans forward, peeking out into the audience. "God, what a crew! Look at that old dear in the front row—she's already starting to doze off! And she's got a tash!"

He's trying to get me to laugh. He needn't bother.

"And there's that prick from *The Financial Times* . . . I'll never forgive him. Called my Oberon 'A spineless, energy-sapping non-entity in tights.' Never even bothered to mention my legs!"

I grin in spite of myself.

"Oh my God! Look!" He pulls at Sam, who plays Clarence. "In the middle of the front row in the dress circle!"

"Hey, mind me chains, mate!" Sam looks out. "Fuck! You're right! Gotta go. Good luck, Evie!"

Michael yanks my arm. "Evie! Look! You'll never guess who it is!"

Sam strides on, flanked by two guards. " 'His majesty, Tendering my person's safety, hath appointed this conduct to convey me to the Tower.' "

"Mikey, now's not a good time," I warn. I need to concentrate. What's my first line? " 'Set down, set down your honourable load . . .' "

"It's that guy . . . you know, from that band . . ." he blurts out. "What the hell is he doing here?"

Pushing him aside, I peer through the curtain.

Sure enough, there, sandwiched between two elderly middle-class couples in the front row of the dress circle, is Jake, wearing a suit.

I step back. Every day for five years, I've imagined what this moment would be like. And now, here it is. Tonight of all nights. How could he have known?

And all the fear on the verge of overwhelming me a second ago distils; sharpens into a thin stiletto point.

This is not the night I fail.

David appears; fussing and restless. "Corpse up!" he commands the

250 ∾ KATHLEEN TESSARO

pallbearers. "It's time. Take a deep breath, darling." He looks at me. "Evie? It's time. Did you hear me?"

Reaching up, I pull the long black veil over my face. "I'm ready."

ANNE

Thou wast provoked by thy bloody mind
That never dreamt on aught but butcheries.
Did thou not kill this king?

RICHARD

I grant ye.

ANNE

Dost grant me, hedgehog? Then God grant me too
Thou mayest be damned for that wicked deed!
O! he was gentle, mild, and virtuous!

RICHARD

The fitter for the King of Heaven that hath him.

ANNE

He is in heaven, where thou shalt never come.

RICHARD

Let him thank me, that holp to send him thither;
For he was fitter for that place than earth.

ANNE

And thou unfit for any place, but hell.

RICHARD

Yes, one place else, if you will hear me name it.

ANNE

Some dungeon.

RICHARD

Your bedchamber.

As the curtain comes down on the first half, Anthony grabs me by the waist, kissing me full on the lips; he's sweating and revolting. "If only good old Janice could do *that* every night! I'm telling you, I nearly got an erection, you were so good! Oh, look! I think I'm getting one now!"

I shove him away. "Easy come, easy go." I'm pretending to be less shaken than I am.

He gives my hand a squeeze. "I was really dreading it, second night and all. But you blew me away, kid." His eyes twinkle. "Go on! Spit at me again! I love it when you're mean!"

I take off my crown and step down from the thrones. My legs threaten to buckle underneath me, but David rushes up and I rally, flashing him a smile.

"Well, bugger me! Who would've guessed you were so fierce!" he gushes.

All the way down to the dressing room I parade through congratulations. Even Boyd strides into the middle of the ladies' dressing room, without even a knock on the door, and gives me a kiss.

"Now you've done it!" He's beaming. "You know, Frances Guin from the casting department was sitting next to me." He shakes his head. "Get ready, Evie! That's all I have to say. Get ready!"

A bottle of champagne appears, the girls pop it open, passing round plastic cups.

"Five minutes to curtain up," the stage manager announces over the tannoy, sparking a flurry of last minute preparation.

And amid the chattering and teasing, I slip into the ladies and stand with my back pressed against the cool metal door. No one will ever know what a tremendous act of will that was for me . . . but underneath even all that, Jake's presence thumps away like a heartbeat . . .

What's he doing right now?

Signing autographs? Having a drink?

What does a rock star drink?

Champagne? Scotch?

If it's Jake, it's both.

Something long buried stirs in the pit of my stomach.

So, he's here.

The announcement comes over the tannoy again. "Visitor for Ms. Albery at the stage door."

Michael pops his head into the dressing room. "Come on, Evie! You're coming, aren't you?"

"Sure!" I wave him on. "I'll be there in a minute. Go on without me."

They're all headed for the Dirty Duck across the road. Every time I think I'm alone, someone else pokes their head round the corner, offering to buy me another drink; even people who aren't in this production—other actors who've just heard the news. I should be thrilled. I was a success when failure loomed. But now, as I sit here, wiping the last traces of mascara from my eyes, the sick lurching feeling is back, as if the night weren't over but just beginning.

He's there; waiting for me.

"Will Ms. Albery please ring the stage door."

Releasing my hair from my ponytail, I brush it through. I wonder how he knew I was here? Perhaps that man, Alfred, keeps him posted. No matter. There's nothing he can do to me any more.

I put the hairbrush down neatly on my dressing table and examine myself in the mirror.

I'm not the same. I'm different. The last time he saw me, I was a stupid, awkward kid. Now I'm a real actress; the actress who just walked onto the main stage of the RSC tonight and blew them all away.

Michael comes rushing back in. "Oh, my God! Evie! You'll never guess who—"

"Darling," I interrupt him, "will you do me a favour and chat to him? I don't want him to get bored."

"How do you know him?" He blinks. "Is he—"

"A second cousin," I cut him off. "Do you mind?"

He nods enthusiastically. "My God, but you're a dark horse!" he laughs, before hurrying back upstairs.

Jake will be surrounded, of course. Signing autographs and flirting. They're used to big names at the stage door, actors mostly; Hollywood in town to see their chums. But nothing like Jake.

The phone in the corner of the dressing room rings.

I let it.

Slipping my feet into my sandals, I pick up my handbag and turn out the light. The backstage area is empty; I weave through the dusty hallways, lined with costume rails and props. I press open one of the emergency exits, then slip, unseen, out of the side of the building into the cool night air.

The theatre's surrounded by an elegant park, which borders either side of the River Avon. Walking through the darkness, I can hear the sound of the rushing water and the wind through the trees. Across the road, there are gales of laughter and music coming from the Dirty Duck. At the end of the park, there's an ancient churchyard and a long residential street; one side is darker than the other. I cling to the shadows, walking home. I'm invisible; enjoying my secret adventure to escape without being detected.

Outside the city centre a euphoric sense of freedom overtakes me. A glimmer of triumph; he's just standing there, while call after call's put out for me, surrounded by people, all watching.

Why is it still so sharp, after all this time?

He's got everything he ever dreamt of—fame, sex, money—but he wants forgiveness too. I've groped blindly, numbly, from day to day, struggling; a single angry shard glowing inside me, vibrant and warm.

All I have left is my silence. And as long as I have the power to hurt him, I'll use it. It's the only part of me that feels truly, painfully alive.

But none of that matters; tonight changed everything.

I can breathe now. This is what success feels like—like finally being able to breathe. It's been a long time coming. And I like it.

The fields on either side of me whisper, stars glimmer in the velvet sky above. The corner shop glows in the distance. There's the Old Rectory with its long drive. Home is only a few more yards away. I've made it. The gravel crunches beneath my feet. I reach into my handbag to get my keys.

Suddenly a car swerves into the drive, headlights blinding

I keep moving, eyes front.

A car door slams.

"Evie!"

I jam the keys into the lock. The door swings wide.

Jake throws his arm across it, holds it open. "Evie! For fuck's sake!"

I don't want to look at him; don't want to see him, hear him, touch him.

"Leave me alone." I lean my full weight against the door.

"Five minutes! I just want five minutes." He presses it open.

"I'll call the police!"

He forces his way inside. "Go on! Call them."

It's almost impossible to see. Stumbling in the half-light, I lunge for the phone. He reaches behind me, rips the cord out of the wall.

I'm left holding the receiver.

"All I want to do is talk to you!"

I pitch the phone at him; he ducks and it crashes against the far wall.

"You're mad!" he shouts.

"No, *you're* mad, Jake! Why are you following me? How did you even know I was here?"

He stops a moment, catching his breath. In the dim light, I can make out the same aquiline features, the long, angular limbs, set off in his tailored suit; thick hair tumbling almost to his shoulders.

"Alfred's a fan. You were good, you know—"

"What do you want?" I cut him short.

"Damn it, Evie!" He pounds his fist against the wall in frustration. "Why do you have to make everything so difficult! I just want to . . . to talk to you . . ."

"I don't want to talk! I don't want anything to do with you! No money, no property . . . what you owe me, Jake, money can't buy!" Tears burn my eyes. I won't cry. "Leave. Just leave. It's over."

"No. No, it's not!" He's suddenly lost; displaced, in the middle of the floor, shaking his head; pulling at his hair.

His agitation's distressing. I wish I could cut myself off from him. "Go home, Jake," I say quietly.

But he paces back and forth; a wild animal, trapped.

"So, this guy you're seeing? Is he nice? I'll bet he's a real nice guy, Evie!"

I don't know how he knows about Evan, but it unnerves me. "Fuck you!" I step past him, up the stairs.

He grabs my arm. "You and I are alike—we understand each other."

"I'd rather die than be like you!" I wrench my arm away.

"Why? Look at me!" He catches me about the waist. "Look at me! I've changed!"

I struggle to free myself. He falls, pulling us both halfway down the steps. "I'm clean!" He grabs my hands. "I've been clean for three months, Evie!"

"So what? What's that got to do with me?" I try to twist my hands away but he holds them tight. "You expect me to believe you?"

He pulls me closer. "You have to believe me!" I can smell the alcohol on his breath.

"Why?"

"It makes all the difference!" He's staring at me; his eyes wild and dark. "Things would be different now."

"What are you talking about?" A thin, icy strand of terror builds inside me. He's high or mad or both. "Get away from me!" I push him off, running back up the stairs.

He follows me, moving slower now. "We've got money, we won't be poor, living in shit, I can do it right this time . . ." He tries to touch me. "Do you see?"

"Get away from me!" My heart's tearing in two. "Look at you! Do you think you can just come here in your . . . your fucking Armani suit!"

"You don't like it?" He pulls off his jacket, throws it on the ground. "You don't like this suit? Here!" He tears off his shirt and turns around.

For a moment, I can't place what I'm looking at and then, suddenly, I can't even breathe.

Moonlight spills across his bare torso and there, tattooed onto his shoulder blades, in incredible, painstaking detail, is a pair of enormous black wings. They spread ominously, suspended in full flight, reaching all the way down to his waist. Along his arms there are more designs—all intertwined with the same name, again and again . . . Raven, raven, raven . . .

"You're the only thing I can feel . . ." he's speaking softly, moving closer, "the only thing I've ever really felt!"

"Oh, don't, don't!" My head's bursting.

"I was so in love with you, I used to stare, watching you while you slept!"

"You're lying!" I'm crying; it's unbearable. "Stop it!" I strike his face as hard as I can. The palm of my hand stings but he doesn't even flinch.

I hit him again, harder.

And again.

He grabs my wrist. "Go on, tell me how you love your nice boyfriend!" he whispers.

And then he pulls me to him, forcing his mouth over mine.

I beat on him with my fists but he holds me tighter. I bite his lip but he kisses harder; the taste of warm blood fills my mouth.

"Say you don't love me!" he demands.

"I hate you!" I spit the words out at him. "I hate you more than anyone I've ever known!"

"I don't care! Tell me you don't love me."

"You've ruined my life!" I'm flooded by him; dangerous, intoxicated.

"And you've ruined mine." He presses me harder against the wall. "I have nothing, feel nothing!"

"Leave me alone!" I collapse my head against his chest. Something in me breaks; brittle and slender, like a dry twig. His skin's warm, smooth, smelling of tuberose and sweat . . . almost imperceptibly, I raise my chin towards his lips.

He lifts me up, carrying me into the next room. "Never."

He strokes my face. "You're so beautiful."

I lie very still; every bit of me aches.

Somewhere, in the thick, dark night, a nightingale sings.

"Do you remember? How we danced? With the old people."

I close my eyes; a tear falls down my cheek.

He curls himself around me.

I'm floating, somewhere far above my body . . .

He presses himself closer; his arms are covered in track marks. "I'll make it up to you. You're the only thing I ever loved. We can go back."

I'm drowning, saturated with self-loathing and disgust; the water's far above my head.

I force myself to sit up.

"I despise you," I whisper, watching his face change. "And I'll never forgive you."

I stumble into the bathroom, lock the door and crouch, naked, until I hear him leave.

The car engine roars to life and the brakes screech.

He's gone.

I open the door. It's still dark.

And lying on the bed, curtains drawn against the dawn, I'm sobbing; inhaling the smell of him that's soaked, like perfume, into the pillows, the sheets and me.

It's late afternoon. I'm standing in the queue at the corner shop, buying a pint of milk and some aspirin. The man in front of me is buying a paper. There's a picture on the cover.

A black car, ploughed off the road, door open. A dark haired man, pale, lips tinged blue, head lolled back against the driver's seat.

ROCK STAR SUICIDE BID the headline reads.

My hand moves in slow motion. I pick up a copy.

The man behind the counter's speaking to me.

I hand him a fiver and walk.

He calls after me. I keep on walking.

As soon as I close the front door, my legs give way.

I tear the paper open. Words float in front of my eyes: "car found in a ditch near Coventry . . . overdose . . . prescription sedatives . . . possible brain and liver damage . . . stable condition . . . performance of the RSC . . . suicide note . . ."

Another photo: Jake's hand, clutching a small piece of paper.

And then the piece of paper, smoothed out, a single line, scrawled in Jake's handwriting.

"Where are we now?" it says.

*I*T'S LATE.

    I walk silently up the stairs.

    Robbie's words play on a loop tape in my head. "What are you so afraid of, Evie?"

I pause on the landing. Allyson's gone now; moonlight illuminates the barren walls of her old room. The empty wardrobe, whose doors swing open, invite someone new to fill them. I pass Piotr's door, closed. I lower my head anyway, as if he might sense me, passing outside. He leaves early in the morning, practices at the Royal Academy, comes in late.

He's avoiding me.

And I've stayed out of his way.

It's been almost two weeks now.

Climbing up to my bedroom, I take off my coat and turn on my bed-side lamp. There's a chest at the bottom of my bed. And, opening the lid, I take out a battered blue box file.

I haven't done this in a long time.

I sit on the bed and open the lid. It's just an ordinary box file—from Ryman's—filled with old photos, papers, letters . . . I spot the faded trademark pink of *The Financial Times*. It's worn and delicate; the pages brittle with age.

I unfold it carefully.

Filling in for an indisposed Janice Waites, Eve Albery proved a fero-
cious, intensely sexually charged Lady Anne, matching Anthony Kyd's
sybarite Richard at every turn of their first scene, hurling the verse with
an assurance uncommon in such a young actress. The emptiness of
Lady Anne's grief in Albery's capable hands is transmuted at lightning
speed to something far more potent and dangerous, at times overtaking
the character itself; there's a powerful moment at the end of that scene,
when she stands, baffled, an uncomprehending victim of her own
strength of feeling. I'm certain that we'll be seeing a great deal more
from her in future.

There were other reviews, the *Telegraph* and the ever popular *Warwick
Bear,* but this one was the best; the one that haunted me. Now, to my surprise, I feel strangely detached.

I riffle through the contents of the box: Alex's birth certificate, a pair of
tiny white knitted baby socks, an old passport, postcards, divorce papers . . .

And a letter, sealed and addressed to Jake, care of Messrs Strutt and
Parker.

It's not very long; I know it by heart.

Dear Jake,

Your son, Alexander, was born on April 14, 1997. He is a healthy, un-
commonly beautiful little boy.

I only thought that you should know.

Yours,

Evie

Of course, the envelope is yellowed now; the stamp out of date.

And across the address, someone has written "Return to Sender."

It came back with a brief note from Alfred Albert Manning, informing
me that Messrs Strutt and Parker were no longer employed to handle Mr.
Albery's affairs. But by that time, there was very little left to manage. The
band had dissolved; the third album abandoned, the tour cancelled; houses
and cars seized by the Inland Revenue.

And Jake had disappeared, in the way that only the famous can after
something like that. There were rumours of a celebrity rehab in Antigua; a
house in Geneva . . .

Alex sighs in his sleep, turning over in the next room. I listen as he settles again.

It was incredible that he survived at all; that's what the papers said.

It was only later, days later, that I realized the pill box was missing.

No one knew he'd been to see me. To anyone else, it appeared as if
he'd waited at the stage door in vain.

I tried contacting him, but the hospital was swarming with reporters
and paparazzi. Once I knew he would recover, I realised, to my shame,
that I didn't know what to say.

Then the unthinkable happened; the impossible.

I was pregnant.

I'd gone to the company GP complaining of flu symptoms. It never
occurred to me she'd test for it. But she just smiled and said, "You're having a baby," as if it were the easiest, most natural thing in the world.

"That's not possible," I said.

She looked at me sideways. "You have had sex, haven't you?"

I stared at her, stunned. I'd broken up with Evan. The only man I'd
slept with was Jake.

After I left her office, I bought as many home pregnancy tests as I
could afford; lining them up, one after the other on the bathroom windowsill, terrified that even one of them might reveal she was wrong. But
they didn't. And as two months grew into three and then four, the cage in
my heart creaked open again.

There was never any question about what to do.

There's something else at the bottom of the box. I pull it out from beneath the pile of papers; a stack of loosely bound pages, curling at the edges,
covered in slightly off centre typeface. It's the old script, from the pub theatre days. *Innocents in the Underworld: A Love Story.*

I never finished it.

Maybe it wasn't a love story after all.

What kind of love tears people apart the way we did?

Yet has the power to create the most unfathomable passion of all?

PART FOUR

December 1997

*I*T'S A WET DECEMBER MORNING. The black cab turns into the narrow street in Fulham; the windshield wipers flick back and forth, back and forth. Outside, rows and rows of identical little houses pass by. Finally he pulls up in front of one with a bright red door. "Here we are," he says. "Number fourteen."

I hand him the ten-pound note I've been clutching ever since I got in, back at Euston Station.

It's raining harder now. I pull my coat tight but it doesn't fit any more. I can't get it round the growing bump. I open the cab door, struggling to lift my case.

"Leave that, luv." He quickly gets out. One of the few pleasures of being noticeably pregnant is the sudden heroism of strangers. He lifts the case easily, gallantly, getting drenched in the process, while I waddle up the front path after him.

I ring the bell and there's the sound of dogs barking; scrambling; their little doggy toenails clicking against the wooden floor inside.

"Quiet! Heel!"

They pay no heed, barking louder as she descends the steps.

"All right, then?" The cabbie nods hopefully.

"Yes, thank you. You've been so kind," I say. He runs back, ducks into his cab. And I watch as it trundles down the street.

The door opens.

"Come in! Oh, Evie! Yes, you are getting big, aren't you?"

I smile. In many ways Gwen looks exactly the same as when I first met her, all those years ago, in the basement offices of the Actors Drama Workshop Academy. She has the same sharp bob, only greyer now; the same quick smile and intelligent, animated face; the same fondness for long, slightly bobbly wool cardigans and layers of chain necklaces strung round her neck.

"Here, let me help you." She drags the case inside; it's full of clothes I can't even squeeze into but that I had to bring away from Stratford anyway. My Japanese lodger has several more months to go before I can move back into my room. And now I'm too big, too pregnant to continue my contract with the RSC. I found myself suddenly out of both a job and a home. It was Boyd who suggested I contact Gwen. Apparently they're looking for an extra pair of hands to man the office at the academy. He also urged me to apply for the Speech and Drama Teaching Course at the Guildhall to qualify as an acting coach. He's become my dearest ally.

"I think this is so exciting." Gwen pushes a scraggly looking terrier away with her foot. "So nice for me to have company. Down, Mordrid! Get down!"

Mordrid, a drooly little pug with a black, squashed face, is doing his best to climb up my leg. I pat his head warily.

"Just give them a shove," she instructs. "They're both quite old and a bit deaf. This is Parsifal." She indicates the terrier, smiling wistfully. "My son was an enormous fan of *The Once and Future King*. Shall I make us a cup of tea? Let's go into the front room."

I follow her through the dark red hallway, lined with piles of books on makeshift bookshelves. The front room's painted an amazing bottle green; walls covered in paintings and sketches, their colours mirrored in the spines of still more books stacked heavily on to the bookcases on each side of the fireplace.

A pair of ancient red velvet sofas sit opposite one another, lined with faded throws, and there's a battered upright piano against one wall, covered in sheet music; mostly musical theatre scores. Small china trinkets are massed on the mantelpiece in no particular order. It's like a house in a Victorian play; overflowing with life, busy with knowledge and experience.

Even the dogs lolling about on the oriental carpet are engaged in battles of good versus evil.

I'm going to like it here; I'm safe.

I settle back into one of the red velvet settees and Gwen goes to put the kettle on. Almost immediately I have to pee; another one of the joys of pregnancy.

As I waddle up to the first-floor landing, I take a peek inside what will be my room for the next few months. It used to be Gwen's son's room years ago, before he headed off to Cambridge and then began filming all over the world as a nature photographer. It's easy to see it's a boy's room. There are clumps of blue tack on the wall where surely posters of Madonna and Pamela Anderson once hung, stacks of old issues of *Viz* and *Private Eye,* and the slightly musty smell of boy, which is really just the absence of any perfumed beauty products. Gwen has made up the bed for me with pretty pale pastel bed linen, underneath the framed photograph of a red Lamborghini Countach. I feel comfortable and welcome; part of a family. I'll be piling my clothes into drawers that once held mismatched sports socks and hidden copies of *Playboy*.

When I return, Gwen's lit a fire and laid out "elevenses"—with a proper teapot, china cups and an assortment of biscuits on a plate. None of the china matches; most of it's seen better days, but it's all extraordinary and at one time would have been quite valuable.

She pours me a cup. "So, here we are." She smiles and I sense a kind of sadness floating underneath the surface. "I hope you'll be all right," she adds quietly.

"I took the liberty of having a poke around when I went to the loo," I confide. "It all looks so lovely; I really can't thank you enough."

She holds her tea, cradling the warm curve of the cup in the palm of her hand. "I didn't mean that. I'm pleased, of course, but I was thinking of you . . ." She pauses. "George's father and I were divorced when he was three. It's not easy, Evie. At least, it wasn't easy then, and I suspect not a lot has changed."

We sit a moment and I stare into the fire. Parsifal rolls onto his back, sighing with contentment at the pleasure of having his tummy warmed by the flames.

"You see, Gwen . . ." I stop.

She takes a sip of her tea, waiting.

"The timing could've been better," I admit. "But I never thought I'd get pregnant; in fact, I was told I'd never have children at all. So something amazing has happened." That's all she really needs to know. "Something miraculous and frightening and terribly, terribly inconvenient," I add.

She smiles again.

"I'm so grateful that you're helping me. My parents want me to live in Ohio. But . . . I don't know, I just can't see myself going back. After everything, London has become my home—the place where all my dreams are."

"And the father?" she asks, gently. "Will he help?"

I focus on the grey sheets of rain. "We're not in contact."

She nods silently; the drain spout taps out a rhythm, over and over.

"Of course," she says after a while, "all that pales in comparison to working with Simon day after day!"

She passes me the biscuit plate. I appropriate a shortbread finger.

"Still . . . what's the word? Challenging?" I ask.

She sighs. "Some characters are too big for any stage. I think you'll like the new office—once we've sorted it all out. It will be so nice to have you around. The studios are really quite wonderful. And Boyd will be taking a few master classes next term."

I smile wryly. How quickly things change: one minute I'm an actress, the next I'm a pregnant secretary, sorting through papers and answering phones for young American students with dreams of taking over the world. God has quite a sense of humour.

There's a twinge in my lower back. I stand up, walking over to the mantelpiece, to examine the various objects crowded upon it. There are tiny figurines, more teacups and saucers, photographs in silver frames . . . and a strange wooden plaque on which the slogan *This Too Shall Pass* is carved.

I hold it up, looking across to Gwen. "What's this?"

"Yes, it is ugly," she concedes. We both laugh at her frankness.

"So what's it doing here, among all these lovely things?"

"I have a particular fondness for it." She drains her cup of tea. "I had a cousin, Ralph; he was extraordinarily bright—a really handsome chap; women adored him. And so funny! He used to drink," she continues. "You know, the way some people do; as if it's a profession. After a while he couldn't hold down a job. My aunt sent him to a place, some institution to dry out. They had a wood shop, which was ironic; Ralph was so clumsy he could barely slice a piece of bread. I visited him shortly after my divorce and he gave it to me. That was years ago." She feeds Mordrid a Jammy Dodger. "It was his way of letting me know that everything would be all right."

I turn it round in my hands; it's a rough, unfinished thing. I run my fingers over the words: *This Too Shall Pass.* It seems such a forlorn sentiment.

"How is he now?"

She looks up at me. "Now? Oh, I'm afraid he's dead. People like that don't often see old age." She stands, brushing the dog hair and biscuit crumbs off her skirt. "But it was so sweet of him to think of me. And of course he was right; nothing does stay the same. Now, shall I help you unpack? I'll just take this into the kitchen or the dogs will eat everything."

She picks up the tea tray and heads down the hallway. I place the little plaque back between the delicate figurines and family photos.

Later that afternoon, after I'm unpacked and settled, I return to my room to have a lie down. There, on top of the dresser, is the funny little wooden plaque. Gwen must've put it there, identifying some layer of significance I cannot see.

But as I lie on my bed, I'm haunted by an image of a handsome man with clumsy hands, working with great concentration, as if something so simple could redeem him.

The Actors Drama Workshop Academy on Bayswater Road looks out over Hyde Park. It spreads over the first two floors of a massive Georgian town house. The lower floor is divided into two large acting studios and a small rehearsal room with offices on the ground floor.

Gwen, a receptionist named Amber (a young singer, with thick red hair and a passion for R & B) and I work in one office. Simon shares his with the accountant, Alan, twice a week. It's perhaps a little cruel on Alan, who dashes out at lunchtime, pale and shell-shocked, heading for the nearest pub, but as he's able to recover for the remaining five days, we all feel it's justified.

The students are gearing up for their end of term showings. They swarm about, slouching in hallways, drinking takeaway coffees from Carlo's, the expensive American coffee chain, which opened around the corner a few months ago. They seem impossibly young and at the same time disarmingly confident, strutting about London with ease, on a constant whirl of theatre outings and regular trips to nightclubs. There are so many more of them than in my day; each term hosts at least fifty students and, accordingly, there are fifty instant Polaroids tacked up on the bulletin board. To them, I'm just a fat, slow-moving adult. Very few of them even know my name.

I spend most of my day unpacking boxes of files, sifting through which ones should be transferred to computer disks and which stored in the archives (a grand way of saying put back into boxes, labelled and shoved into a closet).

In the evenings, I'm studying to teach speech and drama at the Guildhall and occasionally putting pen to paper when I'm not too exhausted. Life has compacted into a neat little rut of work, study and home to the house in Fulham.

It's twenty past five on a Tuesday afternoon in February and the sun's setting. Gwen and Amber are finishing up for the day. I'm putting in some extra time, working on a scene for a master class; Boyd's encouraged me to write something that we can workshop with the students. I'm taking the classic Shakespearean convention of a young woman dressed as a man and experimenting, putting it into modern-day settings, including an exclusive gentlemen's tailor in Savile Row. Whole hours disappear before I know it, sitting in front of the computer, but no one else in the office seems to mind.

Fiona Richards, the well-known stage actress who's teaching the general acting class, strides in, looking for an audience. She's attractive in an eager, overly animated kind of way, with her large brown eyes, short dark hair and lean boyish figure. She takes regular tea breaks while class is still in progress, coming in to regale us with stories of what new tortures she's devised for her students on little more than a whim. Grabbing a mug from the shelf, she leans against a filing cabinet. "I've got them all being cows!" she announces. "It's just *too* funny!"

Amber looks at her in shock. "But that's horrible!"

She waves her away. "Nonsense! Good for their voices! Anyway, they're all mooing in iambic pentameter—the prologue from *Romeo and Juliet*." She can barely contain herself. "It's hysterical! You have to see them. 'Moo mouses most malike in Mignity'!"

I catch Gwen's eye and smile.

"I'll make them be babies now! Anyone want to watch?" And, filling her mug with hot water, she heads back to her mooing charges.

Amber turns to us. "She's mean! You shouldn't let her."

But Gwen just shrugs her shoulders. "She knows what she's doing. Maybe she's a little power crazy. But they all adore her."

Simon veers in, his wild white hair dancing, weightless, round his head. "Gwen! I have an idea! We must open another school in America! Using famous Hollywood actors as teachers! It will be huge! Follow me!" He zips backs into his office.

Gwen continues to flick through her Rolodex. "Here we go. Another plan to rule the world," she sighs, "and it's only Tuesday."

"Gwen!" he barks. "Gwen, this is important! We're running out of time!"

She rises reluctantly, pulling herself away from her desk. "Now he's going to have me here all night."

Amber stands up too. "Tea or coffee?" she offers, switching on the answer phone for the evening.

"Oh, tea!" Gwen smiles gratefully. "I can't face Simon without at least another cup of tea! Evie, do you think you could ring the Peacock Theatre and confirm the use of their stage for the twenty-seventh and twenty-eighth?"

"Gwen! Gwen!" He's sitting in his empty office, shouting. "Get me Dustin Hoffman's telephone number!"

"Of course," I say. "Leave it to me."

Lowering myself into her chair, I search through her Rolodex for the number while Amber makes two cups of tea for Simon and Gwen. She slips on her coat and picks up her handbag.

"Night, Evie. See you tomorrow."

"Good night," I say, watching as she takes the tea into the next room.

These are the moments I love, these rare quiet intervals when there are people around me, and yet I'm alone.

In the corner, the fax machine begins spewing pages.

I locate the number I'm looking for and leave a message, making a note of it for Gwen, which I leave on her desk. Then I wash up the used coffee mugs and tidy the kitchen before collecting the fax pages and stapling them together. They're invariably either for Simon, or Gwen, or occasionally a long letter for a student from an overwrought parent concerned about the rapid drain of money from their account.

I leaf through them. It's my name on the front.

Sitting down, I look through the pages. It's from Robbie, of all people; handwritten in what appears to be a stream of consciousness style.

```
EVIE!
What's all this I hear about you leaving the
RSC?!!! Boyd tells me you're studying to be a
teacher!!!! WHY!!!!
```

My heart leaps into my throat. She's the last person I expect to hear from; the last person who would approve of what I'm doing. She dives headlong into a mile a minute account of her own life.

```
I'm thinking of going back to school, there are so
many things I have yet to do, I find working in the
Chinese herbalists a REAL DRAIN . . . they don't
understand me, don't get creative nature, actually
they fired me anyway—said I couldn't make change but
that's bullshit. I've just been a little . . . I
don't know . . . lately. So I'm taking some life
drawing classes . . . actually, I'm the model . . .
my boyfriend . . . did I tell you I had a
boyfriend? I think he's some sort of underworld
drug baron . . . terribly rich, never says two
words, drives around in a black Mercedes with a
driver and two huge security guards . . . has a
divine cock, makes the Empire State look small . . .
I think he's in love with me . . . anyway, hates
that I pose naked for other men . . . very
possessive . . . finding it hard to concentrate . . .
Evie . . . am feeling a bit down . . . like there
```

are too many things all happening at the same
time . . . do you understand? I thought you
might . . . you were always such a good friend
to me . . . think you really got me . . . do you
remember the House of Chekhov? We will go to
Moscow! We will!
    So anyway . . .

There are three more pages, crammed with writing.

She's worse.

Much worse.

I'm filled with dread. I want to tear the pages up; I wish I'd never seen them.

Fiona strolls back in, chucks her mug in the sink without washing it up. "They're just angels! Rolling around on their backs, sucking their thumbs! I just adore how malleable they are!" She stops. "Are you all right?"

I fold the pages over, pushing them into my handbag. "You shouldn't do that," I say quietly.

She looks at me in amazement; that kind of I'm-playing-to-the-back-row-of-the-Olivier amazement actors specialize in. "What? What are you talking about?"

"They came here to learn how to act." I meet her eye.

"And I'm teaching them. If you can't take a little humiliation, then this isn't the job for you!" Her voice betrays her bitterness. "Besides, most of them will never make it anyway," she adds, sauntering over to the door.

I hate the way she speaks about them; as if they were disposable.

"But they don't know that! And neither do you!"

She narrows her eyes. "I think I do. I've been around long enough, Evie, to recognize real talent when I see it. And anyway, it takes more than that. You have to want it"—her gaze bores into me—"more than anything else in the world. The world's full of would-bes, could-bes, might-bes . . . how many people do you know who'll ever be anything more than that?" And she arches an eyebrow at me, before making her exit.

I shouldn't have done that; shouldn't have spoken to her at all. She's bound to make it into a whole drama and tell Simon . . . I run my hands over my eyes.

A Chinese herbalist . . . a receptionist . . . a teacher . . . what happened to our dreams?

Fuck it.

I press Delete. The scene I've been working on vanishes into oblivion. Fuck all of it.

Fiona's right: the world's full of ambitious failures, clinging to their delusions. Time to live in the real world. Opening my handbag, I take Robbie's letter out again.

Why doesn't she just take her goddamned pills? What am I supposed to do to help her, a thousand miles away?

I tear it into several small pieces and throw it away.

Two days later, Robbie leaves a message on the answering machine at work. "Evie, I was just wondering if you could give me a ring . . . I'm . . . do you think you could ring me?" Her voice is strange. But, typically, she doesn't leave a number.

I tell myself I'll call Boyd to see if he has an up-to-date number.

I tell myself I will, but then I don't.

I don't know what to say to her; what to say for myself. And I can't bear to hear her sounding so crazy. I'll call her later, when things are different. We'll have a long chat, laugh about old times.

Besides, it's not as if either of us is going anywhere.

I'm coming back from the post office, walking along the corridor. The students are having their final run at the Peacock Theatre; the building's almost empty.

My soft-soled shoes make almost no sound, padding slowly along.

I round the corner.

Then stop.

A tall figure moves from the shadows into the light.

It's Boyd.

He looks old, lost.

"There's been an accident, Evie. In New York."

This is how it begins.

I'm nine and a half months pregnant and throwing up into the sink one morning when suddenly, I'm standing in a puddle; a lake of warm clear water.

Water, I think to myself.

How odd. Where did it all come from?

Yes, of course!

My waters have broken.

Gwen's left for work already; she's meeting students at the airport. I'm alone in the house. So I ring a minicab service—the one that keeps shoving their cards through the front door—then heave myself back upstairs.

I struggle to pull on my clothes. There are only two outfits I wear now, alternating them day after day—the blue pregnant pants with the blue pregnant top and the black pregnant pants with the black pregnant top. Today, the most important of all pregnant days, it's the black outfit.

And I feel frightened, thrilled, unusual, as I toss my toothbrush into the bag, The Hospital Bag, that's been standing by my bedroom door, packed and ready to go, for over three months—full of carefully ironed baby clothes and extra large white cotton nightgowns for me and a pair of slippers I've been saving for The Hospital.

Is there anything else? Have I forgotten something?

The cab's on its way and my waters have broken.

It's happening.

I throw in a book (as if I'll ever read again). And wrestle on my coat—the one that just fits over the arms but only just, gaping open ridiculously. Then I go downstairs, lock the door and wait on the front steps in the freezing morning air.

The cab pulls up and the man looks me up and down.

"Where are we going?" he asks suspiciously.

"Chelsea and Westminster Hospital, please," I say, smiling, beaming. And then I'm suddenly overcome by another wave of nausea. I purse my lips and concentrate.

This does nothing to convince the cab driver, who can see me fighting off the urge to be sick. He stands in front of the car door, reluctant to let me in. "This isn't an ambulance," he informs me halfheartedly; unsure that if he fights with me now, I might really, *really* go into labour.

I need to open my mouth. I need to respond convincingly, to seem friendly, lighthearted, not quite as desperate as I am, despite the fact that I'm carrying a suitcase, clutching my lower back and fighting the overwhelming desire to vomit, right here in the middle of the street, with every fibre of my being.

But all I can do is moan and flinch.

This isn't good.

The driver instinctively backs away from me, like I'm going to explode.

The estate agent across the street spots me. He's the one who, despite having a warm, cosy office all his own, seems to find it necessary to spend most of his days pacing up and down the sidewalk, shouting at the top of his lungs into his mobile phone.

"Hey!" he stops in mid-shouted conversation. "Are you OK?"

I nod my head. "I . . . I need to go to the hospital," I gasp. (I don't care if I'm in labour; I absolutely will not throw up in the street.)

The cab driver holds his hands up. "I'm not an ambulance service, man. I'm not taking responsibility for *that!*"

(It's the destiny of pregnant women to lose their identities; we're just pods.)

The shouting estate agent's outraged. "I'll have to call you back." He clicks his phone shut. "You ignorant cunt!" he shouts at the cab driver, who I'm certain is never going to take me to the hospital now (here comes another wave; I feel faint, clutching the side of the car to regain my balance). "Can't you see she needs to get to the hospital! She's in labour, you dumb fuck!"

This isn't what the cabbie wants to hear. He's shaking his head. Climbing back in the front seat. Shutting the door. "You sort it. It's not my business."

"Please!" I can feel the warm trickle of water down my right leg. But he's off. The estate agent shouts, running after him down the street and I start to gag against my will.

This too shall pass, I tell myself. Somehow, some way, I'll get there. This too shall pass.

It's the shouting estate agent who drives me, like a scene from some movie, strapped into the front seat of his Range Rover and sitting on a black plastic bag, just in case. He calls ahead and shouts at the nurses, so that as soon as he drives up, honking his horn in front of Accident and Emergency, one appears with a wheelchair to take me in.

Things are moving faster now.

Fluorescent lights flash above my head as they push me down the hall. Then I'm in a room, the nurse is helping me into a green paper gown. I throw up into the sink, holding the side of the bowl, and behind me the room's filling. Off comes the giant underwear, apart go my legs, there are an army of faces peering at me, fat and immobile. I'm a tortoise turned on its back. I'm public property. My back's snapping in two. My hands shake and the waves are coming. They're strapping the monitors on. And this too shall pass, I tell myself. Somehow, some way, this too shall pass.

It hurts. It tears. I don't know the nurse who's holding my hand but I'm breaking hers; crushing it. Breathe, she tells me. Just breathe. And I want to slap her into next Tuesday. I hate her. I hate this. It hurts, it hurts, it HURTS! This . . . this too shall . . . fuck!!!! This too shall . . . damn it . . . pass!

Then the monitor's blinking—the numbers shooting up, 154, 160, 172, up and up they go.

"The baby's in distress," they say. "Don't push. Stop pushing," the midwife tells me but I can't . . . I can't stop pushing . . . I have to, *have* to get it out!

"Stop," she tells me again, "you have to stop!" But she doesn't understand; she doesn't know that I'm breaking, that I'll die if I don't get this out, and I can't, absolutely can't stop pushing.

The green numbers are flashing. They're prodding me, pulling me, injecting something into my leg and all the time I'm shouting, I want IT OUT! I really want it out! Oh God! Make this pass, make this . . . and they're pushing me, I'm in an operating theatre, a gas mask over my face, the surgeon's staring at me, everyone's moving very quickly and this too shall . . . this too shall . . . this too . . .

I open my eyes.

I feel nothing. Nothing but the constant undertow of sleep pulling me down.

I was doing something. In the middle of something. Something important.

My lids fall shut again. I force them open.

What was it?

And suddenly I'm not alone.

There's someone else in the room; a pink little body curled up like a kidney bean, lying in a clear plastic cot by the side of my bed. He's sleeping, his arms pressed to his chest; and the nurse, the one whose hand I crushed, smiles. Silently, she lifts him and hands him to me.

He's here in my arms, warm, safe, alive. The pain's gone. There's only him. And he's perfect; he's the ceiling of the Sistine Chapel, the swell of a Verdi chorus, the Taj Mahal and the Grand Canyon all rolled into one.

A soft little hand reaches out and wraps its tiny fingers round mine.

I wonder if Robbie can see us now.

And this too . . .

This too shall pass.

> *"O swallow, swallow*
> Le Prince d'Aquitaine a la tour aboile
> These fragments I have shored against my ruins
> Why then Ile fit you. Hieronymo's mad againe.
> Datta. Dayadhvam. Damyata.
>   Shantih   shantih   shantih"

Mr. Hastings looks up.

His forehead's damp with perspiration. He's staring at me; a question in his eyes. For the first time in months I've let him have free rein—not stopped him once. And now he seems distressed; unnerved by the unexpected freedom.

Is it me, or has he skipped a few pages? It didn't feel quite so long this week or so strident. Could it be that Mr. Hastings is mellowing?

The rest of the group are in a stupor, which is to be expected.

I smile back at him, which only seems to disturb him more.

"Well?" he asks irritably.

"Well," I answer, crossing my legs. "So it goes, eh?"

He blinks at me, appalled.

I'm being flippant. I try again.

"Mr. Hastings . . . may I call you Gerald?"

"Yes, yes." He waves his hand impatiently.

"Gerald, why is it that you're so fond of this poem?"

He frowns.

I sense his indignation building. I head him off at the pass.

"What I mean is, what is it that you like about it so much? What appeals to you . . . from a personal point of view?"

And he scowls again, only more intensely this time.

By now the rest of the group have joined us again in mind as well as body. Clive straightens in his chair, Brian loosens his tie, Mrs. Patel can't suppress a yawn. Doris takes a small wooden fan from her handbag, which she waves lightly, seductively, like some character from a Restoration drama, in front of her bosom, a gesture which strikes me to be of almost perverse modesty.

But Mr. Hastings is silent.

There's the slightly tinny sound of water rushing through unseen pipes.

"Well, it's long," he ventures after a while.

Clive smirks.

"And you like that?" I prompt, ignoring Clive.

Mr. Hastings straightens defensively. "When you're my age, people don't often listen to what you're saying. And then, of course, he has so much to say, Eliot. And he says it in these wonderful ways. There are quotes and references; a whole secret language."

I nod.

"And I like," he continues, "that Eliot was a nobody; a bank clerk. A genius without question," he adds quickly, "but no one knew for the longest time. They just thought he was . . . ordinary."

"But he wasn't," Doris affirms, smiling graciously.

And for a moment, Mr. Hastings is distracted.

I lean back in my chair, contemplating the life of T. S. Eliot, hidden genius, poet, playwright and scholar, showing up for work in his grey flannel suit, hands moving mechanically through piles of paperwork while his brain was beset with images of heroes, hot gammon steak and Hindu prayers; an inner world full of the secret longings of ordinary men, if, indeed, ordinary men long to be heroes, eat gammon steak and utter Hindu prayers. Apparently they do.

"But most of all," Mr. Hastings folds the worn edition closed on his lap, "it's sad."

Clive looks up.

Doris stops fanning.

"My father liked this poem. I don't think he understood it. But he wanted to be the kind of man who did."

His eyes meet mine; they have a certain fierceness I've grown quite fond of.

Suddenly a smile spreads over his features. "I've always endeavoured to be the kind of man who reads Eliot."

"And what kind of man is that?" I ask.

"The kind of man who's willing to appreciate what he doesn't understand."

And he leans back in his chair, satisfied.

Class was over twenty minutes ago; the students are gone. Outside, the cleaning lady's metal bucket rattles against the mop as she works her way down the hall.

I'm in my coat, ready to go, and have been for some time. But I just can't seem to pack all my papers and books back into my holdall; I honestly don't know how I got them all in this morning. The more I push, the more difficult it becomes. I've emptied it and restacked them—first sideways and then standing upright . . .

I step back, breathe and try again.

There must be a way.

I cram them in loosely, lean my full body weight down on them and force them in. The side seams of the holdall creak, but eventually I succeed. And, heaving it over my shoulder (the one that's nearly an inch lower than the other from lugging this bag around town, day in, day out), I lumber down the hallway.

As I push through the side exit, I'm greeted by a thin, misty rain. Looking up, I take in the mysterious beauty of this night sky, its moon veiled by a spill of full, dark clouds.

The next thing I know, I'm falling.

I pitch forward, grab the handrail.

The shoulder strap snaps.

And the entire contents of the bag tumble down the steps, landing in a deep black puddle on the uneven cobblestones below.

Shit!

There they all are: my *Norton Anthology of Poetry,* my *Oxford Companion to Literature,* my Chekhov, my Congreve, the red leather John Donne book from the secondhand shop on Charing Cross Road, the Sheridan plays, the War Poets, and worst of all, my *Complete Works of Shakespeare;* the same edition I brought with me all the way from Ohio over fifteen years ago—sopping wet.

"That's a lot of books."

I turn.

Robbie's leaning against the opposite wall, holding R. Fitzroy's blue and white china teacup, still wearing the ugly orange jumper of eternity.

"What?"

She takes a sip of tea. "I said, that's an awful lot of books to have to carry around."

I pick up the sodden Shakespeare. It hangs, dripping, in my hand. I try to shake it out, but the spine, fragile for some time, gives way. It collapses, pages falling away like leaves. "I've had it for years," I say.

"Maybe you don't need it any more. Maybe you don't need any of them."

I stand, staring at the puddle.

The rain picks up.

"But, of course I need those books!" I rub my eyes, irritated and over-whelmed. I'm not in the mood for her tonight. "How am I going to teach? By heart?" Crouching down, I fish out the Chekhov; its pages dissolve beneath my fingers. I drop it, back into the black water. "Damn!"

"It wasn't an accident."

"Of course it was!" I look at her. "I tripped!"

"Evie," her voice is clear and still. "It wasn't an accident. I saw it coming. I could've moved. But I didn't."

Cold rain splashes against the back of my neck, like a cold hand. "What are you talking about?"

She turns her face towards the moonlight, water beading like tiny crystals on her fine features. She speaks carefully, fitting the pieces together for the first time. "It was freezing. The sky was white. You couldn't open your mouth without your teeth aching, it was so cold. I'd gone out without a coat. The guy who sells fruit on the corner called out to me, asking me where I left it. I laughed. I told him I was only going to be a minute, just getting some Diet Coke, but I already knew that it didn't matter if I had a coat or not . . . I knew I didn't want to come back, that the cold wouldn't affect me." She turns to me again. "It wasn't an accident."

"But . . . you said it was . . . you said . . ."

"I know what I said." She's confused now, staring into the china teacup. "But it only came back to me a moment ago. Your foot was on the edge of the step, you looked up at the sky, you kept going, but there was nothing there! And it came back . . ." Her voice is strained with feeling. "I thought I'd been cheated, Evie! All this time, nowhere, stuck! And then, I remembered . . . I never even bothered to take my coat!"

We stand there, looking at one another.

"Don't you see? I made a decision, Evie! I must have!"

The rain falls harder.

She's very still now. Her thin shoulders have sunk forward; wet hair clings to her face. She's even paler, her skin's just a translucent, soft glow. I've never seen her so quiet, so calm.

Raindrops fill the cup in her hand; tiny ripples in the warm tea.

"You never wanted to go to Juilliard, did you?"

I feel as if my heart's been cracked in two; my innermost secret on the brink of exposure. "How do you know that?"

Her voice is gentle. "Because there are no accidents. No mistakes. We don't just fall off the pavement into the abyss, do we? Even if there had been no Jake, you still wouldn't have gone, would you?"

She waits for me to say something.

I open my mouth. No words come out.

"You're not what you think you are."

I can barely find my voice. "And what's that?"

"A failure."

Part of me wants to laugh, from relief. The rest of me wants to cry, for the same reason.

Suddenly the story I've built my whole life around comes undone, dissolving like the pages in the books at my feet. Evie, the failed actress, the

282 ~~ KATHLEEN TESSARO

bad friend, the wayward daughter and cold, unfeeling lover. Evie, who should've been somewhere else, doing something else, feeling differently, achieving more; Evie always scrambling to catch up, lagging, still lagging behind . . .

I close my eyes; tears mingle with the cool drops on my cheeks.

"But failure is the price you pay . . . isn't it? For love."

There's no response.

I open them.

"Robbie!" My voice echoes. *"Robbie!"*

There's no one there.

I'm alone, holding the broken bag.

R. Fitzroy's teacup is on the pavement in front of me.

I pick it up.

It's still warm.

"Excuse me."

It's a woman's voice, soft, with an Irish lilt.

I turn, looking down the hallway.

She's about forty, with long dark brown hair and bright blue eyes. She's carrying a stack of books and a large leather handbag, not unlike my former holdall, is slung over her shoulder, bulging with so many papers, it has no hope of shutting properly, but neither does it look as if she's tried. Dressed in an ankle length black wool dress, of a rather bizarre, asymmetrical design, she's staring at me with a curious look on her face.

"Yes?"

She continues to frown at me. "Excuse me, but where did you get that teacup?"

I look at the cup in my hand. I obviously can't tell her the truth . . . "It was outside," I say wearily. "I found it outside."

She takes another step towards me. "It's just I've been looking for it for months. It belongs to me, I'm sure."

"Really?" It's clear she thinks I'm lying; that I've been hoarding it all this time. "And you are?"

"Rowena Fitzroy," she introduces herself. "I teach playwriting. What was it doing outside?"

I blink. "I guess someone . . . used it . . ." I'm not vindicating myself very effectively. "I just popped out to get some fresh air . . ." I hand it to her quickly. "I'm afraid it's not very clean."

Rowena takes the teacup and then smiles; it's a lovely, genuine smile. I relax. "That's so odd! I normally wouldn't care so much, it's just that my daughter gave it to me for my birthday . . . it's a mother thing, there's something about anything from your child . . ."

I nod. "I have a little boy. I'd rather die than misplace a single glue-encrusted masterpiece."

And we laugh, in recognition of our common bond.

"Hey, what happened to your bag?" She points to the broken holdall, dangling from my arm.

"Nothing. An . . ." It's on the tip of my tongue to say, "an accident," but I stop myself. "Nothing. It was always . . . stressed. I'm sorry about the cup. I really didn't take it—I'm not that kind of person."

"I'm sure," she says. "Well, lovely to meet you and thank you for salvaging it for me. I'll have to be more careful in future; I'm afraid I have a bad habit of trusting to people's better natures. Ellery says I'm mad!"

"Ellery?" I repeat. "Ellery King? The fight instructor?"

She flushes. "Such a cliché, isn't it? A staff room romance! Do you know him?"

I shake my head a little too vigorously. "I've . . . you know . . . seen him around, that's all."

She laughs again, touching me on the arm. "Apparently he kept stealing my chamomile tea!"

And I laugh too; the image of him leaning in to flirt with the red-haired student still floating in my mind.

She's about to go; then she stops. "Listen, I don't even know your name!"

"Evie. Evie Garlick." I offer my hand and she takes it. "I teach, I was going to say an acting class but it's more like a reading aloud class with my lot. I did try my hand at playwriting once or twice . . . it's not easy, is it?"

She tilts her head, looking at me thoughtfully. "No, I suppose it isn't. But then, if you get to a place where not writing is harder than writing . . . have you done anything lately?"

"No, I . . ." I'm longing to give a fascinating, detailed account of why this is true, but this is all that comes out.

Fishing around in her capacious leather satchel, she pulls out a slightly tattered card.

"Here's my number. If you ever want to talk about anything you've written, why not give me a call? Sometimes all you need is an extra pair of eyes to see something that's been right in front of you all along." She smiles again. And I can see why Ellery likes her; there's something sexy about her warmth and immediacy. "Lovely to meet you, Evie. And thanks again!"

She waves and I watch as she walks down the long corridor, the blue and white china teacup rattling in her hand.

The front gate squeals, banging irritably behind me. Climbing the steps as fast as I can, I twist my key in the lock, pushing the door open. I dump my broken bag and coat and race through to the living room.

It's empty.

And my spirits sink.

I thought he might be here; all the way home on the train, I held the image of Piotr in my mind, sitting in front of the piano, perfectly still. But he's not.

Of course he's not.

I sit on the sofa; a dull ache fills my chest. I've been so stupid! So backward and impossible and insane! What was I thinking? That he'd just be waiting here, in the dark, like an idiot?

I bury my head in my hands.

There was a time when my heart was barred against the world. When Alex was born it swung open and a terrifying capacity for joy and fear invaded.

Now something new has taken hold: a fine, rare feeling; at once calm and powerful, coursing through my veins.

Only I've made a mess of everything.

I press my eyes closed.

"Please, God," I murmur, "whatever you are, wherever you are . . . please, just give me one more chance! I beg of you, please!"

Opening my eyes, I look around.

The room's still empty.

I wander upstairs.

It's always the same step that catches me out, third from the top. It groans underfoot and I hear her shift above.

"Evie? Is that you?"

"Yes, Bunny."

"Well, then. Come in and say good night properly."

I push open the door. She's still fully dressed, reading glasses balanced on the end of her nose, sitting at her writing desk in the corner.

She turns, waving me in. "Come and sit down," she commands, gesturing to the bed. I perch on the end of it. She tears a cheque off and slips it into a preaddressed envelope. "There's something I want to discuss with you."

I feel overwhelmingly adolescent, as if I've been caught sipping my parents' sherry from the bottle.

She folds her hands in her lap, looking at me over the top of her glasses. "I normally wouldn't intrude, darling, but has something happened with you and Piotr?"

"Piotr?" I try to sound casual.

She continues to stare at me.

"No, I mean, I . . . why?" I stammer, my face flushing.

"Because he left this morning for Paris."

My heart stops.

"Paris? For how long?"

"He didn't say. It just seemed odd." She turns back to her desk, taking out another bill.

"Did he say why?" I venture, after a moment.

She doesn't look up. "No."

"Oh."

I sit there.

Another minute passes. I stand up. "Well . . ."

"Although," she peers at me again, "I was rather under the impression that he was in love with you."

"Really?" My heart starts again, a secret joy rushing through me. I look at her eagerly. "How do you know?"

"Oh, Evie!" she sighs, shaking her head. "Have you always been this . . . this naïve?"

"Yes, Bunny," I admit sadly. "I suppose I have. What can I do?" I persist. "What can I possibly do?"

She looks at me for a long time.

"You have to wait, darling." She reaches over and squeezes my hand. "You'll just have to give him his time."

I wash my face, warm water against my skin. All I can think of is him; the smell of his hair at the nape of his neck, the flash of his eyes, his boyish, teasing grin, hands that slice the air when he's excited.

Give him his time.

Why is doing nothing the hardest thing of all?

I should be tired; exhausted. But lying in bed, my thoughts ricochet, bouncing around my head. My feelings flame my imagination, setting it alight. But it burns in vain; he's gone.

I turn over, frustrated.

I close my eyes. Images swell to the surface.

Suddenly, something else is setting them off, a small glowing nucleus of an idea . . .

Have I always been this naïve?

Have I always been . . .

Naïve . . .

And then it's there, fully formed.

I turn on the light, peel back the covers. Out comes the blue Ryman's box from the chest at the bottom of the bed; I dump its contents on the floor.

I reach for a pen on my bedside table.

Innocents in the Underworld the old manuscript reads.

I draw a thick line through the title.

"The Ingénue," I write above it.

It stares back at me, clean and sure.

I pile a couple of pillows on top of one another and jam them into place. Then I climb back into bed.

Back goes the title page.

Act One, Scene One . . .

The words come thick and fast, filling the page, as if they've always been there, dormant; just waiting for me to wake up.

The man following Bunny around the house has a clipboard and a pair of narrow reading glasses on his nose. He's wearing a bespoke suit; it's easy to tell it's bespoke by the bizarre combination of rigorously conservative tailoring and the flashes of extraordinary turquoise silk lining in his jacket. They walk, slowly, through each room, pausing to examine certain pieces of furniture or an unusual objet d'art . . . they speak quietly, in low voices, between themselves.

It's only after he's left that I notice the catalogue he's left behind; Christie's Auctioneers.

And there are others, more men; not quite so finely dressed, with tape measures and cameras.

I watch their comings and goings, on my way to make fresh cups of tea before trudging back to my room to continue my work. I'm up early, filling page after page, stealing hours to and from classes on the train, one ear always attuned to the voices chattering in my head and the other waiting to hear his footsteps or the sound of the front door opening, when everyone else is home. Bunny teases me, says I'm possessed.

But I'm not the only one.

She's changed too; she's quieter, more self-contained. She's mulling something over in her mind, a string of suited men for company.

Then it's finished.

It's late. The staff room's almost empty.

I sit down at the wobbly beech table and take out the long brown envelope from my bag. It's a satisfying weight in my hands. Over seventy thousand words in three acts.

A familiar fear grips me.

I don't have to do this.

I can put it back in my bag and no one will know.

My mind contracts, pulling at the question from this angle and that; what could happen, what should happen, what might happen . . .

Suddenly the sound of the dripping tap in the corner is unbearably loud. I look up.

There's the pile of washing up; the same chipped mugs and stained teaspoons, the same brown sponge, worn and filthy, under the same empty paper towel dispenser. And the same indignant laminated sign, curling now at the edges: THIS IS NOT A HOTEL!

No, this is not a hotel.

This is the staff room I've been sitting in, week in, week out, night after night for three, going on four years, hoping that somehow, something, somewhere would change.

As long as it didn't have to be me.

You're the hero of your own story. I remember him saying it, the tone of his voice; he leant against the kitchen counter and spoke of slaying dragons; of happiness . . . Happiness is a shabby little goal.

I didn't understand, then.

There's a peace that comes from the integrity of self that the rough fortunes of happiness can't touch. But it can only be paid for in acts of courage.

I stand up, cross to the staff mailboxes.

Here it is; R. Fitzroy.

I place the envelope carefully, soundlessly inside.

There are no fanfares for the truly great moments of your life. Just dripping taps and the sound of your own footsteps, walking from one room into another.

I pause when I reach the door.

The room's a dingy grey under the blinking fluorescent bulbs. They cast a sick, greenish light on the furniture; chairs that literally cave inward, bearing the imprint of a thousand different lethargic bottoms; coffee tables, so beringed from tea mugs and takeaway coffee cups that it seems a deliberate part of their design, and the ill-fitting, stained carpet tiles.

For a long time, this was the best I could aspire to.

I turn off the light.

As I open the kitchen door, a thick wave of heat and smoke washes over me. It's coming from a battered black skillet, flaming away on Bunny's ancient cooker.

He's bent over a chopping board, sleeves rolled up; a look of intense concentration on his face. He could be Hephaestus at his anvil, forging weapons for the gods in the smouldering depths. But he's pounding a steak with an old potato masher instead.

I've never seen anything more beautiful in my life.

Piotr looks up, pushes his dark hair back from his eyes.

"Hello," he says guardedly.

"You're back!" I'm grinning so wide my cheeks hurt.

"Yes." He smiles softly. "I'm back."

He flings the steak into the skillet. It sizzles and splutters in the olive oil. His eyes meet mine; he turns away shyly. "Why are you looking at me like that?"

"Because I've been stupid," I confess.

I want to touch him so badly; to wrap my arms round his neck and bury my face in his chest.

I trace the edge of the counter with the tips of my fingers. "And you really have no idea how much I've missed you!"

He's quiet.

The steak hisses and pops. The rich, savoury smell fills the kitchen.

He turns it over, one-handed, the other hand slung into the pocket of his jeans. He's got a way of standing, of moving; the assured, swaggering grace of a cowboy.

"Have you eaten?" he asks.

I shake my head.

He nods to a chair. "Sit down."

I watch, a growing knot of apprehension in my stomach, as he pulls the steak from the flames, puts it on a plate. Then he walks over, crouches down in front of me.

Oh no.

Here it comes: the "I don't think we're really suited for one another" speech.

Why shouldn't he feel that way? I look down, biting my lower lip, staring at my fingernails.

Please, God . . .

"Evie look at me."

I force my gaze up.

How could there ever have been a time when this face, these features, weren't dear to me?

"Tell me about Alex's father."

I blink. "Why?"

"Because," his eyes are sad and tender at the same time, "it happens I missed you too. But I won't be on the outside of your life. I want to know all of it."

He stands up, reaching for a bottle of red wine.

"I . . . I don't know where to start," I falter.

He pours out two glasses, handing me one.

And he smiles; that wonderful teasing grin I've missed so much. "Why not start by saying again how much you missed me."

There's a knock on my door.

I poke my head out, as usual, half-dressed and verging on late to take Alex to school.

"Yes?"

It's Bunny. Her expression's grave. "Piotr's smoking," she says. "There's been a phone call and now he's out in the garden smoking!"

"What? Cigarettes?" I ask stupidly.

"Yes." She somehow manages to imbue this single word with profound sinister undercurrents.

I follow her down the steps. Out in the back garden, as reported, Piotr's pacing up and down the length of the lawn, puffing away anxiously. He's clearly a practiced hand at the art of smoking, a skill no doubt perfected during those years in Paris.

Before I can reach him, Alex joins us, racing past me to tackle his legs. "Hiya!"

Most of their bonding follows this basic pattern; Alex hurls himself repeatedly at Piotr and Piotr lets him.

"Oi!" Alex shouts gleefully, as Piotr lifts him up over his head. "Oi, oi, oi! Put me down!"

Piotr twirls him round and then deposits him back on the grass. Alex, giggling hysterically, lunges at him again.

"Are you all right?" I watch as Piotr flings Alex over his shoulder like a sack of potatoes.

"No. I don't think so." He launches Alex on the lowest bough of the horse chestnut tree, where he scrambles off excitedly. "Pogorelich has pulled out of a concert, a performance with the Philharmonia. They've asked me to play Prokofiev Three."

"My God! Piotr! Alex, stop it, now! When?"

Alex wraps himself affectionately round Piotr's leg.

Piotr rests his hand on his head. "Tonight."

"Oh. Bugger!" I think I might need a cigarette too.

"Can I come?" Alex looks up at Piotr. "Can I turn your pages?"

Piotr ruffles his hair. "There will be no pages tonight. Well," he adds wryly, "with any luck there won't." He turns to me. "Do you remember what I told you about? You have to play two concertos in the final round of the Tchaikovsky?"

I nod.

"Prokofiev Three was the one I walked out on. Rostropovich is conducting tonight. The woman from the Philharmonia said he recommended me himself."

"Oh, Piotr!" I'm bursting with pride on his behalf.

He shakes his head. "You don't understand. Already, the head's gone! Pogorelich is an enigma; complicated. The audience will be full of musicians and reviewers . . ." He's pacing back and forth, growing more and more agitated.

"But Rostropovich recommended you," I remind him.

"He remembers a performance from . . . what? Eight years ago?"

"But it's still in your repertoire?"

"Of course it is!" He swings round. "It's my obsession! It keeps me awake at night; I can't close my eyes without hearing it! But that doesn't mean I can play it!"

"Piotr . . ."

He pulls away; sucks hard on the end of the cigarette. "The thing is, I'm shallow!" He sounds appalled. "I want to be liked, Evie!"

I can't help but laugh; this isn't the response he's looking for. "But it's only natural . . ."

He shakes his head, over and over. "It's unbearable! I'm shallow! At the end of the day, I'm just like everyone else!"

"Piotr." I hold out my hand.

He takes it.

Sun filters in through the thick canopy of leaves above us; the air smells of black earth and new grass; fresh and green.

"Are you going to do this?" I ask.

He nods mournfully.

"Well, then. Just stop it." I grip his hand harder. "I admire you. It doesn't matter to me if you do this or not. But why not try? Just show up."

He shakes his head. "So easy, huh?"

"No, not so easy! In fact, the hardest thing of all." And then I say something that surprises me. "It's a matter of faith."

He sighs, rubbing his eyes. "And if I don't believe in God?"

"Then believe in love," I suggest quietly. "Love in a random universe."

Alex races around us; he's found a large stick he's waving about like a sword.

"Hiya!" he yells, beating on the tree trunk.

Piotr's face relaxes, his shoulders fall. He throws the cigarette down, grinds it out beneath his heel.

"It's been a long time," he apologises. "One loses the taste for heights."

He shoves his hands into his pockets.

"Come on." I slip my arm through his and steer him back towards the house. "You need some breakfast; you probably won't have much of an appetite later on. And I don't expect your tails have been dry cleaned recently. When's rehearsal?"

Alex skips ahead of us. "I'm going to make you a sandwich," he announces, brandishing the stick. "You can either have a ham sandwich or a peanut butter sandwich. Or you can have ham and peanut butter but that's *disgusting*! And a juice box," he adds, tantalizingly, a juice box being the most luxurious liquid in his young world.

I push open the kitchen door. "Piotr's playing Prokofiev Three tonight with the Philharmonia!"

Bunny claps her hands. "How thrilling!"

"And," I continue, "he needs a hot bath, mint tea, his suit pressed and a fry-up breakfast before he's too nervous to swallow it."

"I'm not nervous," he protests. "I'm terrified. And you," he eyes me warily, "are very bossy!"

I open the refrigerator, piling eggs, butter, bacon and jam onto the counter. "Scrambled or fried?" I grab a frying pan. "You're getting your bacon crispy unless you speak now. Bunny, what are you going to wear?"

"My black crêpe, of course." She forces Piotr into a kitchen chair. "Where are those tails? Don't worry, I'll find them. I used to press all Harry's suits. And you need a haircut, young man. I won't have you stepping on stage before you've had a trim. I'm calling Newton. He used to valet for the Prince of Wales. He's about eighty but still gives the best wet shave in the business." She pauses on her way upstairs, adjusting the heat on the stove. "The butter should smell like freshly roasted hazelnuts, darling. That's how you know it's at the right temperature."

"So what time's rehearsal?" I switch the kettle on. "Shouldn't you be warming up?"

But Piotr just shakes his head. "I live with too many women!"

Alex hands him a juice box. "Me too."

I'm sitting on the edge of my bed in my bathrobe, my hair wrapped in a towel on the top of my head. Hanging from my wardrobe door is an elegant empire-line dress; layers of gathered chiffon the delicate colour of a thumbnail; not quite pink, not quite peach, dangling from two slender shoestring straps. Allyson gave it to me before she left, claiming she didn't have room for everything and it made her look too gamine anyway. Gamine is just what I need. On my dresser there's a string of pearls from Bunny and a small golden handbag in the shape of an apple. It's an incredible, unspeakably extravagant object . . . "You'll look like Atalanta." Bunny handed it to me gently. "Be careful, unless you are caught!" And there it sits, a golden promise, glittering in the early evening sun.

Here, in this moment, nothing's happened yet. In another minute I'll start to put on my makeup, to dry my hair, to spray my limbs with a thin, invisible layer of rose scented perfume . . . but right now, all is still.

And yet everything's already done.

I know, as certainly as I sit here, that by this time tomorrow everything will be different.

The Royal Festival Hall is overflowing with people, champagne corks echo to good-natured cheers and the air buzzes with conversation. Standing next to Bunny, I grip her hand tightly, trying to keep my nerves at bay.

It's a vast hall; cavernous and grand. I look up at the three enormous tiers, filling with people; the staggered boxes, suspended seemingly in midair. It's a space crackling with anticipation; electric with possibility.

Bunny and I take our seats in the stalls.

A slender man in his forties sits down next to us.

"It's exciting news, about the Prokofiev!" He's apparently unable to contain his enthusiasm. "You know who he is, don't you?"

We nod.

"I've been with Steinway twelve years," he continues. "I can remember when he played in Rome, the Chopin first concerto, and in Berlin, the Diabelli Variations. It's been too long! Far too long!"

The orchestra begin to file on stage.

The leader violin stands up, pressing A on the piano.

Bunny turns to me. "I just thought you should know, darling, I've decided to start seeing other men."

Rostropovich takes the stage amid a roar of applause.

"What?" I gape at her. "Who?"

She's clapping, smiling coyly. "No one you know. A friend of Belle's."

I look at her in amazement. "A friend of Belle's?"

"I've decided it's time to move on, Evie," she says firmly.

Piotr enters, to more applause. He's striking; incredibly handsome with his haircut and tails. Rostropovich takes his hand.

"But . . . I mean . . . it's all so sudden!"

She puts her finger to her lips.

Piotr sits down in front of the piano.

He's holding my hand, pressing me close as we move through the crowd. We can't go two steps before we're beset by more congratulations, invitations. A press photographer takes our photo, talking to Rostropovich, who kisses Piotr no fewer than five times on the cheek.

Bunny stops him. "Oh! Please, I'd love to have a copy of that picture!" She writes her address down on a slip of paper. "A night to remember!" She winks at me.

They're speaking a mixture of Polish, Russian, a bit of French. All I can do is smile inanely, but he won't let go. And I don't want him to.

There are two men behind me.

"What was the encore? Rachmaninoff?"

"Stunning, wasn't it? The B Minor Prelude . . . 'Le Retour'—the return. One of the pieces Rachmaninov wrote when his exile from Russia was over."

I'm radiating pride from every pore.

"Le Caprice!" Suddenly, Rostropovich is addressing me. "Tell him!" he urges me emphatically. "We're all going to Le Caprice!"

But Piotr's shaking his head. "I'm taking these ladies home. There's a peanut butter and ham sandwich waiting for me."

"You're mad!" Rostropovich laughs, slapping Piotr on the back. "Come to Washington! Whatever you want to play! Do you know Franco? Franco Panozzo, the best agent in Europe! Franco!" he shouts, waving across the room.

Piotr turns to me. "You look so beautiful," he says softly. "Is it any wonder that I'm in love with you?"

And, smiling, he turns to shake Franco's hand.

Allyson's dress lies crumpled in a heap on the floor.

"Come with me to Paris." Piotr stretches out on the bed, dangling his feet over the edge. "I want to show you Paris."

I turn over on my back. "All right."

"Maybe I'll move back to Paris." He runs his fingers through my hair. "Want to come?"

"Be serious."

"I am serious."

"What about Alex? And what about me, for that matter? What can I do in Paris?"

He kisses my forehead. "I'll keep you. Like a mistress. I'll buy you pearls and expect favours in return."

"I don't like pearls . . ." I hold his hand out, spreading the fingers wide. "And you can have the favours for free."

"You are so American!" he laughs.

"I'm ignoring that." I press my hand against his, marvelling at the difference in size. "I can't leave London. I mean, I don't want to."

He folds his fingers over mine. "We could go anywhere, Evie."

"We?" I say it lightly, but I don't dare look at him.

"We." He pulls me to face him. "There is a 'we' now."

"Yes, but . . ."

"But what?" He smiles, tracing his finger along my lips. " 'O! My America! My new found land!' "

I laugh, delighted. "When have you been reading John Donne?"

"You forget, mon ange, I have a library card!" And he rolls me on my back, peering naughtily underneath the sheet. "Now, let's get back to this business of you being my bored, exquisite little paramour . . ."

A week later, I'm sitting in a café on Long Acre. My hands are wrapped around a cup of coffee I haven't touched yet and I'm not likely to.

I'm early, of course. I'm one of those people who always arrive early, even for bad news. If I had an appointment at the guillotine, I'd show up with half an hour to spare. But then, if good news can wait, bad news must be taken quickly, urgently, like medicine.

It's lunchtime; all around me waiters are rushing plats du jour to hungry diners, tucking into business lunches. But I have no appetite.

I regret it now, with every fibre of my being. When I gave it to her, I wanted change, welcomed it, even. Now all I want is for things to remain the same; to become invisible again. It was a mistake. And now she's going to sit across from me, smiling, being polite; trying to find the nicest way of telling me my script is a pile of unplayable shit and I should stick to torturing pensioners.

The café doors swing open. I freeze.

Two loud men in suits, slapping each other on the back, enter.

I exhale.

Right.

I need an escape plan. I'll say I have an appointment in ten minutes— an unexpected appointment I can't reschedule. Then at least we can keep it brief.

My coffee's gone cold.

I push it away from me, find I have nothing to do with my hands, and pull it back.

The doors open again.

I can't bear to look, so I stare at the thick black liquid.

"Evie?"

I raise my head.

There are two of them; Rowena and a sharply dressed man who looks to be in his mid-thirties with blonde cropped hair and glasses. He's got his hands in his suit pockets and he's grinning at me.

Two of them?

Oh, God! She's brought a buffer!

I bolt up, nearly toppling my cold coffee.

"Hello!" My voice is far too bright. I extend my hand, even though we haven't been introduced. "So good of you to meet me!" I'm babbling. I have to stop babbling. "Would you like to sit down?"

How can she do this to me?

How can she demolish me in front of a stranger?

I smile even wider. "Coffee? Or lunch? It is lunchtime, isn't it? Would you like to see a menu?"

I search around for a waiter.

"Evie," she begins, pulling out a chair, "I'm sorry, I really should have rung you and asked permission."

Where's that waiter?

"But, being a writer myself, I couldn't resist a bit of drama." She exchanges a look with her bespectacled friend.

I might hit her.

"Anyway, maybe you'll forgive me when you understand . . ."

No, I'll never forgive you.

Where's that fucking waiter?

"But I want you to meet Nigel Watts from the Royal Court."

I stare at her.

She's glowing with excitement.

"He'd like to talk to you about your play."

"Can you get that for me, please! Oh dear! Where's my handbag?" Bunny rushes past me into her bedroom. "He's early! Everyone knows that women are always late . . . how can he be here so early?"

The doorbell rings again.

"Please, Evie! My God, my hair looks like a newsreader!"

"I'm on my way," I call, heading down the steps. "Relax, you look beautiful!"

If I thought Bunny was exacting when she was single, it's nothing compared with when she's actually seeing someone. She's been plucking and preening since noon and it's only their third date. But I enjoy helping her choose her dress and jewellery; playing the mother hen and opening the door. I toy with taking the old boy into the front room and giving him a grilling. "So, where did you meet? What are your job prospects?" She'd be appalled, of course.

I should do it.

I pause in front of the mirror at the bottom of the steps. Since Bunny decided to put the house on the market, many of the older pieces have already been auctioned. But this mirror, fatally flawed and yet all the more fascinating for it, remains. I'm smiling. And I realise that I like the way I'm able to see beyond myself, not just the careful scrutiny of physical flaws and assets.

And as I cross the hall, it occurs to me that I haven't looked at myself in that way for a long time. I can see who I am without searching any more.

I turn the handle.

"I'm on my way!" Bunny calls in a singsong voice. She's starting her grand entrance down the steps as I open the door.

She stops. "Oh dear! You're not who I expected."

I close the door with a bang.

"Evie, you just shut the door on that man!" She hurries down the steps. "Why?"

My hands are shaking.

"Evie!" She peers out of the window. "He's just standing there! No, he's walking down the steps. Now he's stopping . . ."

"Get away from the window, Bunny, please!" My whole body's going numb. I walk into the living room. "Get ready. Your date will be here soon."

"Bugger my date! I want to know why you shut the door on that young man!" She stands in front of me with her hands on her hips.

I turn away.

This can't be happening. Not again. A pressure builds in my head, pressing against my brain. I have to think.

"If you don't tell me, I'm going to go out there and ask him myself!" She waits a moment. Then marches dramatically towards the door.

"He's Alex's father." I say the words as quietly as possible.

She's staring at me; her silence like a weight, pushing me into a vast, unknown space.

I'm cold.

"He's the father of my son." I say it again, louder this time.

It's strange how years of silence can be washed away in seconds.

I turn to face her.

It's done.

"Well, then," she says quietly, "you'd better open the door."

Acacia Avenue is abandoned; the long row of plane trees stretching their thinning branches towards the wash of grey light sweeping across the evening sky. A cool rush of wind scrapes a handful of dry, early autumn leaves across the walk. And they dance, trapped in an eddy, whirling around one another.

Jake's standing, head bowed, near the front gate.

He raises his head.

I know it's him because I recognize his features. But something . . . everything about him has changed. He holds himself differently, as if his whole centre of gravity's shifted; he's more solid, but not any heavier; his hair's clean, short, and there's none of the mercurial agitation I know so well. But now he looks at me, simply and clearly. It's the light in his eyes, the directness of his gaze that unnerves me the most. And I realise with a shock that he has nothing to hide.

I walk down the steps; the cool air blows my hair back from my face.

"I'm sorry," he says, oddly. "I had no idea you lived here."

I don't know what to say or how to begin.

As it happens, I don't have to.

"I saw a photograph in the paper." He's choosing his words carefully, slowly. "You were at some concert. I called the news desk . . . they gave me the name of the photographer and he had this as a contact address . . . I thought the woman, Bunny Gold, might know you . . ." He pauses. "I've been looking for you, Evie." His voice is unspeakably gentle. "I've been looking for you for over three years . . ."

Reaching into his jacket pocket, he pulls out a brown envelope. It's worn and battered, frayed around the edges; it looks as if he's been carrying it around a long time.

"I was going to ask her to give you this."

"What is it?" I sound defensive.

He runs his hands over the surface of the paper, as if he's reluctant to part with it. "It's something that belongs to you," he says at last.

And he hands it to me.

Inside the envelope is a small black leather book.

As I turn the pages, I have a curious sense of falling.

Rome is no stranger to heroes . . .

"You really had a way with words," he says quietly.

A streetlight flickers on, casting a circle of white light around us.

"When did you . . ." I can't speak.

He shifts uneasily. "When Chris made me leave, I found it. I thought, maybe, some day . . ." He pauses, forces himself to continue. "I thought maybe, some day, I might become the man you saw." His eyes meet mine. "I'm so sorry, Evie. For all the damage I've done. To you, to us . . . I know it's not enough—to say I'm sorry . . ." He stops, brow furrowed.

For a moment, I think he's going to continue.

But then he turns and opens the gate instead.

The gate swings shut, banging against the old metal lock.

"Jake!" I pull it open again.

The wind's picking up.

Suddenly, all the pieces fit together. "You're clean, aren't you?"

He smiles a little, running his hand through his hair in a slightly self-conscious gesture. "It's about time, wouldn't you say?"

I should say something, congratulate him. But instead I just stand there; unable to form any words at all.

He must be used to this reaction. "Well . . . take care, Evie."

I take another step. "You disappeared."

He stops.

"I sent a letter, to Alfred Manning." My words echo in the empty street, hollow, vacant sounds. They topple out anyway. "It was returned. And then I thought perhaps it was best if you didn't know . . . you were so, so . . . I didn't believe you could ever change . . ."

"Know what?"

I grip the book harder.

"Forgive me, Jake," I whisper.

I can hear the light footsteps, skipping down the stairs behind me, two at a time.

"Please forgive me . . ."

"Mummy?"

Jake looks up.

"Mummy! Look!"

Alex, his makeshift cape billowing behind him, leaps down the walk, arms spread wide. And he laughs, throwing his head back, a thrilling, uninhibited sound of pure delight.

He's so beautiful, my son. The curve of his lips, the dark, almond shaped eyes . . .

For a moment, he almost appears to have taken flight.

Brian stands up, walks boldly into the centre of the room. He looks around. Then, taking a deep breath, he begins.

> "This world is Not Conclusion.
> A Species stands beyond—
> Invisible, as Music—
> But positive, as Sound—
> It beckons, and it baffles—
> Philosophy—don't know—
> And through a Riddle, at the last—
> Sagacity, must go—
> To guess it, puzzles scholars—
> To gain it, Men have borne
> Contempt of Generations
> And Crucifixion, shown—
> Faith slips—and laughs, and rallies—
> Blushes, if any see—
> Plucks at a twig of Evidence—
> Asks a Vane the way—
> Much Gesture, from the Pulpit—
> Strong Hallelujahs roll—
> Narcotics cannot still the Tooth
> That nibbles at the soul—"

Pulling himself straight, he grins broadly.

"Well done, Brian!" I say, clapping. "What a wonderful reading!"

"Very clear," Mr. Hastings agrees, surprised. "More of the Dickinson woman, I suppose?"

Brian nods, making his way back to his seat.

"Not half bad," Mr. Hastings muses. "Almost as good as Eliot."

"Actually," Brian crosses his legs, smoothing out a crease in his trousers with a careless brush of his hand, "Dickinson was a great innovator. Eliot probably wouldn't exist without her."

A hush descends.

Mr. Hastings's eyes widen. "Well," he says stiffly, "I don't know about that."

"I do," Mrs. Patel cuts in.

We all stare.

This is the first time she's ever opened her mouth.

"It's the weird spinster women, locked away in their quiet rooms, who have the most shocking things to say," she asserts.

Mr. Hastings blinks indignantly, suddenly overwhelmed.

I dive in. "Would you like to read something, Gerald?"

He frowns, slowly unearthing the worn volume of Eliot from his overcoat pocket.

"The Waste Land," I suggest, as brightly as I can. He seems quite old tonight.

But he shakes his head. "No, no . . ." he fumbles with the pages.

There's an almost audible shift in the energy level of the room.

"I would like to read . . . something considerably shorter . . ."

Doris gives me a worried look.

Even Clive seems concerned.

"Something," he rests a pair of reading glasses on the end of his nose, "something from 'Journey of the Magi.'"

*E*VIE . . ."

I look up, surprised.

The woman standing next to me on the corner of Madison and Fiftieth Street, waiting for the lights to change, is staring at me.

"Evie Garlick, am I right?"

There's something familiar about her . . .

"Yes." I'm furiously trying to place her. How many people do I know in New York City?

Pulling her long silver fox fur coat tighter against the arctic wind, she draws a slender black Sobranie cigarette to her lips. She almost appears to be enjoying my confusion. "You don't remember me, do you?" she deduces.

And then, suddenly, I do.

She's older, thinner; streaks of silver mingle indiscriminately with her carefully coiffed blonde hair but her pale grey eyes are sharp as ever; boring into me as if not a moment has passed since our last meeting.

"Mrs. Hale! Of course!" I offer my gloved hand. She squeezes the tips of my fingers.

"So you're a playwright now," she says, tilting her head to one side as she exhales through her nose. "Congratulations."

The light changes. A swarm of people rush past us, jostling for position in the crowded rush hour streets, doing their best to maintain speed on the icy, snow covered sidewalk.

"Thank you." I blush, despite the cold.

"I saw the first one." She nods briskly. "At the Brooklyn Academy. It was good," she concedes. "Are you in town doing another?"

"No, I'm with my husband this time."

"Oh!" She raises her eyebrows, as if this is a turn up for the books. "And what does he do?"

"He's a musician." I'm smiling with pride now. "He has a concert to-night."

"How exciting." And she takes another drag, scrutinizing me through narrowed eyes. "So, tell me, did you ever go to Juilliard? Alice never told me anything."

It's strange, somehow even shocking, to hear Robbie referred to by her real name. I shake my head. "No, I decided not to go. But Ro . . . I mean Alice was such a huge help to me . . ." My voice trails off. I'm unsure of the appropriate etiquette. I don't want to offend her. Robbie stands, al-most palpable now, between us.

She looks away, pulling the coat again with her long, thin hands. And then she smiles, a quick, tense flash of the teeth.

"Well, she had a special talent for make-believe." She sounds weary. "I often wonder what would've happened to her if she'd just stuck it out."

The lights change again. We're engulfed in a fresh herd of people.

"You mean," I'm confused, "you mean with acting?"

"I meant with Juilliard." She sighs. "But call it what you like. It was stu-pid of her to leave after only a year; to waste her scholarship and run away to London." A look of resignation clouds her features. "But then I sup-pose she wasn't very . . . very well."

She turns, waves, flags down a passing cab. "I'm going to be late. Can I drop you anywhere? Where are you going?"

"Carnegie Hall," I murmur.

The cab pulls over. She opens the door.

"I'm headed the other way." She reaches out, squeezing my fingers again. "So nice to see you again."

Frowning, she looks up at the thin veil of snow drifting down. "I hate this weather! You have to be so careful," she warns, "these pavements are treacherous. It's so easy just to slip off the edge!"

The door slams shut. The cab pulls away, disappearing into a sea of yellow, under a freezing February sky.

And that's the final thing you should know about Robbie.

Nothing was ever entirely what it seemed.

Acknowledgments

I WOULD LIKE TO thank the following people for their unparalleled help and support:

Johnny Geller, Lynne Drew, Maxine Hitchock, Meaghan Dowling, Michael Morrison, Lisa Gallagher and Gillian Stern.

My dear friends and fellow writers Gillian Greenwood, Deborah Susman, Annabel Giles, Kate Morris, all the woman at the Wimpole Street Writers Workshop and especially my mentor and inspiration, Jill Robinson.

I owe a special debt of gratitude to Peter De Havilland, Stephen Harris, Dr. Matthew Knight, and Bob and Ragni Trotta for both their precious time and extraordinary generosity.

And, finally, Lucy Mellors. For services so kindly rendered.